CHARMED
CIRCLE

CHARMED CIRCLE

DOLORES STEWART RICCIO

KENSINGTON BOOKS
http://www.kensingtonbooks.com

KENSINGTON BOOKS are published by

Kensington Publishing Corp.
850 Third Avenue
New York, NY 10022

All Kensington titles, imprints and distributed lines are available at special quantity discounts for bulk purchases for sales promotion, premiums, fund-raising, educational or institutional use.

Special book excerpts or customized printings can also be created to fit specific needs. For details, write or phone the office of the Kensington Special Sales Manager: Kensington Publishing Corp., 850 Third Avenue, New York, NY 10022. Attn. Special Sales Department. Phone: 1-800-221-2647.

Kensington and the K logo Reg. U.S. Pat. & TM Off.

ISBN 0-7582-0301-2

First Kensington Trade Paperback Printing: November 2003
10 9 8 7 6 5 4 3 2 1

Printed in the United States of America

For my daughter,
Lucy-Marie:
"Anything is possible."

ACKNOWLEDGMENTS

My heartfelt thanks for the inspiration and support . . .

To the Saturday circle: Christine, Cynthia, LaVerne, Marilyn, Muriel, Nancy—and especially Rick—for their patient listening, valuable insights, and sense of fun.

To Joan Bingham, Nancy Erikson, and Anna Morin—the best of friends and readers.

To my editor, Ann LaFarge, whose confidence and wise perception have meant so much.

To Sandra Beach, who has fine-tuned both *Circle* manuscripts with exceptional care and understanding.

Esbat of the Seed Moon

An enchanting afternoon in April, windows wide open to the scent of lilac and ocean breeze freshening the house—my spirit should have been lifting and soaring like a gull over the waves, but here was Deidre sipping tea and dispensing gloomy suspicions at my kitchen table.

"An entire family doesn't simply disappear into the blue!" I declared while I gently packed my blended herbal chakra oils. My friend Deidre Ryan would sell them at the shop she manages, Nature's Bounty, at the Massasoit Mall. "Perhaps the Donahues went on vacation. They could be at Disney World this very moment."

"Do you think the Donahues took Candy out of second grade in the middle of the term without informing Miss Hassel? Besides, Candy would have said something to my Jenny—they're best friends. They share every intimate detail of our family lives with one another, and you can just imagine how annoying *that* is. Last month on Parents' Night, while we were both waiting to see Miss Hassel, Denise Donahue asked me if I'd left the Church, just because Jenny told Candy a few little tidbits about our circle. I had a word with Jenny, told her how such gossip might affect her friendship with Candy. But I doubt I got through. You know how girls are." Deidre shook her short, blond curls in parental exasperation.

"There's no hiding what we do since Q's trial last year, Deidre. That dumb headline—*Local Witches Hex Sex Killer.* Maybe a relative of the Donahues died suddenly, and the family was too distraught to tell anyone they were going to the funeral." Tenderly, I tucked shredded paper around the richly-colored bottles, each tint representing a different chakra.

"Their Irish setter Patsy has been found wandering around the neighborhood, hungry and abandoned." The kettle began to whistle. Deidre put another tea bag into the pot and poured in more boiling water. The pleasant odor of ginger wafted out of the spout.

"A pox on them, then. It ought to be a felony to neglect a pet. Where's Patsy now?"

"Watch those casual curses, dear. Where do you think Patsy is? Heather took the poor matted thing to Animal Lovers until we find out what's what." A sister member of our Wiccan circle, Heather Morgan, was practically supporting the animal rescue shelter with her lavish trust income. "She's ready to murder the Donahues. Unless, of course, they're already murdered."

"Who would do such a thing? And why?" I taped up the box of oils, ready to stash them in Deidre's Plymouth Voyager. My home-based business—Cassandra Shipton's Earthlore Herbal Preparations and Cruelty-Free Cosmetics—was flourishing, thanks to Deidre's marketing skills and the success of my *Herbal Delights and Potions* catalog. A nice, steady little income to keep me and my dog companion, Scruffy, comfortable in the pleasant seaside home I'd inherited from my grandmother.

"Actually, I was relying on you to do one of your vision things to explain all that," Deidre said, her childlike, round blue eyes looking at once hopeful and apprehensive. Since her own area of expertise was in making poppets and amulets, Deidre was in awe of my clairvoyance.

"I don't *do* visions. They happen all on their own. And I have no control over when or about what." Sipping my fragrant tea thoughtfully, I wondered what it would be like to get a handle on those weird experiences, turn them on and off at will. Too much responsibility, I decided. Deidre and others would only plague me the more. What no one understood was the shock and pain of clairvoyance—except other clairvoyants, perhaps. It was like Alice falling down the rabbit hole, trapped in the weirdness of Wonderland. Visions never seemed to be about anything agreeable—winning the lottery or finding the man of one's dreams. More likely, they would be grim snapshots of where the bodies were buried, or worse, how they got there.

Deidre must have pushed the right buttons in my psyche, however, because later that afternoon, just as I was leaning over to settle the box of oils in the back of her Voyager, I got the first insight.

"Oh, sweet mercy!" The shutter of my inner eye blinked open for a fraction of a moment, then shut tight. What I saw was a pink sneaker sticking out of the earth. A nauseating vision I wished I hadn't had. This was all Deidre's fault.

"What? What? Tell me what," Deidre kept saying insistently.

"I think you're right—the Donahues are in deep trouble," was all I could bring myself to say.

It was almost time for Beltane, May 1, a joyous High Sabbat of creativity and fertility. So naturally I was feeling somewhat depressed that my lover, Joe Ulysses, was in jail again, this time in British Columbia. I'd fantasized about making love outdoors at night. If the weather is warm, and you're not buzzed by little flying insects, and no one catches you at it, a woodland tryst is truly magical, an ideal way to celebrate the return of spring.

A ship's engineer, Joe worked for Greenpeace, an organization that frequently ran afoul of the law during one of its quixotic crusades. This time Greenpeace activists had attempted to block an access road on King Island in British Columbia. The Canadian government had awarded a logging contract to Interfor, allowing the company to clear-cut an ancient temperate rain forest also claimed by the Nuxalk natives of Canada. After confronting the Royal Canadian Mounted Police, the young activists had been rounded up, jailed, and were now awaiting trial. Joe, who should have stayed aboard ship, apparently couldn't resist jumping into danger himself. I suppose I admired that quality. In fact, I found Joe himself a gamble that couldn't be resisted. *Ah, well . . .*

After Deidre departed in the late afternoon to make one of her microwave specials for her three small children and her fireman husband, Will, I continued to have misgivings. "Oh, I don't want to get involved in this," I told Scruffy. For those who live alone, there's a great deal of comfort in talking to a dog, a cat, or even an iguana, if only to hear one's own voice saying what one truly feels. Most times, a pet listens in sympathetic silence, but Scruffy had a personable knack for making his own opinions known—at least, it seemed to me that I heard him clearly.

Hey, Toots, let's go out for a walk and forget all these hassles! Cavorting near the kitchen door, Scruffy nosed his leash invitingly. He's a bit too big and clumsy to be cute, a cross between a French Briard and the randy, sandy-colored mutt who fancied her. Some so-called friends have commented that my hair is the same color as Scruffy's, and about as neat.

"Oh, all right. Maybe the Atlantic will clear my brain of that pink sneaker. Ugh." I put on my old green lumber jacket that hung on the same hook as Scruffy's leash, and we set off down the rickety, rotting stairs that led from our neat little saltbox home to the rocky beach below, where Plymouth Harbor seemed not to have got the news that spring was here. An east wind roiled the waves to white froth. It would be mid-July before this water warmed up enough for the hardy to swim.

The dog and I took a good, long tramp along the beach. The sun lowering behind our house gilded the sails of a few brave boats. A school of bluefish began to agitate the water, and a host of screaming gulls gathered in a feeding frenzy. I let Scruffy off-leash to play *fetch the stick* as we walked. As the solitude bore down on me, the pink sneaker refused to fade in my mind's eye. *It's dinnertime, dinnertime!* Scruffy looked at me meaningfully and turned back toward the stairs. Dogs always know to the minute the time at which they should be fed, and they push it ahead by a quarter of an hour any chance they get.

"What a nag you are," I scolded him but changed course obediently. Maybe leaving the house would attract that desirable red flicker to my answering machine. One of my children might have called—that would be a nice change—or maybe even Joe. I certainly had been working on his release with all my spells and crafts.

I love messing about with herbs, oils, and creams; it's a kind of enriching, aromatic, creative playtime. I suppose that's how Phillipa, my friend who writes cookbooks, feels about cooking. Tactile joys. For her, it's the squish of hand-mixing meatballs, the scent of baking bread filling the kitchen, the satisfaction of whacking a winter squash with a sturdy cleaver. That Saturday afternoon before our April Esbat, I'd decided to concoct a Wise Woman Herbal Tea Blend, a mixture of sage, nettle, lemon balm, chaste tree berries, and dried orange zest. Perhaps I would add a little motherwort or elder flowers. My hand was drifting between the two jars, waiting for inspiration to illuminate the recipe, when there was a knock at the front door.

Scruffy leaped up from his midmorning nap under the kitchen table and began to bark in the frantic manner he assumes when he's been caught sleeping on the job. *Stranger! Danger! Let me out, out, out, and I'll chase it away.*

"Quiet, you mutt. It's probably a neighbor," I said. "Go around to the back door," I shouted. For generations, the cranberry-painted, broad-planked front door of this old house had been opened only to take out bodies feet first, and it was strangely reluctant to be employed for any less solemn purpose. If one tried to open it on some lesser occasion, the door creaked, groaned, stuck, and warped to express its displeasure. I tended to leave well enough alone. Closing the two jars of herbs, I dusted off my hands and went to unlatch the kitchen door, which is on the seaside, along with an architecturally incorrect porch.

"Hi. Are you Mrs. Shipton?" The teenaged girl standing in the doorway could have been something left over from Halloween, with short, spiked black hair, dark brown lipstick, starkly pale skin, and so many layers of sooty eyeliner, they were turning the whites of her eyes red. Amber-colored eyes—a rare shade, I noticed. She wore a half-dozen thin, gold rings in one ear; a pentagram hung from the other.

"Yes, I'm Cassandra Shipton." Scruffy had stopped barking and was sniffing the girl's imitation alligator boots with great interest. Her thighs were a chilly blue in that leather miniskirt, and there didn't seem to be too much warmth in the ratty, spotty fur jacket, either. Maybe it was April, but the blast off the Atlantic was back in the middle of March. "Would you like to step inside? That wind is fierce today."

"Sure. Thanks." She shook Scruffy off her boots and patted his head absently.

She smells good, like hamburgers and fries. The dog's nose twitched appreciatively.

"I'm Freddie. Winifred McGarity." Freddie's amber gaze was busily scanning my kitchen as if looking for clues to a mystery. I was suddenly conscious that the countertops were cluttered with the tea blend in progress. "I'm here about the witch business."

"Witch business?" I wondered what the word was around Plymouth these days concerning our circle. It was hardly a secret anymore, as I'd pointed out to Deidre. Although we weren't being denounced from pulpits, this wasn't Salem where witches were needed to draw the tourist trade to the Gallows Tree and other local attractions. We were tolerated but not welcomed, like a flock of grackles who'd descended on bird feeders meant for finches and chickadees.

"Please don't screw with me, Mrs. Shipton. I'm a sincere person, you know what I mean?"

"I'm sure you are, Freddie, but as it happens, I'm in the herb business, not the witch business."

"Everyone says there's a coven right here in Plymouth, and you and your friends are it. So I'd like to apply for membership, you know what I'm saying? Do you have an application I could fill out or something like that?"

"Why don't you sit down, Freddie, and I'll make us a nice cup of tea."

"Hey, what's in that stuff?" Freddie asked suspiciously as I spooned teaspoons of the new mix into my sturdy brown teapot, then added boiling water from the kettle on the stove.

"It's a new blend I'm creating. It's supposed to make you healthy, wealthy, and wise. Or at least wise." I filled a plate with ginger cookies. The girl looked borderline anorexic. Scruffy's nose followed my every move with rapt attention.

"Yeah. Well, you first."

"It has to steep a minute or two. Soooo . . . tell me, Freddie . . . *why* do you want to be a witch?"

"I already am. But I think I need, like, some training in the fine points. Sometimes things go wrong, you know what I mean?"

"What makes you think you're a witch? In fact, do you know what a witch is?"

She was silent for a few moments, glancing through the kitchen door to the rooms beyond—looking for what? Satanic effects? I poured the tea, noting that it had a pleasing fragrance. Adding a spoonful of honey, I passed the syrup pourer to my guest, who was now feeding a ginger cookie to Scruffy under the table. He lay down on the fake alligator boots in total devotion.

"I can bend spoons."

I laughed with relief. This was just a romantic teenager who needed a stiff dose of reality. But my gaze couldn't help going to the two stainless steel spoons I'd laid haphazardly on the table.

And Freddie saw me looking. She sighed and studied the spoon nearest her cup. Then she raised her hands over the table, not touching anything on it, and I noticed that each of her fingernails was painted a different dark shade, from deep plum to black.

After a few moments, her spoon appeared to shudder or shimmy. Then, as if the table had tilted fractionally, ever so slowly the spoon slid toward her. When it had reached a stopping place at her saucer, she picked up the spoon and rubbed it gently as if to warm the metal. I was transfixed and silenced by what was going on in front of me, and so lost track of how long in actual time Freddie spent stroking the spoon. But our tea had not yet cooled before the spoon folded over like a piece of foil. Not the thin neck of it, which is easy to do. The thick bowl of the spoon was bent double.

"There, like I told you, I'm a witch," she said and handed me the crumpled spoon. It was hot, as if it had been standing in boiling water.

I needed time to think. I wished I didn't harbor the inconvenient notion that anything or anyone who comes to my door is my business, a cosmic nudge to action. "Drink your tea before it gets cold," I said. "And have some cookies. You'll find the combination of sugar and ginger helps with the nausea that follows extreme psychic effort."

"No shit?" said Freddie. "See, I knew you'd have something to teach me." Obediently, she sipped and nibbled. After a time, she said, "Well?"

"When you say you're a witch, how do you define that? What do you mean?"

"It's, like, I have this power that other people don't have, you know what I'm saying? It works with machines, too. Especially computers. Those retards at school call me The Virus because I can screw up a computer any time I want. And sometimes when I don't want."

"Can you restore the computer, or just savage it?"

"Don't know. I'm not allowed in the computer room anymore.

They say I planted something, but I didn't. I just held my hands over the keys."

"What you have, Freddie, is a talent for psychokinesis. But that doesn't make you a witch. A witch is a follower of the Wicca, the oldest religion. She's a celebrant of the natural cycle of the year. She believes in a universal spirit that includes feminine as well as masculine elements. In Wicca, there's no central organization or leader or dogma, so some witches belong to traditional religions as well. And although we believe in the potential for psychic power in everyone, a witch may have no special talents at all."

Freddie chewed on a cuticle thoughtfully. "Well, what's the point then? I mean, don't you want to have Satanic powers and control over things?"

"Satan is a recent invention. He has no place in Wicca, which predates Christianity and Judaism. Since we don't credit Satan, he has no power with us. Yours is a rare but *natural* talent." Why was I taking on this teacherly role with a pushy teenager?

"Natural talent like being double-jointed or a math whiz?"

"Not exactly. It's more like being a healer or a telepath. You'll find there are many people, even when they see what you can do with their own eyes, will claim that you faked it, because your ability scares them. So you'll get into trouble."

"I already have." Freddie put her feet up on one of the empty kitchen chairs. Scruffy jumped up on her legs and looked straight at her with his top-dog stare. She stared back until he turned his gaze down and returned to his postulant pose.

"What do you think?" I asked, bending down to scratch Scruffy's chest, a bliss spot. He stood quite still with half-closed eyes, as if hypnotized, and took his time about delivering an opinion. *She's all right. Let's take her for a walk and see if she can do something fun like throw a stick.*

"Let's go for a walk with the dog," I said, "and you can tell me about the trouble. Do you want to borrow a longer coat? It's chilly on the beach."

I gave her my old lined raincoat, which at least would cover her goose-bumped thighs. The way she belted it tightly and turned up the collar, it acquired a certain rakish style. I wrapped myself in Joe's pea jacket, inhaling his lingering spicy scent, and we went down the shaky wooden stairs to the rock-strewn beach below. The wind had abated, but it was still quite cold. Where the shore curved, the windows of the houses ahead of us caught the rosy brilliance of the lowering sun, like the fable of the Golden Windows.

"Some things have happened that I didn't mean to do," Freddie said. She stooped to pick up a piece of driftwood and threw it as far as she could, which was quite a distance. Scruffy scampered after it joyously.

"Like what?"

"Oh, the damn fire alarm went off and no one could shut it."

"That was your doing?"

"I hadn't studied for the history test. But it didn't matter because we got sent home early. So that night I cracked the books and ended up with a C-plus," she said proudly.

"Could have been a coincidence," I suggested.

Scruffy was hitting on her legs with the driftwood in his mouth. She pulled it away from him and heaved it back down the beach. "Yeah? Then how about this. Miss Manson, who runs the computer lab, yelled at me in the parking lot when all I did was ask her to give me a chance to fix them. She goes, *I don't ever want to see you near those computers again*, slams the door of her car, and revs the engine. And I go, *You'll be sorry*! but I don't think she heard me. So when she drove off, her brake fluid ran out. I could see it trailing after the car. She hit a tree down the road, trying to avoid some kids crossing at the light. She's okay, but her jaw is broken."

We walked a way in silence, listening to Scruffy's happy barks, the gulls' rapacious cries, the incoming tide swishing the shore. Finally I said, "Yes, I'd better help you. I'm not saying that was your fault, since I don't know what was in your heart at that particular moment, but just in case . . . We are very careful about causing any negative reaction, because it comes back—threefold, sometimes. Did anything happen to you?"

"Maybe that was why my cat got run over. Patch the Pirate. Usually he was so street smart. It didn't make sense, you know what I mean? I'd had him forever, ever since I had the chicken pox."

"I'll talk to the others," I said. "Maybe you can come to an Esbat in May."

"Oh, cool! Do you dance naked?"

"That's called sky-clad. No, we don't. And if you'd like to blend in, we don't dress in mourning or wear pounds of dark makeup either."

"May's a long time off, though. Maybe I could come back for a visit in the meantime?"

"I guess that would be okay. How about this time next week?"

"Do you mind if it's later? Usually I'm working after school and on weekends at Hamburger Heaven, but today something went wrong with the fryer, like these clouds of black smoke you wouldn't believe, and we had to close."

"We'd better talk again. So, if Saturday's out, how about eight o'clock next Wednesday? Or later?"

"I'll be here. Absolutely."

"We need your help, Fiona, to do a finding," Deidre told the oldest member of our circle a few days later.

At Deidre's insistence, the police had entered the Donahues' home to have a look around, even though no one had filed a missing persons report. They found no evidence that clothes had been packed. Paul Donahue's keys were lying on his bureau, Denise's handbag was on the bed. In the laundry room, the iron was still plugged in, but it was the kind that shuts itself off when not in use. There were dirty dishes in the sink, spoiled milk in the refrigerator. It appeared that Deidre's suspicions might be confirmed.

Deidre had insisted I go along with her to Fiona's in case I might have a useful vision, which goes to show how clueless she really is about clairvoyance.

It was difficult to believe the change that had come over Fiona Ritchie since she'd taken on the task of raising her grandniece, Laura Belle. The child's mother, Belle MacDonald, unmarried and bound for law school, had been foisted on Fiona by her family during the pregnancy. The intention had been to put the baby up for adoption and let Belle get on with her schooling. But when it came down to it, Fiona couldn't let Laura go, and Belle welcomed a way to have her baby and her career, too. Now the formerly book-cluttered, cat-hair-infested, grisly and grimy, fishnet-draped cottage near the center of Plymouth had become a neat, cozy child-centered home. Here indeed was magic!

Fiona sat in her favorite easy chair with her beloved green reticule leaning against it and her plump Persian, Omar Khayyám, lounging nearby. The venerable carryall, formerly brimming with all manner of esoteric pamphlets and witch's simples, now over-flowed with a cascade of soft toys, juice bottles, tissues, linen books for infants, pacifiers, and the like. Her carroty-gray braids were neatly coiled on top of her head, with a crochet hook stuck through them that she would be looking for later. In her lap, which was enveloped in a patchwork apron, delicate little Laura Belle sat comfortably surrounded and enthroned by loving arms, not at all restless, smiling her rose-petal smile and listening to our talk as if her year-old mind could perfectly comprehend its meaning but she simply wasn't ready to join in just yet. Her huge eyes were the color of morning glories at dawn. How could such a small bundle of life, only recently come to consciousness, be so self-possessed? It was enough to make one's breath stop to think that this child might have been given away to strangers. Fiona held fast.

"So . . . a finding." Fiona nuzzled the top of Laura Belle's dark curls and looked absently out the window. "Why are we interested?"

I actually didn't want to speak to that point, but my better nature prevailed. "Because I saw a pink sneaker sticking out of the earth."

"You never told me that!" Deidre looked at me accusingly.

"Somehow they've come to our door," I said. "People do that sometimes, and then you have to do something for them if you're going to be a human being."

"Yes. All right, then. Where's my pendulum, I wonder." Fiona commenced taking stuff out of her reticule. I guessed she no longer kept a pistol in there. She needed the room for teddies and rattles.

"Is it crystal? Is that it hanging from the window frame?" I noted that Fiona's windows sparkled. The books that lined every wall were neatly arranged. As a former librarian, she treasured her several collections of arcane volumes, which in the old days had been picturesquely festooned with cobwebs.

"Oh, now I remember. My little Tinker Belle likes to see the light reflecting through it, doesn't she, precious! Let's put this little girl into bed for her nap, and then we'll see. No, not you, Omar." Surprisingly spry, Fiona rose while holding Laura Belle and rocked her way upstairs to the nursery, a dainty little room whose walls were stenciled with cute, magical animals—deer, owl, fox, otter, and turtle. We'd talked Fiona out of bats and snakes. Time enough for the mythology of transformation when Laura Belle was a teenager wearing a spandex miniskirt.

Scooting Omar out of the way, we spread a map of New England on the scarred oak coffee table while Fiona warmed up her pendulum, rubbing it between her palms and humming to it, some tuneless chant of her own devising. She stilled the crystal above the map, then let it go as it willed. The pendulum swung wildly in circles. After a minute or two, the circles became ovals, elongating gradually, until the pendulum might as well have been a straight line pointed toward Maine.

"This is not what I would call coming to our doorstep," Deidre complained.

"You started this, my dear," I reminded her.

Fiona got an atlas and laid it open to the state of Maine. The pendulum swung repeatedly in the direction of Bangor.

After fortifying ourselves with cups of Irish tea and a plateful of Fiona's miniature cream scones, Deidre drove me home. "Does Fiona swing that thing around the map on purpose, or does it have a life of its own?" she mused.

"What does it matter? However she does it, she's usually on the mark. But for the record, I go for the extrasensory explanation," I said. "Should we doubt one another's magic?"

"It's just human nature to doubt someone else's psychic skill. I mean, how much faith do you and the others have in my amulets? But you're right, we shouldn't mistrust these abilities. Have you thought who's in Maine at this very minute?"

"Phil!" I exclaimed. The fifth member of our circle, Phillipa Gold Stern, who had recently married Stone Stern, a member of the State Police Plymouth Detective Unit, was on a tour to promote her just-published cookbook, *Native Foods of New England*. Her agenda included an appearance on a Bangor news channel that was scheduled for this week. "Do you know where she's staying?"

"No, but Stone will. How much shall I tell him?" Deidre drove into my driveway and braked the car. Scruffy immediately began to bark. I could see his shaggy face at the bay window in the living room.

"He already knows the worst about us. So we'll tell him about my vision and Fiona's pendulum. He may even welcome looking into the Donahue mystery. Plymouth isn't that fertile a field for detective sleuthing. I wonder that such a bright man can be satisfied here."

"We seem to be doing our best to present him with challenges. I'll tackle Stone, and then you can call Phil and fill her in on your latest project."

* * *

By now, Stone was used to my visions, and even had a sneaking respect for them—which might explain why he invited Deidre and me to walk through the Donahues' split-level ranch house and give him our impressions. To banish any negativity, she and I had brushed certain protective spices on the soles of our shoes—ground clove and frankincense—so I hoped we wouldn't leave brownish footprints on the Donahues' pale green wall-to-wall carpet.

Vacant homes are especially evocative to me. But I do try not to waft along like a phony television psychic saying some inane thing like, "I sense that someone has died in this house," when we all know that any house that's been lived in for over fifty years may very well have witnessed a death scene. Nevertheless, I often get a sense of the emotions lingering in empty rooms. This time, though, I wanted more—a picture, a vision, some real clue.

It was not to be, however—not now, anyway. "All I can say is that I could feel fear in there, especially in the bedroom," I said to Stone and Deidre. That was, of course, a major understatement. The moment I'd walked into that pleasant, yellow room where a shiny, white leather handbag lay neatly on the bed, where bottles and jars were arranged according to size on the vanity, an unbridled terror had raced through me with its accompanying wild rush of adrenaline. I could hardly keep myself from running down the stairs and outdoors to throw up. What would the calm, professorial Detective Stern have thought of me then! Just a hysterical female. I kept control of myself firmly.

"This place reeks of trouble!" declared Deidre, shaking her hands to dispel the negativity, and for good measure, stamping her enchanted shoes on the mat as we left the house. "What *are* you going to do, Stone?"

When we had seated ourselves in his silver-gray Audi, he looked at us both over his oval-framed glasses with an air of disappointment—as if we were schoolgirls failing the subject he taught. "I've contacted the two families. Reluctantly. After I told

Paul's mother as gently as I could about the unexplained absence, she had to be sedated, and his father was treated for chest pains shortly afterward. But Denise's mother and father, Bea and Harry Hawkins, have assisted us in filling out the necessary missing persons reports. They own an antiques business in Scituate, which is not all that far away, but I got the impression there was a little coolness. Bea Hawkins said there's a chance that the family may have gone to Atlantic City for an impromptu holiday. Her son-in-law, she tells me, loves to gamble above all things, and he's taught her daughter to enjoy it, too. Paul might not have bothered to notify the school that Candy would be absent, Mrs. Hawkins said, but her Denise certainly should have done so."

"What about work? Paul Donahue wasn't the type to take off from work without a word to his staff." Deidre shook her blond curls in disbelief.

"Financial counseling firm. The major portion of his work was accomplished outside the office, calling on customers. He didn't have to touch base with his staff on a daily basis, although he usually did. A secretary-receptionist and two young assistants, fresh from business school, one working on estate plans, the other on investments." Stone drummed his long, tapered fingers on the steering wheel. "It's a mystery, all right. What would have been the source of the Donahues' fear, do you think, Cass?"

"Maybe he has some dissatisfied customers." I heard my own voice and wondered where *that* idea had come from.

"Maybe he does," Stone agreed. "We'll be looking into that angle."

"Then look for someone who's a hunter," I added, still off the top of my head.

"Of course! Maine!" said Deidre. "But it's not the right season."

"Depends on the game," I said.

I'd left a message at Phillipa's hotel. That night she returned my call. "At last I'm in my room having a drink," she said. "What a day—you wouldn't believe!"

"What marvelous native dish did you whip up for the cameras today?"

"Braised Fiddleheads on Polenta, which the host persisted in calling 'cornmeal mush.' It's fiddlehead season in Maine, you know. Nasty little things to clean, I must say. But I wonder what *you've* been eating, Cass—hallucinatory mushroom soup? What's this Stone tells me about a missing family? And why are you and Dee involved?"

"Dee's fault. The missing girl, Candy Donahue, is a friend of Jenny's. But then I got this glimpse of a pink sneaker sticking out of the ground. So we had Fiona do a finding with her pendulum, and it came up Bangor. Has Stone contacted the police there?"

"What's he going to say? His *psychic friends network* said to look for a pink sneaker in Bangor?"

I could hear Phillipa taking a sip of her drink, the ice cubes clinking against glass. It sounded good. I stretched the phone as far as it would go to open the refrigerator door where there was an open bottle of chardonnay. Instantly, Scruffy stuck his nose in the refrigerator and inhaled deeply.

Any of that roast chicken left, Toots?

I took out the wine and closed the door firmly. "Well, he should do something," I said.

"He did. He faxed the missing persons reports to a friend on the force, told him he had a tip that the family might have been taken against their will to some place in the Bangor neighborhood."

"Good. That's a start."

"Listen, Cass—that's not the news."

"What, then?"

"I had some free time this morning, so I looked up Tip's mom—just to see how things were going. She's still living on Indian Island."

At the mention of Tip, the boy I'd wanted so much to adopt, I felt the kind of shock-pain you get from accidentally touching a hot burner, only all over.

"But Tip's not," Phillipa continued. "Mary, the mother, told me that she and Tip's stepfather had been fighting a while back, and Tip ran away from home. She doesn't know where he is, and she hasn't bothered to call Tip's father in Plymouth. So I figure you may want to call, to see if he's gone there."

"Of course I will. Thanks for visiting Mary. Brilliant idea." I was trying not to let hurt feelings quiver in my voice. "But I wonder why Tip didn't get in touch with me. I told him to call me collect any time there was a problem."

"Maybe he will yet. But you know that age—thirteen, isn't he? Tip always was an independent kid."

"What about the younger brother, Lib—did you see him? What did he say?"

"Mary said he's living at a Catholic school in Bangor run by a Brother Francis. The school is funded as a missionary. They take in Native American children, get them ready for high school. She said it's easier for her, and the kid's happy there. But Brother Francis thought the name Little Bear wouldn't blend very well into Bangor High, so they've renamed the boy Christopher. I called the school and spoke to him but he didn't even know Tip was missing. And didn't seem too interested. So there we are. Try not to take it to heart," Phillipa said.

But that's right where I did take it.

As soon as we hung up, I called S. E. Thomas, sometimes called Sam. He sounded drunk as usual. "So Tip took off and left that bitch, did he? Well, if he comes back here, he'd better be ready to shape up," said Tip's father.

I wanted to hang up on him, but instead I said, as pleasantly as possible, "Please be sure to let me know if he calls or turns up. Promise?"

"Oh sure, sure. Nothing to worry about, though. The boy can take care of himself pretty good."

The pink sneaker receded from the foreground of my anxieties as Tip's disappearance took over center stage. When we met at Heather's on Tuesday for an April Esbat, which was to be partly a full moon ritual for new growth and the release of old issues, and partly a planning session for Beltane, I was looking forward to getting some spiritual reinforcement from the cone of power our circle had raised many times.

We gathered first in Heather's conservatory, which had been swept bare of dog toys, dog beds, and water bowls for the occasion. Heather never had fewer than seven canine companions wandering around her Federalist mansion—and sometimes as many as a dozen. The larger breeds were bedded down in the converted three-car garage, the smaller ones generally shared the conservatory, but tonight they'd been relegated to the kennels as well. The faint odor of doggie fur and some citrus disinfectant wafted between the potted trees and cane chairs. After scrubbing the place, Heather's disapproving but loyal housekeeper, Ashbery, had made a tray of smoked salmon and watercress sandwiches and a frosted gingercake, then departed for the weekend to her sister's home in Vermont. I could just imagine her stamping the dust of witchery off her Wellingtons as she tramped out to her old Dodge.

The April evening was fresh and cool, but not too chilly to work outdoors. A few dark clouds scudded over particularly brilliant stars, the moon just rising in full glory. The grounds were well-screened from the street by an ornate board fence and thick pines. Recently, Heather had landscaped the far backyard with a circle of large, round stones and a flat altar stone at the center. Except for the hazard of dancing about at night in an area where dogs roamed freely by day, Heather had created the perfect place for outdoor ceremonies. Now she cast the circle with her silver-handled athame, and we stepped inside the space between the worlds where magic is worked. I asked my sisters to bring light to the disappearance of Tip. After the ceremony of raising power, chanting and dancing, ending as usual in breathlessness and laughter, we dispersed to the house for refreshment.

"Fiona, you're our finder. What do you think?" I asked our

frowsy oldest member, who was shivering slightly in her softly-faded coat sweater of many colors.

"I think that I can't stay long," Fiona said, a harried look in her eyes. "I promised my neighbor who's sitting with Laura Belle."

"What did you tell her? Bridge game? Church bingo? Assertiveness training?" Phillipa's eyes sparkled with mischief.

"A housewares party," Fiona confessed. "Hosted by a dear friend who needed my support. So Martha, that's my neighbor, asked me to buy her a pie birdie. Now where in Hades will I find that?"

"No prob," Deidre assured her. "I know just where to find that at the mall—a pretty bluebird. I'll pick one up for you tomorrow and drop it by."

"Just take a few minutes to help me," I pleaded, bringing her a cup of coffee from the buffet. "While you drink this, for the drive home."

"Tip is all right, all right," Fiona said absently. "That boy knows his way around the woods on his own, better than most men."

"Is that where he is? In the woods?" I refrained from shaking my pixilated friend.

"Don't worry. Where he is, he's right at home."

I said I didn't like the coincidence of Tip's being in the same woods with the pink sneaker.

"Oh, come now," said Phillipa. "There's hundreds of miles of woodlands in Maine. No reason to suppose that Tip will encounter the pink sneaker of your nightmares. Which reminds me, I hear it from my well-placed sources that Paul Donahue was about to be the subject of an SEC investigation. The complaint is that he had to reimburse a union pension fund for money he'd speculated with and lost in the market. So he used monies from smaller investors, and then was unable to replace those funds."

"One of my husbands was a financial planner. Roberto the Hyena." Heather twisted the end of her burnished chestnut braid, her hazel eyes flashing sparks of anger. "I've never trusted those bastards since. That Paul Donahue might have fled the country to avoid prosecution. All those guys have their tropical islands—and their off-shore banks."

"I don't see how he would hope to disappear with his whole family," Deidre objected. "Where would Candy go to school? And besides, you had to see that house. Not a toothbrush missing. The iron was still plugged in. No woman runs away from home leaving an iron plugged in."

"Fiona sees them in the Bangor area," I reminded Heather. "Maybe one of the small investors caught on to the embezzlement."

"That's what Stone wondered," said Phillipa.

Then we talked about Beltane, deciding we could risk a little fire to leap over in Heather's sheltered stone circle. Fiona thought she would bring Laura Belle if she couldn't find a baby-sitter. That reminded me of Freddie McGarity.

"So the thing is, she's amazingly psychokinetic and completely without any control. I fear what may happen to her and to others if she might accidentally direct her energy against them. She already broke a teacher's jaw and possibly caused her own cat's demise," I concluded my report on my encounter with Freddie. "She wants to join our circle, but of course I discouraged that idea."

"Out of the question," said Phillipa vehemently. "Absolutely the wrong chemistry for our circle. Why don't you just take her on as your own protégée, Cass? Maybe Freddie will satisfy that Earth Mother complex of yours, still mourning over Tip."

"Really, Phil, you can be so cutting at times. Where's your sisterly empathy?"

Deidre came to my rescue. "Let's allow the girl to come as a guest at one of our Esbats and we'll see. She may prove useful. You know, those psychokinetics can positively wreck sensitive machinery, and you never know when such a talent might prove useful to us. If we're going to keep allowing Cass to lead us into lives of crime, that is."

"Do you happen to recall who blew the whistle this time, Dee?" I asked. Deidre merely smiled—she knew I was well and truly hooked.

"Well, I think we should have a look at the girl and judge for ourselves," said Heather. "We don't want any other animals to suffer because of her misdirected craft."

"Yes, yes, let's give her a hand," Fiona agreed. "But not on Beltane. Might give her a pheromone surge or something. What about the Esbat afterward? Deidre's the hostess of that, and she's willing. But now, by golly, I have got to get home."

And so, the circle agreed to look over my so-called protégée. Freddie would be thrilled.

There was a message on my answering machine, blinking its cheery red eye. "Hi, Mom. It's Becky. Ron and I have some very special news to share. Call me when you get the chance."

Great Goddess! Maybe she's pregnant, I said to myself. Am I going to be a grandmother before I even get married again? Immediately, I was assaulted by guilt like a big, salty wave that takes the ground right out from under your feet. A new life— women were supposed to feel pleased about things like that; it's part of the program. Well, I *would* be ecstatic if that new life were growing in me instead of in my daughter. I wasn't ready to step into the role of crone just yet. I made myself a cup of ginseng tea and rocked for a while in my grandmother's chair, a sage green upholstered rocker, armless, designed for child cuddling. It faced my first-floor bedroom window, looking out on the herb garden just coming into leaf. After a few minutes I felt Grandma's spirit hovering around me like a warm shawl. What was the matter with me? If Becky has a baby, I would be wise and wonderful like my own grandma had been with me, or at least I could try.

Once I got my exclamations of delight ready and in order, I called Senator Winslow's office, where Becky worked as an executive assistant—which meant she did everything from ordering Chinese to rewriting an impromptu speech.

She was at her desk, her voice a bit strained. "Listen, Mom—it's better if I call you later. Will you be home around dinnertime?"

She didn't want them to know at work yet, I concluded. "Sure," I replied.

The call came just after our dinner and most likely before hers, since two working people often dine out or late. "It's such big news, Mom! Ron's going to run."

"Where?" The light dawned slowly over Marblehead. "I mean, for what?"

"The party wants him to run for state representative. Isn't that grand?"

"It certainly is! He's such a brilliant, well-connected attorney, a Lowell in Boston, for heaven's sake. Young, of course, but the party must have taken that into account. Are you quitting the senator, then, to help in Ron's campaign?"

"Yes, of course. But I haven't given my notice yet. We're so excited, Mom—I feel this is only the beginning. Who knows how far we could go?"

"Who knows, indeed! The White House has occasional vacancies."

"Listen, Mom . . . Ron asked me to ask you for a favor."

"Sure, honey . . . anything to support my favorite candidate."

"Ron said it would be helpful if you stayed out of the news. Like, no involvement in local crime, and no Halloween specials on what the neighborhood witches will be doing for trick or treat. Okay?"

"It's Beltane, not Halloween, Becky—that's the next High Sabbat, the first of May. Tell Ron, with my love, that I'm not giving any interviews. I *was* planning a news release on Wiccan fertility rites, but out of family affection and responsibility, I'm cooling it."

"I hope you're taking this seriously, Mom. It means a lot to us."

"I know, honey, I know. I promise that you and Ron can count on me not to embarrass the campaign."

That wasn't exactly a false promise. It's just that I was born under some quirky star that keeps following me with a spotlight when I'd be perfectly content to remain an anonymous private person.

I nearly gave up on Freddie when she didn't show up for our Wednesday appointment until after nine. But her tardiness gave me a chance to realize that I would be disappointed indeed if I didn't learn more about this extraordinary girl. She was still wearing her Hamburger Heaven uniform—winged cap and ketchup-red smock—with the ratty, spotted-fur jacket over it. She'd brought a greasy hamburger for Scruffy, which he gulped down ecstatically, vowing eternal friendship with a soulful gaze. Her dark, heavy eye makeup was beginning to run down her pale cheeks, giving her the look of a sad-faced mime. With difficulty, I stifled the suggestion that she wash her face. The habit of maternal command dies hard.

"Have you talked to the coven yet? Are they going to let me join?" she asked eagerly while I poured out two steaming mugs of mulled cider, with plenty of relaxing allspice and ginger. We took them into the living room, where Freddie perched on the windowseat. Scruffy jumped up beside her, resting his head on her knee, and she obligingly scratched between his ears.

"We don't call ourselves a coven. We prefer 'circle,' which is less offensive to the community," I explained. "For the same reason, we'd rather say 'Wiccan' than 'witch.' Wicca is simply a nature spirituality religion. And we Wiccans *are* inviting you to visit us at an Esbat in May, just to meet as friends for whatever help we can give you. But you wouldn't want to join us older women, dear—it would be like joining one of your mother's clubs, the bridge or quilt-making sort of thing."

An uneasy look crossed Freddie's face. I must have made a tactless assumption. Maybe her mother wasn't the bridge type. "Why don't we start with your telling me about yourself and how you discovered your psychokinetic abilities."

"Here's the thing . . ." Freddie chewed on her smudged lip. "I have to tell you I didn't get along with my folks—like, *big time*—so they got me sent to a Catholic training school for a while. The nuns kept us busy with classes and chapel and working in the laundry, so we wouldn't have time to fool around, you know what I mean? I got to be a pretty good ironer. But things would go wrong wherever I was assigned. Like, the mangle would short out or the washing machines would overflow or the underwear we hung in our own backyard would end up hanging in a tree down the street. The nuns didn't believe in electric dryers, I guess. But they did believe in Satan. So, after a run of incidents in the laundry, they thought I was possessed of the devil."

"What did you think was happening?" I asked.

"I didn't think it was all that weird. Like, shit happens, you know? But then my aunt Sofie—Sofie Papas—needed some help when she got the arthritis, so she took me in. Not my real aunt, just a landlady where me and my mother lived before she got married again—an old Greek lady who used to bake clove cookies that would break your teeth if you didn't watch out."

"Clove cookies sound harmless," I said. "Clove oil is often used to kill tooth pain."

"She put in the whole cloves," Freddie explained. "But she told all us kids to call her 'aunt.' No kids of her own, you know? Aunt Sofie had friends at the convent, so one day her nephew brings her to the school to look for a suitable girl. She's like, clumping around in her walker when she spots me bringing a basket of towels upstairs to the linen closet, and she goes, *Oh, it's my little Winnie. The Lord must have sent her—surely she's the answer to my prayers. Please let me take her home with me. I'll see that she goes with me to Mass every Sunday, and Sunday school, too.* You can bet I got my shit together fast and ran down to the front parlor before Aunt Sofie could change her mind. No one else gave a damn. Like, some of those old nuns crossed themselves as I went out the door." Freddie gazed out the bay window into the misty April night.

"Your Aunt Sofie's been good to you, then?"

"She's dead. And don't you go thinking I had anything to do with that. She was a great old gal, and I got to like her a lot. But after the funeral, I figured the nephew would try to jump my bones and then haul me back to the school, so I took off on my own. I'd been saving the odd dollar here and there, so I had a little stake. Enough to move in with some friends and have a room of my own."

"What about your parents? Didn't you get in touch with them?"

"Are you kidding? No, I was lucky there. They'd moved to Florida and didn't have a clue that I wasn't still ironing for the nuns. Sometimes I worry about my brothers, though. Jack and Jim, what a couple of brats, they're younger than me. I figure I'll get in touch with them again in a couple of years, when I'm eighteen."

"But you stayed in school—that's terrific!" I thought how tempting it must have been to Freddie, finding herself free of adult supervision, to get some full-time, dead-end factory job instead of sticking with U.S. history and English composition.

"I mean to make something of myself, Mrs. Shipton."

"You can call me Cass." I was going to say 'Aunt Cass,' but I caught myself in time. "Where, exactly, is this place where you're living?"

"You aren't going to turn me in, are you?—no offense, Cass."

"You wouldn't have told me your story if you thought that. I believe you read people very accurately, which is the mixed blessing of psychics. Are you psychic as well as psychokinetic?"

"Read minds, and like that?"

Scruffy stood up and stretched. He'd be wanting his evening run, made even more inviting by the prospect of chasing rabbits out of my herb garden.

"I'll take him out," Freddie offered. "If you mean, like, being able to sort out men, maybe I *am* psychic. Isn't everybody?" She headed for the kitchen and took down the leash from its hook beside the door. "I'll just take this along in case we need it. Let's go, Sport," she said to the dog dancing around her studded boots. "We'll be back in a jiff."

Putting our empty cups into the sink, I had the wild thought that Freddie could help me with the problem of the pink sneaker, even though I wasn't entirely clear on how. *Sort out men*, indeed! I put my car keys on the kitchen table.

The light mist had turned to rain. When Freddie came back, I wiped the mud off Scruffy's paws with a towel kept for that purpose on the cellar doorknob. "Wow, you're really a neat freak, aren't you?" the girl commented.

"Let's sit here," I suggested. "I want to see what you can do with these keys."

"Hey, Cass, that's too many. Just put out one or two."

I took the garage key off the ring and laid it down between us.

"Wait. I got to warm up, you know what I mean? She rubbed her arms on the thin Hamburger Heaven jacket, then warmed her hands by shoving them under her armpits. "Funny you should pick a key. The first time I ever did this, my stepdad had locked me into a closet, but he left the key in the lock. I used the end of my barrette to poke the key out so that it fell on the floor outside the door. Couldn't reach the key from under the door. The barrette wasn't long enough." Freddie fell silent and looked at the key steadily. Then she stretched out her hands toward the key, without touching it. After a while it zigged a bit. I waited silently. *Zig. Zag.* A minute passed. *Zig. Slide. Zag. Slide.* And so on, five minutes or more. Freddie was no longer cold. There was sweat running down her forehead into her eyebrows. Finally the key reached the tips of her fingers, and she grasped hold of it with a triumphant smile.

"I bet your stepdad was mighty amazed. *I'm* amazed," I said. "Now don't you twist and fold that key," I added hastily. "I may want to lock up the garage some day. What we need to work on here, Freddie, is *control*. It's fine to use that marvelous gift for some good purpose, but never mischievously."

"Yeah, like, it doesn't always work the way you want, you know what I mean?"

"I know exactly what you mean." I'd had my own struggles against black thoughts, black art.

"What about your coven—I mean, circle. Do they have 'gifts' or don't they?

"Nothing outrageous. We have a finder, a Tarot reader, and a visionary. That's my talent, if you can call it a talent." I omitted Deidre's ability with poppets and amulets, Heather's candle-burning rituals and curses.

"No shit!"

Later, over her protests—*Hey, I can thumb*—I gave Freddie a ride home. The commune where she was staying was in a run-down part of Plymouth, but even on Prospect Street, it was the only house with a gaping hole in the side, broken columns on the porch, like a smile of crooked teeth, and a leaning gravestone in the front yard. Stolen, probably. Two teenage girls were sitting on the porch roof under an umbrella, an open window behind them.

"That's my room up there," Freddie pointed proudly to the next window where only a small light shone. "And that's my new cat, Shadow, in the window."

"*I have a little shadow who goes in and out with me,*" I recited. "All black, from what I can see. Listen, Freddie, how would you like to help me in a little investigation I'm running?"

"Is this one of those good purposes you were talking about?"

"Trust me. When's your afternoon off?"

"I don't really have one. But I usually can get off on Monday—it's the slow day at Heaven."

We agreed that I would pick her up after school, 2:00 P.M. Before then I'd have to purloin a list of Paul Donahue's irate investors. And a plausible excuse for calling on them. I mentioned to Freddie that we would be visiting some businesspeople, so she might want to wear something appropriate.

* * *

Researching Paul Donahue didn't turn out to be all that difficult. The media had zeroed in on the missing family, a quirky enough occurrence to make the story a headliner. When the SEC investigation came to light, news reports implied that the Donahues may have run to avoid his imminent arrest. Various bilked investors were stalked by predatory reporters. A few were even persuaded to comment on their situation. A high school senior spoke on camera about his grandmother's loss, her late husband's entire retirement savings, over $350,000, money she'd planned to live on for the rest of her life. It made me wonder how people could be so trusting. Paul Donahue must have been a pretty persuasive fellow, probably a Pisces.

Unlike the media, I didn't believe Donahue had gotten off scot-free. So I began to compile a list of his financial victims and potential avengers. I checked out my slate with Phillipa, and she filled in the names I hadn't learned, privileged information from Stone that she was not supposed to discuss. I won't say what she threatened me with if I ever squealed, but it wasn't pretty. One never knew what a witch—a Wiccan—might be able to accomplish with a heartfelt curse.

Some names, like that of the destitute grandmother and her young grandson, I could cross off as unlikely. Plus a few people I happened to be acquainted with who didn't seem right for the slaying of an entire family—Bunn the Baker, for one. No one who produced a bread as honest and reliable as his caraway rye could be fiendishly vengeful. So after my purely subjective deletions, I found myself with a half-dozen names—residents of Plymouth, Scituate, and Duxbury—only one Boston address. It was doable. But did I really want to continue with this unlikely project?

Well, why not just start, I thought, as I fixed myself a bracing cup of mid-morning coffee—have a talk with those living nearby and see how it goes? But I would need a cover story for introducing myself and Freddie to these people. Heather's shelter for abandoned dogs and cats, Animal Lovers, came to mind—a noble cause for which to solicit funds. Encouraged by this brainstorm, I called Heather immediately.

"Listen, Heather, how would you like me to hit on a few businessmen I know of for some substantial donations to Animal Lovers?"

"What the devil are you up to now?" Heather asked.

I told her. "And I'm taking this girl Freddie with me. She has some of the most impressive psychic gifts I've ever witnessed."

"When it comes to sorting the human chaff from the wheat, you can't do better than a dog," Heather confirmed her usual bias. "Never mind Freddie. Take along the Donahues' dog Patsy. There's a good chance that she may have witnessed the kidnapping, if there was one. Say, has anyone considered alien abduction?"

"It wouldn't surprise me to hear that some reporter gets desperate enough to suggest it. Have you checked the headlines of the supermarket tabloids this week?"

"Please—that trash. So, then, how about Patsy?"

"Maybe. Why do I have the nasty suspicion that you're looking for an easy mark to adopt the poor mutt?"

"If you're so psychic, how come you need Freddie? Believe me, you'll get a lot more love and gratitude from a dog than a teenage delinquent. Come on over for lunch and meet Patsy. You're going to adore her."

Having checked that Ashbery was on duty, I agreed at once. Lunch at the dog mansion was not to be missed when Heather's housekeeper was whipping up her magic in the kitchen.

At noontime, when I stepped out of the Wagoneer in Heather's driveway with Scruffy trotting beside me, a soft breeze was strumming on the barely budding branches and sunlight was pouring down in its warm, promising April way. The huge old magnolia was in full glory, the forsythia hedge was blooming, and

Heather's motley crew, fenced in away from the driveway, was howling, barking, and snapping in various degrees of alarm.

Ignoring them, Scruffy merely curled his lip, peed on the magnolia, and strutted past the fence to the front door. *I hope you don't expect me to socialize with that low-class crowd.*

"I expect you to behave yourself like a perfect gentleman," I replied as Heather opened the door. By her side was a freshly groomed Irish setter. A jaunty green scarf with shamrocks on it, worn askew about the dog's neck, had been slightly chewed.

"This is Patsy," Heather introduced us as if to an honored guest. I almost expected Patsy to extend a dainty paw, but instead she glared at Scruffy and emitted a *sotto voce* growl, so low that Heather didn't notice.

Scruffy did, however, and responded by taking a startled step backward. *Hey, Toots—what's with the nasty redhead?*

"Play nice, children," I admonished. We sidled by Patsy in a respectful manner, and Heather ushered us into the conservatory, where a luncheon table was arranged between the potted palms and an array of rubber chew toys. A wine cooler stood nearby, filled with crushed ice and a bottle of Moët.

While Patsy busied herself pushing the chew toys into a heap and guarding them from Scruffy, Heather and I lunched on lobster bisque, delectable little biscuits, and a salad of ripe pears, toasted walnuts, and Stilton cheese. When Ashbery brought out the chocolate mousse and Heather opened a second bottle of Moët, I was softened up enough to agree to anything.

"How are Patsy's manners in a new situation?" I asked. "She's going to be meeting some total strangers in professional settings."

"As you see, she's a perfect doll," Heather assured me.

A nasty little bitch, if ever I met one. Scruffy lay on my feet under the table, brooding.

When Heather wasn't looking, I dropped a biscuit on his paws to cheer him up. Heather thought that feeding dogs "people food" ruined their health and appetite. Her animals were fed a scientifically formulated, weight calculated, high-protein chow with a spoonful of canned beef mixed into it for flavor—day after day after day. Scruffy, on the other hand, got whatever I was having with a little chow stirred in. He was especially partial to baked stuffed bluefish, turkey meatloaf, or lasagna.

Patsy, wearing her own dainty green leather collar and leash, accompanied me good-naturedly when she saw that a car ride was in the offing. She hopped up in the front seat beside me and gave Scruffy the merest lifting of her lip to indicate that his occupation of the backseat would be tolerated.

Whose car is this, anyway? Believe me, Toots, I've met mean old cats with better manners than this babe. He hunkered down on the backseat with his nose between his paws, refusing even to gaze and sniff out the partially open windows.

"Patsy may be a bit standoffish right now," I reassured him, "but in time I'll bet you two will be the best of friends. Come on, now . . . isn't there one little, little nice thing you can say about Patsy?"

There was a long silence in the backseat. Scruffy was not much for playing "the glad game." Finally, though, he came up with what was, for him, a happy thought. *She smells pretty good. She's not fixed like the rest of the surly females at that place.*

"Uh-oh," I said.

Wearing a short, black dress with narrow straps and a lacy bolero jacket, Freddie bounced down the high school stairs in clunky red platform heels that matched her lipstick. A diminutive red patent leather purse swung from her shoulder by a long gold chain. This was, no doubt, her conservative outfit, not much different, I told myself, from the little dresses worn by models in the *New York Times* fashion supplements. Only considerably cheaper, if purchased in Plymouth. And I infinitely preferred her vivid new lipstick to the brown stuff—a purely personal prejudice since both shades were equally unnatural.

"Very nice," I commented. "Okay, dogs in the rear, people in the front—that's my rule." I backed up my words by shoving Patsy up over the back of the seat until she got the idea and jumped. Scruffy moved over and stuck his nose out the window behind the driver's side, elaborately ignoring Patsy, who whined over her demotion.

"Here's the plan," I explained to Freddie. "We're going to call on a few people soliciting donations for Animal Lovers, a shelter for abandoned pets. If it seems feasible, we're going to take this Irish setter—Patsy is her name—to see how she reacts."

"Same as you're taking me, I guess," said Freddie. "What are we nosing around to find out?"

"Someone who's been swindled and may have been angry enough to go after a whole family."

"Hey, is this the Donahues you're talking about? Wow. Was Patsy their dog? Are you working with the police or anything?"

"No. I'm following these leads on my own."

"Maybe you're a P.I. then?"

"No. Not that, either. I just feel I have to follow up on a few leads I have in my head. Does that bother you? I guess it's probably more than I should be asking of you. It's okay if you want to back out. You can still come to the Esbat."

"Hey, you rule, Cass! This is awesome. Who's our first suspect?"

It seemed ironic to be soliciting a donation from the Serendipity Shoppe, a down-at-the-heels emporium crammed from grimy counter to dusty corner with every conceivable collectible. It didn't look like a very profitable operation; a Wal-Mart it wasn't. The yellowed window sign read: "WE BUY JUNK AND SELL ANTIQUES. *S. Fiddle, Prop.*" But I had seen the financial losses of the firm and knew the owners had made—and then lost—over half a million somehow, somewhere.

"Good afternoon, Mr. Fiddle," I said as we trooped in the door—all of us, that is, except Scruffy, who was sulking and whining in the Jeep.

"Mr. Fiddle has been dead as a doornail for a decade. I'm Bill Wade, sole owner and proprietor. What can I do you for?" offered the dark-browed man behind the counter. Lounging at length in a Mission chair tipped back at a dangerous angle, he wore black jeans, a black cowboy shirt with shiny studs, a turquoise bolero tie, and an enormous black Stetson. A greasy, dark ponytail hung over his collar. Somewhere between thirty-five and forty, I guessed. A slight bulge was beginning to inch over his beaded belt with the silver pony buckle.

"I'm Cassandra Shipton and this is Freddie McGarity," I introduced us. "I think I've seen you before, Mr. Wade, at the Bettridge estate auction perhaps?"

"I take an interest in furniture from time to time. You in the market?"

"Not at the moment. But my friend Heather Morgan may be looking for a Chippendale period highboy. Would you have such an item?"

"Captain Morgan's granddaughter? Lives in that big Federalist place up near Harlow's Landing with all the wild dogs? Tell her to give me a call. I show the good stuff by appointment only. If I don't have what she wants, I can get it."

"I'll tell her. Do you have another shop somewhere?"

"It's more like a warehouse. Not for your casual browsers."

In an instant, a vision flashed across my inner eye of Wade at the door of a big, old building with a peeling gray exterior and boarded-up windows. It was late at night; two men were carrying in several pieces of furniture wrapped in padding. I had the strong feeling that they were stolen goods. The image vanished as quickly as it came and left me staring into space, feeling stupid.

But Bill Wade was looking elsewhere. Eyeing Freddie appreciatively, he gestured toward Patsy. "Nice bitch," he said.

"Glad to know you're a dog lover," I continued my charade with forced cheeriness. Already I didn't like this cowboy character. "Since I'm here to ask you to donate to an extremely worthy cause . . ."

He paid scant attention as I went into my Animal Lovers spiel, stressing the Heather Morgan connection. Freddie was smiling enigmatically while running her slim fingers over the smudged glass case stuffed with an incredible array of vintage jewelry and small items of dubious value.

"Nice trash," she said. "Do you have crystal balls?" The cowboy's chair slid a fraction toward falling, but he grabbed the counter and righted it until all four legs were grounded. Excellent reflexes.

I wrenched my attention away from this interplay to watch Patsy. She stood near the door in her sporty shamrock scarf, ears pricked up as much as an Irish setter can manage, giving the cowboy a canine once-over. She ventured no nearer, but she didn't back up or growl, either. Nor did she relax and flop down on the floor while we continued our chat.

"No crystal balls, little lady, but I might have something else that would interest you." He directed a speculative look at Freddie's earring. "How about a sterling silver necklace to match that pentagram? Or a Ouija board? Genuine shrunken head?"

"Awesome." Freddie said, looking up at the three shrunken heads hanging over the jewelry case. They looked like shriveled coconuts with noses and hair. "So, what do you say about that donation?"

"Sorry, no can do. This little shoppe has fallen on hard times, I regret to say." Bill Wade stood up, as if to hurry us on our way. He was even taller than he had appeared when stretched out horizontally on a tilted chair. "Despite this excellent location, classy merchandise, and constant stream of discerning customers like yourself, this is not a good day to hit us up for a handout, so you and your little doggie might as well get along."

"How picturesque," I said. "Your current crisis wouldn't have anything to do with Donahue Financial Trust and Development, Inc., would it?"

The cowboy hit the counter with his fist, rattling the crystal beads and painted brooches into a heap. "Are you some friggin' reporter come sneaking in here under false pretenses?"

"Don't get your boxers in a twist," Freddie said pertly. "We only stopped into your cruddy *shoppe* to get a few bucks for some down-and-out dogs and cats. But apparently my associate here has hit upon a raw nerve with her casual remark."

I thought it was time that I took back control of this interview. "Are we to take it then that you are one of the victims of Donahue's alleged swindle? I mean, it's common knowledge that several shop owners had investments with Donahue. It just popped into my head that you might be one of his victims. Sorry. No offense meant."

"That bastard and his family have been living high off the hog on other people's hard-earned savings," Bill said, kicking the Mission chair sharply with the toe of his black boot. "They deserve to be taught a lesson they won't soon forget. And that's all I got to say about it. Now if you don't want to buy something, I'll thank you to let me get back to work." He sat down, leaned back, and tipped the Stetson over his eyes.

Before we left, I glanced again at the gruesome, glossy shrunken heads. No resemblance to the Donahues, I decided, as we left the dusty shop and thankfully breathed fresh air again.

It's about time you came back, Scruffy complained while we were installing ourselves in the Wagoneer. *How come you took Nasty Patsy inside with you and left me out here?*

"Patsy had some tracking work to do," I explained to Scruffy, who harrumphed his derision. "But Bill Wade didn't seem to provoke any reaction," I said to Freddie while we were buckling up in the Jeep. "What was your impression of him?"

"That Buffalo Bill wanna-be? Hot air and a soft gut. I bet I could have gotten a few bucks out of him for the little ones, though, if we'd had a bit more time. But I figured us private investigators have our schedule to maintain." Freddie examined a chip in her purple nail.

"Anything else?"

"Well . . . I wouldn't tell your friend to buy a Chippenwhatzis from that character if it's the sort of goods that can be traced, you know what I'm saying? Might be hot."

"My very thought," I said, starting the motor. "But I'm fairly well convinced that Bill Wade hasn't had anything to do with the Donahue disappearance. Maybe the popular conception is right, and the whole family simply has fled to a pleasant little island where they can spend their ill-gotten money while getting a great tan. I'm stuck with the notion, however, that they're all buried in a shallow grave in the woods. Maybe Maine woods."

Patsy chose that moment to utter several heartrending cries, but when I turned around to look at her, she was nosing out the window silently.

"What's next on our list?"

"The Doll House. How'd you get hooked by the Donahues, Cass?" Freddie took a lipstick out of her red patent leather shoulder bag, turned down the passenger mirror, and reapplied the vivid crimson to her lips. She flicked some black stuff out of one of her amber eyes with a green fingernail.

"It was sort of a vision thing," I explained lamely.

"Far out," Freddie said. "See—I had you pegged for a real witch. But you just go, *I'm in the herbal business, not the witch business.*" Her voice imitated mine in an annoying falsetto. "But just once, wouldn't you like to pick up on the million-dollar Lotto numbers? I mean, instead of where the bodies are buried?"

"That would make a pleasant change," I admitted. It was a question I'd often asked myself.

Woolley's Doll House & Seasons Shop, located near Plymouth Center, was a neo-Victorian building with a surfeit of gingerbread decoration painted in three candy shades of grape and one of raspberry. The windows were enchantingly peopled with dolls and stuffed animals of every style and nationality. One could glimpse inside the store doll dwelling places from Victorian mansions to California ranch houses. Life stories of dolls and teddies were told in large, glossy volumes or adorable little pamphlets. Signs promised after-Easter sales of bunnies, chicks, baskets, and chocolate eggs at a fifty percent discount. I wondered who would be provident or confident enough to tuck away Easter goods for the following year.

"Oooooh," said Freddie. "This is, like, totally awesome. Don't you just love those teeny-weeny Beanie Babies? Wouldn't you want to buy some cuddly bear for your very own?"

"Who needs a Teddy when I have Scruffy? Speaking of which, if we have a problem getting Patsy into the shop, we may have to identify her as a registered service dog. They can go anywhere."

"Is she a service dog?"

"My friend Heather gave me a certificate I can use. She's very resourceful."

"You mean, like, one of the witches—Wiccans—does forged dog papers? Wow."

"Let's go around to the delivery door. That might be easier," I suggested. It didn't seem to be a busy time for doll fanciers. There was no one in sight in front or around back. With a reluctant Patsy in tow by her green leash, we slipped inside. "Let's try the second floor. I think that's where the business offices must be." We made our way up the back stairs, and sidled around a mountain of doll carriages, doll beds, and tiny rocking chairs. I opened the door marked "AUTHORIZED PERSONNEL ONLY."

"I'm looking for Mr. or Mrs. Woolley," I explained to an anemic young woman with a great mane of brown hair who ambled by me toward the stairs, looking as if she were wrapped in an inviolate dream. Salesperson, no doubt. The kind I always get.

"They're in the office," she said, waving vaguely away from the stairs. "You can't miss the yelling."

True enough, I could hear that some sort of an argument was escalating as sounds emerged from the open door at the end of the hall. We moved sideways between walls lined with stacks of stuffed frogs, lobsters, alligators, dolphins, whales, and sharks with velvet teeth. Did the fire inspector ever check this floor?

"Here, Freddie, you hang on to Patsy." I knocked on the open door to interrupt a rotund little woman with improbable blond hair and a pink Cupid's mouth seated at the desk, a cup of tea in front of her, and a tall, round-shouldered, balding man leaning over her, chewing on a cigarette holder with an unlit cigarette, horn-rimmed glasses propped on his shiny head. "You always blame me." "If you weren't so stupid . . ." "We weren't the only ones." "I told you right from the beginning . . ." were some of the phrases being shouted simultaneously by two angry people. I gathered that it was the roly-poly woman who was on the defensive.

"What's that dog doing in here?" demanded the woman the moment she looked in our direction. "Take Froggie Foggie Dew out of its mouth this minute. Dogs aren't allowed on these premises. Remove her immediately!"

"Mrs. Woolley? Gee, I'm sorry. I didn't mean to startle you. Oh, don't worry about Patsy," I said, turning around to find the Irish setter dangling a stuffed green frog from her mouth.

Pressing the dog's upper jaws against her teeth, I muttered, "Drop it, drop it, that's a good girl." Patsy hung on stubbornly to one green arm. It was a perfect match for her scarf, I had to admit, but I didn't think it would last long in a tug-of-war. "Patsy's a registered service dog. I guess she just forgot herself for a moment when she fell in love with her frog prince."

"What the hell do you want?" asked Mr. Woolley, the cigarette holder still clutched between his teeth. Of the two, I preferred Patsy's hang-up.

I went into my prepared speech about Animal Lovers while the couple looked at me with expressions that were both incredulous and infuriated. At the same time, I eyed Patsy for signs of traumatic memory, but she seemed completely occupied with chewing Froggie's limp arm.

"Didn't you see the sign downstairs? *No pets . . . No solicitors!*" demanded Mr. Woolley.

"We came up the back way," I explained. "I didn't want to disturb your customers. Listen, I'll pay for Froggie. I guess I got you people at a bad time."

Freddie offered Patsy a Tic-Tac. Instantly the dog dropped the stuffed frog to grab the breath mint, but the little green fellow was looking definitely the worse for wear.

"Gee, Mrs. Woolley," said Freddie ingenuously, "didn't I see you on TV when the Donahue scandal broke? Aren't you, like, practically famous now?"

"No, you did not," snapped Mr. Woolley. "It was that bubble-headed Shirley Bean and her feckless grandson. Dragged her onto the six o'clock news so she could look like a damn fool. Nothing sacred to you young people these days. Shirley and my wife, what a pair, dumb and dumber. Went to the same seminar that crook gave and ate it up, both of them. Next thing I know, I'm broke. A lifetime of careful savings down the drain."

"*Now* who's blabber-mouthing?" said Mrs. Woolley, narrowing her china-doll blue eyes at Mr. Woolley. "*Your* idea of financial management is to stick good dollars under the mattress and come back five years later to see if they've had offspring." She smiled disparagingly and took a long swig of her tea.

"Hey, you're not a reporter, are you?" Mr. Woolley looked at Freddie savagely. Then he flipped his glasses down from his forehead onto his nose and looked again. His expression mellowed, but his eyes were speculative as he looked her up and down from spiked black hair to red high heels. His expression was hardly avuncular as his gaze lingered on her long legs in sheer black stockings.

"No, sir. Not me," Freddie said. "I'm just a high school girl working on my Girl Scout Community Service badge by canvassing for donations to worthy causes."

"Funny, you don't look like a Girl Scout," said Mr. Woolley. "What's that thing you got hanging from your ear?" He reached over to touch Freddie's pentagram earring, and suddenly he seemed to have something large and furry hanging from his arm. It was Patsy.

"All right, I've had about enough of this," said Mrs. Woolley, standing up to her full height of just over five feet and pursing her little mouth into a pink dot, while Mr. Woolley howled and cursed. "You get that attack dog out of here this very instant or I'm calling the police. Do you realize that's a genuine cashmere sweater that mutt is mauling? Registered service dog, indeed! *Junkyard dog* is more like it."

"Fuck! Fuck! Fuck!" said Mr. Woolley as a sort of punctuation to Mrs. Woolley's speech, while I pulled Patsy's jaws apart and dragged her into the hall.

"Give the lady one of my business cards from my pocket, will you please, Freddie. I'm deeply sorry, Mrs. Woolley. Please send me a bill for the sweater. And the Froggie. I'm afraid Patsy thought that Mr. Woolley was going to strike this young lady, but I don't think the dog's broken his skin or anything." Still murmuring apologies, I departed like a Japanese peasant bowing out of the provincial lord's presence.

Patsy brought her drooping green captive with her to wave in front of Scruffy, then snatch away when he nosed at it. *What's that dumb thing?* Scruffy pretended indifference. Patsy made some soft doggie sounds. *Nasty Patsy says she protected my hamburger friend from an attack person. That's my job.* Scruffy's nose was definitely out of joint.

"I'll take you with me at our next stop," I promised, knowing it was Plymouth Pets Day Camp, so no problem. "What did you think about that couple?" I asked Freddie. "And what did Patsy think?"

"Mean old sots, but not psycho," was Freddie's character summation. "Mrs. Woolley's tea reeks of whiskey, and Mr. Woolley would be a letch if he got you alone, but other than that . . . Patsy didn't react to them at all until the old man started to get ideas, if you know what I mean. Good girl, that Patsy. You gonna keep her?"

Both noses in the backseat swiveled away from their respective four inches of open window and turned toward me. Two pairs of ears perked up attentively.

"Quiet, those two are listening," I said.

Freddie was reapplying her red lipstick. "I suppose now you're going to tell me you witches talk to the animals. Like Doctor Dolittle, maybe?"

"Not all witches. Scruffy and I have a special relationship."

"No shit. Like a 'familiar'? Scruffy goes out and does your bidding at midnight? Sometimes I think I hear what Shadow's saying, but it's not in words, you know what I mean?"

"Yes, I do believe it's possible to understand animal language. Don't know about the 'familiar' part, though . . . I'll settle for simple obedience commands—never mind training Scruff to carry out spells and curses."

"Hey, Cass—you and I could probably make a fortune as pet psychologists. 'When you gotta know what your pooch thinks—who ya gonna call? The Pet Shrinks!' Like it?"

If you want to know what Nasty Patsy's thinking, just ask me, Toots. Scruffy snorted in the backseat. *She's getting tired of her new chew and thinking about chomping on the seat here. Hey, it's no fur off my tail, but this redhead has no house manners at all. Best thing would be to drop her off at the pound.*

We had just enough time for another stop before everyone would be wanting dinner. Not that I had to worry about Freddie, who had no family waiting at home to check the kitchen clock and worry about her. Freddie's folks had gone off blithely to Florida with her siblings Jack and Jim, leaving Freddie to iron her way into heaven. They had no idea she'd escaped, and if they'd known, may have opted for another so-called training school. So Freddie had to parent herself and make her own home in a run-down runaway's commune. Well, wasn't that every teenager's dream?

As I fell into a driver's mindless coma, slowed by late-afternoon traffic on the one-lane road to Plymouth Pets Day Camp, while Freddie peeled the color off her fuchsia nail, I got this picture in my mind's eye of those two empty guest rooms, one rose and one blue, sweetly tucked under the eaves upstairs at home. More of an image than a genuine vision. I struggled to keep it from surfacing. Alone is good, alone is free, I reminded myself. I'd better talk to Phil. She always straightens me out when I get some dewy-eyed notion. I'll tell her that Heather's trying to foist Patsy off on me, too.

It wasn't the best time of day to corner Jack Reardon, the Plymouth Pets owner and head trainer. Patrons were pulling in and out of the parking lot, picking up their canine charges as if they were kids at kindergarten. Freddie, Patsy, Scruffy, and I crowded into the long cement waiting room. There were bright blue appliquéd rubber paw prints on the floor and dog posters on the walls. Some soothing étude by Chopin was playing over the loudspeaker. In this dog-centered setting, we didn't seem at all conspicuous. A woman with an expensive blond haircut and a sailor's tan arrived to retrieve her companion bulldog. I wondered if she let him slobber like that on her plush new BMW upholstery.

We stayed as close to the wall as possible while the blonde retrieved the ugly old fellow's leash from a red plastic shoebox labeled *Winston*, one of many colorful boxes on three shelves, each with a dog's name, *Spike . . . Princess . . . Biscuit . . . Britta . . . Niko . . . Dusty . . . Daisy . . . Snickers.* Some contained extra collars and leashes, others held soft toys or baggies full of treats. This nursery school atmosphere must be reassuring to dog parents who left their little ones here for the day while they went to work, secure in the knowledge that their pets would have plenty of exercise and attention. Beyond the waiting room, behind a mesh fence, there were two playrooms. Larger dogs were joyously nosing around a beach ball in the farther room, where a stocky young woman with very red cheeks was supervising. Smaller dogs—beagles, cockers, and toy poodles—were pattering about in the nearer room. Both walls were lined with crates for "quiet time."

"Was Winston feeling social today?" the blonde asked the tall, smiling camp counselor as he tried to separate Winston from the other dogs, who were all eager to squeeze though the gates with him.

"Oh yes, Winston made a new friend today . . . Nellie. That's Nellie there, the English setter. Winston's doing just great."

"That's a good boy, Winston," cooed the blonde. Winston stared at Patsy, his eyes narrowing. She glared back, her ears sleeked for action. Scruffy moved up beside Patsy and showed his front teeth just enough to deter the bulldog from making any aggressive moves. The blonde continued a monologue of dog chitchat and baby talk as she moved out the door, dragging a reluctant Winston behind her.

Jack Reardon leaned out his office door, looked around the waiting room, and couldn't place us among his regular customers. "Did we have an appointment?"

"Ah . . . no . . . but we'll only take a few minutes of your time." He waved us into his inner sanctum, dogs and all. Scruffy hovered at my side. Patsy leaned against the closed door but otherwise did not seem the least bit intimidated by Jack, a middle-aged man of thickset build with thinning red hair and a florid complexion. He would have looked right at home behind the bar in a pub, polishing glasses and pouring draft beer. When he smiled broadly, his pale blue eyes nearly disappeared into puffy lids. Since I didn't want him to take us for real customers and be disappointed or angry, I hurried into my prepared plea for a donation. Before I could finish, he had already taken out his checkbook. I shook off a twinge of impostor guilt.

"This is the best I can do at present," Jack said, handing me a check for $25.00 and eyeing Scruffy. "Bet you got this fellow at Animal Lovers. Part French Briard, and part God-knows-what-mutt," he decided. "Been through an obedience course, has he?"

"Oh, there's no need," I laughed at the idea. "We've been together for several years now, and Scruffy's got me well enough trained to suit him."

Jack looked at me as if I were speaking in tongues. Then he

glanced at what might be another prospective customer: Patsy, glued against the door. "Say, I know this little girl. Patsy Donahue, isn't she? Denise Donahue used to bring Patsy here twice a week, for playdates with the other doggies." His expression darkened. "You mean, they didn't take this pretty girl when they ran off with everyone's money?" Clearly, this was some new low of treachery, in Jack's book.

"Just left her to wander around sad, starved, and matted." Freddie said. "Animal Lovers is her home now. That's why your donation means so much." She actually batted her sooty, black lashes at Reardon.

At the thought of Patsy's plight, Jack opened up with a vicious tirade that started out inveighing against animal neglect and escalated to indicting all wily embezzlers who bilk innocent businessmen.

"Did you get stuck, too?" I inquired sympathetically. "We've talked to other local people who've lost money with Donahue. Wonder where he's run, don't you?"

"What a bastard," Jack said, getting even more red in the face. "Told me I could realize twenty percent or more on my savings if I had the right investments. Named other Plymouth businessmen who were taking advantage of what he had to offer. I even talked to a couple who claimed to have made a bundle, but it turns out now that his early marks may have shown a profit on paper but they kept reinvesting it with Donahue. No more savvy than greyhounds racing after that fake rabbit." Suddenly, he seemed to think he'd said too much, and he shut up, gesturing at the check in my hand. "Well, that's all I can do. I'll be lucky if I'm still in business next month."

"But Plymouth Pets Day Camp is such a popular idea," I said, watching the dogs dashing around the two playrooms.

Not with me, it isn't, Toots. Scruffy was not amused. *But say, why don't you park Patsy here? Let her trot around after that dumb beach ball.*

"Not popular enough yet. Like anyone else who goes into

business, I have loans, obligations. But you're not interested in
my problems. So if you'll excuse me . . . don't forget, though, if
you decide to polish up your significant canine's manners—what
did you say his name is? Muffin? We can schedule an evaluation."

"Thanks. I'll think about that." I ignored Scruffy's mutterings,
and we left with dogs in tow before Jack Reardon could throw us
out of his office. Scruffy marked the azalea bush by the front
door, and we piled into the Wagoneer.

"What did you think?"

"Harmless," Freddie said. "Patsy didn't twitch an eyelash."

"Maybe that's enough for today. Aren't you getting hungry?"

If you ask me, it's hours past dinnertime, was the grumble from the
backseat.

Freddie was consulting our list. "Yeah, but it's only quarter to
five. How about we make one more stop? That clock shop is just
up the street."

A few minutes later, we were parking in front of Gere's Clock
and Watch Repair, the shop's name lettered on an antique
wooden sign, a clock face that creaked back and forth in the April
breeze.

"Scruffy, you're going to have to stay in the car this time, but
we won't be long," I promised, while he tried to shoulder Patsy
out of his way. "Sorry." I pushed him back inside and hurriedly
shut the door, a maneuver at which I have become necessarily
adept.

In the shop's window, a few porcelain clocks were arranged on
satin-draped pedestals. There was a discreet sign lettered in
Gothic style in the lower corner of the window: *Help Wanted.
Inquire Within.*

Inside the shop, a round-faced man with a monk's tonsure
bald spot was bending over a wooden clock case, the counter lit-
tered with brass parts. He had pale skin with a pronounced "five
o'clock shadow," and right on time, too. The little stack of business cards on the counter read *Thomas Gere, Timepiece Restorer.*

Just as Thomas Gere looked up and smiled, the hour struck

with a vengeance. Suddenly, the quiet shop turned mad with a cacophony of bells, beeps, cheeps, bings, and dings, along with a few cuckoo calls and a tiny tin horn blowing. Patsy howled and bolted. She dashed around the shop like a mad dog, then dove behind a fine, old grandfather clock, which rocked in an alarming fashion on its base. Freddie threw her arms around the timepiece and held it firm, while I hauled Patsy away toward the door, mumbling apologies.

"No dogs, no dogs!" Gere cried out, too late. Patsy leaped upon my shoulders and looked pleadingly into my eyes, at the same time clicking her teeth together in a menacing fashion. "No dogs, I say. Get that beast out of here at once!"

Still in a panic, Patsy jumped off me and turned on Gere with a snarl. In an instant, her front paws were up on the counter and she was curling her lip back over her teeth. The brass clock parts scattered, some of them falling and rolling behind the counter. Gere stepped back as far as he could go, against a shelf of glass-domed clocks, rattling them dangerously. His eyes were wide, his pale face a shade more ashen under the beard. "No dogs, no dogs," he whispered.

"Here, let me," Freddie said, grabbing the leash and pulling Patsy sharply down from the counter. It took real muscle, but apparently the girl was strong, because she managed to drag the stubborn dog across the wooden floor. I could hear Patsy's claws scraping as she struggled to hang on, but Freddie got her right to the door and I flung it open. Outside, Scruffy was barking and jumping against the windows.

I decided against asking Thomas Gere for a donation to Animal Lovers.

After I'd apologized profusely and left the premises, while Gere still had his hand on the phone threatening to call the police, I got into the car with the yowling dogs and we dashed away from Gere's shop with a squeal of tires.

After a while, when the dogs had quieted down and I could hear myself think, I said, "Was it the clocks or the clockman?"

"That's what I wonder," Freddie said. "But you know what I feel? Something icky in there. I mean, I know we were only there a few minutes, and it *might* have been the clocks all going crazy, but on the other hand, Patsy didn't just get spooked. She was damned mad, you know what I mean? I'd like her to have another chance at Gere, wouldn't you?"

"I wouldn't want her impounded as a dangerous dog."

"Yeah. I guess. So then, what if *I* try to get in there. Maybe Gere could use someone to watch the shop afternoons. Leave him free to go out back to play with his clockworks or terminate someone else. I'm mighty sick of hamburgers anyway. Like, the fat smell gets into everything."

I laughed, my big mistake. "Gere's not going to take you on after the havoc we caused today."

"Oh, yeah? What do you want to bet he won't even recognize me?"

I shouldn't have taken the bet.

"Who's the Greek dude?" Freddie asked over a plate of braised chicken with vegetables. She motioned toward the framed photo on the kitchen desk, Joe smiling jauntily, standing at the railing of the *MV Greenpeace*. How did she know he was Greek? The Greek fishing cap? Her psychic nature?

"My significant other," I replied.

"So where is he?"

"In jail. British Columbia."

"Far out," Freddie said.

"Hey, not drugs or anything heavy like that. Just an environmental protest, obstructing loggers who were out to clear-cut an ancient forest." Instantly, I was sorry I'd said *just*. I would have to admit to myself that I was not the environmentalist at heart that Joe was—or Heather. Well, maybe I would be if it were an animal rights issue. I could imagine myself breaking into a lab to free caged animals, providing they weren't rats and mice. Beatrix

Potter aside, I couldn't warm up to rodents. "He's with Greenpeace," I amended. "A ship's engineer."

"Hey, cool!" Freddie was even more impressed.

Scruffy and Patsy had wolfed down their dinners in short order—dog chow with a little chicken—and were thumping their empty stainless steel dishes against the kitchen cabinets. Braced to intercede in canine food fights, I'd been pleasantly surprised at how mannerly Scruffy had behaved with Patsy. I gave them each a dog biscuit, and they trotted off to find a decent rug on which to crunch them. "They're getting along okay. Isn't that surprising?"

"Patsy's running out of options." Freddie analyzed the situation as she stacked our plates and brought them to the sink. "She's been abandoned to the streets, so she knows the score now. *Fit in or shove off.* Dogs have a sixth sense, you know what I'm saying? Same as us."

"Yes, I see." Same as Freddie, I thought.

As I came in the door from driving Freddie "home," if you could call it that, the phone was ringing. *Joe!* Free at last of Canadian legal hassles, he'd been presented with an honorary membership in the Nuxalk nation and his personal totem pole, which he was having shipped to me. I couldn't imagine where I would put it. The side yards were a maze of herb plots and brick paths. Out front were a dog-ravaged lawn, various flowering bushes, notably my grandma's favorite lilac now in full glory, a small grove of pine trees near the road, and a flagstone path that bypassed the front door, which was never used anyway. In the back of the house were clusters of birch trees, more pines, and a slope with rickety stairs that led down to the rocky beach. In a flash I could see the totem as a post at the top of the stairs. In my mind's eye, it looked as if it belonged there. Good shaman magic. Cool, as Freddie would say.

"When will I see you?" I was careful not to sound too plaintive.

"It's all I'm thinking of," he said, his voice getting husky, a tone as intimate as his fingers brushing across my skin. "After this incident, I figure Greenpeace owes me some leave. I should be flying into Logan within a week. I'll call again once I have a confirmed reservation."

"Shall I meet you at Logan?"

"No, because I won't know when I'm going to get another assignment and have to take off suddenly. I'll arrange for a rented car at the airport."

He wasn't even here yet, and already he was planning his escape. "It's Beltane on the first of May," I said wistfully.

"I don't think that holy day's listed in my missal. Great time, is it?"

"You'll love it," I said, lowering my own voice to a honeyed purr.

"I can't wait. So, what's new with the circle? All's quiet, I hope. You're not tracking down any evil-doers, right? Just a little local magic and mayhem?"

"Hmmm. Where shall I begin? The cosmetics and potions are selling briskly, and I've expanded into dream pillows, herbal pillows, and aromatherapy wish candles. I have a new protégée named Freddie who's psychokinetic. A whole local family has gone missing. Possibly dead. And we—Scruffy and I—have an abandoned Irish setter staying with us."

"Oh, Jesus, I suppose you're investigating," he said. "Don't do anything crazy."

It's so satisfying to realize you can surprise someone you love and give him a nice little anxiety attack.

"And who the hell is Freddie?"

"A very remarkable person. Be sure to let me know when to expect you so that I can have everything ready."

"Such as . . . ?"

"Oh, wish candles . . . scented massage oils . . . that sort of thing."

"Soon, very soon," he murmured.

* * *

The next morning, I dropped in to have a cup of coffee with Phillipa. Only nothing's that uncomplicated in Phillipa's state-of-the-art kitchen. It was cappuccino with whipped milk dusted with cinnamon cocoa and an assortment of biscotti, those rock-hard Italian things that are double-toasted to break the teeth of anyone whose name doesn't end in a vowel. Possibly they originated with the ancient Roman army, a durable sort of biscuit to take on forced marches.

"I've been collecting donations for Animal Lovers. Hitting up that little list of financial victims you gave me." Surreptitiously, I stuck my almond biscotti into the cappuccino. Some of the sliced almonds fell off into the hot brew.

"You're keeping that our little secret, right? In order to avoid any marital misunderstanding between Stone and me." She passed me the plate of biscotti, but I waved them away with the half-nibbled, soggy one in my hand.

"Oh, absolutely. I would never want to be responsible for letting you loose in the singles market again. I remember how it went before. But here's the thing. Patsy has put her paw on a suspect. And since I'm not supposed to know who the suspects are, I'm puzzling over how to get Stone to investigate the guy."

"Which guy?"

"Thomas Gere, the clock repairman."

"You're out of your mind. As usual. Listen, my older brother Dan went to school with Tommy Gere—they graduated in the same year, class of '71. They weren't real close—Dan was a sports jock—but I did see Tommy occasionally at the house or some school event. Then Dan went off to med school, and Tommy was sent to 'Nam. I remember him as a mild, pale tinkerer who spent his happiest hours in shop. A juvenile Mr. Milquetoast. Certainly not someone to make a ten-year-old sister's heart beat faster."

"That's what people always say when interviewed about the local ax murderer. Your family wouldn't happen to have a yearbook? I know that was a while ago, but . . ."

"As a matter of fact, I have Dan's yearbook. And my other brother Josh's—class of '75. And mine, of course. Somewhere." Soon we were deep in dusty attic trunks. I kept losing Phillipa to fits of nostalgia as forgotten treasures were unearthed and admired. The Silver Lake High Yearbook, Class of 1980—Phillipa, her raven-black hair parted in the middle, spilling over her shoulders, her expression ethereal. Soon we were laughing affectionately over those innocent times. Although I'd graduated from an entirely different high school three years earlier in Salem, I saw myself at eighteen through Phillipa's dreamy yearbook gaze. It seemed we were other people entirely then, perhaps distantly related to our present selves, like third cousins. Which was literally true. Everything we'd believed then had been displaced by lessons in the real world as surely as every cell in our bodies had been changed and renewed every few years since. Except for the abiding spirit within.

And there, with Dan and the Class of '71 was the young Thomas Gere, recognizably himself. Unlike women, who often change their names, their hair color, and their style, men tend to remain very much the same. *Chess club. Drama. Archery.* Voted *Most Likely to Build a Better Mousetrap.* The quote beneath his photo read: "*In any weather, at any hour of the day or night, I have been anxious to improve the nick of time. . . .*" —Thoreau.

"Patsy had an adverse reaction to Gere, Phil," I said when we had descended to the orderly, gleaming kitchen and washed off the dust. "Do you think you can give Stone a little nudge in that direction?"

"I'll see what I can do," she promised. "Could I say you had a vision, do you think? He's a convert to your visions, you know."

"Stone's been very supportive, but there is that line he draws between what's his business and what's our domain. What sort of a vision?" I felt uncomfortable lying about my episodes of clairvoyance, although I could, when pressed to the wall, lie quickly and convincingly, like any survivor of an abusive marriage.

"Hmmm." Phillipa wandered over to the long herb planter

under her two kitchen windows and sprayed its fragrant, green plantings with a copper mister. She picked off a wilting basil leaf. "What if I say you 'saw' Patsy snarling at Thomas Gere. Which you actually did, but not psychically."

Did our other world, the spirit realm, distinguish between creating a deliberate misconception and telling an out-and-out lie? "Okay, try that one. It's almost true. Maybe your esteemed husband will be moved to investigate further. Meanwhile, I'll see if I can find out anything else about Gere on my own."

"Talk to Dee. Perhaps Will knows something useful."

When I opened the door, a fresh-faced young woman was standing on the mat. "I got the job," the stranger said with a triumphant grin. Scruffy wasn't barking. He was nosing the girl's hand for pats and treats.

My ginkgo biloba finally kicked in. "Great Goddess, what a change!" I realized I was looking at Freddie, reborn into the Brady bunch. No makeup, except for a little coral lipstick that complemented her amber eyes. Actual freckles visible across her nose. Spiky hairdo metamorphosed into soft, brown curls, which I later learned was her hair's natural state. White blouse with Peter Pan collar, gold heart-shaped locket her only jewelry, Black Watch plaid skirt hemmed just above the knees, and wonder of wonders! navy blue kneesocks!!! The earring holes were still visible, but only if you looked really close. "What did you do, rent that outfit?"

"Mostly leftovers from parochial school. Like, I know I should have dumped them, but they were in this box where Shadow likes to sleep. Sort of a nest, you know what I mean? I gave Shadow my old Hamburger Heaven smock instead."

Freddie stepped into the kitchen and took her usual chair at the table. I took the hint and put on the kettle. "Want a sandwich?"

"Yeah, well, I didn't get my regular Saint Peter Burger after school, because I didn't go to work. I went over to Gere's Clock instead, to apply for an after-school job. And guess what—I got it!"

"He didn't remember you?" To tell the truth, I wasn't surprised. She'd nearly fooled me, although Scruffy had sniffed out her identity fast enough.

"Clueless. Very pleasant, too, if a person weren't savvy. I told him I was called Winnie, in case he would remember your saying 'Freddie' when we were in his shop before."

"Your kind of savvy *is* psychic—most people don't have intuitive talent very well developed. But the thing is, I don't like your getting this close to him, Freddie." I sliced cold chicken and arranged it on white bread. Freddie liked salt, pepper, lettuce, and lots of mayonnaise. Well, she could use a little fattening up. I started on a second sandwich.

"Oh, come on, Cass. This is so cool! What could be better than having an undercover agent right on the premises? Mr. Gere says he'd been thinking of advertising for someone to help out afternoons. Then he goes, 'I'll have to ask you for references, dear, because of the nature of my merchandise.'"

"I don't think my name would do any good. In fact, I think my name is 'mud' with Thomas Gere."

"I didn't use your name as a reference. I used the names of your friends. I figured you could get them to help out, you know?"

"Freddie!" I stopped spreading mayonnaise, holding the knife in midair as if I were a statue. "Just where and how did you get the circle's names—I take it that you do mean the circle?"

"Well, that didn't take any big occult genius, you know what I mean? They're right there on your kitchen phone, your most frequent calls programmed for one-button dialing. Fiona Ritchie, Deidre Ryan, Phillipa Stern, and Heather Morgan. Who else could they be but the other witches?"

"Very resourceful," I said dryly, handing her a plate of sandwiches and a mug of my new Wise Woman tea blend.

"I hope you remember our bet, Cass. You said if I could fool Mr. Gere, after that major screw-up in his shop, you'd teach me some real Wiccan spells on a regular basis, just like piano lessons, you know?"

"*Moi?* I said that?"

"A promise is a promise," Freddie pronounced sentence on me with great satisfaction, then turned her complete attention to her sandwiches.

"I'm zeroing in on Thomas Gere, who has that clock shop in Plymouth Center," I told Deidre. While the April afternoon was teasing us with an unseasonable 70 degrees, Deidre and I were sitting out in her fenced backyard with her youngest, Bobby, her toy poodles, Salty and Peppy, and my two dogs—as I now thought of Scruffy and the Irish setter—all of them milling about our dusted-off lawn chairs. "We visited most of the Plymouth businessmen who got stung in the Donahue con. Gere was the only one of the lot who turned pretty Patsy into an attack dog. So I'm wondering if Will could tell us anything more about Gere. Do you think Will might know him?"

"I'm sure he knows the shop. I'll ask him. But it's difficult to believe that some nice local guy could do away with the Donahues. Our evidence is a bit on the flimsy side, I have to admit. All we know is that the family has gone missing, you've had one of your funny spells featuring Candy's pink sneaker, and Patsy has taken a dislike to Gere. It could be just as reasonable to suppose that the Donahues are in Rio de Janeiro living it up on everyone's life savings, Patsy was spooked by the clock chimes, and you've been hitting the chardonnay too enthusiastically. Speaking of which, would you like a beer or a cola?"

"No, thanks." What I would have liked was a tall glass of iced tea, home brewed, with a little sugar and a lot of lemon, but I knew from experience that Deidre would only have that powdered stuff. "You don't really believe that Rio de Janeiro scenario. After all, it was you who rang the first alarm."

"True enough. And I'm trying to think how I can help. I mean, I don't do visions, or findings or candle spells or Tarot. I suppose I could make a little poppet of Mr. Gere, in case we decide to put the squeeze on him. What's he look like?"

"Promise—no black arts, right?"

"Right," she said insincerely.

"Round face, a bald spot on the crown of his head, pale skin, and a heavy beard. Sort of looks like someone who's been working in the cellar for weeks."

"Maybe he's got them buried down there. Ugh."

"Not unless his cellar has a dirt floor, if my vision is to be believed, and besides, Fiona found for Maine."

Bobby, who'd been grabbing hold of Scruffy's fur and trying to hoist himself astride, was now sitting on the ground, crying. "Bad dog, bad dog," Deidre said and shook her finger at Scruffy as she rescued her son.

Dumb kid, dumb kid. Why doesn't he get a horse? Scruffy shook himself disdainfully and stalked off to brood under the forsythia bush. I almost heard Patsy laughing at him. She had been occupying herself by terrorizing Salty and Peppy, then piling all their rubber bones and balls in a heap in the grassy corner of the yard she had staked out for herself.

"Play nice, children," I said weakly. The unexpected warmth of the sun was too sensuous for positive parenting. Let them sort out who's top dog by themselves, I thought.

"Just look at my baby! He's all muddy now," Deidre continued to scold.

"He was trying to ride on Scruffy's back," I explained. "Dogs don't go for that, unless they've been trained to accept it."

"Have you ever considered bringing Scruffy to obedience school?" Deidre asked.

"No, never. We suit each other well enough." I was tempted to ask if Deidre had considered obedience school for her crew, but I held my tongue. "Do you ever sell any of your dolls? They're really quite adorable—most people wouldn't imagine they have any use besides decoration."

"I do enjoy making them, too. I put a few up on a shelf behind the cash register at Nature's Bounty just before Valentine's Day. They were love dolls, actually. Each one had a tiny red heart

painted on its chest under its clothing. You know, like Raggedy
Ann's heart. I sold several practically at cost, and then some irate
person came steaming in to demand the return of the pitiful
price of the boy and girl dolls she'd bought."

"Why ever?"

"Well, I'd made the dolls anatomically correct, and apparently
this person didn't think her daughter should know what little
boys are made of."

Later, at dinnertime, Deidre called me. "Will says he doesn't
know Thomas Gere personally, but some of his friends at the
firehouse do. A couple of the guys have gone hunting with Gere.
During the bow and arrow season, you know, that precedes the
regular hunting season? They rented a hunting lodge and had a
high old time. The cabin was somewhere near Bangor, Maine.
Fiona gets high marks for finding, I'd say. Will's going to find out
whose cabin and exactly where it's located. So . . . how's that for
sleuthing! Do I get the prize or what?"

"Now we're getting somewhere," I agreed.

"And I'm making a little bow and arrow for my Gere poppet,"
said Deidre.

"Yes . . . well, resist that impulse to stick the arrow somewhere, my dear. We're going to do this the right way . . . or
should I say, the white way?"

"Don't be a spoilsport,' said Deidre.

Beltane—May Day, Feast of Fertility

To me, every High Sabbat is the best ever. At Samhain, I delved deep into the mysteries of life and death; the significance of other holidays pale in comparison. At Yule, my spirit would be entirely occupied in encouraging the frail winter sun to grow vigorous. And at Beltane, I forgot all that supportive stuff and threw my heart into the fertility of Maytime, thinking it the most beautiful and vital of all the High Sabbats. I didn't know if my melding with each season, my identification with its essence, was a sign of strength or weakness. As a Libra, I felt I should be striving for a more balanced view, even while I prepared for Beltane with joyful abandon—the loveliest of holidays!

I brought into the house great armfuls of woodruff with its fragrant white blossoms. Never used for a curse, a conjure, or a cure, sweet woodruff was solely a flavoring for May wine, although sometimes I would include it in a wish pillow, as a whiff of Beltane, for someone who wished to be pregnant. After filling vases and jars with enough bunches of woodruff to make Scruffy sneeze, I presented a bouquet to Heather for the May Bowl.

"Oh, how exquisite," she exclaimed, barely audible above the canine chorus of welcoming and warning barks. Dogs of all sizes and smells milled about her legs as we headed for the conservatory where there was a thermal carafe of coffee. She poured a cup for me. "How are you getting on with Patsy?"

"Better you should ask how Scruffy is getting along with Patsy. The answer is, he's becoming more resigned to her intrusion into our household, and she's less greedy about toys and tidbits than she was at first. But I can't tell you yet if I'm going to keep her for always. She is a dear, sweet girl, though."

"Patsy's probably five or six years old. Who's going to adopt her if you don't? I hear she's taken a dislike to Thomas Gere."

"Yes. And Will tells us that Gere went hunting last fall up near Bangor. Some bow and arrow macho thing that happens just before the regular hunting season."

"So what are we going to do with this information?"

"Phillipa's pouring it all into Stone's ears. Deidre's making a poppet, which is more of a concern than a help. Fiona's been finding for us rather accurately . . ."

"And I'm doing this great candle ritual I just unearthed from some old book of Fiona's. It's an open-the-grave, unlock-the-secrets spell, green and brown candles. Do you know how difficult it is to find brown candles? It's the one color no one makes."

"How did you compensate?" I had thought Heather could always buy anything she wanted.

"Ashbery and I made the candles ourselves. I didn't tell her what they were for, of course, but she still thinks I'm demented. Chunky mushroom shapes with dark, twisted wicks. I included bits of brown leaf, twig, and bark to make them rough and earthy. They're so fantastic I'm tempted to market them."

"I could put them into my catalog for you. What did you scent them with?"

"Wood rot and asofoetida."

"Well, maybe my catalog isn't quite the right outlet for such a specialized product."

"Help! I need a baby-sitter for Beltane," wailed Fiona on the phone. "My regular is going off on a garden tour. I wonder if you'd recommend your protégée—and if she'd be interested. I never dreamed, at my time of life, that I'd have to be out beating the bushes for a baby-sitter. It's so ironic!"

"Freddie's a very capable young woman, and she's cleaned up very nicely to get a job at the clock shop."

"I know. Gere called both me and Phil for a reference, with no idea that we'd never met the girl. Luckily, we're both canny enough to figure what you two were conjuring. Along with knowing Phil's family from school days—friends with her brother, I believe—our hometown boy was acquainted with my poor, dead Rob Ritchie. Gere had repaired that antique ship's clock you've seen on my mantel for Rob. But aren't you afraid you've put Freddie into the path of danger?"

"Hey, it was her idea," I said defensively. "But, yes, I am afraid for her. Also, with her psychokinetic talents, who knows what may happen in a clock shop? It bodes ill all around. Have you tried to tell a teenager what to do recently?"

Fiona laughed, and I couldn't help smiling at my end of the wire. She had this deep, good-humored laugh that made one think of an aging but infinitely charming cabaret hostess. "Here I am childless, and you with children grown. How do we get ourselves into these briar patches?"

"It must be karma. It seems as if we draw kid troubles as nectar draws the bees."

"Perhaps we'll get royally stung. But Laura Belle is such a doll, I could never regret her. She's changed my life completely."

That was an understatement! Frowsy neglect had given way to neat efficiency in Fiona's picturesque cottage. "I hope you're preparing yourself for the day when Mommy Belle arrives at your door—a successful lawyer with her own apartment and a nanny on order—to claim her daughter."

"By then it will be too late. The wee darlin' will be imprinted with all my arts and talents, and her sensible mother will be clueless."

"That's a fairly dark idea, Fiona." There was a touch of the fairie about little Laura with her face so sweet and pink-cheeked and those morning glory eyes so knowing.

Fiona laughed again. And when Fiona laughed, I just had to join in her merriment.

When I arrived at Heather's on May 1, I found my woodruff put to its traditional use. Heather's crystal punch bowl, filled with white wine and strawberry liqueur, was garnished with sliced, fresh strawberries and scented with woodruff. This delicious punch went down rather too easily, and we were all pretty much in the mood for dancing by the time we went outdoors to Heather's new stone circle for our celebration. Although we usually alternate hosting, all of us had wanted to consecrate this perfect stone circle with a High Sabbat ceremony, one of the four most important celebrations in the cycle of the year.

At our mature ages, dressed in our flowery dresses, with Phillipa in her wide-brimmed straw hat, we looked more like a suburban garden party or May wedding reception than a Wiccan coven preparing to celebrate a pagan fertility rite. I wore my new jumper, mint green sprigged with tiny yellow flowers, and a white silk T-shirt; the rest of the circle looked as if they'd shopped in the same Talbots catalog as I had.

But once we got down to it, we tossed off our shoes and entwined our ribbons around the Maypole in quite a merry mood, and, later, leaped between the two fires with plenty of spring in our steps. Especially Fiona, who has that enviable talent of being able to put on a glamour, a subtly altered appearance that made her seem taller, younger, and more attractive. No more the fifty-ish grandaunt with childcare worries weighing heavily on her brow, tonight she'd become a graceful, radiant maiden. Maybe it was partly the forgiving firelight, but I vowed to keep working on the art of glamour, a magic well worth every effort.

As I drove in my driveway long after dark, I could see Scruffy and Patsy sitting upright, side by side on the living room windowseat, waiting for my return like two suspicious parents—the canine version of *American Gothic*. Dogs never believe those excuses you give them for being later than you promised. After I'd handed out biscuits, I sank into a bathtub full of hot, lavender-scented suds. It was heaven—so of course the phone rang. Why don't I have a cordless phone like everyone else in the world? I asked myself, dripping my way from bathroom to bedroom, wondering who was dead or dying.

"I tried to reach you earlier before I got my flight, but you weren't home," Joe complained. "You were gone for hours and hours. Where were you?"

"Oh, thank the Goddess, it's you. Out celebrating May Day. Did you call earlier? I guess I forgot to check my answering machine when I got home. How wonderful, darling! Where are you?"

"Logan. I'm just about to pick up a rental. I know it's late, but would it be okay if I drove out there now? You know I can't wait to be with you, Cass . . ."

It was after midnight, and I was in my Victoria's Secret green silk pajamas, curled up on the living room sofa, nearly drifting into sleep, by the time Joe arrived, his solid male presence so amazing and breathtaking after weeks without him. He surrounded me with strength and warmth and the delicious fragrance of herbs in sunlight. I loved the way he looked, his features rugged, his body compact and strong. His hair was crisp and curly, black touched with gray, and his eyes pure Mediterranean blue. He wore a neat beard that excited my skin like a feather drawn slowly and softly across breasts and thighs. Even though we didn't romp through the woods by moonlight, our celebration of Beltane in the time-honored way was entirely magical.

"How long can you stay?" I finally asked over a very late breakfast.

"Barring the odd environmental catastrophe, I have a week's leave before we embark on the *Arctic Sunrise* to stop the pirate fishing off Mauritius. Which is top secret information, by the way." He poured himself and me another cup of coffee. "We've had word that some Belize-registered vessel is illegally hauling up Patagonian toothfish and unloading the catch at Mauritius."

"Is that somewhere in South America? I've never heard of the Patagonian toothfish."

"Mauritius is an island in the Indian Ocean off the southern tip of Africa. Near Madagascar. And you'll hear of the Patagonian toothfish once we get there. Awakening public interest is our game, as you know. That makes being hauled off to jail a publicity plus, so I'm a temporary hero taking a well-earned rest. Now, what would you like to do with our week? I mean, what *else*?" He winked at me lewdly, and his smile was richly satisfied with himself.

"How would you like to take a drive up to Bangor? I know it's not as romantic as Madagascar, but . . ." I began to clear the table.

"Bangor?" The smile faded to bewilderment.

"There's a hunting lodge I want to check out."

"For?"

"Bodies."

"I'm off work until Monday," Freddie explained when I opened the door to her familiar black-spiked hair, sooty eyes, multi-earrings, and leather miniskirt, "so I dropped the disguise. Whose Rent-A-Wreck out there? Hey, is that the Greek dude? So, I guess you want me to fade, right?"

I did, rather, but I didn't want to lay any more rejections on Freddie. "Come on in and meet Joe. And fill me in on anything you've learned at Gere's Clocks. You can join us for lunch."

"Lunch? At three? Far out." I managed to keep a dignified expression despite Freddie leering at me. Scruffy and Patsy changed the subject by leaping upon her with abandon, each vying to be the dog who looked most closely into her eyes and got the most licks in all over her face.

Freddie had many questions about Greenpeace, and Joe had rousing stories to tell, so the two were soon chatting like old friends. By the time I dished up aromatic double-fish chowder, a combination of salt cod and fresh cod, I thought Freddie was about ready to join up and see the world from a Greenpeace dinghy rocking on the waves over various environmentally challenged seas.

Freddie ate as if she hadn't had any lunch yet, or breakfast, either. When tales of daring Greenpeace exploits began to wane, between bites of crusty French bread laden with olive tapenade, she said, "Cass is teaching me to be a witch—I mean, Wiccan practitioner. She says I'm a natural psycho-something, you know what I mean?"

"Psychokinetic," I corrected, not overjoyed with the turn our luncheon conversation was taking. Joe looked as puzzled as I had been over Mauritius, so I explained. "Mind over matter. Freddie can move things without touching them. And she tells me she can addle machinery and electronics, too, although I've not asked her for a demonstration."

Joe raised an expressive black eyebrow. "Rather like an albatross, is she? I'll keep her off the *Arctic Sunrise*, then. And did I hear Cass say you're working in a *clock* shop?"

"Hey, it's a necessary risk, just like the Greenpeace gang takes all the time. Cass and I are nosing around there, if you know what I'm saying. We think maybe the clock man, Tom Gere, has offed this whole family, the Donahues, who disappeared in Plymouth a month ago. Cool, isn't it?"

"Is everyone ready for coffee and apple tart?" I asked.

"Sure. Very cool," Joe said, glancing my way just briefly. "And why would Gere do such a thing, do you suppose?"

"I'll have some tart, thanks," Freddie said. "Because Paul Donahue ripped off half the businessmen in Plymouth, which included Gere, that's why. I've been meaning to tell you, Cass. Just at the end of the week when he paid me—it was under the table, you know, so he wouldn't have to do any paperwork—Gere was packing up some of his precious antique clock collection and sending them off to an auction in New York. He must have needed the money real bad, because he had tears in his eyes, real tears, when he was deciding which ones to sacrifice. He acted as if someone was making him chop off his fingers one by one. You would have loved me being all sympathetic over those weird old things."

"Seems we'll have a lot to talk about while we drive north." Joe gave me a meaningful glance.

"Hey, you two grabbing yourselves a little vacation time? Excellent." Freddie approved of us with a beaming smile outlined by brown lipstick. "Want me to house-sit, watch the pups, or anything?"

"If this were a vacation week, I'd be delighted," I said, "but you do have to be in school, and now you have this job with Gere. All I want is for you to keep a low profile over there for a few days, and be safe. I'll call you every evening at your place to be sure you're okay. Scruffy and Patsy can stay with Heather or at the Animal Lovers Shelter—they'll be just fine."

"So, do I get a demonstration?" Joe asked. "Of this magic talent of Freddie's?" The unbelieving twinkle in his eyes did not escape Freddie's attention.

"Sure," she said. "I do better when I'm running on empty, but I'll give it a try. What do you have with you that's made of metal?"

Smiling, I stacked the last of the dishes and brought them to the sink.

"How about this?" Joe took out his pocket compass and laid it on the now-cleared table.

Freddie leaned over to admire the ornate case without touching it. The needle began to tremble. "Awesome. Looks like a family antique, am I right? Probably too heavy to move," she said, but she stared at the compass and passed her hands over it. After a moment of gyrating wildly, the needle pointed solidly at Freddie and stayed there. "Just call me True North," she said.

"My God, she's magnetic!" Joe exclaimed. "Let me see your

hands." He examined Freddie's hands front and back for some device that would explain what he had just witnessed. But she wore no rings or bracelets. Perhaps she had found them an interference. As she winked at me over his head, Joe said, "Is it something in this dark nail polish?"

"It *is* like magnetism," I agreed. "But you won't find any rational reason for the compass needle settling on Freddie. I think you're going to have to shake off this skepticism, darling, if you're going to hang with me and my friends. Freddie, please do a spoon, if you're not too tired."

Freddie sighed. "Got an old fork, tablespoon, anything you don't want?" I found an odd fork and put it in the center of the table. "I'm too full," she complained, but she held her hands above the fork, her brow beading with perspiration as the fork slowly slithered toward her. Then, suddenly, it stopped and lay motionless. "That does it," Freddie declared, falling back into her chair. "Any more and I'll have to barf."

I was gratified to see Joe looking properly astounded. After Freddie left, he said, "So the young lady has come to you for instruction, is that it?"

"No, Freddie doesn't need teaching, she needs control. I'm hoping to help her gain a handle on this weird ability of hers before she does something she'll regret very much. But I wouldn't want anyone to know about Freddie, Joe—think of it as *my* top secret—because Freddie could be a valuable commodity to the wrong types of people. Imagine being able to jimmy locks, screw up computers, and sabotage machinery."

"Terrific business opportunity for a witchette," Joe agreed. "But now I want to go for a walk on the beach in the May sunshine while you tell me all your dark secrets, absolutely everything about this Donahue mystery, and about Freddie, and what do you hear from Tip?"

I felt the air go out of me in a long sigh. It would take a month of May sunshine to exorcise those three worries.

*   *   *

On Friday morning, we drove north in my Wagoneer, Joe and I switching off at the wheel about every two hours. It was delightfully mesmerizing just to drive along beside him, the trees zooming past us, the motor humming with soothing competence. We played CDs, Vivaldi and Dvorak, spelled by rollicking sea chanteys. Although May had not yet fully awakened the landscape, Maine was as magnificent as always—but, to me, depressing. The melancholy sight of so many rundown homes with derelict cars rusting in their front yards took the shine off the beautiful vistas. It seemed colder than spring should be, but was seasonally correct, of course, for Maine. As always, I missed the enclosing roads of home, where hills and trees cut off the longer view, allowing the possibility that surprise would await the traveler around the next bend. Here we could see for miles, groves of startling white birch or rich, dark pine. It's no wonder that there's so little witchcraft Down East, so unlike cozy, secretive, inbred Massachusetts. Maine is a kind of psychic wasteland, despite its elemental splendor.

There are few ghosts, too, that the natives will admit to encountering. But we happened upon a pair of British innkeepers, Cecile and Nigel Usher, who had been brought up on tales of something clanking on the castle stairs at midnight and who still reveled in revenants. We had decided to stay at the Bone Rock Inn, perched on a ledge above the town of Northeast Harbor. Surrounding the inn, a dense forest kept the place in firewood for cool days and nights—they were all chilly, in my opinion. Bone Rock was a private and inviting place for lovers, though—haunting and haunted.

As she brought in a welcoming tray of strong British tea with scones to our room, Cecile said, "If you happen to look out your window after midnight, don't be surprised if you see a lady in mauve wandering through that old herb garden. The locals won't discuss the matter, but the librarian tells me that she fits the description of a young woman named Grace Meade who lived here in the early eighteen hundreds."

"This place is right up your alley," Joe muttered, tossing his duffel bag into an antique pine armoire.

"How interesting!" I exclaimed, giving him a warning glance which he likes to call my *evil eye.* "A love story? Her captain didn't return from the sea?"

"No, not that," said Cecile. "He returned, all right. A whaler bringing her a two-year supply of soiled shirts and some rotting pineapples. She poisoned him, so they say, but no one knew why, nor was she ever charged. The townsfolk made her chew up a handful of every herb—roots and all—that she had growing in her herb garden, but nothing sickened her and nothing could be proved."

"Typical herbalist," said Joe.

"Very knowledgeable, indeed, as you say, Mr. Ulysses. A great one for the herbal cures, she was," Cecile agreed. "A few brave souls continued to seek remedies from Grace Meade through the years. She lived to be very old, ninety-odd. They say she took many lovers among the men in town, although the women shunned her. They called her a witch, poor superstitious sods."

"I'll keep an eye out for her," I promised. "Will I be able to call home on this phone? I have an AT&T credit card."

"Just dial nine before the number, luv," Cecile said. "There's going to be an early moon rising tonight, too. Gracie favors the moonlight. Shall I make a dinner reservation for you in our dining room?"

"I wouldn't miss it. At seven, please."

It was a serene and comfortable room with pale yellow antique wallpaper, a large mahogany four-poster bed, and double windows overlooking the garden. I left my practical forest-searching, body-hunting Maine gear in the suitcase, and shook out the one all-purpose dress I had packed, moss green jersey—it would do—and a fine wool shawl, pale gold, that had been a gift from

Joe. Would I wear my pentagram inside or outside the dress? Outside. Cecile seemed to be a broad-minded soul.

Then I made my calls. As arranged, I called Freddie at a time when Gere usually went across the street to the Plymouth Diner for a quick meal.

"Gere's Clock and Watch Repair," Freddie sang out happily.

"How are you? What's new? Any problems?"

"Everything's cool. You two having fun?" she purred suggestively.

"None of your business."

"Sure. Hey, I do have one thing to report."

"Yes?"

"Tom asked me if I could take over tomorrow. He's going to be away for the rest of the weekend. A good chance for me to snoop around in his office, right?"

"Wrong! You stay out of there. Clock people are precise, tidy types. If you mess around in there, he'll know it. At least with Gere gone, I'll know you're all right. You must be doing a great job there, if he trusts you to close up."

"Yeah, I guess so. But Saturday is no big deal. Just drags along, you know what I'm saying? The real clock nuts come in earlier in the week."

"Anyway, take care of yourself," I warned.

Then I called Heather to check on Scruffy and Patsy. "Oh, they're having a marvelous time—don't you worry about them," Heather assured me. "Dogs love to romp with other dogs, you know. The old pack instinct. Personally, I think Scruffy has been a bit lonesome being the only dog. You can tell that from the way he's been running back and forth in the yard, barking at everything."

I could just imagine what version of these same events I would hear from Scruffy when I returned home.

After dinner—some fantastic shrimp thing, and pear pie with ginger—we wandered around outdoors with the other guests who had been tantalized by Cecile's ghost stories. The moonlight glistened in the high branches of pine, the tiny new maple leaves were silver-tipped, and the old herb garden fragrant with ancient, woody thyme and hardy woodruff. But it was a fruitless and chilly vigil from which we were glad to retire to our splendid four-poster. Joe lit the fire that was laid in the small tiled fireplace.

"No decent person goes to bed before nine," I said.

"All the better," he replied.

There's something about making love in a strange bed in an unfamiliar town that feels deliciously illicit, as reckless and anonymous as strangers on a train. We tangled together so hotly, it put all thought of ghostly pursuits and Grace Meade right out of our heads. That made it all the more surprising, just after the grandfather clock on the landing struck half past midnight, when Joe sat up in bed and said, "*Jesu Christos*, what's that?"

I looked across the room toward the dying embers of our fire. We'd left the window shades up, and although the moon was higher in the sky now, light was streaming in. A fine, misty glow seemed to be wavering between us and the fireplace . . . fluttering like pale moths . . . rising . . . dissolving . . . then returning to a clearer definition, now like a mauve silk robe caught in a breeze. Then as I watched, dumb and frozen, holding the quilt wrapped tightly around me, the mist darkened and hollowed, like armless sleeves reaching out toward us. Its motion was subtle, gentle, hypnotic. I heard a *hiss hiss* sound, and smelled the odor of something ugly and mousey. To me, unmistakable.

"That's hemlock, Joe. It's Gracie," I whispered.

"That's crazy, Cass. Must be something leaching out of the fire," Joe whispered back, his hand touching the gold cross that hangs around his neck.

I screwed up my courage. After all, I'm accustomed to the comforting ghost of my grandma. And I'm in touch with the invisible world, I reminded myself, the limitless dimensions beyond our own, the dazzling alternate realities, and all of the fairie-spirit realm—so why should I not communicate with this spirit? Let the embracing, loving light surround me, protect me, I said to myself. The misty thing seemed to be bubbling now, murmuring incoherently. "What is it, Grace?" I asked aloud.

The hissing sound rose and fell like snake music. The dark arms flailed and reached and folded in on themselves, waves of the universal sea. *Shhhhh. Sssssss. He'ssssss heeeeere. Shhhhhh. Seeeeeee. Heeeeeee. Heeeere.*

The image pulled in its waving mauve appendages, turned paler, and like a wisp of fog, floated away and became one with the last vestiges of moonlight lapping the windowsill.

"Would you want to be rid of your ghost?" I asked Cecile the next morning. We were breakfasting at one of the two round oak tables in the kitchen where she served buttery scrambled eggs, crisp bacon, and hot oatmeal muffins. "I mean, I might be able to help with words and things to dispel any lingering spirits."

"Not on your life, luv." Cecile stopped right in the act of flipping fried apple slices and turned toward me. Her sky-blue eyes twinkled shrewdly. "That's money in the bank, our Gracie. We're written up in other states, you know—guests bring away stories. Not in the Maine papers, of course. Mum's the word on ghosts Down East."

"Oh, of course. I see."

"So, you met up with Gracie somewhere upstairs, then?"

"I'd have that fireplace checked into, if I were you," Joe said. "Something peculiar drifts out of it, and it smells bad, too."

"Hemlock," I said.

"Yes, it grows wild in the fields around here. Looks like parsley, if you don't know your plants. None of it on our grounds, though. Gracie was no fool."

"Does she ever speak to your guests?"

Cecile turned back to her cast iron frying pans. "Once in a blue moon. Kindred souls, you know. Once a yoga teacher stayed in your same room and told me she wailed and flailed at him.

Then his car went off the bluff up north. No one can really understand her, you see, luv."

But I thought I had understood Gracie, and I was about to find out.

"I guess I'll just have to get used to weird things happening when I'm with you," Joe reflected as he drove us toward Bangor after breakfast.

"Makes a change from Greenpeace commando raids, does it?" I was more than a little exhausted, letting the motion of the car flow over me restfully.

"*Our* confrontations are all rather straightforward. Huge banners, loudspeakers, the media alerted—no visions of murdered families or screaming banshees in the moonlight. If you ask me, it should be Gracie's husband who walks through Bone Rock Inn at midnight."

"Maybe he does," I said thoughtfully. "In which case, we should catch a whiff of dirty laundry and rancid pineapples. Or maybe Gracie is merely a projection. When you get to Bangor, follow the signs to Old Town."

"Say again?"

"When you get to Bangor, keep going on to Old Town. We're going to need a guide, and Phil said that might be the place to find one."

"I mean about Gracie."

"She could be a projection of Cecile's desire to make Bone Rock Inn rather special."

"Then why our room? Why us?"

"Another projection. A way for my clairvoyance to deliver a little advance warning."

"You mean, like channeling?"

"Something like that."

"Does this mean Gracie is going to travel around with us, hissing in times of danger?"

"Not a chance, unfortunately. Ghosts tend to haunt places rather than people. Perhaps a ghost is like a hologram of leftover life energy."

"Good. I'm glad that wraith won't be following us. I'm counting on having you all to myself." His hand on my thigh moved higher, causing a rush of heat to flow through me. For one wild moment, I thought of giving up this whole crazed search and returning to Bone Rock Inn for a little siesta.

At the barbershop where I made Joe ask the patrons to recommend a guide, the consensus was that Willie Joseph would do fine if we wanted to traipse through the mud up there in the woods and get eaten alive by black flies. Following the directions they gave Joe, we drove over the bridge that crossed the Penobscot River to Indian Island. Brilliant rays of sunlight suddenly pierced through dark clouds that had been gathering all morning, turning the river into a placid curve of silver.

We found Willie's place, a tiny cedar-shingled house on River Road, and Willie himself sitting out front on a weathered oak rocker, making a basket. The rich, sweet smell of the grasses wafted toward us as Willie's nimble brown fingers continued their work while we talked. He was slender and shy, with piercing gray eyes and white hair that contrasted handsomely with his leathery skin; his smile showed a tooth missing in front. His jeans were faded to a soft color that all the stone washing in the world can't reproduce, his flannel shirt was an earth-tone plaid, and his belt colorfully beaded with a wolf's head silver buckle. I wished I had brought my camera, but then I would have felt stupid taking his picture, like a gauche tourist who tips the native a dollar to look picturesque. Willie making a basket, I thought, is one of those pictures best kept in memory alone.

But as soon as we mentioned the hourly rate we would pay, Willie ruined the portrait in my mind's eye by clapping on his head a baseball cap bearing the legend *Penobscot Little League*.

"Sure, I know that Gus Lewis camp. I'll take you up there, but you'd better grease yourselves with some potent bug-off. You just want to look the place over, is that it?" When Willie stood up, he seemed to unfold, half a head taller than Joe. The knowing little smile that played around his mouth suggested he thought we were cracked but he was used to eccentric white folks.

"I have my own brand of insect repellent," I said. The combination of essential oils I had mixed into a witch hazel base would ward off an army of black flies. We anointed our exposed faces and hands while Willie stored his basketry and locked up.

"Are any baskets like yours for sale?" I asked as we started out for the Lewis cabin. Joe drove with Willie beside him, while I sat in back. How typically female of me, I thought. A salute to macho country.

"All kinds of them at the shop." Willie gestured toward a gift store located near the bridge, as we drove off the island. "Or I can make something to order. Medium-size sewing basket will run you three hundred fifty dollars. Lost art, you know. I'm one of the few still weaving. Kids couldn't care less."

"How long does the sweet grass in a basket smell sweet?" I asked. I was wondering how that delicious fragrance would work in aromatherapy. I rather thought it would be a reviver, like jasmine.

"Years sometimes." Willie paused to direct Joe. "Take that road on the right. It's a dirt track and rutty, but the Jeep can handle it. You work with herbs?"

"Yes, how did you know?"

"Guess I have a sense for it. You've got herbs in your bag—I can smell them. And you mix up your own bug-off. Joe here, he's either a fisherman or merchant marine. It's in his walk and his sea tan."

"Elementary, my dear Cass," said Joe. "I used to be merchant marine. Now I'm with Greenpeace."

"Oh, the crazies," Willie said.

I thought Joe would be offended, but he just laughed as we bounced along a muddy track canopied with tree limbs. "Hunters and loggers would say so, I guess."

"Since their last mission in Canada, Joe's been made an honorary member of the Nuxalk nation. They presented him with his own personal totem pole," I bragged.

"Well, that's something different." Clearly, Willie was the non-committal type. "Bear right at that fork. Lewis place is about a mile up the road."

A few minutes later we arrived at a neat, one-room log cabin in a tiny clearing. "Guess I'll turn the Jeep around now to make sure it's possible," said Joe. "I wouldn't want to have to back up all the way to the fork." The Jeep grunted and lurched in the mud, but Joe gradually shifted it around so that it headed back the way we'd come, a move for which we would soon be thankful.

We got out and looked around. How quiet it was, like an empty church, except for the black flies buzzing around us. The heavy pines surrounding the cabin had discouraged undergrowth so that the surrounding woods looked like a park. The strong smell of pine sap was nearly medicinal. May sunshine shone through the thick branches in ethereal beams. What peace, I thought, wondering if I'd like to own a cabin like this in the Maine woods. But it's so isolated, I concluded. I sure wouldn't want to stay here without Grandma's rifle.

"Now that we're here, what exactly did you want to see?" Willie asked. "I suppose I could get you into that camp, but it wouldn't please Gus much if I broke the lock. I'd have asked him, but he's way the hell up north guiding a party of sports to the good fishing."

"No need. I just want to look around the woods here." This sounded so idiotic, even to my own ears, I figured I'd better give Willie some explanation. "There's a family missing in Plymouth, friends of a friend, and I received some information that they might have come to harm near here. I did contact the police, but there's little enough they can or will do on a mere suspicion. So since Joe and I were driving through Maine, I thought I'd just have a look myself."

"Takes all kinds," said Willie. "Look all you like, it's a free country, especially in these parts, and Gus wouldn't give a damn. I'll just take a little rest here by the Jeep so as not to disturb your search. You want me, just give a holler." He lit a cigarette, an unfiltered Camel, tipped his hat so that it shaded his eyes, and lounged against the Jeep. Body language for *Suit yourself—I'm not interested, and I'm not watching.*

"Let's work in a circle," I murmured to Joe, taking his arm and setting off to survey the immediate grounds. Beyond the rutted, muddy driveway, the grounds were fairly dry and smoothly carpeted with pine needles that appeared to have been undisturbed for some time. As we walked, we widened our circle, brushing away the flies and ducking the occasional low branch. As our circle got wider and more ragged, the woods got denser, nearly impassible.

"I don't know that we can go much farther," Joe said, steadying me when I stumbled on a leaf-hidden rock.

"This must seem like a glorious fool's errand to you, I know," I admitted ruefully.

"Fool's errands are my business, don't forget," he replied cheerfully. "Besides, I've come to have faith in your hunches."

"One more circle," I suggested. "Aren't these pines wonderful? So aromatic. Wouldn't you love to live in the deep woods?"

"Visit here, yes, but it's too far from the ocean for me," Joe said. "Where I grew up, I was always in sight of the sea. It was like my second mother."

"All right. Let's go back, then. I don't know what else we can do."

"Shhhh," whispered Joe. "What's that?"

"What's what?" I whispered in return.

"I thought I heard a rustling sound over that way."

"Might be a deer. I certainly hope it's not a moose. Or a bear. Or . . ." Gracie's warning flashed into my mind. *He'ssssss heeeeere.*

"Might be anything. Quiet for a minute."

But I can never be quiet when I'm nervous. I *had* heard something hitting against branches. "I can't see the cabin from here, can you? We aren't lost, are we?"

"Not while we can see where the sun is. The cabin is west of us. Wait. There, I heard it again."

"Let's get back. Maybe Willie can tell us what we're hearing."

Joe took my hand and hurried us back in a beeline. Wonder of wonders, we came out of the woods right at the cabin. Willie looked up and was about to speak when something whizzed between Joe and me. My first thought was to marvel at the size of that black fly.

"Get flat," said Willie urgently, plunging behind the Jeep.

Joe grabbed me and pulled me to the ground, half in the mud. "What in the world are you doing?" I cried.

Silently he pointed toward the cabin. Sticking into the door was a lethal-looking steel arrow, still vibrating.

"Some idiot white man out there," Willie said, reaching up cautiously to open the Jeep door. "Crawl over here, and let's get moving before he lets loose with another zinger. Fool ought to be locked up."

"Cass, I want you to climb into the car without lifting your head above the door," Joe ordered. "Can you do that okay?"

His hands were urgently prying me out of the mud. It's harder than one would imagine to creep forward on one's elbows. My jaunty blue L. L. Bean windbreaker, new jeans, and the beaded white moccasins I'd bought in Bangor were now a uniform sodden brown as I pulled myself into the backseat and crouched in a heap. Joe slid in the passenger's door, then over to the driver's side, Willie got in and slammed the door.

Somehow Joe started the Jeep without lifting his head higher than the steering wheel, and we careened out of the clearing, hurtling down the dirt road as fast as possible without crashing into the underbrush. As we bumped along to safety, we gradually sat up.

"Those wanna-be nature boys usually come up here in the fall," Willie commented. "Don't know why they're so set on hunting the hard way. All of us up here use rifles now unless we got to guide a party of the bow-and-arrow sports. Some funny stories come out of those trips back into nostalgia country, you can bet. But the point is, what's that dickhead doing up here in May—spearing black flies?"

"Maybe he's trying to warn us off Gus's place," I suggested as I scraped mud off my neck and hands.

"You don't suppose it was Gus Lewis himself come home early?" Joe wondered.

"Naw," said Willie. "Gus doesn't own a bow. If he did, he wouldn't shoot it at a trespasser. Worst he'd do is shoot a rifle in the air. But if Gus did shoot at someone, even if he was drunk, he wouldn't miss and destroy his own front door."

"Will you report that shooter to the police, or shall I?" I asked.

"Better you than me," Willie said. "You got the theory about your missing friends. And right now I wouldn't laugh that off. But if I go into the station with a story about being scared off by a stray arrow, they'll be making a joke of me for the next twenty years."

"Don't worry," Joe agreed. "We tourists will make the complaint, and no one will snicker—at least not to our faces."

And so we did. The understanding older police officer who took our information was nearly straightfaced, unless you looked quite closely at the corners of his mouth.

"Why exactly were you up there at Gus Lewis's cabin?" the officer asked.

"Well, there's this family in Plymouth . . ." I began.

"Looking for a place to rent for the hunting season, and maybe a guide as well," Joe quickly interrupted, giving my moccasin a gentle prod under the table.

"Yeah. Well, Gus is okay. You could do worse than Gus Lewis."

We transported Willie back to his cottage and paid him what we owed, plus a good-size tip for the added element of risk he'd endured so stoically. He pocketed the money without counting it, for the first time in our acquaintance looking at me directly with his piercing gray eyes. "You got the sense, too," he said. It was a statement, not a question.

"Yes," I said. "I think Gus or someone is going to find a grave up there someplace. Might have three people in it, one of them a little girl in pink sneakers."

"Jesus. Got a card? Leave it, in case."

I handed him my business card: *Cassandra Shipton, Earthlore Herbal Preparations and Cruelty-Free Cosmetics.* I shouldn't have been surprised when he reached in his pocket and fished out a card in exchange: *Willie Joseph, Handcrafted Basketry, Certified Maine Guide.*

"There's something else I'd like you to keep on the watch for." I told Willie about Tip running away from home and disappearing, that he might have taken up residence on his own in the woods. "The boy is very dear to me," I added.

"I see that. I'll let you know if I hear anything. Indian boy that age can manage okay in the woods, but it'd be better if he got himself back into a school." Willie waved and turned away.

As we drove off Indian Island, somehow I felt reassured, as if this trip hadn't been entirely wasted. That night we spent at the Bone Rock Inn before driving back to Plymouth was in itself worth the trip north. The tall, four-poster bed seemed to throb like the deck of a ship, carrying us to higher and higher crests. Although Gracie didn't materialize, our lovemaking was thrilling enough without the *ménage à trois.*

I'd decided to tackle Stone at home, with the hope that Phillipa's backing would give my theories more credence. My friend was little help to me, however, as she divided her attention between some grilled duck thing that had to be finished "just so" and a risotto that needed constant watching. Balmy and blossomy May had invited Stone and me to lounge outside with our glasses of wine, a lovely Verdicchio, while Phillipa basted and fussed. Although the ocean was out of sight, it was only a short walk away; one could smell it in the soft, salt air and hear it in the distant cries of seagulls.

I outlined my evidence. Stone was a trained listener, giving his complete attention and not interrupting. I could almost see his brain cataloging the bits and pieces of my discoveries into a reasoned whole. He combed back his fine brown hair with thin, nervous fingers, the creases in his forehead suggesting that he was mulling over my findings and considering his reply with care.

Finally he said, "Let's assume that anybody could have shot off that arrow for any reason. We can't take the incident as proof positive that the Donahues came to grief at this Lewis place. I know you have your . . . sights set on Thomas Gere. It's true he rented that cabin for bow-and-arrow hunting, but that was last fall. I admit Gere does have a motive, but so do a dozen or so other businessmen in Plymouth. It's all rather tenuous for me to be asking Bangor to dig around in the woods up there."

"But, Stone, remember that Gere turned his shop over to his teenaged assistant and went off somewhere last weekend. He could have gone down Maine to check that everything was still undisturbed. Then he caught sight of Joe and me poking around in the woods near the Lewis cabin. He might also have recognized the same Wagoneer he'd seen in front of his shop in Plymouth on the day Patsy attacked him. Maybe Gere had his crossbow with him and decided to give us a little warning."

"A lot of maybes," Stone said, refilling my glass before heading to the kitchen to finish the salad, his allotted chore. Phillipa's new husband enjoyed cooking, and was quite a good chef, but she was not pleased to have him muddling about in her kitchen domain. Chances are he would forever be relegated to drinks and salads. Still, for a man who'd been a bachelor until his forties, he seemed cheerful enough about Phillipa's quirks. And it was obvious that they were very much in love. A luminous aura shone around them when they were near each other. I admired the choreography of their interactions as they worked together— pure harmony.

Chalk one up for late marriages, I thought, watching Stone and Phillipa gazing at one another fondly. How I wished Joe could have been here to be impressed by their domestic bliss, but on Monday he'd had to fly away to Africa to rescue the Patagonian toothfish. Oh, why couldn't I find a man who wanted to rescue *me*? Aren't forty-something "wise women" as endangered a species as some fish no one every heard of?

"So, aren't you going to do *anything*?" I asked in plaintive tones, not entirely because of Stone's rejection.

"Yes, Stone," Phillipa's crisp tone cut in. She had finished the last basting of the bird she was calling Duckling *Veronique* and was garnishing it with dark, sweet grapes that Stone had been assigned to seed. "What are you going to *do* about the Donahues? Cass may seem spaced out to the casual listener, but I've known her long enough to realize that her obsessions are generally proved justified in time. So I say, light a fire under those Bangor cops," she commanded as she poured warm brandy over the duckling and lit it with a wooden match.

"You have a real flair for showmanship, Phil," I said. "Have you ever thought of having your own cooking show on television?"

"In my dreams. Do you realize how many more books I'd sell if I had my own show?"

"All right, all right," Stone sighed heavily. "I'll see what I can do to stir up a search. But it's their jurisdiction, and I can't do anything about that."

"Kidnapping across state lines. You could bring in the FBI," I suggested.

"Much as I respect your hunches, Cass, I'd much rather be embarrassed with the Bangor cops than with the Feds, should nothing come of this effort."

"You could do a little investigating of Thomas Gere right here in your own jurisdiction," Phillipa countered, dishing up the risotto for our first course. "Agree to that, and we'll have no more talk of murder and kidnapping and where the bodies are buried until after we've enjoyed this excellent dinner."

"I'll have a closer look at Gere," Stone promised. "And you two witches will stay out of this while I do."

"Scout's honor," I swore. Behind Stone's back, Phillipa winked at me wickedly.

Esbat of the Flower Moon

When the Esbat after Beltane arrived—a full moon cere-mony between the high holidays, the Sabbats, the May Esbat particular to feminine energy—it was time to introduce Freddie to the circle as I'd promised. If only she would maintain that sweet-sixteen disguise she'd adopted to disarm Thomas Gere into giving her a job! To my eyes, she looked so much more attractive in a simple blouse and skirt, with her hair reverted to its natural soft brown, and her mouth colored a hue reminiscent of human rather than vampire lips. As the mother of three teenagers, now grown to adulthood, I should have known better than to raise my hopes. Freddie appeared at my door in an outfit that she must have imagined would help her to blend right in with a circle of Wiccans. She was so thrilled and excited, she ap-peared to be dancing just above the floor, so how could I be cruel enough to pierce the bubble that kept her aloft?

"You look so interesting, dear," I said. "What color is that in your hair?"

Scruffy nosed her affectionately. *She smells different, but I know her anyway. It's the hamburger girl.*

"Midnight in Moscow. Awesome, isn't it? You just do this mid-night black thing, then highlight with luminous silver. Like starlight, you know?" She reached down to ruffle the fur between the dog's ears. He stretched appreciatively, then flopped on her fake alligator boots.

"Yes, possibly. And the lipstick shade?"

"Crimson Slash. I knew you didn't like the brown stuff, so I chose something bright since these are your coven-mates. Or do you call them sisters?"

"Friends. I just call them friends. Why don't you take it easy, have a glass of milk or something, while I finish this herb bouquet. It's a little early still."

" 'Friends' sounds like Quakers. Got any Dr. Pepper Lite?"

"No, but there's sarsaparilla or ginger beer in the fridge. I make them myself."

"No shit! I thought that stuff was born in little brown bottles. Sure, I'll take a hit of beer." Freddie rummaged in the refrigerator, her black leather skirt hiking up her backside. "Okay if I have some of this cheese, too? So what's with the herbs? Gonna get mellow?"

"Help yourself. These herb sprays are for the fire. Woodruff, mugwort, sea fennel, rosemary, lavender. Not a single controlled substance among them. Sorry to disappoint."

Freddie brought out the cheese, bread, and mustard to make herself a sandwich along with the ginger beer. "So what *are* those dry things good for, then?" She slathered rye bread with mustard, added slabs of cheddar, and bit in with a sigh of satisfaction. I wondered when she had eaten last. Flipping off the bottle cap with a purple-painted thumbnail, she took a long swallow of ginger beer from the brown bottle. Maybe she hoped it was alcoholic. The metal cap flipped around the table into her hand. Well and good, I thought; her talent is high tonight.

Scruffy did his best to remind Freddie that he was a cheese aficionado by pressing his nose against her knee. *Hey, Toots . . . don't forget your little buddy here.* She passed him a small piece of sandwich under the table.

"Aromatic herbs affect mind, spirit, and energy level," I explained. "Nothing goes to the brain faster than scent."

"You ought to know, I guess—being in the herb business and all. Is that what you're going to wear tonight?" She gestured toward my ivory linen slacks and T-shirt.

The slacks were new, and the T-shirt was sage silk. I thought I looked just right. I clipped on gold earrings.

"You ought to have your ears pierced, Cass," Freddie advised, "so you wouldn't have to wear those retro hoops. I could do it for you, you know. Doesn't hurt hardly at all. You just keep sliding the thread back and forth for a while, and you're set. I've only ever had one infection in all of these." She gestured toward her ear with the row of tiny gold rings.

"Thanks. I'll think about that," I said, taking my light windbreaker off the hook by the kitchen door. "Scruffy, you guard the house while we go out for a while."

Scruffy groaned and flopped under the kitchen table. *You mean stay here for hours all alone? Where's that nasty Patsy?"*

"You know very well that Patsy is at Animal Lovers overnight so that she can be nicely groomed."

"You talk to Scruffy just like he's a human person," Freddie commented. "That's how I do with Shadow. Sometimes I think he speaks to me, whispers in my ear, you know what I'm saying?"

"Yes, Freddie, I know exactly what you're saying." I took my athame off the kitchen shelf and snapped it onto my belt.

"Holy Mother of God," said Freddie, on whom a Catholic education had not been wasted. "I didn't know we were going to be carrying. Are we expecting to be raided or something?"

Maybe I was a little pleased to have surprised the unflappable Freddie. "It's an athame. Not a weapon, but a sacred tool used in Wiccan rituals."

"No shit! What for? Some kind of sacrifice? I don't do too well with blood, you know what I'm saying? If you're going to cut up something alive . . ."

"No, no Freddie . . . we don't traffic in that weird sort of thing. Everything we do is on the white side, not the side of darkness. An athame must never touch any living being or anything that once had life. It's used to consecrate the circle where we work and to cut through negative vibrations. Mostly, it's symbolic, part of the uniform."

"It sure looks wicked," Freddie said admiringly, peering at my belt. "And sharp."

"That it is. Traditionally, the athame is threefold sharp, both sides and the point."

"Maybe I ought to get me one of those, then—if I'm going to be a witch. Wiccan, I mean."

I thought about Freddie strutting around with a dagger in her belt—that could be pure trouble. This called for a new Wiccan law, in a good cause. "The athame must be presented by the full circle to a Wiccan who has spent a year learning and preparing herself, or it's very bad luck," I improvised.

"Cool!" said Freddie.

We met at Deidre's place, a brick-fronted garrison Colonial brimming with her homey arts and crafts, from embroidered cushions with quaint sayings to braided rugs to flea market furniture "finds" refinished to a shining new life. And, of course, her collection of homemade dolls, looking quite innocent, propped on benches and shelves.

Freddie's soot-lined amber eyes seemed to miss nothing of this Laura-Ashley-Country-Life ambiance but she said little and behaved in a subdued, shy manner while I introduced her to the circle.

The backyard was partly screened by newly-leafed maples and a stockade fence, sufficiently separated from other properties, since houses in this area were set on acre lots. Some of the neighbors might get interesting glimpses of our rituals from upstairs windows, but their views would be dappled by trees and obscured by darkness. And in her usual efficient managerial fashion, Deidre had encouraged her husband Will to work nights this week rather than later in the month. Her three small children were bundled off to her mother-in-law's. The field would be semi-clear for raising a cone of power tonight.

I could count on my tactful friends not to embarrass Freddie with outright scrutiny, but they certainly sized her up, each in her own covert way. And vice versa. I wondered if Freddie was feeling somewhat disappointed in her friendly neighborhood witches, who appeared to my eyes as ordinary as any women's gathering—Friends of the Library or Women in the Arts, for instance. But how did they appear to Freddie? Perhaps it was like meeting a gaggle of eccentric aunts.

"Mrs. Ritchie looks like a fairy godmother with a swag bag," Freddie whispered as we wandered around Deidre's backyard, waiting for the moon to appear over the horizon. "What's her game?"

"Glamour," I said. "She can change her appearance to blend or to attract attention."

"No shit! A makeup artist?"

"More like an illusionist."

"And your friend—Phil, is it? The one who's a dead ringer for the wicked stepmother in *Snow White*. I like the black leotard, though." Freddie plunked down on one of the jungle gym swings, dragging her boots on the scarred ground as she swung lazily back and forth.

"Tarot."

"Cool! Would she read for me, do you think? And your other friend, the Maid Marian type with the Gucci boots and Hermès handbag? Excellent stuff, but definitely scuffed and scratched. Lost the family fortune, did she?"

"No, Sherlock. We should all have a stock portfolio like Heather Morgan's. The leather accessories must date back to the days before she gave up the exploitation of animals. But I can see you know your quality labels. There's hope for you yet. Heather does candles and things. And our hostess, Deidre, has a fair hand with crafts."

"You mean like all those dollies? Where does she stash the ones with the pins in them?"

An orange glow rose over the dark trees. "Quiet, now. We're going to begin."

Freddie bounced up, leaving the swing twisting to a slow halt. "You don't even have thirteen. That's why you ought to take me on. You need more witches to make a quorum."

"Thirteen was a conjecture of the Dark Ages inquisitors. Magic can be worked even by the solitary practitioner. As you have discovered to your chagrin. Or what was it you thought happened with the teacher who runs the computer lab, poor Miss Manson? So enough with the kibitzing—listen and learn," I said, ending our whispered conference as Deidre cast our circle with her athame.

"It's nine feet because nine is the essential multiple of three, and the work is always accomplished threefold," I explained to Freddie before the invocation began.

Phillipa lit a small fire in a brazier at the circle's center, adding a few of my dried herb sprigs. Soon the pungent fragrance rose and circled in the air like invisible, scented arms surrounding us. Moonlight shimmering on her golden curls, Deidre drew a pentagram in the air between us, then raised her arms and began a crooning chant that Phillipa had made for us, invoking and drawing down the moon's force into herself for her role as priestess in this night's ceremony.

> *Like a wave of the sea or a leaf on the tree,*
> *Like all bright things that live and be,*
> *We come from the goddess, the great and the small,*
> *And dance through her seasons, the mother of all.*

Soon the silvery luminescence caressed her shoulders. Her arms and fingers seemed to glow with a cool, dancing fire. Deidre's transformation appeared splendidly visible for a breathless moment before it faded to a quiet radiance. Beside me, I could hear Freddie's very soft whistle of admiration. "Shhhh!" I warned her in a whisper.

After we had shared a few minutes of meditation, Heather came forward to light the work candle and passed it to Fiona, who drew up her shoulders in some way that made her appear tall and queenly, the talent we all envied and practiced secretly. Then when the moment seemed right to her, Fiona passed the candle to Deidre.

So the light began to move clockwise around from hand to hand, with pauses for each of us to speak aloud or consider silently whatever she would like to manifest. Freddie's wishes were among the silent ones. Whatever was desired, we all visualized for each other. If no details had been given, we simply focused on imagining a beneficent light surrounding the petitioner.

Now we were ready to raise the cone of power. As I concentrated on feeling my connection with the spirit of the universe, I began to feel a tingling from the top of my head to my hands. I don't know what the source is of this physical reaction, but I know I can summon it with some effort, and it's a very real sensation. I think it must be close to what nurses feel happening in their hands when they summon the healing touch. Whatever it is, more than any spell or incantation, it's this sacred energy that interconnects all things and makes magic possible.

Again beginning with Fiona, we allowed this energy to flow from one to another with squeezes of our hands, faster and faster. Suddenly, when Deidre gave the signal with her athame, we threw up our arms and hands toward the moon, releasing the cone of power, and with it, all our stated and unstated wishes and desires.

"Awesome," Freddie murmured. "That was wicked awesome."

"What did you feel?" I asked as neutrally as possible. An important question. All the studies in the world won't make a

Wiccan if one feels no connection to the natural power of the universe.

"Hey, what a trip. Extreme. I mean, outer space. I mean, that was like the other thing I do, but to the tenth degree, if you know what I'm saying."

"You felt the energy being passed between us?"

"Like lightning, babe."

Later, we went indoors for wine, tea, and a buffet of snacks set out on Deidre's country maple dining room. A stern glance from me warned Freddie to take her hand off the wine bottle. As she piled her plate high with every cookie and pastry in sight, I wondered if she visited a dentist regularly, living on her own as she did.

I ought not to worry about such things, I admonished myself. What's next? Agonizing over her report cards?

"Cass has told us of your psychokinetic talents, Freddie. We all hope you'll give us a demonstration this evening," Phillipa said in what she may have believed was a kindly fashion, not realizing that she had already been pigeonholed as a wicked stepmother type.

"Okay, if you want," Freddie said thickly through a mouthful of strawberry napoleon with whipped cream. "Only I do better on an empty stomach. Too late for that!"

"For goodness sake, Phil! Let the girl finish her food before she has to sing for her supper," Deidre ordered, putting an arm around Freddie's waist, showing clearly that Freddie was both taller and bonier, an angular adolescent.

When Freddie had consumed the last morsel and swig of her snack, Deidre settled her on the sofa with the round oak coffee table in front of her. We sat around it, Fiona on a rocking chair, the rest of us on embroidered floor cushions bearing such legends as *Two Hearts, One Love* and *Friends Are Forever*. Between scatter rugs that Deidre had braided herself, the pine floor was smooth and shining, reflecting the many lit candles. Salty and

Peppy, Deidre's toy poodles, curled up beside Freddie. The girl's shoulders were hunched, her eyes looking inward.

The spoon I put on the table I had brought with me, not wanting to be responsible for the crumpling of some matched set of Deidre's. My spoon was plain stainless steel flatware, heavy enough to be impressive. Freddie gazed at it impassively and laid her right hand on the table about three inches from the spoon. The room was eerily silent except for the heavy breathing of the sleeping poodles. I don't know how long we sat there, quietly watching that motionless spoon.

I felt rather than heard Phillipa's sharp intake of breath when at last the spoon barely twitched, then lay still again. After another span of time, perhaps three minutes, it twitched again, a bit more, hitching toward Freddie's fingers. Then, with agonizing slowness, in fits and starts, it moved inexorably into her grasp.

"Sweet Mother," exclaimed Fiona. "That's the real thing, all right."

"Wait," I whispered. "Watch."

Freddie caressed the compliant spoon. Her face was damp with exertion. Now she gazed off into space with a dreamy expression. A very little time went by before the bowl of the spoon gave up its rigidity and folded over, malleable as butter.

"Here, let me see that," demanded Heather, imperiously reaching across the table. Coming out of her trance-like state, Freddie smiled and gave over the trophy willingly. "It's hot!" Heather exclaimed. "Here, feel this." She gave the folded spoon to Fiona, who held it briefly, then handed it to Deidre. Quickly the scrunched thing passed around the circle.

"Freddie came to me for help," I explained as if I hadn't already told them all this privately. "Sometimes her abilities manifest in ways she didn't intend, and they cause harm. As I've explained to her, black thoughts and acts can rebound into her own life. The recent loss of Freddie's cat may have been the result of an accident that befell one of her teachers. Although she's too young to join a circle of crones like ourselves," I continued,

ignoring Phillipa's raised eyebrow and Deidre's smile of disbelief—none of us wished to embrace the crone mythology, no matter how old we got—"I'm hoping each of you will offer her your
own insights and guidance. And that she may occasionally attend
an Esbat, as this one tonight."

"*Of course* we must take her under our wing," Fiona agreed at
once, "before she conjures up something . . ."

"Tell the circle about Miss Manson, Freddie," I interrupted.
"Begin with The Virus."

Looking shy for once, a diffident Freddie related her tale of
accidentally jinxing the computer lab and her subsequent expul-
sion from the class. "The thing is, I was doing excellent in the
computer lab. It was crazy what I could do that the others couldn't
even follow—my super best subject. But then Miss Manson ac-
cused me of cheating, said I must be getting illegal help somehow. So she gave me a failing mark. That's when the computers
went la-la on them. And now they're all calling me The Virus."

"Oh, everyone has weird accidents like that when they're
starting out," Deidre assured her in a motherly fashion. "Once
when I had a little argument with the clerk in the kitchen appli-
ance department at Sears, all the electric mixers began to . . ."

I shot her a warning look. "Wait, Deidre. There's more."

Freddie continued her tale through Miss Manson's loud refusal to allow Freddie to make amends in the lab, the teacher's
driving off in a huff, a sudden leak of brake fluid, and the ensuing
mishap. "Miss Manson's jaw was broken. It was quite a while before she could speak again. Then my little Patch got hit by a car.
And Cass says there could be a connection," Freddie wailed.
"How can I quit this shit if I don't know how I did it?"

"You must remember, dear, that *thoughts are things.*" Fiona
launched into one of her favorite lectures. "Anyone who has a
strong psychic power has to be especially aware of that. Because
there are two laws at work here. The first, the Law of Cause and
Effect, means that thoughts—like words, images, and rituals—

can bring about change according to will—that's Spirit, the invisible world, manifesting in the world of form."

"In other words, *magic*," Phillipa murmured.

Fiona ignored the interruption. "The second law, or maybe it should be first, is that whatever you send out into Spirit returns threefold into your own life. 'Bread cast upon the waters.' If you send healing thoughts to someone, you'll be surrounding yourself with good vibrations. But if you think hatefully of someone, wishing them ill, they may be harmed, and so may you."

A dawning comprehension lit up Freddie's face, but it was instantly negated by her normal expression of suspicion. "Yeah, right. So if someone slaps me down, I'm supposed to, like, turn the other cheek? I've already heard all this crap from the nuns. I really was hoping you witches would be more down to earth, you know what I mean?"

Phillipa chuckled, her Wicked Stepmother chuckle. "Listen, young lady, you're here to learn, and we've agreed to teach you. Your role as a novice is to listen respectfully. Naturally, you're going to have negative thoughts . . . that's only human, and as you pointed out, you're not applying for sainthood. But you do have control over your wishes. And you *may not* wish harm, especially you psychokinetics. Or if it happens before you know it, you must immediately expunge the evil wish. Say it out loud at once and with feeling: 'No . . . take that wish out of the law!' It's like when you make a disastrous mistake on the computer, you instantly press the 'undo' icon, right?"

"What's all this with the 'laws'?" Freddie looked bemused. "What's the good of being witches if you have to stick with some goody-goody rules?"

Easier said than done, I was thinking. But we never heard Phillipa's rebuttal because just then Fiona screamed and fell forward, her head striking the rocking chair arm. Freddie screamed, too, and huddled back into the sofa cushions as if to avoid some contagion. For a moment I froze in an icy blast of fear. Had someone opened the door to winter? Then I was scrambling to my feet with the others to rescue Fiona.

"Don't be alarmed, Freddie," Deidre spoke above our clamor, as Heather and Phil took hold of Fiona under the arms and dragged her onto the couch. "It's just a trance. She's fallen into a trance." Freddie sprang out of their way and hurried to my side. Salty and Peppy instantly took fright, yipping and turning tail as they scampered out of the room.

In the midst of Deidre's calm reassurances to our guest, there occurred a truly spooky event. A family of Deidre's rag dolls, for no apparent reason, flew off their perch and hurtled across the room into the fire. A shower of sparks erupted onto the braided hearth rug. Abruptly letting go of Fiona's arm, Heather jumped into action, stamping out the smoldering bits with her leather boots, as if performing a native war dance. Another cascade of sparks flew up and out, circling Heather's head, the burnished chestnut braid of her hair swinging in points of light like stars.

Coming out of my glacial coma, I screamed, too, "*Watch out*, Heather!" Heather bounded away from the sparks, slapping her head like a madwoman. The dolls had begun to burn. They smelled like compost on a searing summer day, a heap of decay laced with rotting peels and animal feces. My stomach acid rose to taste level, making me cough and nearly retch.

"Whew," said Fiona, suddenly sitting upright, flinging away from Phillipa, who was patting her wrists. "What *is* that stink? Not smelling salts . . ."

With a cry of disbelief, Deidre rushed to rescue her handi-work, encountering another flaming shower of sparks. I caught hold of her arm and pulled her back. "Get away! Something weird is happening there," I said.

"No shit," said Freddie, who had remained by my side, mov-ing as I moved, sheltering herself from the revolting conflagra-tion in the fireplace.

Now Phillipa, fearless among cringing companions, strode over to the fireplace, wielding her silver-handled athame, which shone like an avenging sword. "Banish, you Evil Ones! Out, out of our circle! Be gone, be gone!" she commanded the grinning, crumbling, blackening dolls in her deep, compelling voice.

A head fell off one of the dolls and seemed to jump the screen onto the rug. I grabbed the fireplace shovel and scooped up the smirking, black thing, tossing it back into the flames.

Freddie shrank back toward the sofa, and I thought I saw her cross herself in a moment of retro-religiosity. Fiona was rubbing her forehead where a bruise had begun to form. "Will you people quit fussing around with that fireplace and get me some ice in a towel," she complained. Reaching up, she dragged Freddie down next to her, putting an arm around the pale girl. "You sit here with me, honey."

Stunned and silent, we continued to watch the dolls collapse into ashes. "Did you see that!" Phillipa exclaimed. "Those dolls just shot across the room, all on their own." She paused for a sharp look at Deidre. "Unless they were on some kind of trip wire."

"Are you nuts?" asked Deidre. "I don't know what got into the damned dolls. This must be Fiona's doing."

Sitting down on Fiona's other side, Heather handed her a cold compress she'd fetched from the kitchen and looked at her questioningly. "So, where did you go off to, Lady Fiona?"

"Woods," Fiona replied uncertainly, pressing the wet towel against her forehead. "Someone was guiding me, the spirit of a woman. It was all thick woods, brambles, broken branches, thorns, stones—a heap of stones. Maybe he didn't get the little girl after all. He thought she was dead when he went to get a shovel out of his van. I think the girl got away. He searched, but I don't believe he found her."

"Didn't *any* of you see how my dolls got into the fire?" Deidre wailed.

No one had time to come up with a theory, because just then the phone rang. Maybe we were still in an impressionable state, but it was as if we already knew what we were about to learn. It was Stone. Phillipa talked with him for a moment, or rather he talked and she listened, ashen-faced.

After they'd hung up, she said, "Listen, everyone—they found the Donahues. Stone said it was that guide you hired in Bangor—Willie Joseph. Apparently he followed some trail or other on his own time and found them. Denise had been asphyxiated with a plastic bag over her head. Paul Donahue was shot through the heart with a crossbow."

Deidre screamed, a kind of thin wail closely related to keening. "Oh, Great Mother!" she exclaimed when she could speak. "What am I going to tell Jenny? Her best friend Candy . . . so cruel a death . . ."

"Snap out of it, Deidre! Candy wasn't there," Phillipa said. "Just her sneaker. No one knows what happened to Candy. They've organized trackers, but an awful lot of time has gone by for an eight-year-old girl to have survived in the woods up there. That is, if she really got away."

"Patsy!" Heather declared in sudden inspiration. "They'll need Patsy to find Candy."

"Were the sneakers pink?" I asked.

"Yes, Cass."

"Where were they found?"

"Just one. Half-buried between the rocks. Denise and Paul were entombed in an abandoned root cellar, almost completely overgrown."

I nearly lost it right there, but Heather was saying, "Let's just talk about this manifestation for a minute. See if we can make sense of it. What happened with those poppets? And the stench! Was it Fiona's trance that caused it? Is Freddie a poltergeist?"

"None of the above," I said. "We summoned the cone of power ourselves, all of us together. No use complaining that the magic worked rather oddly."

"She has a point," said Phillipa. "But personally, I was surprised as hell."

Later, I reassured Freddie, "Our Esbats and Sabbats don't

usually include fireworks, you know. This was quite out of the ordinary."

"Far, far out," said my chastened protégée. "And you witches are going to teach *me* control?"

"Wiccans," I corrected her absently. I was thinking that powers unleashed might not be so easy to get back into the bottle.

The following day, Heather drove up to Maine with Patsy to help in the search for Candy, joining hundreds of other searchers. I suggested she stay at the Bone Rock Inn above the town of Northeast Harbor. Apparently, Heather didn't remember my earlier tales of Gracie the ghost, so I reminded her. "For whatever . . ."

Meanwhile, Fiona did a finding for Candy with her crystal dowser and came up with someplace farther north than the Bangor area. "Does that mean she's still alive?" I asked. Fiona said, not necessarily, but she thought so.

"Listen, Fiona, see what you can dig up on Gere's past, will you? I don't know how much investigating Stone may have done. All he's told me, or rather told *Phil,* is that the man is a decorated Vietnam war hero with no criminal record. What are we missing here? However enraged he may have felt over being swindled, why would he try to slaughter an entire family? That's taking revenge a bit over the top."

"Maybe to him it was warranted response, an execution of sorts. Must be a really sick character," she said, promising to look into Gere's past. Fiona's research skills were formidable, a combination of psychic talent, access to unlimited libraries, and a weird network of Internet contacts.

Scruffy moped around listlessly but staunchly denied that he missed his red-furred friend, Patsy. Whenever Heather called me on her cellphone, however, which she did at least twice a day, Scruffy strained to listen for that familiar scolding bark in the background. "Candy's disappeared into thin air," Heather complained time and again. "Not a trace to be found by woman nor dog."

I really wished I was there with Heather, but I felt I needed to keep an eye on Gere as the local news began feasting on every shred of information about the Donahues. Perhaps the descent of media vultures on juicy bits of the murder would cause Gere to break down and reveal himself. But my after-school shopgirl spy, Freddie, reported no erratic behavior, just one odd thing. Important antique clocks from Gere's personal collection had begun disappearing from the shop.

"He's squirreling them away in some safe hole, or selling them for a stash of getaway cash, you know what I'm saying?" Freddie's theory was much like my own.

Storing or selling his treasures, Gere must be getting ready to run. He ought to be terrified that Candy would be able to finger him. It must be that he was as much in the dark about her whereabouts as we were—if he weren't certain that she was dead.

Somehow, Tip kept coming to mind. Lost children in the never-never land of the Maine woods. Children with no homes, no lanterns in the windows, no loving arms reaching out for them. Did they fly through the pines at night? Sleep huddled together in tree houses? Catch fish in the streams and fry them over campfires? Steal milk from grazing cows, eggs from chicken houses, blankets from clotheslines? Stay young forever?

"Earth to Cass, Earth to Cass," Freddie said one afternoon while I was deep in this fantasy. "Want another cup of ginger tea? Hey, I'm getting to like this stuff, can you believe it? So, how about your helping out Ms. Heather's search with one of your famous visions?"

"I wish. Unfortunately, they're not on call."

"Maybe you could try, though. Like you keep telling me, you know. Get some control over your powers."

After a week of tramping fruitlessly about the Maine woods with a paw-sore Irish setter, Heather gave up and drove home. "Your herb bug-off stuff saved our lives," she said as we drank iced mint tea in my backyard in the late May sunshine, where Scruffy and Patsy were playing tug-of-war with a fallen birch branch. "Those black flies were big enough to carry off a small animal. You can bet I kept Patsy on leash the whole time we were outdoors. *And* what about that eerie inn!"

"Great food, and a lovely herb garden, right?" I prompted.

"Yeah, but that creepy *thing* wafted through our room at midnight and gave Patsy fits. I couldn't get her out from under the bed."

"Gracie," I said. "The resident ghost. Did she tell you anything?"

"I hardly believe it myself. But, yes, I did think she spoke to me." Heather paused to dab my chamomile skin-soother on her poison ivy. "Don't you have anything stronger than mint tea around here?"

"Wormwood," I suggested. "And the ghostie said what?"

"Well, it seemed to me that Gracie was moaning *sheeeee's noooooo heeeere*. The curse of a vivid imagination, I suspect."

"Fiona said to look farther north."

"Oh, sure. Big help. Does that mean, at least, that the little girl is okay?"

"Maybe, according to Fiona. Would you like a glass of May wine?"

"I thought you'd never ask."

Scruffy and Patsy loped into the house with me for long, cool drinks of water that left the kitchen floor flooded as they took turns at the dish, jowls dripping liberally. *Me first. Me first.* In a canine way, they were having as good a time together as can be had without laughing. I had the sinking feeling that, when this whole Donahue conundrum was solved, I wouldn't be able to turn Patsy over to Animal Lovers for adoption. Even now, I'd agreed to allow the Irish setter to bunk here for the time being. What was it with me anyway? A born sucker for kids and animals. Mother Earth in herb-stained sweatpants.

While I was in the house pouring the woodruff-scented wine, a ray of sun streaming in the kitchen window caught the clear liquid in a sparkle of light, and I started to feel faint. I sat down at the kitchen table for a moment, leaning over my knees. At once I was out of myself—walking in the deep woods toward a clearing where I could see a small, neat house with several ramshackle outbuildings. As I walked toward it, a plump woman came out with a girl close beside her, both of them carrying dishpans. The girl was wearing overalls turned up at the ankles. They stepped inside a wire enclosure around one of the outbuildings and began to scatter the contents of the dishpans on the ground. Chickens came running, but there was no sound. It was like watching a silent film. A word popped into my mind: *volaille.* Chicken! Then I looked up, and I was back in my own kitchen. *Well, finally*, I thought.

Putting the two glasses and a bottle on the tray, I went unsteadily to my guest in the backyard. A slight breeze over the herb plantings brought the strong, reviving scents of sage and thyme. I breathed in deeply. "She's alive," I said. "Candy's alive, living with some nice, motherly-looking woman. The clothes the girl's wearing must have belonged to someone else. They don't fit her."

"Oh, goodie. You've had a vision," said Heather, swinging around in the chaise longue to reach for a wineglass. "Let's make sure that a photo of Candy is being circulated in the northern part of Maine. Although surely the TV news reports . . ."

"Actually, I think it's Canada . . . Quebec . . . perhaps Candy cannot make herself understood, or she's so traumatized . . ."

". . . She's afraid to say who she is, or she can't remember—and that would explain why she's not been found." Like any good friend, Heather finished my sentence for me.

A bank of cirrus clouds began to drift over the sun, turning the temperature back to early April. Just as Heather was getting ready to return to her dog-centered mansion, with a care package of anti-itch lotions and natural flea powder from my stockroom, Fiona called.

"He *is* the sick bastard I took him to be," she began without preamble. "As an expert in timing devices, Gere found his niche in Special Ops demolition during his tour of Vietnam. Sure, he was a hero, so that's why they hushed up a certain incident that didn't reflect much glory on his unit. You remember how youngsters sometimes were involved in attacks against our troops? Gere tracked a few of them down to a small village, and the next thing we know, most of the place was blown up. By then, there were no adult men left in that village, just women, children, and old people."

"Great Goddess! The army must have wanted to keep that one under wraps. How did you find out?"

"Don't ask," said Fiona.

I grabbed Heather, who was on her way out to her car. "Pick up the extension in the living room. You have to hear this." Then I made Fiona repeat everything for Heather's benefit.

"But wait, there's something else," Fiona said. "When Gere got home from his stint in Vietnam, his fiancée dumped him for another guy—and get this, the other guy was a financial whiz, just like Donahue. Only this guy handled investments for Plymouth Trust—not a freelance adviser like Donahue. Coincidentally, there was this tragic accident that took the lives of the young couple. Their house blew up with them in it. The theory is that it was a natural gas explosion. I suppose the evidence was there, but it's mighty suspicious to me."

"Where was Gere when it happened?" Heather asked from the extension.

"In Maine. Bow-and-arrow season. Brought home a deer, too."

"Now, why didn't Stone tell us all this?" I complained.

"Maybe he didn't dig deep enough," Heather suggested. "The Plymouth cops ought to deputize Fiona as an honorary detective."

Most of the time when I talked to Stone, it was privately and informally, but with Fiona's findings, which were matters of fact, I felt I could call him at the Plymouth County Detective Unit's office. Perhaps I wanted to be sure he'd take us seriously as informers. Not surprisingly, Stone already knew that Gere had been in Special Ops demolition—and even that he'd been one of those rogue officers who were suspected of taking unsanctioned revenge on villagers, the innocent with the guilty. But what Stone hadn't considered or connected was the mysterious death of Gere's ex-fiancée and her new husband—an explosion officially explained as accidental. But curious indeed, considering the clockman's motive and means.

"Hmmm," said Stone. How I wished I could see his expression! "Okay, I'll have a look at that report. You say Fiona came up with all this? What I'd really like to know is . . . where the hell does she get all her information, Cass?"

"Oh, some Internet contacts," I said vaguely. "And I have something else for you, too—just one of my own ideas this time."

"Okay. Is this a vision thing? I never thought I'd be one of those detectives who worked with psychics, but my life took this strange twist when I met Phil . . ."

"You're lucky," I assured him. "You've discovered a network some people never know. Sometimes we tap into information that can never be found in a file . . . it's just out there in space, like radio waves."

"I like it better when you *don't* try to explain what you do to us mundanes. Okay, out with it then."

"I think you'll find Candy Donahue in Quebec, just over the Maine border. Look for an isolated farmhouse, maybe a poultry farm. A nice, elderly woman, rather plump, French-speaking. I don't think the woman knows who the child is. Candy may have tried to tell them and can't bridge the language gap or is too frightened to attempt explaining herself. If I'm right and you do find her, she must be able to tell you who abducted her family."

Stone sighed heavily. "Right. I'll contact the Mounties, then. I do hope I'm not going to make a major ass of myself."

"Trust me," I said, wondering myself if I was on the right track.

As soon as I hung up, I called Phillipa and Deidre, so that it wouldn't be thought that Heather and I had been holding out on the circle. Guilt . . . guilt. We were getting to function like a real family. Phillipa especially should not learn about Fiona's news from Stone. I called her first and repeated everything I'd just told her husband.

Her response was less than approving. "I really wonder if we ever should have got ourselves mixed up in this Donahue mess," she declared tartly. "Now Stone's going to chase after your vision, and if it's a red herring and he falls flat on his face with the Mounties, he's going to blame *me*. Why didn't we discuss your vision in the circle before we decided to consult Stone?"

"Stop whining and think, Phil," I said, reaching into the refrigerator for the rest of the May wine. "There's a young girl whose parents have been murdered. She's lost somewhere up north. There's a murdering bastard who'd like to shut her up, if only he could find her. If I have information on her whereabouts, should I sit on it while our Wiccan committee reaches a consensus on how to handle the matter? It isn't as if we ever reach a consensus on anything."

Phillipa laughed. "Oh, we're not that bad—*sometimes* we agree about *some* things. That's why our circle works. Okay, I'll give you that you had to act fast. But I'm still going to worry about Stone pursuing this will-o'-the-wisp of yours. I guess it's time to read the Tarot and see just how much trouble there is ahead."

"Splendid idea! Call me when you've seen whatever . . ." and I made her promise to keep me informed. Then I hung up and dialed Deidre.

"I just hope Gere never finds out where Candy is. You know he'll try to kill her, don't you?" Deidre warned. "Even if the Mounties do find her, she'll have to be held in protective custody. I think it might have been better, Cass, if you hadn't told Stone about your vision at all. If you'd only talked it over with me first. That farm might be a therapeutic setting for a while. At least Candy's safe there."

"I don't know how Gere *would* find out," I said, with the sinking feeling that accompanies an unwelcome truth. "Stone's very discreet. Bordering on the paranoiac."

"Oh, yes? Well, he'll have to make calls, send faxes, whatever. I'll bet you that my Will and the whole firehouse will have heard about Quebec and the nice poultry lady before he gets home tonight. News travels like the wind on the Plymouth shoreline."

"Thanks, you've been a great comfort," I said, draining the last of the May wine from the bottle into my mouth.

"Well, you want the truth, don't you?"

"Never," I said. "I want cheering, consoling lies at all times."

Which I didn't get from Phillipa when she called me the next day. "Dark . . . dark . . . dark," she intoned. "A long, difficult journey. Deception. Destruction. *Double, double toil and trouble . . .* After the sixth card, I wouldn't turn over any more. I think I'd rather allow the future to surprise me this time. You going to the funeral? Stone tells me the medical examiner is going to release the remains of Paul and Denise."

So many of Plymouth's residents attended the Donahue funeral, they couldn't all fit into the Garden of Gethsemane Church. Hundreds had to stand outside on the lawn to hear Reverend Peacedale's eulogy for the martyred family whose Northern Irish roots and upwardly mobile aspirations had brought them to this popular Presbyterian congregation. Liberally larded with the theme of forgiveness, the pastor's words were broadcast outdoors through a speaker system. The church was a neighbor, so I'd walked over there with Freddie, who was in punk mourning—black jersey, black miniskirt, black platform shoes, spiky hair, and jet earrings. By the foresight of arriving over an hour early—actually because I wanted to study the arriving mourners—we were able to be seated inside.

The circle was there, too, in full force, although before the service ended, Fiona had to leave when her grandniece Laura Belle began to wail mournfully. Deidre and Will were wedged behind a column. I could just see her blond curls and her hand waving at us. Phillipa and Stone stood in back by the big double door. She was looking very elegantly witchy in a wide-brimmed black hat. Heather sat by Freddie and me, muttering "What am I doing here? I loathe funerals."

Among the mourners, I noted the presence of some who might feel that a higher justice was being served in the grisly death of Paul Donahue. Mr. and Mrs. Woolley of the doll shop were some of the last to be admitted, she being a trifle unsteady, as if overcome with grief, and in need of the support of her tall, balding husband.

"Drunk again," Freddie observed *sotto voce.*

"Lucky her," Heather whispered.

"Quiet. And look over there in the third row. The black pony-tail."

"Yeah. Like, Bill Wade is really crying his eyes out over Donahue. I don't see Reardon, the pup person, though." Freddie swiveled around, counting the house like a pastor's wife.

"Maybe he's outside, although he didn't strike me as a gloater. He seemed more concerned with Patsy's fate than his own losses."

"Geeze, Cass. For a witch, you sure are trusting."

"It's my instincts I trust, Freddie, which is quite within the psychic character. Speaking of which, I don't see your employer anywhere."

"I doubt he has the balls to show up here, you know what I mean? That would be too extreme." She continued to survey the rows in back of us. "Oops!"

As Freddie gave a small squeal, she seemed to sink down into our pew. I looked to see what had startled her. It was Gere, all right, leaning against a pillar at the rear of the church and gazing right at us. A curious twitch at the corner of his mouth might have been a sardonic smile. I hoped Stone could see him smirking; they were not far apart.

As the choir sang a resounding chorus of "Amazing Grace," I prayed Gere wouldn't recognize Freddie—I was, after all, in the right place for a meaningful prayer. Surely Freddie wearing her present punk look bore little resemblance to the demure preppie type he'd hired to work in his shop. Recently she'd added a black spider tattoo to her shoulder and a tiny gold nose ring that hurt me to look at. The nose ring was a fishhook shape, removed when she was playing sweet sixteen.

As the hymn soared to its conclusion, sobbing could be heard in the front row. Both the Donahues had living parents to agonize over this tragedy. No matter how Paul Donahue had swindled the small businessmen of Plymouth, no one deserved the fate that he and his wife had suffered. I knew I'd never be easy until somehow they were avenged and their daughter was safe.

As the two coffins, trailed by weeping relatives, moved up the main aisle of the church and out into the sunshine, we edged into the crowd of exiting mourners. I glanced around again for Gere, but apparently he had already slunk away. On the trampled lawn outside, I shook hands with Reverend Peacedale, muttering something about "this sad occasion" and his "consoling words." Although our relationship had got off to a rocky start, with much suspicion on each side, we'd both mellowed out over the past year. Peacedale had stopped chasing Scruffy off the church grounds, and I no longer suspected the minister of planning a block exorcism against me.

"Reverend Peacedale, I'd like you to meet my friends, Heather Morgan and Winifred McGarity," I said when they had elbowed their way through the departing crowds to join me.

"Lovely eulogy. So meaningful," Heather said softly in her most patrician tones.

Freddie shook hands solemnly. "I'm Catholic, myself," she said, as if fearing that he would shanghai her into the church for a forced baptism. "Nice little place you have here."

"Thank you, Miss McGarity," said the cleric gravely. "It seems as if this tragic event has brought the whole town together."

"Don't you worry, Reverend, sir. Ms. Shipton and Ms. Morgan

here are on the trail of the murderer. Cass is working through her psychic visions, and Heather burns homemade candles, so it's only a matter of time before the killer is brought to justice. Well, criminal justice, you know what I'm saying?. The Big Dude Upstairs will get him later."

"We really must go now, Freddie," I said. "There are others waiting for a few words with Reverend Peacedale. And we have friends here who might want to come back to our place for coffee."

"Or brandy," Heather whispered in my ear.

"Let's get together at some quieter time, Mrs. Shipton," the minister said. "I'd enjoy learning more about your visions."

"Yes, yes," I agreed, pushing Freddie and Heather along, intent on reaching Phillipa and Deidre before they could disappear in the sprawl of parked cars. "Another time."

"It's only a matter of time. Get the pun, Cass?" Freddie enjoyed her own little joke. "Time . . . clocks . . . Tom Gere. He's gone, you know. I don't think he recognized me, do you?"

"I sincerely hope he didn't. But I think it would be a great idea if you'd be, like, a little more discreet about our detective work and my visions, you know what I mean?" It's a weakness with empaths like myself, that instinct to blend. Now I was picking up Freddie's speech habits.

Phillipa's hat was easy to follow, and she and Stone sauntered our way when I beckoned. I never did corral Deidre and Will.

With all the circumstantial evidence linking Thomas Gere to the murder of the Donahues—the undeniable motive, the bodies being found near a Maine cabin Gere and his buddies had rented, the steel-tipped arrow like those Gere used for hunting— what more could the attorney general want? If only the Mounties had located Candy, but so far their search, which I suspected was desultory anyway, had come up with no unexplained child staying at a poultry farm.

"No, it's not plenty of evidence, Cass. It's not even enough,"

Stone explained in a patient tone as we sipped Phillipa's cinnamon-frothed cappuccino on the patio. He looked dispirited but resigned. "Or rather, it's all circumstantial. Yes, Gere has a motive, but so do the rest of Donahue's marks. Did you know that Bill Wade of the Serendipity Shoppe was also among the men in that hunting party?"

I'd never thought to check on the other hunters. Thanks to Patsy, I had concentrated on Gere to the exclusion of all other possibilities.

"I thought not," Stone continued. "Although Paul Donahue's wound *is* consistent with a steel-tipped arrow, we can't tell *whose* arrow. Archery is a popular sport. There's an archery club right here in town with over forty members, including both Bill Wade and Jack Reardon of that Plymouth Pets outfit. Reardon is their best marksman, I understand, although he's dead set against hunting and has made his feelings known to one and all. Again, I see you looking dumbfounded. Yes, Cass, and the situation gets even more complicated. A Boston-based gym proprietor whom Donahue also fleeced, a fellow named Buster Moon, owns a hunting lodge not two miles from the one Gere and his pals rented, and even nearer the old root cellar where the two bodies were found."

"What about any other evidence?" I asked in a small voice.

"We couldn't find a print or a shred of fiber anywhere on either of the Donahues, or in the root cellar. Whoever killed them never took off his gloves and must have worn a cap, also—didn't leave so much as a hair on the victims. All we have is one footprint, a common sort of L. L. Bean work boot. Gives us a general idea of the height and weight of the perpetrator, but too new to be helpful as to a distinctive wear pattern, but we will have a look at Gere's wardrobe if ever I can find a judge to issue a warrant. Which is not yet."

"What about tire tracks?"

"Yes, we got those, too. Possibly belonging to a Dodge van. The vehicle registered to Thomas Gere is a Bronco. Police reports show a Dodge van stolen from an Orono shopping plaza about a week before the Donahues disappeared. Never recovered. Anyone could have stolen that van, if it was the vehicle used to transport the bodies."

"I told you that prospects for a quick arrest looked bleak," Phillipa said. It was this viewpoint, offered on the phone earlier today, that had sent me scurrying over to confront Stone, who had the nerve to be enjoying a Sunday afternoon at leisure instead of getting on with the investigation. But my righteous indignation had been deflated like a punctured tire.

"I'm certain it was Gere," I said. "Remember how Patsy reacted to him?"

"But, Cass, you told me that all the clocks in the shop were striking," Phillipa reminded me. "Isn't that enough to spook any animal?"

"What if I give Patsy another go at Gere," I wondered aloud.

Stone sighed deeply and glared at me over his trendy oval glasses in the manner of a high school teacher confronting a truant. "Absolutely not, Cass. If this man is as dangerous as you believe him to be, it will be nothing to him to add you to the body count. You *must* leave this matter to the police to investigate. Phillipa? If you value your friend Cass, I want you to make her swear by whatever you women find holy that she will stay clear of Gere."

Phillipa looked at me conspiratorially, the ghost of a smile hovering over her lips as she considered the problem. "Cass, Stone is quite serious about this. So you must swear by the Triple Goddess you'll not mess about with a murder suspect *on your own*."

I got her drift and vowed to Stone, by the Goddess of a Thousand Names, that I would take no solo action. Still he looked at the two of us suspiciously. It had been too easy.

"Have a biscotti. This one's chocolate tangerine and that one's cherry almond," Phillipa passed the dish to me. "I always think having choices is important, don't you?"

* * *

The next morning, Monday, I called Heather. "I need your help to give Patsy another sniff of Gere," I explained. "I swore to Stone I wouldn't do anything on my own, but if you go with me, I'll be keeping my promise in a way. Besides, you better than anyone ought to be able to read canine reactions."

"Sure, I'll help. But there's no big trick to figuring out if a dog views a particular person as an enemy to be feared. Ears laid back, eyes narrow, muzzle snarling. What's the plan?"

"Well . . . that part's not quite clear in my mind yet."

"Hmmm. Listen, there must be twenty or more clocks around this mausoleum. Let me see if there isn't one that needs some work, and then we'll have a legitimate excuse to call on Gere."

"Yes! Great idea. Let's try to drop in between striking hours, though."

"Oh, right. Say, considering the scene that you caused last time, maybe it would be better if I went in with Patsy alone."

I was loath to admit it, but she had a point there. Disappointed at the thought of being left on the sidelines, I realized that there was something in me that actually enjoyed stirring the cauldron of mischief. Maybe that's what Stone had detected in me, what worried him most.

Later that morning, Heather called me back. "There's a pretty little Delft clock with a detached pendulum in one of the guest bedrooms. I've packed it up, and I'm ready to skirmish. Why don't we take my car in case Gere made a note of yours last time you were there. I'll pick up you and Patsy in a half-hour or so, okay?"

As soon as Heather arrived in her drool-spattered Mercedes, we took off with Patsy and Scruffy riding in style in the back seat, noses sniffing rapturously out the partially-open windows. We parked under a shady tree down the street from Gere's shop and waited until just past eleven o'clock. Heather, looking casually classic in crisp white pants and a navy silk blouse, her long chestnut hair worn in one glossy braid, took hold of Patsy's green leather leash, and tucked the boxed clock under her right arm.

"Now we'll know," she said, winking at me, then turning to stride down the street.

I watched her enter the shop, feeling left out. Maybe I would just stroll slowly along the street in case it turned out that Heather needed help.

"You guard the car," I said to Scruffy. He gave me the same disgusted look as always and plumped himself down on the seat with a deep sigh. *Boring . . . boring.*

Before I left, I took the keys that Heather had left in the ignition and locked the car doors. I edged against the buildings until I was very near the entrance. It was no more than five minutes since Heather had entered when I heard a noisy commotion erupt—vicious growling, something large and breakable toppling to the floor, and hysterical shouting. Heather backed out the door, struggling with Patsy, who dug her nails into the threshold and then the pavement, straining against her collar and snarling, which caused her to drop something she'd been carrying in her mouth. It looked like a long pot holder.

Catching sight of me lurking in the shadows, Heather tossed the clock package like a football, so she could use both hands to hang on to Patsy and drag her toward the car. By some miracle, I seized the box in midair, and we both dashed toward the Mercedes.

Gere came out of the shop, still shouting, looking disheveled, wearing a sweater with one sleeve ripped away. "You're going to pay for this grandmother clock your little bitch just destroyed!" He started to follow us down the street toward the car. Patsy bared her teeth and snarled at him. Heather kept hauling her away, and I hurried to unlock the car, trying to keep my face averted. As soon as I opened the car door, Scruffy leaped out to defend us, ready to do battle with tooth and claw. I grabbed his leash, at which point Gere got a good look at me.

"You, again!" he screamed. "What the hell is this? That's the same attack dog you brought in here before." At the same time, he prudently backed away from the two snapping and snarling dogs. I saw his lips move soundlessly for a minute. Then he shouted, "I've got your license number, you two. I'm calling the police. You'll pay for this." And he disappeared into the shop.

"Uh-oh," I said as we drove away. "I hope Stone doesn't hear about this."

"Don't worry," said Heather. "Not only did Patsy recognize *him*, he remembered *her*. She must have been there when he kidnapped the Donahues. That man is not going to call the police and stir up trouble for himself. On the other hand, he may look for some sort of retribution for that handsome clock that crashed to the floor. I sure hope he won't be able to trace my license number."

"I doubt he'll have to," I said. "You're quite a looker, you know. If he asks around town—*who's the tall, attractive dame who drives a Mercedes filled with dogs?*—half the shopkeepers on this street could tell him your name."

She was silent for a few moments as we inched along with the usual noon traffic on the narrow streets of Plymouth Center. In the backseat, Patsy was still trembling. I reached back to stroke her soothingly, and she jumped right over the seat into my lap. An Irish setter is not what I would call a lapdog, but there she was, hanging over me on both sides.

She gets away with everything. Grumbling and sighing, Scruffy turned away and took a disdainful pose, gazing out the window.

"Well, you can't expect her to be as brave as you are." I turned to speak to the offended dog in the backseat. Scruffy puffed up his chest a little at this diplomatic suggestion.

"Still talking to dogs, Dr. Dolittle?" Heather inquired. "I should know better than to hang around with you. You're definitely hazardous to my health. How do you get yourself into these things? How do I?"

"We can't just let Gere get away with it. Think of that innocent little girl. But Stone says they haven't enough evidence yet to make an arrest and the Mounties must be dragging their heels in the hunt for Candy. So much for that 'they always get their man' shit."

"Really, Cass, your language is becoming as coarse as Freddie's. Well, isn't this just great! A crazed clock person with a vendetta against me is free to come and go just as he pleases. You'd better come back to my place for lunch so we can plot our strategy."

"A vendetta against *us*," I corrected her. "Is Ashbery cooking?"

"I'm the one who careened into Gere's beloved grandmother clock. And don't worry that I'm going to cook up something myself. I'm no Phil. When I left the house, Ashbery promised me a crabmeat quiche and an avocado salad. A chilled Pinot Grigio with that, I think."

"Sold," I said as I gently scratched Patsy's chest. "Now tell me exactly what happened in that clock shop."

"Sure. Just picture this, will you! We open the shop door, the little bell jingles, and a minute or two later, Gere comes out from the back room, all smiles. As soon as Patsy catches sight of him, the hair on her back stands up in a ruff, and she bares her canine teeth. I can barely hear that low, motorboat growl in her throat that means real trouble for someone. No more than two seconds later, without warning, she leaps, like a K-9 attack dog jumping to bring down a suspect, a perfect arc to take her over the counter if I had not pulled her back with all my strength. Patsy gets caught up on the counter, betwixt and between. I fall backwards. The grandmother clock rocks away from the wall. Gere screams and dives to save it, but Patsy scrambles off the counter and grabs hold of his arm. Luckily, he's wearing a thick coat sweater. I don't think her teeth quite get through it when I yank her away. She won't let go of the sleeve, which rips off. The clock topples to the floor. I pull Patsy out the door, and Gere follows me, shouting. Now, I think I deserve a combat medal, don't you? A silver pentagram at least."

"You did nobly. And so did our prime witness, Patsy. If only we could bring her into court to face Gere."

"Yeah? Well, count me out. Now, let's go home and open that bottle."

A few minutes later, heartened by a glass of chilled white wine, I had a bright idea. "Do you think if we let it out around town that Gere is a suspect, we could force him to do something crazy the way criminals usually do when they get cornered?"

"Criminals and rats," Heather said. "Not my favorite cornered creatures. Let's get serious here. What's the point of honing our craft to a fine edge if we don't turn a sharp little spell against this guy? I say, let's call in the others and take care of matters ourselves. Yes . . . we'll do it this afternoon."

There was no dissuading Heather with reminders about our pledge to *do no harm.* As soon as we'd reduced Ashbery's excellent quiche to crumbs, she was on the phone. An emergency circle was called for the next evening, Tuesday, at Fiona's. After Heather had driven me and the dogs home, I soaked away the haze of Pinot Grigio in a steaming lavender bath. I would need a clear mind for the decisions that lay ahead.

The vote was three against two. Deidre and Heather had opted for a direct hit on Gere but Fiona, Phillipa, and I didn't want to risk the rebound effect.

"Not everyone subscribes to that threefold business." Heather carried in a steaming teapot and a trivet from Fiona's tiny kitchen and placed them on the much-scarred cherry coffee table where Omar, the fat cat, was lounging on the *Pilgrim Times*. He sneezed and glared, departing with great dignity for his padded shelf on the windowsill. "Some occultists say it's moralistic nonsense, a fear of punishment. Others say that Wiccans, being in tune with divine energy, are naturally ethical."

"It's in such a good cause," Deidre lamented. "I bet I could do it with one of my little dolls, just tie him up in knots for a while until Stone turns up some hard evidence."

"Think of your children, Dee." Fiona poured the orange-scented herb tea into mugs. "You don't want to take the chance of those black vibrations boomeranging into their lives. I know how I feel about my own dear Laura Belle . . ."

"Well, children are not *my* worry," Heather declared with an air of satisfaction. "I could hole up in my turret workroom and light a few appropriate candles . . ."

"Ah, but what about your canine family?" I reminded her, passing the honey.

"Damn and blast it to Hades," Heather said.

"Spells are tricky work," said Fiona, rummaging in a glass-fronted bookcase where she locked up her arcane literature. She pulled out a moldy leather volume, reeking of mildew, much thumbed and bookmarked. I could have sworn that book had live cobwebs hanging off the binding. "But I think I may have something here to help."

As always, Fiona enthralled us with her serendipitous lore. We crowded around for a closer look at the dubious relic. Faint purple letters etched into the black leather cover read *Hazel's Book of Household Recipes*. "Where in the world did you unearth this relic?" Phillipa wanted to know.

"Yard sale," Fiona said. "Obviously, they didn't know what they had here. Misled by the title, just like you, Phil. Oh, the 'household recipes' do include stews, soaps, sachets, and cough syrups—regular early nineteenth-century necessities. But the book also includes recipes with magical ingredients and purposes. It would be interesting to learn more about Hazel's life, whether she prospered or was persecuted. Plainly, it's a book of shadows. Look at this, for instance . . ."

Fiona turned to a handwritten recipe for Thieves-Away Sachet. Juniper, mistletoe, rosemary . . . I was fascinated, my thoughts leaping ahead—did these recipes really work? Could I incorporate them into my own herbal preparations? How in the world could I advertise such things? On the opposite page was a recipe for Familiar Spirits, which appeared to be a food supplement for enhancing the natural abilities of dogs and cats. Brewer's yeast, barley, buckwheat ... "Fiona, do you think I might borrow ..."

Fiona had already turned to the page marked by an old-time ferry schedule. Just Desserts! the title proclaimed in ancient black ink, with a thick exclamation point like a dagger with a drop of blood. Deidre, who'd edged in beside me, whistled. "Oooh. This Dispelling Demon Entities with the blue candles and mirror is awesome. And an herbal concoction for you, Cass. What do you think it will do?"

"Jalap powder, tincture of benzoin, orris root, patchouli oil, brimstone ..." I read the rest of the recipe with fascination. "What a weird mixture. You dry it and make a kind of incense cubes to burn on the nine nights."

"Look here," said Heather, pointing to a note at the bottom of the page. "We're to begin on a Tuesday—that's because it's Mars day, battle day—during a waning moon, for that which must be decreased. And I have the blue candles—I made them a bit on the dark side, but they'll do. More of a midnight blue."

"Hey, no black candles," I insisted.

"What about this picture thing?" Phillipa asked.

Deidre read aloud, " 'Make a small painting of the demon and glue it to a mirror, facedown. All harm the demon intends will be reflected back unto its being.' I'll do that part—it's my sort of magic."

"There was an article about Gere's shop in the *Pilgrim Times* ... oh, maybe six months ago," Fiona said. "With a photograph, as I recall. One of those local business write-ups that are a regular feature of the paper. Maybe people pay for them, I don't know. They're always flattering. I'll make you a copy of it from the library microfiche."

"I'd just as soon skip this 'sweeping out the negatives' bit, though," Phillipa said. "Brooms are so predictable."

"Okay, Tuesday, a week from today," Fiona said. "I'll bring a nice apple cake, shall I?"

"What does she think this is," Phillipa whispered in my ear, "a P.T.A. meeting?"

"Sure. Psychic Threefold Attack. Be there!"

"Hey, Ma!" Adam's voice sounded tinny in the answering machine I turned on when I arrived home from our council of war at Fiona's. "I'm on my way to Canada. Going to stay with friends in Montreal for a week or so. Finally getting some time off. Anyway, I'm stopping by your place first—because I have something for you. It's Friday, quarter to eight—I should be there by half past nine. I hope it's okay if I stay the night, or as long as it takes."

I hadn't seen my son since Christmas, nor heard from him since I'd called him in April, so this sudden stopover was more than a surprise—it was pure shock and delight.

I wonder what he's brought me, I thought. A daughter-in-law? A rare herb plant? A pet to take care of, just like the old days? It's a good thing Joe isn't here on one of his lightning visits. What a perfect Penelope I am! Perhaps I should take up weaving.

I glanced at the kitchen clock—it was already quarter to ten. Just as I was getting ready for some serious worry, however, Adam sped into my driveway, jumped out of his car, and shouted for help. "Better open that old front door," he said, hauling several big boxes out of his dashing gray Lexus. Scruffy, who'd come out into the driveway with me, jumped around Adam, barking with excitement. "Easier getting this stuff into the house through the front. Hi, dog! What's his name again?"

Hey, Toots, I think I've smelled this guy before—but what's all this stuff, stuff, stuff! Scruffy turned his attention to the packages in the driveway. He lifted his leg slightly.

"Oh, Adam, it's so wonderful to see you! Scruffy, don't you dare! It's okay. You remember Adam." I warned off the dog from his marking inclination and rushed back to the kitchen for the house keys.

"What's all this, honey?" I wrestled open the cranberry-colored front door. It creaked and protested as usual.

With the flurry of packages being efficiently unpacked, I seemed to be missing the chance to greet Adam with a proper hug. Later, I thought, when we get settled. Deep inside me burned a guilty secret I hid from everyone, even from myself most of the time. Although I loved all my children, I felt there was a special understanding between Adam and me that was different, more restful and reliable, than my relationship with the girls. I hoped I wasn't favoring him for being male.

"Ma, I *told* you I was going to design a computer system for your herb business. Not just bookkeeping, but also a Web site for customer orders. Well, here it is, finally. I'll set it up tonight, tomorrow we'll get you online, and then I'll teach you to use it. I've registered your domain name as it appears on your business card—hope that's okay. I don't know how you've gotten along all this time without a computer."

" 'The shoemaker's children often go barefoot.' Or, in this case, the shoemaker's mother," I said, feeling slightly overwhelmed by the magnificence of the gift—and the giver. "What a terrific idea, and the best part is having you here to guide me into the twenty-first century. I guess you know I could never do this without you. My, you look marvelous! What happened to my unkempt computer genius? Is that cashmere?"

"Hey, I'm not a nerd anymore, Ma." Adam was standing still finally, in the middle of my living room, surrounded by a fort of boxes. His head almost touched the low Colonial ceiling, his dark blond hair was attractively tousled. He wore a handsomely-styled leather jacket over a beige turtleneck sweater with cotton canvas jeans and expensive-looking boots.

How little he resembles Gary, I thought, feeling pleased in a mean sort of way. More like my dad at that age, especially that charming, lopsided smile. Except for the green eyes—my eyes.

"So, come on, Ma. I have been meaning to get this system set up since Christmas. If you only knew how busy I've been." He hugged me back for a moment, then ducked out of my embrace. "Our place has just gone berserk. I'm lucky I got away at all."

Our place was Iconomics, Inc., a leading business software company that was, in my view, using up Adam's brainpower at a blazing rate and would leave him, like an overplayed athlete, completely burned out at age thirty. Although I couldn't exactly comprehend what Adam did at Iconomics, I was filled with pride at his brilliance.

I cleared some desk space in my office, formerly my grandma's sewing room, and Adam went right to work. Thinking how tired he must be after the long drive, I made some rather strong coffee and put a mug of it into his hand. He sipped at the brew while uncrating the awesome equipment I was sure I'd never learn to use. Scruffy lay yawning in the doorway where we had to step over him each time we entered or left the little room. *Hey, Toots— isn't it time we all hit the sack?*

"You go ahead to bed if you like. You're in the way here anyway," I replied.

"I assume you're talking to the dog. I guess that happens to old ladies who live alone," Adam teased, as he began to attach the various electronic marvels to one another.

"Maybe I should get married again," I needled back. A momentary film clip of a life with Joe—dazzling as Aegean sunlight—played in my mind's eye.

Adam frowned, not entirely at the mess of electronic equipment confronting him. "You're going to need another phone line to handle all this without tying up your regular phone. We'll order it in the morning. Got anyone special in mind? Is that Greek guy still in the picture? Becky said she thought he was long gone on some environmental quest."

"Joe. His name is Joe Ulysses, not 'that Greek guy.' It's reassuring to know that you and Becky take an interest. You may tell her that he still drops by between adventures." I felt a certain satisfaction in actually having a love life to hint about, infuriatingly, to my children.

It was a matter of pure amazement to me to watch Adam make sense of that tangle of power cords. By one in the morning, he had everything up and running to his satisfaction, but he himself was ready to crash. After shutting down the whole system, he wolfed down warmed-up soup with a side of toasted cheese and stumbled upstairs to the blue bedroom. I was exhausted, too, but also exhilarated and grateful, although I hardly knew for what. I found Scruffy asleep in my downstairs bedroom, his legs jerking, anxiously dreaming of a chase.

Opening the window, I was lulled sweetly toward sleep by the fragrance of my grandma's lilacs wafting in over the lawn and thoughts of a wedding—mine. I pictured a pale green dress, something floaty and very feminine, a circlet of flowers in my hair. Or would that be too jejune? Would I ask the Reverend Peacedale to officiate? Perhaps I should choose a handfasting ceremony instead of a church wedding, with Fiona tying the knot. That was a pretty thought, but when it came right down to it, I guessed I'd rather we were bound together in a more traditional and legal way.

But wait a minute . . . what about that gold cross hanging around Joe's neck? Wouldn't he insist on a priest?

As the argument inside my head heated up, sleep slipped away from my grasp, so I got up and leaned on the windowsill, listening to the smack-and-swish of the waves hitting the seawall at high tide. Maybe I should table the details of my wedding until I had an actual proposal from an actual Joe. And who said I want to get married again, anyway?

Snapping on the light to change the subject, I picked a book that Adam had asked me to study, *PCs for Dummies.* That did the trick. I was fast asleep before I got past "Making Friends with Your Computer."

The next morning, I'd just put on a pot of coffee, and was sautéing onions and chilies for Adam's favorite *huevos rancheros* when I heard Freddie clattering up the back stairs on her platform sandals.

"Yo, Cass," she called in the kitchen window that was open to the porch, and beyond the porch, to the Atlantic, calm and gray-blue in the May sunshine. It hurt me to see her looking so lonely and hungry. I wondered if her after-school stint at Gere's and occasional baby-sitting for Fiona were paying her enough. At least when she worked at Hamburger Heaven, she could always eat her fill. It just wasn't right for a teenager to be living on her own as she was, no matter how scaled-down her expenses were at the commune.

"Just in time for a big, big breakfast," I said. "No work today?"

She's here! The girl is here! Scruffy rejoiced, sniffing her bare toes with abject delight.

"Cut it out, Scruff—that tickles! I'm not due at the clock shop until two. So I thought I'd hang with you for a while and find out what's new in the witch business. Maybe you ladies are getting ready to turn Gere into a toad or something fun like that?"

"Hush!" I commanded. "I have company."

"Uh-oh. Joe here? I'd better split then and leave you two lovers to roll around in the herb pillows."

"No, it's not Joe. And I'll thank you to speak more respectfully. Or better yet, don't speak at all. Just make yourself useful by setting the table. Or maybe you could pick a few wildflowers for that little green glass vase."

Freddie looked aghast. "You're not two-timing Joe, are you?" she whispered.

"Hey, Ma!" Just then Adam shouted from the stairway. "Did that damn dog take my boot?"

"Scruffy," I said sternly. "Where did you put Adam's boot? If you chewed up one of his boots, you're in deep trouble."

That man up there left some cow's hoof thing on the floor. How did I know he'd want it back? Scruffy lay down with his nose between his paws and rolled his eyes at me.

Adam came downstairs, wearing only a towel and a scowl, stunning Freddie into open-mouthed awe. She looked as if a god had just descended into our midst from Mount Olympus.

"Oh, sorry." Adam disappeared again into the shadowed stairwell. "Ma, would you see if you can find my boot, please?"

"That's my son, Adam," I explained unnecessarily to Freddie. She'd seen him at all stages and ages in my framed photographs. "I'll just go check in my bedroom for his boot. Scruffy likes to leave stolen treasures under my bed. Meanwhile, as soon as the paralysis leaves your limbs, why don't you check out those flowers over beside the garage. Make a little spring bouquet for the table. By then, Adam will be dressed, and you can meet him properly. And you will *not* bring up anything about Gere or our circle, *please*. It will only worry him unnecessarily. Adam's here to bring me out of the Dark Ages with a computer setup you won't believe. He's a whiz at that sort of thing."

"Oh, cool!" my protégée said, still motionless, as if one glance at Adam in the flesh had turned her to girl-shaped marble.

Later, over the spicy eggs and tortillas, Freddie questioned Adam in detail about the Web site he was setting up for me. She seemed to understand his replies, which was more than I could do. His amused smile revealed that Adam was pleased with the quickness of this funky teenager. As for Freddie, she seemed to have cleaned up her usual salty language for Adam's benefit. Once, when he turned his back, I could have sworn she was on the verge of what we would have called in my younger days a swoon. Poor little girl, I thought. She's right at the age for some serious hero-worship.

As I watched them chattering away in computer jargon at the breakfast table, and later, continuing in my office, I remembered how Freddie had been nicknamed The Virus in the school computer lab—for good reason. Surely she wouldn't put her hex on my fledgling system! Not on purpose, of course, but her wild energy was rather like a loose wire snapping free from the pole.

"This is really simple, Ma," Adam kept telling me as the lessons began in earnest. Then his fingers would race over the keys, causing list after list—or *menus*, as he called them—to flip by faster than the human eye could read.

Adding to my chagrin, Freddie, perched beside Adam, kept

nodding her head knowledgeably and saying things like, "Got that. Okay. No prob. What's next?" until I could have brained her. Happily, maturity prevailed, and I realized that Freddie's annoying expertise actually could be a great asset.

"Remember when I asked you to send me your catalog, Ma? That wasn't just idle curiosity. I've scanned the catalog, graphics and all, into your Web site so that people can order from you online once you've arranged the credit card thing," Adam explained proudly. "Listen, I've even added music." One click of the mouse and medieval strains of *Greensleeves* played on a mandolin rose evocatively out of my brand-new speakers.

"What a perfect choice! This is super, darling. I'll just slip away and put on the kettle," I said. "Why don't you keep on explaining the Web site thing to Freddie, how to receive orders from my catalog, hook up with credit card companies, and so forth. Then she can fill me in later."

The kettle was beginning to whistle when Adam followed me into the kitchen. "I didn't realize that Freddie works for you, Ma," Adam said. "I thought she was another of your—well, you know, like Tip."

"Freddie doesn't work here regularly, but now I'll really need the help," I said. "And she needs employment, Adam. Freddie's completely on her own, living in a run-down commune on Prospect Street. Lately, she's been assisting at a clock shop, but I don't think her paycheck is stretching far enough. And sometimes she baby-sits for Fiona."

"She's a natural. Even as we speak, your Girl Friday is browsing through the programming. Freddie has the makings of a great hacker," said Adam, washing up at the sink. "Got any beer?"

"Root beer."

Adam's eyebrows rose and he sighed. "No, thanks. I'll settle for the tea. How did you happen to take on this tough kid, Ma? You'll only get your feelings hurt again, like when Tip went off to Maine with his mom."

"Shhhh!" I didn't want Freddie to overhear Adam's careless analysis. "I think she has a crush on you, so don't you dare hurt her feelings. Also, watch out, because she's psychokinetic."

"Oh, God . . . what's that? Are you still dabbling in mystic stuff?"

It occurred to me that I myself had brought up the very subject which I'd forbidden Freddie to mention. I explained Freddie's talent, rather lamely, while Adam shook his head. But his sympathy for his eccentric mother won out, as proved by the heartening hug he gave me there in the kitchen. "It's okay, Ma. I know you just want to help the girl. So what can she do besides bend spoons and throw a psychic monkey wrench into machinery?"

"I shouldn't have told you even that much. I'm just taking her under my wing so that she'll learn to control her natural abilities."

"Oh yeah, like you, *ho ho*!"

I poured hot water into the teapot, set out cups and cinnamon rolls, and called Freddie to join us. When Adam couldn't resist glancing at Freddie's spoon in a speculative manner, I tried to kick his ankle under the table, but Scruffy was lying in the way. *Ouch. What was that for?* The dog groaned, rolled over, and nuzzled Freddie's hand, angling for a handout.

But Freddie's thoughts were a thousand miles away. "So a virus is like a spell, and a spell is like a virus," she ruminated, while she idly stroked the spoon in her hand. It was starting to soften. Now my toe wanted to kick Freddie into awareness. "Maybe I should lay a virus on Gere's clocks, just to addle him, you know what I mean?"

"Who's Gere?" asked Adam. "What are you up to these days, Ma? No more voodoo sleuthing, I hope. *I* don't care, but Becky will, with Ron running for state representative."

"Oh, sh . . . sugar," Freddie said, snapping out of her meditation with an apologetic glance at me.

"Thomas Gere is a local repairman who's had a little trouble in his shop, that's all. Nothing for you to be concerned about, Adam."

"Yeah, and don't go blaming your mom," Freddie defended me. "She's only trying to bring a murderer to justice with a little help from her friends. Like, didn't you read about the missing family, the Donahues, how they found a couple of them whacked and dumped in a root cellar in Maine? The kid got away somewhere, we hope, and everyone is looking for her, even the Mounties."

"Listen, Freddie—don't help me," I said. Too late. I was in for one of those galling lectures that grown children feel entitled to deliver from time to time to their troubling parents. By the time I got Adam back on the road north, I'd had to listen to several stern talks between computer lessons.

The next day, Sunday, the clock shop being closed, an eager Freddie arrived early to work with the new Web site. Her excitement fizzled out fast, however, when she learned that Adam was already on his way north to enjoy the rest of his vacation, and I had no idea when he might return. "Wow, that son of yours is *wicked hot*, Cass." Freddie was full of admiration for Adam's expertise as she pointed and clicked her way through our new system. "Now what I'm wondering is, can a witch's hex be sent out over the Internet like a virus?"

I rejected the notion firmly. "We Wiccans don't do Windows, Freddie."

"Not yet, maybe. Soooo—how old is Adam?"

"Too old. Twenty-four."

"Yeah? I've had older, you know what I mean? But I don't guess I'm his type. What *is* his type? You're his mom—you ought to know."

"A mother is the *last* to know. Grown-up, for one thing. And I think he goes for the natural look." Actually, I had no idea. Even when he was in high school, Adam had always kept his crushes entirely secret from his sisters and me. But there was always the hope that Freddie would ease off on the sooty mascara and purple nail polish.

"Hey, Cass, I'm no kid anymore, you know? I'm out on my own and all that. I'm practically seventeen." Freddie's fingers never stopped moving as she argued her case.

"Are you really? When's the big day?" There'd be no one to make a fuss over Freddie's birthday except me, so I'd better find out when.

"June 13. Couple of weeks. I don't, like, celebrate it or anything. Just another day of the year, you know what I mean?"

Of course, a Gemini! Mercurial, versatile. "Thirteen's a lucky number for Wiccans." Already I was thinking of a festive cake, one chocolate layer and one vanilla, in honor of the celestial twins.

Esbat of the Dyad Moon, the Honey Moon

As directed by Hazel's book, we began on a Tuesday when the moon was waning. The ritual for Dispelling Demon Entities was evoked in Heather's turret room, where our candles, incense, and mirror spell could be left undisturbed for nine days. We didn't really believe it would cause Gere to vanish in a puff of smoke, but it might very well cause him to lose focus and put himself in harm's way. Freddie was not invited to this session, even though I'd begun to introduce my protégée to Wicca, magic, and herbs.

Often Freddie came for supper after the clock shop had closed, full of gossip and speculation about Gere. The most interesting tidbit was that Gere's own prize antique clocks were still disappearing from the shelves.

On the thirteenth, I invited Phil, Stone, and Heather to share our dinner—Freddie's favorite, lasagna—served in the dining room on my herb-patterned best dishes from a pottery in Maine, instead of our usual kitchen table supper with dogs underfoot. After dinner, I brought in the candlelit cake, which, like all my other homemade birthday cakes, had a slight depression at the center masked by extra frosting. I hoped Phillipa wouldn't notice.

When we sang the traditional birthday song, led by Stone, who had quite a pleasing tenor voice, Freddie dashed away moisture from her cheeks with the palms of her hands and blew out the candles in a quick, almost angry burst of breath. At that exact moment, a dining room curtain rod popped off its hook and drapery slid to the floor, taking two potted African violets with it. Phillipa lifted her eyebrow and glanced at me significantly, not needing to say the word on her lips: *poltergeist.*

After we cleaned up the traumatized violets, the reluctant birthday girl was overwhelmed by the red canvas overnight bag I gave her, Phillipa's funky watch with changeable wristbands, and Heather's gift of a tailored black leather jacket. Rushing out to the kitchen with a tray of endangered dishes, Freddie got a chance to sob by herself. We let her alone, even when we heard the unmistakable sound of a plate breaking.

Hey, don't blame us. Scruffy defended himself and Patsy.

"I'd be surprised to learn that Freddie has ever had a birthday party." Phillipa pushed away her cake plate. As luck would have it, she'd been handed one of the slices that was half frosting.

"I wonder if aloneness and neglect hasn't contributed to her psychic energy," Heather observed.

"Maybe a little love in her life will lead to control," I said. I hoped it would be in time to save my good china.

Freddie continued to share her PC expertise with me. She seemed able to solve any computer conundrum that puzzled me. I suggested that she quit the dangerous job with Gere and work for me instead, managing the computer orders for my herb products that were coming up in increasing numbers.

Even though she no longer smelled of hamburgers and fries, Scruffy was still delighted with Freddie's company. He demonstrated his affection by constantly thrusting his shaggy head under her arm, the better to be scratched on the chest, a caress that hypnotized him with pleasure.

Why doesn't the girl live here? I could share my sheepskin with her. The L. L. Bean dog bed topped with faux sheepskin had been a

Christmas gift to Scruffy, a prize possession he steadfastly guarded from Patsy when she tired of her own bedding, the folded green wool blanket I'd arranged for her.

"Holy shit, there's a bunch of poisons in these jars," Freddie exclaimed when I showed her around my cache in the cellar. "And that's just the ones with names. What about these numbered babies back here? Am I looking at some witches' favorite controlled substances here?" Freddie peered at dried herbs I preferred to label in code for just such curious browsers.

The walls surrounding us were lined with sturdy pine shelves where Grandma used to store a winter's supply of home-canned foods. Now gallon-size glass jars were packed with my own herbs. They filled those same shelves, along with dark bottles of tinctures and vials of essential oils, plus beeswax, incense, charcoal, unbleached linen, and other staples of my inventory. Upstairs in the kitchen I kept some of Grandma's old Ball mason jars filled with herbs I used often, but this was my real storeroom.

In the center of the room was an ancient, scarred gateleg table, missing its leaf, but otherwise heavy and serviceable. Brass scales glowed softly under the green-shaded hanging lamp. The room was dry and dusty, thick with competing fragrances, the corners hung with inevitable cobwebs—maybe a little scary to an outsider.

"It's all a question of degree," I explained. "Most medicinal herbs are poisonous if you administer an overdose. Many poisons are harmless in minute amounts. An herbalist has to be thoroughly learned and highly ethical."

Freddie held up a labeled jar of dried green leaves that looked like parsley. "*Yeah, right* . . . so how much of this hemlock would it take to wipe out some rival witch?"

"Hemlock is a sacred herb of consecration. It's never taken or administered internally anymore, although it was used in medieval times as a sedative."

"Good night, sweet prince . . ." Freddie murmured, chuckling. "That Joe Ulysses had better watch himself."

"The strawberry-rhubarb pie you're so fond of could be poisonous, too, if I included some shredded rhubarb leaves with the stalks, my dear. The lesson here is, know your herbs."

"And make sure the tea you're offered was brewed from a teabag . . ." finished the irrepressible Freddie. "Anyway, *I* don't need all these weeds to be a witch."

"Herbs are peripheral, I agree. But I seem to have a natural affinity for herb work, so it's an ideal living for me. Even though your skills are in a different sphere, you need to learn about herbs if you want to be a well-rounded Wiccan. You never know . . ."

"Hey, Cass . . . you rule. Whatever you want to teach me . . . go for it."

For a moment I wondered if I should bring this talented girl into the web we were weaving around Gere—but I decided in favor of discretion.

Three days into Hazel's *Dispelling* spell, Gere began to behave erratically. Our after-school spy Freddie reported these details without realizing that we'd been concocting some real magic. Gere made wrong change, lost irreplaceable clock gizmos, forgot deposits, and otherwise seemed to be strongly affected, if not by us, at least by guilt and fear. Unfortunately, Gere also found out who we were and that Freddie was not his innocent girl helper in a baby blue twin set but our own punk protégée. Having left her out of the loop, Freddie didn't have the protection we'd arranged for ourselves. She got the full blast of Gere's murderous anger.

"I was lucky to get out of there with my skin intact, if you know what I mean." Freddie sipped the steadying kava tea I'd brewed for her and related her story to Phillipa, Heather, and me. "I guess I was pushing the envelope, taking in that Donahue funeral with Cass. He must have got a good look at me."

"Even I wouldn't recognize you when you wear those preppie clothes," Phillipa said. "How did he?"

"Say, that nut's been out of his tree all week. Yesterday he messes up the thermostat, and the temp in the shop goes sky-high. Like, I'm dying, so I slip off my cardigan. Mistake. I'm wearing a tank top underneath. Right away he spots the Grandmother Spider tattoo on my shoulder. Next thing I knew, he grabs my arms and he's in my face like it's a winning lottery ticket. Whatever came over him, it was awesome. Then he goes, *You're the little bitch with all the earrings, aren't you?* I mean, that dude was screaming. Up close and personal like that, he catches on to the holes, you know what I mean? Especially this one on my nose that's still a little sore. I had to knee him in the balls to get out of there." She sighed. "Guess I got to change jobs *again.*"

"Yes, I think you gave your notice," Phillipa said dryly. "I wonder how Gere found out about our circle. And how many of us he knows."

Freddie put down her teacup and began to rummage in her beaded shoulder bag. "Easy. Lifted this out of his wastebasket in back. There's another copy on his desk, with addresses, even e-mail, and phone numbers." She unfolded and tried to smooth out a much-creased sheet of paper. Heather's and my names were in the middle, with black arrows pointing to other names, Fiona, Deidre, and Phillipa, and a red arrow linking her husband Stone Stern to us.

"Sweet Mother!" exclaimed Heather.

I filled a large teapot with kava leaves and added simmering water from the kettle. We *all* needed some calming herbs.

"Now he's got another connection—me to you, Cass." Freddie's appearance of sangfroid was unconvincing. She still had bruises on her upper arms where Gere had grabbed her. Thinking of how alone Freddie must feel in the disordered commune she called home, I invited her to stay with me anytime she felt anxious.

"But I've got my cat Shadow," she reminded me, nevertheless looking hopeful.

I hope you don't expect me to tolerate some miserable black hairball hissing and spitting fish around my place. Isn't it enough that I have to put up with the Irisher? From his cool sprawl under the kitchen table, Scruffy huffed and sighed his opinion of animal boarders.

I gave the dog a cautionary nudge with my toe, although no one really listened to him except me. "How about the people you live with?" I asked. "If the necessity arose, would someone there watch out for your cat for a few days?"

"Are you kidding? Most of those crackheads have shit for brains, you know what I mean? Pardon my French . . ."

"Shadow can board with me. I'm sure he'll be sympatico with Zelda, since they're both a minute past midnight." A surprising offer from Phillipa, who at one time refused to own a pet and had to be ambushed by Fiona into adopting the feline waif found in a Dumpster. "You need to expand your vocabulary, young lady— you know what *I* mean? 'Shit for brains,' for example, might be more effectively expressed by any number of pejorative terms— ignoramus, bungler, simpleton, numskull, blockhead, exasperat- ingly obtuse—whatever might best describe your roommates in their drug-induced lethargy."

Freddie, for once, was struck dumb. The kava having steeped sufficiently, I filled china cups—tea never seems to be as flavorful when drunk from mugs—and passed them around, accompanied by a pitcher of local honey to ward off allergies.

"On the other hand, what about a weekend job at Animal Lovers Shelter?" Heather suggested. "That would solve two problems—a source of income for you and a place to board your cat companion whenever you need to."

Freddie poured honey into her second cup of kava with a thoughtful expression. "So . . . what would I be doing . . . like, shoveling sh . . ." she glanced at Phillipa, who was scowling. "Shoveling excrement?"

Heather laughed. "Yes. And feeding and walking and playing with a bunch of abandoned, love-starved animals who need as much TLC as you can give. And the salary *is* a bit more than minimum wage."

"No sugar! And I could still work Cass's computer after school on weekdays," Freddie murmured under her breath, her new job schedule suddenly looking good to her. But I had the rather disturbing notion that the vengeful Gere would be drawing another red arrow on his chart—aimed at the animal shelter. I said nothing, however, not wanting to spoil this rather decent opportunity for Freddie.

As it turned out, our nine-day spell to shake up Gere and force him into some behavior that would bring him to the attention of the law showed signs of working. But the protective aura we'd conjured around our circle, unfortunately, was not as effective.

"Gere's flown the coop!" Heather exclaimed a few days later in an excited phone call. "The sign in the window says CLOSED UNTIL FURTHER NOTICE. And there's a phone number to call if you want to collect a clock. It's just a service—I called it. The girl said if I was desperate for my clock, she had a key and could arrange to meet me there to pick it up, but she'd rather wait until Mr. Gere returned to settle accounts properly. Where'd he go? I asked. She said, Maine. For how long? She's not sure—it was something about somebody's terminal illness."

"I bet," I said. "What if Deidre was right about police business getting around town, and Gere did hear rumors about our search for Candy?"

That night we celebrated our June Esbat, the full moon of all twosomes, from twins to handfasting couples. Our circle met at Fiona's. After she drew our circle with her antique athame, we did the rituals for love that are always part of June's magic. We sought wisdom and endurance in all things, especially in our confrontation with Gere. And we celebrated Earth's bounty. The Esbat left me feeling peaceful and hopeful, despite all contrary signs.

The next morning, Phillipa dropped in with a basket of Madeira scones she was testing and the latest news from the Mounties—which wasn't good.

"Stone said to tell you they found the place where the kid

must have been staying. Not a poultry farm, but the couple who live there do keep some chickens and geese." Phillipa plunked the basket down on my kitchen counter and poured herself a cup of coffee. "Let's go out on the porch and breathe deeply. What a glorious day!"

"What do you mean 'probably'?" I asked as we settled ourselves in my old green wicker rockers and were wrapped in the scent of salt water. The Atlantic was in a kind mood, mildly rippled in permutations of blue.

"This nice old farmer and his wife found a girl wandering in the woods—scratched up, starving, and incoherent—they couldn't understand a word the child said," Phillipa continued while sipping her steaming coffee. "They cleaned her up and let her rest for a few days while they decided what to do. Apparently they concluded she must be a gift from God to them personally."

"Oh, Christ," I said.

"Exactly. They're a childless couple, and the woman had been praying to some recent candidate for the sainthood up there. But when their priest heard about the couple's miracle, he immediately informed the Mounties. Meanwhile, the girl regained her strength. Then some tourist stopped by the farm to ask directions, and Candy took off out back through the woods before the Mounties could rescue her. She hasn't been seen since."

"What tourist? Did anyone get a look at him?" I wondered if Gere could have gotten there ahead of us all.

"Nope. But he was driving a shiny black van. The farm couple couldn't say what make. They're very distraught, as you may imagine. Might have been an innocent coincidence, but the kid got spooked."

"Might have been Gere."

"There's that," Phillipa agreed. "Well, our intention was to shake him up. Now what do we do about Candy?"

A short time later, Phillipa left to cook something *haute cuisine* for Stone, passing Freddie, who was arriving on her bike. "Yo,

Cass," she greeted me. "How's business in cyberspace?" I thought her eyes were a tad less sooty, the whites clearer than usual. After helping herself to a couple of scones, my new data processor went directly to my newly organized, pristine electronic office to make sense of the recent e-mails. Since the Cassandra Shipton Web site had gone online, orders had begun to arrive with gratifying regularity. The Herbal Dream Pillows were especially good sellers, with the Love Potion Pillow taking the top slot.

I threw together a fast supper, microwaving leftover meatloaf and vegetables for Freddie and me, with scraps plus chow for Scruffy and Patsy. The dogs wolfed down their dinners and were checking out each other's food dishes before we slow humans had picked up our forks.

"Enjoy having Patsy here a little?" I asked Scruffy, since I'd half made up my mind to take on the bereaved Irish setter full time.

Arrrgh. I'd rather have ticks and burrs. Scruffy assumed a disdainful mien and stalked off to crunch his after-chow Milkbone in private. I didn't believe him for a minute. Just too stubborn to admit he'd begun to welcome Patsy's company. The Irish setter seemed to be smirking as she settled herself on the braided rug in Scruffy's favorite kitchen place.

After dinner, I drove Freddie home to feed Shadow and to study for her finals. School would be out soon, another ten days. In contrast to the glory of spring elsewhere, the commune looked even more depressing than usual with its yard full of waist-high weeds, trash barrels overflowing with aluminum cans, and a gaping black hole on one side of the house. Freddie ran inside with a blithe wave.

While I sat in the car waiting for the light in her room to turn on, just in those moments of unfocused attention, a vision flashed across my eyes of the front hall smoldering, stinking like a burning tire. I shuddered as a chill began at my forehead, ran over my scalp, down my neck and the backs of my arms.

Imagining that someone in the house, or everyone, was a careless smoker or haphazard cook, and the whole place was a disaster waiting to happen, I got out of the car and followed Freddie up the stairs—the house was never locked—and banged on the door of her room. "You'd better get your things together—everything you value—and come home with me. Bring Shadow," I said without preamble. "I don't like the look of this place tonight."

She looked at my face, startled, and seemed persuaded by what she saw there. "What about the others?"

"Warn them, and make it convincing. I'll corral the cat."

Returning a few minutes later, Freddie said, "Practically no one's at home. They come and they go, you know what I mean? Just the jerks in the back bedroom, and I told them to get their shit together and take off. I said the cops were going to raid the place for drugs. That should do it."

Twenty minutes later we were on our way, with Freddie's gear in the red canvas bag I'd given her for her birthday and an old green duffel bag. She didn't have much. Shadow traveled in a cardboard cat crate. His litter box was an empty plant tray that could be filled with sand. I thought of what care and effort, and how many headaches, it would take to move me with all my worldly possessions. There was something to be said for Freddie's lighthearted gypsy style.

Litha—The Summer Solstice

Was I a real clairvoyant—or simply a nutcase? That's what I was asking myself the next morning when the battered commune house was still standing, unscarred and unsinged. And so it continued throughout the week.

Then on Friday, out of the blue, there was the sublime excitement of Joe dropping into my life again. We'd not been together since that enchanted week in May when we nearly got skewered with a steel-tipped arrow in Maine. He'd called from San Francisco at midnight on Thursday to say he was on his way.

Since 711 Prospect Street was still in one piece, more or less, at breakfast Friday morning Freddie had tactfully suggested that she move back there for a few days to give me some space and Shadow a break from boarding at the shelter. Eager to be alone with my lover, I ignored the omens for once and agreed. After stuffing a few weekend necessities in her red canvas bag, Freddie wheeled off on her bike for school. As she disappeared around the turn in our road that led to the main route, the small frisson of guilt that plagued me was soon dispelled by anticipation of Joe's arrival. By Friday noon, he was standing at my kitchen door, gloriously filling it with his robust reality.

Suddenly all of my senses—even the sixth one!—were involved with his Mediterranean eyes, rich spicy scent, skin-teasing beard, and fiery thoughts. When he took me into his sturdy arms, murder and mayhem fled from my consciousness like gulls before a gale. Our kiss was hotter than hot—I felt as if my midsection were melting away.

After we'd paused to breathe, he brought back reality, asking, "How are you, love? Any new dangers for me to worry about? What skullduggery have you and your circle been up to lately? After our exciting little holiday in the Maine woods, I feel I should be prepared."

"Later," I said, pulling his mouth down to mine, kissing away the troublesome questions. And it was much later when I did catch him up on all that had happened. Our phone conversations during the past weeks had been few and too precious to waste on local crime reports.

Joe had an annoying habit of thinking before he spoke, and he thought a long, long time before replying, "*Jesu*, I wish I had more time off."

Now that the pirating of the Patagonian toothfish had been exposed to the world, my Greenpeace guy had been granted only a few days leave before he would be needed on the *Arctic Sunrise*. The ship's next mission, about which I was sworn to secrecy, would be to delay a third Star Wars system test at Vandenberg Air Force Base in California. Only later did Joe confess that meant positioning the vessel in a dangerous location when the missile was launched. The California missile was supposed to be intercepted and destroyed by a "kill vehicle" launched from the Marshall Islands at the same time—a result the government had yet to achieve. Since the first two tests had been failures, I wondered why Greenpeace bothered. Why couldn't they just sit back and laugh as our military geniuses blew billions of dollars off the map?

Three beautiful June days later—after Freddie had spread the word that Joe was in residence, so no one in the circle even called me—another terrifying image came to me. It was only six on

Monday morning. Joe was still asleep when I crept softly out of the bedroom to let Scruffy outdoors. Deciding not to go back to bed, alluring though that was with my warm lover still in it, his strong arms unoccupied, I started the coffeemaker burping, and before it had even finished, poured myself a cup of the rich, black brew. A spectacular sunrise lured me onto the kitchen porch to see the gilded ocean. I don't know what it is about staring at a shining surface that triggers a vision, but it often takes me that way. What I saw at that moment, as the golden-tipped waves faded from view, was Freddie leaning over a manila envelope shoved through the mail slot. In the next moment, I was watching an explosion, slow-motion, Freddie falling backward, her mouth open, screaming.

The scream must have been mine. The next thing I knew, Joe had hurtled onto the porch and lifted me off the wicker rocker into his comforting embrace. "Are you all right? Are you all right?" he kept repeating, holding me closer each time.

After a moment, I noticed he was naked. "We have to get dressed," I explained reasonably. "We have to get Freddie before she explodes. It's something in the mail."

"First call 911," Joe ordered as we raced toward my first-floor bedroom, causing the dogs to yelp and jump around us, sensing a game was afoot.

Hooray! Hooray! Let's go! Scruffy was always ready for action.

"Can't," I explained shortly to Joe, as I flung on my slacks and shirt. "I don't *know* anything. It's one of my vision things."

"Call them anyway. What do you care?" he argued, pulling on his blue jeans. "They'll get there faster than you and I. Never mind, I'll call them." He strode to the phone decisively and punched in the three numbers.

"It is 711 Prospect Street," I said, hanging over his shoulder.

Joe told the responding officer that we'd had a strange message—an inspired way to phrase it, I thought—that there was trouble, possibly a bomb, at 711 Prospect Street. He said a young friend of ours was in residence, and asked them to send a cruiser pronto to check out the place, and not to let anyone pick up the mail, as the explosive might be in a package or envelope. He gave his name and my address, banging down the receiver on any further questions. Leaving two disgruntled dogs yapping at the living room window, we took off in the nearest car, which was his Hertz rental, a red Toyota.

Joe squealed into a parking place in front of 719; we jumped out of the car and raced toward the scene. Visions are so peculiar. I always have to remind myself that the dimension of a vision is timeless, and so may vary considerably from expectation. This time, all to the good—the mail had not been delivered yet! But there were three police cruisers parked in the middle of the street. The local bomb squad arrived right after we did—one van, four guys in black spacesuits, a bomb-sniffing canine, and a bomb containment vessel on a trailer. The "bomb pot" looked like a squat, thick rubbish can, except that it was white with a blue horizontal stripe around its middle. Freddie was on the doorstep, wide-eyed, holding Shadow in her arms. Her horrified roommates were scattering on various errands that might have included hiding their stashes.

All our heads swiveled toward the end of the street where the mail carrier, a fresh-faced young man already in his summer uniform of postal-blue Bermuda shorts, was coming down the porch steps at 703 Prospect, whistling "June Is Busting Out All Over." A member of the bomb squad stepped away from their black van, lifting a megaphone to his mouth. "Stop where you are, postal worker!" he bellowed to the surprised mailman. "Don't move. We're going to approach you and remove the mailbag from your shoulder. Stay calm. Do *not* drop your mailbag. Wait for the officer to take it from you."

The mail carrier froze in place, his mouth open, the mail for 705 Prospect grasped in his outstretched hand as if arm, hand, and envelopes had been welded into a solid steel bar. Two other members of the bomb team, wearing helmets, face masks, and body armor, moved as if in slow motion toward the postal statue. One of the black-armored officers gingerly lifted the mailbag off the young man's shoulder, fixing it to some sort of long-handled grabber. The other officer removed the mail from the mail carrier's clenched fingers. Tiptoeing toward the van, the bomb squad guys lowered the mailbag and the handful of loose mail very gently into the bomb pot.

"Hey, what's going on?" asked a sleepy-eyed man in a plaid wrapper who had emerged from 713. "What about my mail? What's with the space cadets?"

"I think the delivery will be delayed today," I murmured, watching another of the bomb team members, the one who seemed to be in charge of the German shepherd, take his dog into the commune to begin checking for other explosives. I wanted to follow and grab Freddie and Shadow off the porch, but Joe took my hand and was pulling me toward the nearest cruisers.

"Might as well get this over with," he murmured to me, then spoke to the chubby officer leaning on his cruiser, surveying the house. "Hi. I'm the person who phoned in the alarm."

Immediately, the officer was all attention and suspicion, wanting to know the source of Joe's information. Rather than allowing Joe to get himself in deep trouble, I stepped forward to interfere. After all, this was my problem. "Before we discuss this further, I'd like to speak to Detective Stone Stern. I'm sorry we can't say more, but it's a confidential matter."

After a thoroughly threatening argument, the officer, whose name was Bill Bridges, finally agreed to call Stone. "I've got a man here who's reported a bomb threat. His companion claims they can only reveal their source to you. Shipton. Cassandra Shipton and Joseph Ulysses." There was a pause while Bridges listened and Stone talked. "Well, I don't know, Detective. It's highly irregular. This better not be a false alarm. We got three cruisers and the bomb squad out here. Right. I see. Yes, I see. You'll take the full responsibility then, sir? Right." With a disgusted expression, Officer Bridges ended the call with a fierce punch of the "end" button. "Okay, you two stay right here until Detective Stern arrives. He's on his way now."

When he arrived, Stone looked less than pleased to be routed away from his work to rescue us, but rescue us he did. Soon we were free to collect Freddie and Shadow, crated in his cardboard carrier, to drive home. I wondered how Stone had explained matters to Bridges—not, I'll bet, as a psychic vision.

"Say, Cass, what's all this about a bomb? I just about peed my panties when all those cops showed up at our front door. Jesus help us!" Freddie exclaimed as soon as we were safely on our way.

"I saw it. In a vision, that is. It was an envelope you opened in the mail, Freddie. We had to stop that delivery before something happened."

"Aw, Cass. I hardly ever even bother with the mail. There's no one I know who sends me nothing, you know what I mean? Most of what we get at the house is junk, anyway. Look, when you all peeled into Prospect this A.M., I'd just snatched up this batch off the floor from yesterday. You got me so scared, I stuffed it all here in my bag." Freddie began to pull catalogs and envelopes out of her Guatemalan shoulder bag with the beaded fringe.

Joe slammed on the brakes.

"Gently, gently," I cautioned. "Just lay all those down on the car seat and step outside, dear. Leave your bag, too. Bring the kitty with you, that's a girl. Now we're just going to move away from the car with Joe for a few minutes."

Shortly afterward, Freddie and I were crouched behind boulders in a nearby field. Summoned by Joe on my cellphone, a cruiser peeled onto the road's shoulder with Stone in the passenger seat and the chubby, suspicious cop at the wheel. They were closely followed by a dark blue bomb squad vehicle with two members of the squad in full protective gear, who were soon peering into the front seat of the red Toyota. I felt a tiny bit ashamed of my secret relief that we hadn't driven to the scene in my Wagoneer. I'd grown rather fond of it.

The officer got out of his cruiser and began to block the road to traffic, directing vehicles back to detour through the nearest side road. This favorite shortcut of mine was not a heavily traveled route. Motorists were sparse and obliging that morning, except for the Channel 6 news van, whose driver refused to move away, arguing loudly. The second cop got out of the cruiser and joined his partner. A young woman, whom I recognized as a lowly at-the-scene reporter, Dawn Fox, and a cameraman hopped out of the passenger side, leaving the driver to maneuver his van into a parking place as near to the scene as the officer would allow.

Motioning everyone to stay far back, one of the helmeted men, holding a shield in front of his chest, manipulated a long-handled, padded grabber in the other hand in order to lift piece after piece of mail out of the car and lay it out on the road's shoulder. Watching as each appeared in the grabber's beak and was tenderly disposed of on the grass, I could just make out that most of the mail consisted of catalogs, as Freddie had explained.

Then the grabber began to lift a plain manila envelope from the seat of Joe's rental. Luckily that grabber had a really extended pole, because en route to its removal something went wrong, causing this envelope—which may have bounced around safely in post offices and mailbags for a week or more—suddenly to blow up like a souped-up cherry bomb. A sharp explosion, a flash of fire, and billows of black smoke rolled out of the open car door. Anyone holding that envelope would have caught the blast directly in the head and hands As it was, the letter bomb knocked the bomb squad man on his ass. As his companion shouted at him, the fallen man rolled over instantly, got to his feet, and began to run toward the shoulder, throwing himself over it onto the grass beyond just as there was another, larger explosion. Good-bye, Toyota!

"Holy Mother of God," moaned Freddie. "I could have been toast back there, you know? Burnt toast. And Shadow, too."

"What the devil have you got yourself into now?" Joe murmured, softening the criticism with a hug that took in me, my shaken protégée, and her traveling cat, now yowling pitifully and scratching at his crate. "Not to mention your little friend, here. There's a murdering bastard out there, and how am I going to draw a peaceful breath knowing he's targeting you and your circle? And what the hell am I going to tell the Hertz Company?"

You could stay around and protect me, I thought, instead of throwing yourself into the path of a much larger bomb in the Pacific. I was saved from voicing this reasonable rebuttal by an onslaught from a different direction.

After making a thorough nuisance of herself at the scene, Dawn Fox discovered us—Joe, Freddie, Shadow, and myself—ducked down in our safe hiding place. Already we could hear fire trucks and more cruisers screaming toward the flaming wreckage. While the cameraman kept filming the immolation of the Toyota, the newswoman stalked us with her microphone. "Is that your car, sir? Was that bomb meant for both of you, ma'am? Say, aren't you Cassandra Shipton, from the Plymouth ladies club or something like that? Weren't you involved with a serial killer last year? Do you have any idea who may be responsible? How did you feel about someone threatening your lives—again? Are you upset? Angry?"

In the heat and smoke of the moment, I didn't know what I replied until later when I saw myself on the six P.M. local news broadcast pointing my witch's little fingers at Dawn Fox and calling on her to *Begone!* in the ringing tones used to exorcise a demon. Hands pressed to my aching temples, I hoped nothing would come of this unwanted exposure. Wrong!

Tipped off by Phillipa, who'd received a weary report from Stone, everyone from the circle called me *before* the segment aired, vowing not to miss a nanosecond of it. Phillipa worried about Stone's inevitable involvement with us witches. Fiona was simply and warmly glad that we were safe. Heather congratulated me on rescuing Shadow from the endangered commune. And Deidre offered to blow up a little poppet of Gere to give him a taste of Wiccan tit-for-tat.

But *after* the broadcast, it was Becky howling at me, "MUTH-ER . . . you promised you'd stay out of trouble during our campaign, and now I see you on the six o'clock news, screaming like a banshee in the midst of a nasty explosion with that Greek guy and some punk kid. Ron's beside himself."

"His favorite position?" I asked crisply. "We're fine now, dear. So nice of you to ask." Really, where were her priorities?

From there the conversation went downhill, with Becky abruptly hanging up. A half hour later, she called back to apologize, admitting she was pleased that her mom hadn't been blown to smithereens. We made up. I *promised* to avoid any more embarrassing publicity, but really, who can predict what the fates have up their sleeves? Perhaps it was just my karma to stumble into the path of madmen, or they into mine.

I wondered if Gere had caught the news and realized he'd failed to dispose of his spying shop assistant. Would I ever dare to open a manila envelope again? I should have realized that Stone would arrange to have the mail of everyone in the circle intercepted and vetted before it ever reached us. By the time I got my credit card statements and utility bills in the weeks ahead, payments would already be overdue. But late penalties were a small price to pay for safety.

Meanwhile, life quieted down from sheer screaming terror to an undercurrent of ordinary, unspoken anxiety. Joe's leave was up. When his tender concern about me conflicted with his assignment to help Greenpeace delay the third Star Wars systems test somewhere between California and the Marshall Islands, I urged him to fulfill his commitment and then maybe take a longer leave next time.

"Then you and I can assist in tracking down Gere. I don't think I'll rest easy until he's safe in the justice system."

Joe laughed. "Now *there's* an oxymoron. The Justice Department has no system."

"I guess I forgot for a minute you're no admirer of the law—in fact, you're quite an anarchist, or perhaps I should say *outlaw.*"

"I admit to a certain prejudice. They're all riddled with inefficiency and corruption. Every system, darling, not just so-called Justice. Personally, I'm in favor of vigilante action." We were having this conference at midnight. Joe sat up in bed, the gold cross on his dark chest glistening in the moonlight.

My crusader, I thought admiringly, sitting up beside him while his arms drew me close.

"But I sure wish *you* weren't involved. This Gere is an expert devil. I don't want to frighten you, but I'm horrified at how easily he could conceal a device in a package or a vehicle."

"I am scared," I admitted, after a long interval of comforting. "And don't you find that fear makes you absolutely ravenous? Gere wouldn't be so despicable as to booby-trap my refrigerator, would he?" Joe put reassuring hands on my shoulders and began to trace his lips and silken beard down my neck toward my breasts, a trail of fire. Feeding my hunger took a different turn just then, and I forgot all about food until breakfast the next morning.

Joe's packed duffel bag standing near the kitchen door drew Scruffy's rapt attention. He sniffed it all over with satisfaction. *That furry-faced person is going away again.* If a dog can look pleased, Scruffy did. In the absence of the Toyota, I had to drive Joe all the way to Logan Airport. Not knowing how traffic might be snarled around the inevitable construction, I left Scruffy and Patsy at home. More lonesome noseprints on the bay window!

"Maybe you'd better try a different rental agency next time," I suggested.

"Thank God I got the extra insurance." Joe insisted I not get involved in long-term parking, so I dropped him off at the Departures gate, kissing him good-bye until the uniformed traffic person made me drive along.

After Joe left, things really did appear to be back to normal. Gere had disappeared into Maine, and the shop remained closed. Stone reported that Gere's bank account had been cleaned out.

All the really important clocks that were part of Gere's collection had been auctioned in New York while Stone was still deciding if he had enough circumstantial evidence to question the man.

I struggled with myself and, for once, won. Not a single "I told you so" escaped my lips. After another letter bomb was identified and disarmed before it ever got to me—it had been mailed at the same time as the one addressed to 711 Prospect—Stone finally got his warrant to search Gere's premises, shop and home.

With so much time allowed for Gere to tidy up, very little incriminating evidence was found—just the merest trace of Semtex, a plastic explosive sometimes used in letter bombs. Even the tools that might be used to construct explosive devices were missing, but wall hooks showed some suggestive empty places. This was not reassuring. Gere, who considered us his nemesis, was out there somewhere with his bag of tricks. There seemed no way to shield oneself from so clever a clock- and bomb-maker, except to throw up veil after veil of misty psychic protection, which we did at every meeting of the circle. That constant effort of ours had probably been responsible for deflecting the letter bombs.

Fortunately, just as my faith began to erode in the long, nerve-wracking silence of Gere's absence, there was a welcome distraction. Someone precious and lost came back into my life—my young friend, Tip "Thunder Pony" Thomas.

Once I had fantasized about adopting this Native American boy whose alcoholic father seemed hardly to care about him. Tip and I had developed a strong and, I thought, lasting bond, but he had decided to fulfill a long-cherished dream when his absentee mother reappeared in his life and offered to take him away with her to Maine. A new stepfather and a younger brother had rounded out the promise of renewed family security. After a few months of thoroughly dysfunctional family life, however, Tip's youthful hopes had disappeared like morning mist, and he'd run away.

Talk about *déjà vu*! The youngster who'd disappeared from

my life for most of the past year just unexpectedly appeared at my door—exactly as he had once before. Scruffy began to bark excitedly, signaling that someone was outside. Only this time Patsy chimed in, making a fearful racket. I shouted "Around to the back" through the pine-planked front door. Going out to the seaside porch to greet the visitor, I saw through its screen door the dear, familiar, thin brown face and solemn gray eyes.

"Tip!" I cried, flinging the door open.

"Hi, lady. Did you advertise for a handyman?" As he repeated his former self-introduction, Tip's broad grin, as always, turned his eyes Asian. I hugged the boy awkwardly while he was only half in the door and Scruffy was leaping upon him eagerly, yelping. *He's here! The boy is here! I like him!* Patsy hung back, as dogs do when they're not personally acquainted with a welcomed stranger. Sniffing the scents of the newcomer. Making up her own mind. "Got yourself another dog, I see," Tip said.

"I guess so. Or she's got me. Come on in here and let me get a good look at you." Tip's shock of stick-straight, dark hair was longer now, held back in a ponytail that fell below the collar of a new denim shirt with a tiny ship embroidered on the pocket. While taking in these details, I asked him a half-dozen questions at once. "Where have you been? Why didn't you call? Have you seen your father? Where are you staying? Are you hungry?" and more in that vein.

Scruffy was equally elated and curious. *Where were you a long, long time? What's that strange-place smell? Want to run outside with me and play ball?*

When the excitement had abated a little, and Tip was seated familiarly at the kitchen table, still grinning, with a plate of sandwiches and a glass of milk in front of him, Scruffy lying contentedly beside him, gradually a coherent story emerged.

For several weeks after Tip ran away, he'd stayed by himself in a deserted hunting lodge in the woods north of Bangor, buying a few provisions at the general store, learning to track from the "old guys," hunting small game, and generally fending for himself until his odd-job money ran out. An empty larder coupled with a miserable rainy spell drove the boy to find refuge with his father's younger brother, who worked at the shipyards in Wiscasset. This big, red-haired, blue-eyed uncle looked like no one else in the family and was never taken for a Native American. Nor did John Thomas care a whit about embracing his heritage; he thought all that sort of thing was nonsense.

"Said he'd had enough of pathetic powwows and ersatz shamans," Tip said with an embarrassed grin. I couldn't tell if the boy had been convinced or not.

Tip's uncle knew enough about his family to understand why the boy had run away and didn't insist on contacting either parent. He'd simply given the boy a bed and a corner of his own, as he might have taken in any stray, but insisted Tip go back to school. Since no one had reported Tip as a missing person, it took some months after his school records were transferred before his father found out where the boy was.

It happened that S. E. Thomas ran into the middle school track-and-field coach at Mike's Mayhem, a favorite local bar. Why the devil had Thomas let his son move to Wiscasset? the coach had demanded angrily. Tip had been the team's best runner.

As far as he knew, Tip told me between bites of his sandwich, his father hadn't bothered to contact his former wife, Mary, in Maine with news of her son's whereabouts. Nor had Thomas called his brother John to check on Tip's welfare. For some months, Tip had felt he was "home free," keeping up with his schoolwork, playing clarinet in the band, getting a little part-time work at a hardware store, and generally enjoying a spartan bachelor life with his big, uncomplicated uncle in Wiscasset. Then fate stepped in, tripping up S. E. Thomas as he staggered home from the Mayhem one night after the closing bell had rung.

The complicated break in Thomas's left leg had required a cumbersome cast. Tip's father needed some help around the house. "What the hell you doing with my kid?" he bellowed over the phone to John. "You have no business interfering. I thank you for taking the boy in and straightening him out, but now I want him home—pronto. I'm laid up here with a bum leg—can't even make myself a decent meal." School had just let out for the summer in Wiscasset. That very day, John put Tip on a bus to Plymouth with a duffel bag full of new shirts and jeans, and ten dollars in his pocket. "If it gets too bad you can come back any-time," he said, giving the boy a manly pat on the shoulder. "You get yourself back in school first thing next fall. Don't let your dad talk you out of that."

Tip *would* get himself back in school, he told me. No time for the clarinet, however—and no clarinet at home to practice with. Tip's mother had sold the one I'd given him last year. In Wiscasset, the bandleader had loaned him an instrument, but now Tip wouldn't have time anyway. He was kept busy fixing stuff around the house, cooking meals, and doing errands for his dad, who'd lost his job at Plimouth Plantation and was collecting unemployment. (I suppose Tip's too young for trips to the package store, I thought.) Rather than sulking about his lot, Tip was as cheerful as always, possibly even pleased to be needed by his parent for a while.

"Dad said I could quit school, if I want, as soon as I'm sixteen, and work on the cranberry bogs, but I dunno," Tip said, avoiding my grimace by taking his plate and glass to the sink. "I kinda promised Uncle John I wouldn't do that. Quit, I mean. And if I was going to quit, I could make better wages in Wiscasset—all year, too, and not just in cranberry season. Except that then I couldn't take care of Pa."

"I'm going to ask you for the same promise," I said. "If you need to earn money, you can work after school. I'll ask around. As soon as your father's a bit more mobile, we'll find you something, I'm sure."

Scruffy followed Tip to the sink. *Hey, boy—what's for me?* Patsy, who had been studying the boy from a discreet distance, en-sconced on Scruffy's favorite braided rug, sashayed forward now to claim her share. Tip handed both dogs a few saved bites of ham and cheese, thus making another friend for life.

"Does Joe still come here sometimes?" Tip asked wistfully after we had installed ourselves in the old green wicker rockers on the porch. Both dogs now lay half-circling Tip's chair like furry parentheses. "Sure would like to see him again."

"You just missed him, Tip. He's off on another Greenpeace adventure that will probably be a news item any day now. But he'll be back." (If he doesn't end up in a federal jail, I thought.) "And I know he'll be very glad to see you. Almost as glad as I am. You had me mighty worried when you ran away, you know."

"How'd you find out? Ma call you?"

"No, she probably would have, but Phillipa Gold—she's Mrs. Stern now—was down Maine on business and talked to your mother in person."

"Pa says you got yourself mixed up with another crazy crime, about the Donahues and all. Says you're after Thomas Gere. I was kinda surprised about that. I met Mr. Gere once down Maine when I was working for the guides, helping get the sports through the woods without them killing each other."

"Some of those old guys knew you were up there living on your own in the woods? And they didn't say anything to your mother?"

"Just a bunch of strong, silent Injuns, Miz Shipton." Tip grinned mischievously.

"What did you think of Gere?"

"Dead shot with his bow. Aren't too many shoot that well. Bow and arrow is a different season, you know, Miz Shipton. Most of us guides would rather take a party of rifle-armed sports up in the woods than that bow-and-arrow bunch of crazies. But, I thought Gere was okay. He tipped me five bucks, I remember that. How come you witches got the whammy on him?"

"I see word still gets around like lightning in Plymouth."

"Like smoke. Us Injuns use smoke signals."

"Okay, smartie. For your information, it was Patsy here who

fingered Gere as a suspect. Patsy was the Donahues' dog—evidently a wordless witness to their abduction. Not a silent one, though. Twice we've taken her to Gere's shop, and twice she's gone for the jugular. And now he's looking even more guilty since he's run away."

Tip rocked gently, thoughtfully, more like an old man than a kid of thirteen. "What about their little girl—was her name Candy? Pa said she got away but she's lost somewhere in Canada. Maybe I could help find her. Me and Patsy, that is. I'm a good tracker, and I bet she is, too."

Scruffy lifted his head from a deep snooze and snorted. *That redhead couldn't find her way out of a biscuit box.* Having delivered his scornful opinion, his head instantly dropped back to whatever game he had been pursuing in sleep.

"Heather Morgan already tried that."

"Maybe so, but she's not me."

Tip's innocent confidence, however misplaced, was rather endearing. No way was I going to let him lose himself down Maine a second time. Just as I was underlining that resolve in my mind, Freddie, who was staying with me again since the letter bomb scare, came around the side of the house and clomped up the stairs in her platform sandals, with a bulging backpack and a stack of books under one arm. Draped over one shoulder was the shirt I'd made her wear over her skimpy cerise tank top. Five gold rings in one ear and a silver pentagram dangling from the other. At least she wasn't wearing her nose ring. As usual, her news spilled out the moment she spied me on the porch, while the dogs rushed to greet her and smell her shoes for gossip from the great world beyond the trees.

"Hi, Cass. Good news! Miss Manson finally let me back into the computer lab. Only I have to sit in a corner away from everyone, you know what I'm saying? Like some sort of friggin' leper. Now for the bad news! A shitload of homework. Want me to check the orders off your Web site first? Won't take me a tick . . ."

Tip's rocker had half-hidden him behind its cushioned back.

Suddenly Freddie's monologue trailed off, and she looked at me questioningly. "This is my friend Tip, Freddie. You remember my speaking of him before, and what a great help he was to me last year. Tip, this is Freddie, my administrative assistant. Freddie's boarding with me until her own apartment is ready." *A friend! He's a friend! Don't scare him away.* Assuming various play postures, Scruffy scampered back and forth hopefully between the two teenagers and was completely ignored by both of them.

"Hi." Tip's solemn face broke into an instant grin.

Freddie eyed him coolly, "Hi. Nice to meet you and all that. Well, like I said, I got to keep moving. Later!"

"Have something to eat," I hollered after the retreating purple spandex miniskirt. Freddie strode back to my study, now an office filled with PC, modem, printer, scanner, fax, computer manuals, arcane herb references, and a maze of electric cords. Her bag and stack of books could be heard hitting the floor as she abandoned them to boot up the computer.

"Wow!" said Tip.

"Wow, what?"

He looked down at the toes of his moccasins and blushed. Then a fleeting expression of sadness crossed his thin face. "Well, guess I'd better get home now. Have to pick up some food and stuff. Just thought I'd drop in to say hello while I had the chance."

"Oh, Tip, I sure have missed you! Listen, how did you get here? Walk? No bike? Well, the pups and I are going to give you a ride home, and, don't worry, we'll stop wherever you wish on the way. Why don't you take a couple of apples with you—for the road."

Scruffy's ears pricked up and he bounced into the kitchen to sit under the hook that held his old soft leather leash and Patsy's sporty new green lead. *Come on! Come on! We're going with the boy.*

"Did you know that raw potatoes taste almost like apples?" Tip remarked, causing me to vow silently to check into his diet.

He picked up an apple from the bowl on the table and polished it on his shirt.

When we'd all piled into the Wagoneer and were on our way to Angelo's Supermarket, I used the opportunity to pry into Tip's life at home. In the mornings, the boy told me proudly, he cooked breakfast and cleaned up the house. Later, he did whatever repairs or errands were necessary. The errands took longer because he had to walk everywhere. If there was time and daylight, he practiced his tracking skills, following small animals to their lairs. Then, he made supper, did the dishes, and read some of his books. A stipend from worker's comp was keeping the household going. The pickup truck was gone, sold before Tip had arrived home, and the few hundred dollars it had brought was nearly all spent, mostly on electric bills and a steady supply of whiskey and cigarettes for his pa. An old-fashioned woodstove served for both heating and cooking—in really hot weather, they used an electric plate. Recently, the phone had been shut off. Tip badly wanted a good-paying job.

"I'll find you something," I promised him. "And you're going to need a bike, too, if you're going to get to work on time and do your family errands. Freddie's working at Animal Lovers, and maybe there'll be a place for you there. I'll talk to Heather Morgan tonight. But how will I let you know if the phone's cut off?"

"Freddie's working there? Wow. I'll come by again tomorrow, then. I don't mind walking. I done a lot of walking down Maine. Living in the woods, and when I was a hunting guide with the old guys from the rez."

"I take it that you were favorably impressed with Freddie?"

Tip blushed again. "She sure is awesome," he mumbled. "Got no time for girls, though."

Just as well, I thought, *since Freddie brushed you off like a piece of lint. Maybe I should have a little talk with that girl. At least she can be pleasant and friendly.*

*   *   *

"She's jealous, that's all," was Heather's verdict. After dropping Tip off with his shopping bag full of canned beans, hash, salt pork, cornmeal, and Wonder bread, I'd stopped by the canine-crammed mansion to hit Heather up for the job I'd promised Tip. To continue with our conversation, I had to follow her into the kitchen where she removed a bottle of wine from the temperature-controlled wine closet and opened it expertly. "Bring a couple of glasses, will you, Cass?" She gestured toward the glass-fronted cabinets in the butler's pantry. "I think you'll like this—it's a rather dry marsala. Listen, you've shown a lot of affection for Tip whenever you spoke of him, and now he's back to claim the attention you've been giving to Freddie. Poor little Tip better watch out that she doesn't zap him with that special whammy of hers."

Trailing Heather back to the conservatory while a sea of dogs milled around us, my own two looking quite disdainful among them, I protested, "Oh, she wouldn't."

"She wouldn't *intend* to—consciously." Heather filled our glasses, then, holding her glass by the stem, uncoiled gracefully onto a cushioned wicker chaise longue. Must be something a girl learns at Vassar, I thought.

"But you know the kid is barely in control of her powers," Heather scolded me. "Remember Miss Manson's broken jaw. Maybe you'd better work with Freddie a little more intensely."

"I will. Definitely. Now how about that job? And is there any way a company bicycle could go with it?"

"You don't want much, do you? Sure. We can always use another pair of hands. Especially now that we're building that addition for special needs animals. I suppose we can bring in a secondhand bike or two for the staff. Rather a good idea, that. Every job should have its perks."

"Listen, it's my idea. I'll pay for it."

"Don't be silly, dearie. That's what trust funds are for. Now, what do you think of this wine?"

* * *

It was five when I got back. Before going into the house, I took Scruffy and Patsy for an invigorating run along the shore, as much to clear my head of the marsala aperitif as to give the dogs a chance to race the waves and chase the cheeky seagulls, who were still impudent after a winter's total command of the beach. Patsy was in her glory, a graceful streak of chestnut silk, easily able to outdistance her chunkier companion, while Scruffy made up for this indignity by barking incessantly.

I must cut his bangs again, I thought as we three breathless creatures labored up the steep cliff stairs. He can barely see through that mess of hair in his eyes. And they both need a good brushing. But first, I'm having a quiet little sit-down and a nice cup of tea.

It was not to be. A blue streak of curses emanating from the office was accompanied by sobs, screams, and the occasional thump of furniture being kicked. Obviously, Freddie had hit a computer snag. I rushed to the rescue, even though I knew it would be like the blind trying to lead the sighted.

"Shit. Shit. Shit," was the litany in my office.

"Take it easy, Freddie. What happened here? Surely it can't be *that* bad."

"It sure as shit can be that bad," Freddie sobbed. "I think I crashed the whole friggin' system."

I looked at the screen, where error messages were flashing nearly too fast for the human eye to read. There seemed to be a different one each time, as if the brain inside were running through its entire repertoire of abuse. This was accompanied by a strangely irritating humming and scraping noise from the hard drive. Bursts of intense poisonous green occasionally highlighted significant words such as "illegal" and "fatal error" and "system failure."

"Oh, come on, Freddie—it's not that bad," I lied. "It's still running, isn't it? Stop blaming yourself. This can't have been *all* your fault. We'll work it out, whatever it is."

She gazed at me woefully, her tear-streaked mascara giving her the look of a tragic mime. "It's just the way it happened at school before, you know what I'm saying? I was in one of those black moods. Oh, I'm *so* sorry, Cass."

"What black moods?" Heather's warning was fresh in my mind.

"Like PMS, you know? Don't you witches ever get PMS and then odd things happen to things and people around you? Even what you only *think* about?"

"No," I lied for the second time. "That never happens any more once you learn to control your powers, whatever they are. Which is what we're going to concentrate on as soon as we straighten out this computer problem. The first step—we call our hot line . . . and that's Adam. And we say our words of power that the help we need will be available to us."

For a moment, a wan smile flickered over Freddie's tearful face. "Oh, okay. I could do that. But won't he be, like, seriously pissed about this mess?"

"And we're going to work on your language, too. I sense some lack of vocabulary here. For instance, you could have said, won't he be *exasperated, enraged, infuriated, incensed, annoyed, irate,* or *riled*—rather than *pissed*—you know what *I* mean?"

"Okay, okay. Don't get your britches in a twist." Freddie was already trolling through my Rolodex for Adam's number.

Later, when I came back to call her for supper, I heard her murmuring, "Oh, I hope you won't find this too *exasperating*, but we seem to be having some sort of *annoying* malfunction here." Meantime, the mouse in her right hand clicked away obediently in response to Adam's directions. I tiptoed away. The ziti with herbed tomato sauce I'd made for her could wait, although that, too, would have its calming power, with the particular herbs I had chosen. Adam's salubrious effect on Freddie might make all the real difference.

And so it did. By the time she'd finished her hour-long conversation with Adam, the PC was purring like a satisfied cat, and so was Freddie. Later that evening, over cups of kava tea, I taught her the breathing exercises that have an instant calming effect on me—not only breathing from the diaphragm but also the trick of breathing through alternate nostrils when she needed to fill her lungs deeply, and mindful breathing as an exercise in control.

And I would teach her the words of power I used—perhaps to-morrow.

Tomorrow, as it so often turns out, was not the quiet day I ex-pected. "Life is what happens while you are making other plans."

Right then, life had a few zingers up its sleeve. State troopers in Maine found Candy safe with two older women at an Old Orchard Beach trailer park. After she'd run away from the Canadian couple, the resourceful little girl had hitched a ride in the back of an empty antiques van. Curled up in the packing blankets, she'd slept until the driver stopped at a rest area near the ocean. Thinking she must be close to her home in Plymouth, Candy had hopped out and run toward the shore. The two women, who did short-order cooking at the amusement park, had found her stealing food from trash cans. They'd cleaned her up, fed her chowder and apple pie, and called the police. Even before Candy's maternal grandparents arrived to claim her, tearfully and gratefully, Candy had identified a photograph of Thomas Gere as the man who kidnapped and killed her family.

Although Candy was understandably confused about her es-cape, the woman police officer assigned to question the girl gen-tly continued until a few facts emerged, partly in words and partly in pictures the child drew. "The bad man" had put a plas-tic bag over her head "and Mommy, too, so we would go to sleep." Candy didn't know how long it was before she "woke up." Gere was gone—perhaps back to the van he'd been driving, to get a shovel—and no matter how hard Candy tried, she couldn't get her mother to move or speak.

When she heard Gere's footsteps returning, Candy had run

away through the trees. She'd crawled into a hollow log and pulled some leaves in after her. Gere had kept on searching and calling for her, but she was afraid to answer. Then she'd fallen asleep "for a long, long time." The doctor thought it more likely that she passed out from shock and fear. When she opened her eyes, the sun was high in the sky. She'd walked through the woods until she came out near a diner. Crawling into a produce truck parked there, Candy had hidden between crates of strawberries stacked in the back. She'd eaten handfuls of fruit and napped off and on, with no sense of where she might be heading, which was to Canada.

Finally, the truck stopped at a farmer's market. Candy scooted away and slept that night under a porch. She kept on running, afraid that Gere was still chasing her and would kill her if he could—she was right on both counts. The next day, she'd wandered down the road from farm to farm, always hiding from cars and people. The couple in Canada had found her in their chicken house, looking for eggs. She was eating them raw from the shell.

The farmer and his wife were very kind to her, but she couldn't understand what they were saying, although she could tell they prayed a lot. One day a black van like Gere's stopped by the house, and Candy ran away again, this time to Old Orchard Beach, where she was now reunited with her grandparents at last.

As if that story weren't enough excitement for one day, postal authorities, still monitoring our mail (for all of the circle plus Freddie), had intercepted a package bomb addressed to Cassandra Shipton's Cruelty-Free Herbal Products. It looked alarmingly similar to a shipment of essential oils such as we receive regularly from Minnesota, except for the return address, which turned out to be a porno shop in downtown Boston. Stone told me about the threat as gently as possible, but it still gave me icy shivers from neck to spine. If either Freddie or I had opened that package, we would have been blown clear to Summerland.

"At least, with Candy's identification, you can go after Gere with a warrant now," I said to Stone while Phillipa busied herself in my kitchen making coffee.

"I have to give you this, Cass—you were right all along."

"Patsy was right. Dogs never lie." I hugged both dogs, who were huddled against me, sensing my anxiety. With a twinge of regret, I realized that Patsy would be making her home with Candy now. Candy would surely need her.

"Tell her about *America's Fugitive Files*," Phillipa said to Stone, with one of her wicked grins.

"Oh, what now!" I was in no mood for further complications.

"The producer called, Una Grimm," Stone admitted. He ran his fingers through his fine, brown hair, pushing it back. "You know, *AFF* really does have a great success rate. Great media coverage for difficult cases. And this case has exactly the dramatic elements they go after."

"Complete with a circle of crime-fighting witches." Phillipa's tone was pure mischief as she set out cups and saucers, a pot of honey, and some deliciously fragrant ginger-pear muffins she'd brought with her. Perhaps I was going to pull myself together, after all.

"Surely they haven't learned about *that*!" I exclaimed. "I have to keep a low profile, you know, for Becky and Ron. Ron's running for something or other."

"Keeping a low profile has never been your karma," declared Phillipa. "I just hope we can, though, for Stone's sake."

"This could be a royal mess," Stone agreed. "Not because of you and the circle, Phil," he added loyally. "But that Grimm woman. She kept saying, 'Here's what I want from you,' and every time she said it, she had a different vision of my role in the segment. I don't know if I can cope with her and Gere, too."

"Hey, we're not helpless here," I said. "If you don't like what they have in mind, you can refuse to cooperate. And I sincerely hope they're not planning to interview Candy or her grandparents. They've been through enough!"

"Indeed they have," Stone agreed. "Still, AFF *does* reach a vast audience."

"And it would be great to get Gere off the streets before any of us opens one of his surprise packages," Phillipa reminded us. "I say, let's go for it . . . but let's keep Candy out of their clutches."

"Don't worry about that," Stone said. "I've moved her into protective custody, poor kid—just until we apprehend Gere—with her grandmother for moral support. The grandfather is staying at home to mind the store—literally. Bea and Harry Hawkins own a little antiques shop in Scituate."

"Something about this *America's Fugitive Files* deal gives me the willies," I said.

Stone grimaced in a way that made me believe he agreed. "The final decision won't be mine, you know—if someone upstairs wants to allow Una Grimm to do her worst—and her best—I'll have no choice but to cooperate."

"Maybe we can get Freddie a job 'assisting' the cameramen," Phillipa said, winking at me broadly. "That should throw a jinx into the production."

"No, you don't, Phil. I'm in the midst of teaching her to control all that."

"A little psychokinesis can be a mighty useful tool," Phillipa murmured. "Control, yes. Weakness, no."

"Somebody upstairs" must have waved the checkered *go* flag. Barely two days later, Una Grimm sent her stylish assistant, Kimberly Wu, to interview the detectives and anyone else closely connected with the Donahue tragedy. A disheveled writer, Brian Soule, accompanied her to work on the narration. As yet, none of us had met the frenetic Ms. Grimm or *AFF*'s sexy host, Charley Capotosto, whose square jaw and cleft chin were vaguely reminiscent of Dick Tracy. Of course, we'd all seen him on television, if only for a few moments while browsing the channels for more intellectual fare. I have to admit to a frisson of thrilled anticipation. Our *cause célèbre* would be publicized from coast to coast—and Stone Stern was going to have his fifteen minutes of fame.

Unlike other true-crime shows, *America's Fugitive Files* did not present a dramatization of the crime. Needing less lead time and no actors, *AFF*'s strength lay in being able to move fast, snatching stories right out of the day's headlines, the scary, scandalous, bloody crimes that everyone was talking about. With shorter segments, its one-hour Sunday night time slot could spotlight a quartet of dangerous fugitives. *AFF* concentrated on making a crime-watch community out of millions of viewers. Subtracting time for commercials, those four segments boiled down to less than twelve minutes each. The Donahue-Gere story shouldn't take very long to tape, I thought. I was wrong.

When the camera crew arrived a day later, they began by interviewing Stone and his partner Billy Mann for most of a whole day—working at their desks, walking through headquarters, talking outside the building, relaxing at the local coffee shop, and reviewing the scene of the kidnapping. Billy, who was rough-cut and shy, opted out of the next stage, so that night, Stone flew to New York—with Phillipa insinuating herself into the deal. This was, after all, an adventure too good to miss! They stayed in a rather swank old hotel overlooking Central Park in a suite that was permanently reserved for guests of the show, so that the next morning at the *AFF* studio, Stone could exchange a few words on camera with Charley Capotosto, known as CC to his staff.

CC's deep voice throbbed with sincerity. "Candy Donahue, the little girl orphaned by her family's tragic kidnapping and murder—is it true that she, as the only survivor, can identify Gere as the perpetrator?"

"I'm not prepared to comment on that while the case is still under investigation," Stone repeated for the umpteenth time.

"But you have placed the child in witness protection?"

"Yes."

"So she must be a material witness? What about the grandmother and grandfather?"

"Candy and her grandmother are together. And that's all I'm prepared to say at this point."

"The grandfather, then, he's back at his shop?"

"I don't know where he is." The lines around Stone's mouth tightened.

Putting on the glasses he was holding in one hand, CC portentously consulted his notes. "*AFF* has received information from a reliable source that Gere was trained as a special forces' demolition expert, and that he's sent at least one letter bomb to someone involved in this case. Who was that person?"

"Sorry. In an ongoing investigation, I can neither confirm nor deny that such an incident has taken place." Stone's hands clenched on the arms of his chair.

"So Thomas Gere is out there somewhere, on the run and perhaps in a vengeful mood. What will he do next, do you think?"

"I'm not prepared to speculate on Gere's immediate plans, but I hope they include walking into the nearest police station and giving himself up."

By the time all the hours and hours of tape of Stone trying not to jeopardize his case were cut and edited, the result would look surprisingly coherent. And it would seem as if CC, who never left New York, had actually been in Plymouth. When I viewed the show later, I gained a new respect for the work of film editors. And for Stone, who never did punch CC in his nosy nose.

Meanwhile, at the Donahues' home, the *AFF* cameraman focused on family photographs, the Donahues' wedding portrait, the grandparents smiling in the door of their shop, Patsy as a pup, and, especially, photos of Candy. None of this was a smart idea, but I suppose it was inevitable, justified by the public's need to know, or in this case, to see the victims at a time when they were still smiling.

The Sterns returned before noon the next day. Phillipa immediately threw herself into laying out a luxurious lunch for the TV people before they left town. Kimberly, Brian, and Wilt Halfpenny, the cameraman, having wrapped up a few last details of the locale, including a tape of Reverend Peacedale and his parishioners singing hymns at the Garden of Gethsemane Presbyterian Church, relaxed in the warmth of the Sterns' hospitality. And I was there, too, prevailed upon to escort the only available principal of the crime story, Patsy, for the *AFF* people to admire.

Just about then, Una Grimm flew in to confer with her staff. From Logan Airport, she was transported in a black limo with shaded windows, located her crew by cellphone, and appeared in our midst like a blond Valkyrie bursting out of the clouds in a Wagnerian opera.

"What about the witches' angle," she demanded in a voice that would have resounded through the halls of Valhalla. "Satanic sleuths, etcetera. Do we have any tape on that?" Una accepted a glass of wine and a plate of sandwiches without sitting down, continuing to loom over her minions.

Visibly shrinking into her chair, her assistant replied, "Ah . . . no, that never came up in our interviews."

"Didn't seem to jibe with the true-crime image," Brian added, smiling beamishly over his third glass of chardonnay.

Wilt Halfpenny sighed with resignation and began to check one of his many canvas bags for some equipment or other, possibly more tape.

"How many times do I have to impress this on you?" Una hissed. "*AFF* goes after whatever will make the viewers sit up and beg for more. Like *witches*, you cretins—they're not just for Halloween anymore! The idea that witches have special powers fascinates people."

Suddenly sober, Brian's smile faded, and he nodded several times in an awed and respectful manner. I wondered how much you would have to pay a man to elicit such a slavish reaction. It must be a lot.

"Right, Una," said Kimberly crisply. "So, why don't you give us your vision of the witches thing. We still have a few hours before our flight."

"Wiccans," Phillipa drawled in an authoritative voice that

even got Una's attention. "We prefer 'Wiccans' to 'Witches.' No peaked hats, black Masses, or bloody pentagrams scrawled on the wall. Just a government-recognized religion and a circle of gals who know the phone number of the Civil Liberties Union." Stone groaned, pushed away his teacup, and poured himself a brimming glass of wine.

"I'd better be getting back," I said, picking up Patsy's lead. "Scruffy will be wondering what became of us."

"This must be the dog that fingered Gere!" Una cried in full contralto, grabbing Patsy's head in both her hands and looking straight into the dog's eyes. Taking this maneuver as a confrontation, Patsy jerked away and barked in a particularly nasty manner, her top lip curling over her teeth.

"We've *got* plenty of tape on the dog," Kimberly said defensively.

Dropping Patsy just in time, Una turned, her gaze like a spear pinning me to my chair. "Forceful" didn't begin to describe this lady's aura. "And you're the witch . . . the Wiccan . . . who smoked Gere out with this mutt? Cassandra Shipton, right? Got any spells on Gere? A little doll with pins stuck in his balls? Any visions of where Gere might be hiding out? Brian, didn't you tell me that Shipton was involved in another crime wave last year? Wilt, you can set up right here. Now this is what I want from you, Cass . . ."

Unless I leaped out a window, escape appeared impossible. Wilt had quickly set up his camera on a tripod in the doorway to the deck with the light streaming in over his shoulders, and Brian camped cross-legged in the arch that led to the living room, typing feverishly on his laptop. Might as well relax and enjoy myself, I thought, summoning all I had learned from Fiona about putting on a glamour.

"Hi, Becky. This is Mom. Sorry to have missed you, but here's the thing. If I don't end up on the cutting room floor, I may be a guest on *America's Fugitive Files*. I was trapped into it, literally. I mean, I couldn't even get out the door. A segment about Thomas Gere, the guy who murdered the Donahues. It's scheduled to air a week from Sunday. I hope you and Ron won't be too upset. Just remember, honey—no one blames a candidate for his relatives these days. Not after Billy Beer and all the rest. Talk to you later!"

Calling when I knew she'd be at work, I left this cowardly message after the beep on my eldest child's phone. At least I couldn't be cross-examined about whether the subject of Wicca came into my *AFF* interview.

It did, but I'd taken a leaf out of Stone's book and refused to comment about our circle's ongoing campaign. I declined to name any other Wiccans and denied our use of voodoo dolls. Instead I stressed Wicca's attunement to seasonal cycles, its dedication to nature conservation and animal rights, and its preservation of herbal wisdom.

Freddie was sorely disappointed in my low-profile approach. Watching my cautious responses when the segment was aired, she muttered, "I wish someone would interview *me* about Wicca. Like, I'd really tell it like it is.'

"You don't know *what* Wicca is yet," I pointed out reasonably. "You're still trying to learn hex management."

After Freddie went to bed that night, Scruffy and I watched the tape I'd recorded from the show. There was something fascinating about viewing myself from a stranger's perspective. Then I watched it again, fast-forwarding through everyone else. I looked okay, I thought, not too far over the hill. The soft rose shirt had been a lucky choice. My answers were coherent if not expansive. I might have smiled more, but then it would hardly have been appropriate to grin over the Donahues' tragedy—and besides, I'd been pretty scared looking into that camera, like jumping off the high dive for the first time.

If he wasn't throwing himself in the path of a missile, perhaps Joe would have seen my television debut. No, that Greenpeace bunch probably watched the Animal Planet and Discovery, if they ever watched TV at all. Thinking of Joe on the opposite side of the globe, I sighed heavily. Scruffy put his paw on my knee.

How about a walk, Toots? I need to pee.

Ordinarily, Stone is a gentlemanly soul, but when he got the news about the explosion at Hawkins' antiques shop, The Golden Bee, his language definitely took a turn for the curse. He cursed his superiors who'd put the pressure on him about *AFF,* he cursed Una Grimm for allowing the shop's location to be revealed, and he cursed himself for being a wimp and a fool. By some miracle, the grace of God or Goddess, Harry Hawkins had escaped the demolition, having just gone out back to the Dumpster when the explosion occurred. A malfunction, perhaps, because the package had been designed to blow up when opened, one of several innocent-looking packages delivered to the shop that day by UPS—boxes of carved wooden pigs and roosters and a shipment of Asian teakwood figures—all instantly transformed into a pile of smoldering splinters.

Although protected by the sturdy Dumpster, Harry was not exactly unharmed. Skewered by fear, realizing with horror that the entire stock of The Golden Bee had just been reduced to rubble, he'd suffered a mild heart attack and was now at Jordan Hospital with a uniformed policeman outside the door.

"As soon as he recovers sufficiently, he's going into protective custody with Bea Hawkins and Candy," Phillipa told us.

Realizing we were all in danger, and perhaps could not be protected by the simple maneuver of having our mail waylaid and inspected for explosives, we'd met at Heather's for a council of war on a sensuously green day, a day when we should have been brushing up on our love spells. Heather's dogs and mine were relegated to the enclosure on the other side of the mansion, to ensure quiet for us. With barking at a distance, I could hear a cotillion of insects humming in the field below as we sprawled on various padded redwood deck chairs on the patio outside the conservatory, drinking a perfect May wine from bottles immersed in a copper tub filled with ice. To the casual eye, I doubt we would have appeared to be witches on a crusade.

"I told you so. You should have listened." Reclining on a chaise longue with a denim craft bag even larger than Fiona's satchel at her side, Deidre shook her head in negative wonder that her wisdom had been ignored.

"Oh, any excuse will do for you to whip up some voodoo with those dolls of yours." Heather was scornful, refilling glasses held in indolent hands hanging over the arms of chairs. "Say, remember the night your poppets threw themselves into the fireplace? What a stink!"

"I've always thought that was Freddie's work." Phillipa's tone was thoughtful. "Unconscious, of course."

Fiona demurred. "I had my arms around the girl, and I can tell you she was trembling like a candle flame in the wind."

"Scared shitless, I know," Phillipa conceded. "But it *was* the kind of poltergeist thing one associates with teenagers."

"And all the time, I was blaming Fiona's zooming into a trance state," Deidre said. "A lot of craft work went up the chimney that night! But never mind that—with all that's happened, I say the best defense is that old favorite, a go-for-the-jugular hex."

"I was rather taken with all that 'love of living things' Cass professed to on TV," Heather said. "She made us sound as if we were some sort of cross between the Salvation Army and the Sierra Club. You want us to fall off that high plane, Dee?"

"I'm all for love of the *deserving*. But right now I'm thinking *self-defense*." Putting her glass down decisively, Deidre sat up straight and pulled the denim bag into her lap. From its copious depths, she removed pieces of a disassembled puppet stage, and a moment later was briskly setting it up on a long, outdoor dining table shaded by a beige market umbrella. Reaching again into her bag of tricks, she removed several hand puppets and laid them out in a row on the table.

"Oh, how darling," Fiona gasped, taking up the plump one

with a tiny green satchel and a black cat perched on its shoulder. "If that isn't me! You're so clever, Dee!"

Soon each of us was exclaiming with pleasure over her very own doll likeness. My puppet was crowned with a tiny wreath of woven thyme in her sandy hair, and she wore a canvas apron just like mine; a sprig of rue peeked out of its pocket. In the puppet's hand was a wee bottle labeled *Greek Love Potion.* "It's adorable," I crowed.

"I love this teeny book I'm holding," Phillipa purred. "*The Poetry of Food.* Not a bad idea, that. Where have you stuck the pins?"

"Come off it, Phil," Deidre said. "Would I stick a pin in you? On the other hand, maybe you could use a little deflating."

"Now, now, ladies," Heather soothed. "You've outdone yourself this time, Dee." Smiling her approval, our hostess examined the puppet with the chestnut hair, the Lord & Taylor safari suit, and the leash in its hand attached to a little felt model of Patsy.

"Such gorgeous detail," Fiona agreed. Fiona was not too enraptured with her own replica, complete with tiny coat sweater of many colors, to appreciate the other dolls . . . the Deidre doll with its nimbus of golden curls, the Freddie doll looking like a punk Barbie in a black leather mini, and the Gere doll with a dangling pocket watch and a bomb in one hand. "And what exactly is your plan, dear?"

"*A part for the whole,*" Deidre said. "The first, the oldest law of sympathetic magic. I've already fixed the Gere dolly. I sewed in some hairs from his hairbrush. Now I suppose you're going to wonder how I got them, Phil. You're not the only one with access, but please don't say anything to Stone. You'll only get Will into trouble. My plan is a simple one, the tried and true spell of ancient wise women. "*The play's the thing wherein we'll catch the conscience of the king . . .*"

"That's Shakespeare, not Wicca," Phillipa interrupted.

"Same difference, that old spellbinder. Maybe Shakespeare was really a woman! We'll have to draw down the energy, of course. Then improvise a bit of drama. Bury Gere where he can do no harm. Ideally in the mud from two rivers, but we can make do with the garden hose. Now, who's with me?"

No one—at first. But the more she talked about the danger of having Gere run around on the loose, attacking us with bomb after bomb until we were all turned into a livid pile of hamburger, the more she drew us into her magic play. While Heather pulled on Ashbery's stout Wellingtons and went down to the brook for a tub of mud, we rehearsed the hexes our dolls would invoke against Gere.

"Oh, this is so grand," Fiona breathed, watching Phillipa work the look-alike puppet on her right hand to beat up the miniature Gere on her left hand. "I wish someone could videotape that scene. Children would love it."

"Get real, Fiona," said Heather. "This is not Punch and Judy. And 'keep silent' is always the rule. *To know, to dare, to will, to keep silent.*"

With school schedules, children and dogs to be fed, orders to be filled, and what-have-you waiting for us at home, we couldn't bury Gere that afternoon. Charging Heather to keep the mud moist, we adjourned to our several family duties. But at moonrise, like a sliver of golden melon in the sky, we met again on Heather's patio, and played out our puppet drama for all its worth. Gere's dolly was sunk in wet earth, its eyes, ears, and mouth stopped up, its tiny bomb defused. The tub felt very heavy. It took both me and Heather to lug it into the run-down, unused summerhouse.

"Aren't you just a little nervous about this?" I muttered, as we slid the awkward thing under the old potting table.

"Nope. If it were left to me, I'd have black-candled this murdering creep weeks ago. Maybe then Harry Hawkins would still have had The Golden Bee.

For a few days afterward, I did worry about psychic repercussions, knowing they were bound to occur, wondering in what form they'd manifest—but then, I must confess I forgot all about Deidre's dolls in the local excitement that followed our debut on *America's Fugitive Files*. Not just my own dubious celebrity—an out-of-the-broom-closet witch. At supermarket and drugstore, acquaintances remarked on having seen the show—some looked away nervously, but others asked cordial questions about Wicca. If this kept up, I'd probably find myself invited to give a seminar at the Unitarian-Universalist Church. But it was Stone's predicament that occupied us mostly, especially Phillipa. With literally hundreds of tips and leads to sort through, he and Billy were swamped with follow-up work

"Let Fiona find through them," I suggested to Phillipa.

"He can't do that, Cass. Dowsing with a pendulum simply isn't a sanctioned part of state police procedure."

"Maybe it should be."

Glorious summer had arrived, with those skin-caressing breezes and heartwarming sunshine that New Englanders especially cherish after the chill vagaries of our springtime. With the delightful weather came the onslaught of tourists clogging the narrow streets of Plymouth. Still, for us, not having a murder, an explosion, or a death threat on the immediate horizon constituted serenity. Too much peace and quiet for Freddie, though. And she wasn't pleased about constantly running into Tip visiting me or working at Animal Lovers. The boy continued to worship Freddie, however, although abashed and tongue-tied in her presence.

So, promising to keep on practicing the exercises I'd taught her, Freddie moved back to her room at the commune with her cat, Shadow. A quick study, she'd learned a great deal of control in a short time. Constantly amazed by the girl's ability to move objects and influence outcomes, I wondered how long before she'd try her hand at gambling. She'd be a natural—actually, better than a natural. And she always needed money. Well, time enough to worry about that later. I'd learned a bit more about managing my Web site, taking and filling orders, keeping accounts. Freddie still took charge for a few hours three times a week to straighten out whatever glitches had occurred and help me catch up on back orders. Now that school was out, part-time at Animal Lovers was not enough to occupy her. She looked around for a fast-food job and got taken on as a waitress at Lil & Larry's Lobsters. The "triple L," as we called it, was always jam-packed with tourists milling around the Plymouth dock area.

Tip showed up often for a quick visit between his many chores and the hours he spent at Animal Lovers. Following such a long time of worry, it was a joy knowing that he was thriving now, no matter how difficult his homelife. His father would soon be up and about, he told me. The doctor expected to remove the cast in a week or so.

"I guess I'll stay with Pa," he confided. "I like Maine best. Uncle John would let me bunk there. He's a wild kind of guy, though—likes to take off on his Harley and go wherever the action is on weekends. I guess if he'd wanted a kid to worry about, he'd have got married. So it doesn't seem fair to park at his place. And as long as Ma's living with that mean dude, I don't want to go back there. My brother Lib's in that Catholic school in Bangor, anyway."

"Would you want to go to that school with your brother? Maybe I could . . ."

"Nah. That Brother Francis changed Lib's name and everything. To hell with that." The uncompromising expression that moved over Tip's face seemed to me a preview of how he'd look when he'd grown to manhood. Tip had become proud of his name, Thunder Pony, and Lib was Little Bear, not Christopher. S. E. Thomas, his father, although known locally as Sam, was Soaring Eagle—no matter how much the man used or ignored his son, living with him gave Tip the freedom to be the self with whom he felt at home. Even if his father *was* as much of a drunk as his mother, at least Tip, the champion runner, could escape. Living with his stepfather, Tip would have to endure the sight of his mother being knocked about. I could see that the decision had been made—the least of evils—and it was firm.

So I allowed myself to rejoice in that. I really loved Tip. And if S. E. Thomas got abusive, as he had in the past, Tip knew he could count on me to be there for him. Now that his father wasn't quite so helpless, maybe Tip could return to the track team and the school band. I wondered if I bought Tip another clarinet, would he accept the gift?

After all the spring clearing, pruning, raking, digging, and planting, by the middle of June, my herb beds were gorgeously green, pungently fragrant, the lavender a profusion of purple blossoms, the brick paths neatly groomed. My knees might ache and my hands turn rough, but my stomach muscles had tightened after winter's slackness and, in moments of relaxation, lounging in an Adirondack chair in the midst of my aromatic kingdom, my soul was soothed.

When summer arrives, the intensive labor and mysterious losses of gardening seem worthwhile at last. Into this hiatus of blessed calm and pastoral pleasures, Joe returned to me, having completed his part of the missile protest without being either maimed or jailed. He brought with him an aura of the adventures he had encountered, and he filled up my little house as well as my life with his robust, competent, sexy presence. Everything was different with Joe here. I liked the enriched ambiance, and I loved him. I felt safer, too, not quite so paranoid when I heard a creaking branch outside at night.

" 'There's another nice mess you've got us into, Stan,' " Joe said after I'd described how the bomb package addressed to me had been intercepted, and that information leaked on *America's Fugitive Files* had led to the demise of The Golden Bee.

"Sorry, Ollie. Does this mean you'll be staying for a while?"

"I'm due for a long break, and I've made arrangements to take it. I'd rather not leave you until Gere is caught—or even better, killed."

"Mmmm," I said. "I just know I'm going to sleep a whole lot better with you here . . . in every way."

Sitting on a blanket on the beach, we were toasting the rising moon with an admirable riesling from a case that Heather had sent over to celebrate Joe's return. The gentle summer night was kind to lovers, encouraging minimal clothing and a gentle, lazy mood. Difficult as it was to conjure the reality of death and destruction while Joe's warm hand was tenderly brushing the sand off my back, I finished my tale of woe with the perceived threat to Candy and her grandparents and the resulting protective confinement they would have to endure until Gere was taken into custody. Meanwhile, I still had Patsy to shelter.

The two dogs ran back from their pleasant evening of chasing threatening shadows far down the beach and leaping away from alarming waves. While Patsy sat daintily and expectantly looking at us, Scruffy threw himself onto our blanket, panting. *Water. I need water.* We couldn't very well offer him a bowl of wine—it was time, we decided, to go indoors.

"He's going to miss her a lot," I said as we shook out our blanket.

"Who? Scruffy?" Joe asked.

"Shhhh. Don't mention names. Certain furry folk understand everything."

"Oh, sure they do," Joe laughed.

I said no more. What did they teach them at Greenpeace? Save the animals, even though they're dumb as posts? We trudged our sandy feet up the rickety stairs and into the house.

"So, Cass . . . what hex have you gals put on Gere to prevent any more mayhem?" Joe asked while we were drying each other off after our showers.

The vision of Deidre's Gere doll sunk in a tub of mud in Heather's summerhouse popped into my head like an ugly jack-in-the-box. We should have known better. We *did* know better. "Oh, nothing much, really," I said.

"I don't believe you, and I'm going to torture you until you tell me the truth," Joe murmured against my neck. Sweet torture it was, too, but faced with the gold cross dangling on his dark chest, I kept silent, according to the old way with spells. As children are taught about wishes, they must be kept secret to be fulfilled. Love, I told myself, thrives on an air of mystery and a touch of magic. There were many, many things I would never reveal to Joe.

"Why are your eyes getting greener just now?" he asked.

"I'm thinking of all the secrets you've never shared with me," I answered. In the dim light of the bedroom, I could have sworn he blushed.

After his stint at Animal Lovers on Saturday, Tip wheeled into my driveway on the "company bike." Finding Joe weeding the mint out of the thyme in my herb garden, the boy whooped like a movie Indian, jumped off the bike, and raced to greet him, getting a big, warm hug in return. Tip's blazing smile took over his face, but after we'd talked a bit, on the porch with cold drinks in hand, he admitted to being a little depressed. His father's compensation check was a week late, and the "old man was fit to be tied." Now that the cast was off, S. E. Thomas had thumped with his cane down to the post office and "got a big runaround." Tip had to ask for an advance on his salary at Animal Lovers to see them through the weekend. It was just a few dollars, but every dollar was needed for bread, beans, and his father's whiskey.

A chill of guilt iced through my heart, because I was the one who'd asked Stone to add Tip's address to those whose mail was being intercepted and checked for explosives. I hadn't meant to cause any hardship, only to keep Tip safe in case Gere connected him with me. I wondered if I ought to explain and take the chance of frightening the boy.

"Hey, I've got a job for you worth a few bucks," said Joe. "And I'll pay in advance." He pulled out his wallet and peeled off two fives. "That rental car of mine is looking mighty dusty, and I want to spruce it up before I take Miss Cass, here, out to dinner tomorrow night. Maybe you can find a little time in the morning to clean 'er up for me?"

Tip flushed with pleasure, not taking the money. "Aw, Joe, I'll do that for nothing."

Joe tucked the two bills in Tip's plaid shirt pocket. "Not even we Greenpeacers save the world without getting paid for it," he said.

But the next strike against us wasn't sent to Tip and wasn't intercepted at the post office. This package was sent by UPS to Heather. According to the UPS receipt, the return address was a pet shop wholesaler in northern Maine, quite close to the Canadian border. Possibly thinking it was some fancy new dog harnesses that Heather had mentioned, Ashbery opened the package. The resulting explosion took out the back entry and part of the kitchen of Heather's Federalist mansion. And for Ashbery, life was ended on a glorious June day as abruptly and completely as a balloon is burst when it's stomped by a boot.

From cellphone to cellphone, news of the explosion raced around Plymouth. It hit our circle with cries of anguish—of course, we all thought that Heather was the victim! But Heather had been at the bank that lovely morning, transferring more of her own money to the account for her state-of-the-art shelter and boarding kennel. Animal Lovers was perpetually on the verge of bankruptcy. Meanwhile, a jogging neighbor had witnessed and reported an explosion at the Morgan place.

With two of her house dogs proudly being chauffeured in the backseat of the Mercedes, Heather had driven toward home all unsuspecting, only surprised and curious as fire trucks and cruisers, sirens blaring, speeded past her on the way. Rounding the turn into her circular driveway, she'd encountered the smoldering ruins at the back of her own home, and a cacophony of barking and howling dogs in the fenced yard.

The bomb hadn't been a big one, and the fire it caused was quickly brought under control. Not so Heather, whose screams continued for some time. The loss of Ashbery in such a heinous way was unendurable. That loyal companion, extraordinary cook, and staunch housekeeper, who'd put up with a motley crew of canines, had been like family to Heather, rather like a strict but warmhearted aunt.

When Stone had arrived, ashen-faced with anger at this attack, he'd immediately called Phillipa to come and take care of Heather. Soon we were all there—Joe, too—surrounding her with our love and concern. I felt so relieved to hold her, living and unharmed, and so guilty for my thankfulness, yet crying for Ashbery and for Heather's tears.

"We've got to find him," murmured Fiona. She, too, was looking pale, holding little Laura Belle in her arms so that the child's bright blue eyes were averted from the smoldering doorway.

"Doggies!" cried Laura Belle, joyously pointing to the agitated pack of canines.

"Well, you're our best finder," I said. Joe had gone off to talk to Stone, no doubt to voice the same concerns in more colorful language. I could see in all of us a stronger, stiffer resolve that I felt myself, as if each one was donning some kind of invisible armor in preparation for battle.

That night the circle gathered at Heather's to comfort her in our own Wiccan way. We cleansed and reconsecrated her living space with salt water and dusted it with a protective powder made of crushed, dried basil, elder, valerian, and marjoram. Then we observed a rite of passage for Ashbery's spirit, saying goodbye as she journeyed far to Summerland.

I brought the traditional frankincense and sprigs of rosemary. Their pungent fragrances braced us in our new determination. We lit a fine white beeswax candle with subtle flecks of silver that Heather had made. Each of us spoke in turn about what a wonderful woman she had been. Together we visualized Ashbery rising from the horror of her sudden death into the light of pure love and peace, "to die and to be reborn, the turning of the Wheel."

We mingled our tears with Heather's, and blessed her, too,

with our healing gifts, a feathered dream-catcher from Deidre, a canister of my Wise Woman Tea, crescent-moon cakes from Phillipa, and from Fiona, an invocation lettered on ancient parchment, its source as much a mystery to her as to us. Phillipa, whose voice was trained to poetry, read the verse aloud.

> *My voice, be soft as air,*
> *my hands, be healing as water,*
> *my eyes, be warming as fire,*
> *my heart, strong as the earth.*
> *I am an island in the sea,*
> *a star in the dark,*
> *a staff to those who are weak.*
> *Aye, I do as I will, and I harm none.*
> *Clothed in light, I repel the intruder.*

But two days later, despite our best efforts at consolation and acceptance, Heather still couldn't stop sobbing while she packed Ashbery's personal belongings. There would be a memorial service at Ashbery's sister's place in Vermont on Sunday. Heather was bringing Ashbery's things home to her family. (There were very little remains of Ashbery, and those were still held by the coroner's office.) Ashbery's brother was coming from Augusta, and various nieces and nephews from their far-flung summer jobs.

"No one will ever replace Ashbery. Never, never," Heather wailed as I watched her reverently laying tissue-wrapped framed photos in a handsome wooden box while alternately sipping brandy. "But who the hell am I going to get to feed and water my dogs while I'm in New Hampshire?"

"You aren't driving, are you?"

"No, Dick Devlin offered. Really sweet of him, wasn't it? He had to get someone to cover for him, too." Devlin's thriving veterinary practice had brought him and Heather together during an earlier crisis with her canine corps.

"How about Freddie giving you a hand? She's only working the lunch shift at the Triple L, ten to four. The only problem is what to do with Shadow, but Freddie can board her kitty at Animal Lovers for a few days—how long do you figure you'll be away?"

But Heather was lost in fresh weeping. Through her sobs, I could hear that she was saying over and over again, "I'll kill him. He's a dead man. I'll kill him." It did not bode well for her to be rushing down that negative path. Much as I, too, hated Gere, I resisted the impulse to join Heather's black wishes. The three-fold law was such a strict and confining rule, but I'd seen it in action—I knew it was true.

Finally, I took it on myself to round up Freddie and Shadow from the commune. "Bring enough stuff for a week, in case." I suggested. Before driving to Heather's we installed Shadow in the luxurious cat quarters at Animal Lovers.

The acrid smell of disaster was still in the house, but when Freddie glimpsed the yellow-rose room and private bath that were to be hers for this dog-sitting stint, something between love and wonder shone in her eyes. "Awesome. Totally awesome," she crooned, falling onto the pillow-heaped double bed and flinging out her arms. "It's like a set in one of those swank old movies, you know, *The Great Gatsby* or *Pretty Woman*—something like that." She bounced up again, effortlessly, as if the bed were a trampoline, and rushed into the bathroom to turn on the sink taps full blast. "Holy shit, really hot water. I bet it never runs out, either. Hey, Cass . . . take a gander at this monster tub!"

Perhaps the arrangement with Heather could be a more lasting one, I thought. In her own way, Freddie was a very competent girl and equal to anything Heather needed, except, of course, the long friendship and light pastries that were Ashbery's forte. But Heather would manage decently enough with Freddie's assistance around the house and kennel, and hampers of goodies sent in from *The Plymouth Gourmet*. It seemed really depraved to mourn the loss of Ashbery's delectable quiches when I should be grieving exclusively for her life's untimely end. Phillipa, too, mentioned Ashbery's great artistry with regret and asked me privately if there might be a notebook of her recipes that had survived the explosion.

"I guess that sounds a bit unscrupulous," she'd admitted.

"Besides, with you gifted cooks, it's mostly in the hands and not the recipes," I'd said. "Still, it's a legacy that shouldn't be lost. Remember that nineteenth-century Book of Shadows that Fiona unearthed at a yard sale—*Hazel's Book of Household Recipes?* Soups, syrups, spells . . . what a treasure!"

And that gave me a thought: Hazel might have a good, old-fashioned drawing or compelling spell we could use to bring Gere back to Plymouth. He'd been hidden in that tub of mud long enough—since he was apparently still able to wreak havoc on us.

Before Heather left for New Hampshire, I managed to get Devlin aside and whisper urgently in his ear, "Don't let her burn any candles."

He'd looked at me strangely. "Why would she do that? Oh, you mean at the church service. Not appropriate for a Protestant service?"

"No, I don't mean that. There are always candles at funerals, even Unitarian ones. I mean, in her hotel room. I mean, black candles," I murmured hastily, stepping away when Heather appeared. She was wearing some kind of fitted, dark-navy outfit with a turban that looked Ninja-inspired and carrying her trim Louis Vuitton canvas keepall.

"I wish I could have some workmen come in to repair the damage," Heather said. "I don't know how I can bear to face Ashbery's burnt kitchen when I get back." She paused to wipe her eyes with a hankie drawn from her slim, dark sleeve. An outfit like that probably didn't have pockets. "But the police have tied up all that part of the house in yellow crime-scene tape. They're going to have some forensic experts from Boston down here to gather evidence. Do you think Freddie will be equal to keeping an eye on them?"

"Freddie has surprising depths. But Joe and I will check out the premises from time to time. Perhaps we can reassure all parties."

"That would be really nice of you," Heather said. "I hope you're going to hang onto that great guy. I have a lot of respect for Greenpeace."

"I promise he won't get away from me, except when he's needed to save an endangered animal somewhere in the world."

After I saw Heather off, with Dick Devlin at the wheel of her Mercedes and my friend sitting beside him like a stone statue of Hecate, her mouth set in a line of inflexible resolve, it was still early afternoon, so I decided to stop at Deidre's to discuss my worries about Heather. Deidre didn't work on Saturdays—her two able assistants took over the vitamin shop on weekends. I found her wan and pale in her sunny kitchen, mixing up Kool-Aid for the three youngsters screaming with glee on the jungle gym in the yard.

"No, thanks," I waved away the cherry-colored stuff, remembering exactly how syrupy it tasted when I was young and thought it was delicious. "Plain water's okay. Are you still feeling bad about Ashbery?"

"I'm pregnant," she announced crossly, by which I knew better than to congratulate her. "And I was *so* careful!"

"Well, what a surprise, Dee! I can see why it might be a problem, though." I hugged her limp, depressed shoulders, trying to sound sympathetic. Actually, I thought any new life was a cause for rejoicing, and had thought so even when I was miserably married to Gary.

"It's not a 'problem,' Cass. It's a friggin' disaster." Ignoring my request for water, she took two bottles of beer out of the refrigerator and slammed them onto the Formica table in her jonquil-yellow breakfast nook.

As if to underscore her concern, the screams outside escalated to an ear-splitting pitch, and Salty and Peppy began barking in high-pitched yipes. "Here, let me carry that out for you, Dee." I took hold of the tray she'd prepared, which was loaded with a tall pitcher of red stuff, Mickey Mouse plastic glasses, and a box of Oreos, and brought it outside, hoping the puppies would not ingest too much deadly chocolate. The kids were a hardy lot and would probably survive the sugar overload.

But Deidre knew what she was doing, I realized, when something close to peace descended on the tribe of small Ryans in the yard as we grown-ups sat in the cool kitchen, sipping our beers. Her blond curls looked crushed on one side as if uncombed all morning and her pale blue eyes were watery.

"This year has been really difficult to manage, but it's worked," she said. "Jenny and Will Jr. are in school, when they're not down with some bug, and I've always been able to leave Bobby and whoever's sniffling with my mother-in-law when Will isn't home— he tries to get the night shift as much as he can. But Will's mother has said she's calling it quits if we have, like, one more kid. She has her investment club now, her square-dancing group, her wandering widows Greyhound bus buddies, and her bi-monthly trip to Mohegan Sun. I guess 'grandmas just want to have fun.' So I'm really going to have to leave the mall. I hate that. I loved running Nature's Bounty. I was good at it, dammit!"

She drained the last of her beer and got another out of the refrigerator. I refrained from giving her the fetal alcohol syndrome lecture. This was only one day of her pregnancy, and tomorrow she'd probably snap out of this lugubrious mood. "Maybe the change will have its compensations," I ventured.

She laughed without amusement. "Are you going to tell me how I'll enjoy *not working*?"

"No, dearie. I've served my time at home with three young children and have no illusions on that score. It's not a rest cure. What I mean is, you've always been a fine businesswoman, and these days a business can be run from the home. That's what I do, and I'm making a living, and now that Adam has set me up on the Internet, orders are coming in from all over the country. Why couldn't you do something similar, with your own crafts and maybe other handmade products on consignment?"

Deidre was a crafter of great creative zeal. A glance around at any room in her house revealed the many products of her restless energy, not only the poppets, amulets, and talismen that were her specialty but also samplers with cute sayings, embroidered pillows, afghans, painted trays, hooked rugs, and decorated furniture. At Deidre's, anything that didn't move fast was in danger of being stenciled.

She looked out the window with a thoughtful air. Outdoors, the sugar fix was wearing off. Childish screams of pain or delight—it was hard to tell which—had begun again. Suddenly she sprang out of her chair as if wanting to begin her new career at that very moment—then banged out the kitchen door at full steam, screaming, "Junior, you take that dog off that shed roof at once! At once, do you hear me! And *carefully* . . ."

When she returned, with a toy poodle squirming under each arm, she smiled at me grimly. "Any smart girl can succeed in business while coping with domestic crises? Is that what you're proselytizing?"

"Harriet Beecher Stowe wrote *Uncle Tom's Cabin* at the kitchen table. She had six children and a husband who claimed the study for himself. Apparently, the uproar fed her creativity."

"Very inspiring. Not only domestic crises, but what about the mad bomber? What are we going to do about him? Don't you shudder every time FedEx or UPS drops by with a shipment of goods? How do you handle that? Want another beer?"

"No, thanks. I'm still working on this one. I dowse them, Dee. You know, the way Fiona taught us to do if we suspected poison in food? Silver pentagram on a chain. *Is this clam past its sell-by date? Does this package contain an explosive device?* If the pendant swings in a sedate circle, it's okay. If it makes erratic Z's like crazy, don't touch it. So far, so good. No pendant hysterics. Also, I call the company and check that a package was actually shipped, and when. Then I gently place the package in the garage and leave it there."

"And when do you open it?"

"Never. I haven't opened any," I confessed. "I don't have the nerve. They're all still in the garage taking up so much space that I've had to park the Wagoneer in the driveway. And it's getting to be a serious problem, because I'm running out of stuff I need to make up orders. And Joe is starting to ask questions."

"What are we going to do?"

"Call Gere back, I guess. Settle it with him. That is, if Heather doesn't finish him off with her candles. I wonder if there isn't something in Hazel's book."

"Well, we'd better meet, then." Deidre got up and studied the much-annotated moon calendar on the wall near the phone. "Still a waxing moon on Wednesday night. Ideal, since this isn't a banishing. And Will's on night shift at the firehouse—we can meet here. Why don't you bring Freddie? That girl has sources of power even she doesn't know about."

"Yes, I think you're right about that. And Heather should be back by then. With or without Gere's head in a hatbox. I'm worried about her propensity for negative magic, especially now."

"Well, Dick's with her, so she's not going to spend all her time meditating on a black candle with that good-looking vet around."

"Heather's never really said if they're seriously involved." Whether there was a handfasting in their future or they were still merely friends was a subject much discussed by the circle in Heather's absence. We knew she'd sworn never to marry again after having been swindled in turn by ex-husbands Chet, Roberto, and Norman.

"Of course they're involved!" Deidre declared. "What kind of witches would we be if we couldn't detect those elemental sexual vibes? And just look where it all leads—I suppose I'll even have to give up beer now."

How I envied that fertility she was cursing!

* * *

Troubles always come in threes, as my grandma used to say, I reflected as I drove home. Heather going to the dark side over Ashbery, Deidre in misery over her pregnancy—what next? Tip was next. He was sitting in the kitchen with Joe, drinking cocoa and looking like a lost soul with a marshmallow mustache. Even Scruffy seemed to be affected. Instead of jumping up to welcome me and complain about my absence, he lay on Tip's moccasins, thumping his tail on the floor in lieu of the proper canine greeting that Patsy trotted downstairs to give me—she was fond of napping in the rose guest room.

The boy smells of sadness. Maybe he needs a treat. Or a fast game of ball. Scruffy was counting on me to bring sustenance and cheer.

I dropped a kiss on Joe's wiry hair, hugged Tip's thin shoulders, and slid into one of the kitchen chairs, not forgetting to reassure with pats the worried friend under the table. Life is so precious, so fragile—I needed touch to keep me conscious of my blessings. "What's the problem, guys?"

"Paw's in the hospital," Tip said. "When I got home from Animal Lovers, he was just lying on the kitchen floor. At first, I thought he was—well, you know. But then his breathing was different, and he looked kinda yellow, so I called 911. They took him away in an ambulance. And I got to go with him—they drove really fast, right through all the red lights." For a moment, Tip brightened, but his eyes quickly faded again. "Then after they got Paw into a room, the doctors said I should go home and come back tomorrow during visiting hours."

"Did they tell you what's wrong with him?"

"They're going to test him for hepatitis or some liver thing."

"Cirrhosis?"

"Yeah."

"Okay, here's what I suggest. Joe will give you a ride home to collect your gear, the bike—whatever else you need—and you'll stay here while your dad's in the hospital. Tomorrow we'll take you to see him during the afternoon visiting hours. I'm sure you're perfectly capable of staying on your own, but Joe and I—

and Scruffy, too—would enjoy having you here and making sure you got over to the hospital okay every day. It's a pretty long bike ride, and if you should find yourself coming home after dark, those winding roads can be dangerous. So what do you say?"

Tip seemed surprised and uncertain at the speed at which I planned his life for the next days and weeks, but Joe rescued me. "That would be handy for me, too," he said. "I'm going to need help fixing some loose shingles on the porch roof for Miss Cass." This was the first I'd heard of that project, although I had noticed a creeping stain on the porch ceiling.

Tip nodded in a relieved way. Then I could see a happy thought move across his face, and he almost smiled. "Will Freddie be here, too?"

"Not this week. Ms. Morgan had to go away for a few days, and Freddie's house- and dog-sitting. I guess you probably heard about what happened to the housekeeper, Ashbery?"

Tip nodded, looking tragic. I wanted to reach out and smooth away all those worry lines. "Well, we won't talk about that now— you have enough on your mind. You and Joe go along to your place to pack your stuff and lock up the house while I make supper."

A ride . . . a ride . . . supper! Scruffy bolted from under the table and dashed around eagerly but uncertainly, possibly torn between the chance of a ride and the possibility of a meal forthcoming soon. Patsy sat daintily by the door, simply waiting for her green leash, serene as a princess.

"Hey, boy, let's go—they can come, too, can't they, Joe?" Tip settled the matter.

Before my motley crew could even collect themselves to get out the back door, I had my head in the refrigerator, surveying the possibilities. It would be kid comfort food, I decided. Meatloaf, macaroni . . . No wonder women are so levelheaded in times of trouble, I thought. Even if the sky is falling, and crazed killers are lurking out in the bushes, there are always hungry people to be fed and a household to manage. What was that Zen saying? "After the enlightenment, the laundry."

*   *   *

Stone had put up with a lot of hocus-pocus from us in his gentlemanly fashion, but when Phillipa told him we might be able to draw Gere back into our area for a final confrontation, he was both doubtful that we could pull it off and seriously alarmed that we might be successful. Not that he wouldn't be pleased to collar the madman—but Gere was vengeful and dangerous. Who would he blow up next? Stone didn't want any of us to be scraped out of some fresh smoking hole.

"I don't want you or Cass or the circle to have anything to do with Gere—not now, not ever." Stone's tone was icy but controlled, his chilliest high-school-principal manner.

"Darling, you sound as if you have complete faith in our powers at last," Phillipa said with a winning smile as she kissed him good-bye. I'd stopped in to give her a ride to our conference at Deidre's. "But I'm not sure I do," she said under her breath to me. We made a hasty exit before more objections could be raised.

"Are we real witches, do you think?" Phillipa continued her questioning mode as we drove. "After all, we don't wear robes or have secret names."

"You mean real magic-makers? It's real if it works, Phil. We're out of the broom closet now, so why bother with secret names? Still, if I had a Wiccan name, I think I'd choose Ceres."

"Goddess of grain and harvest—that would suit. You're definitely in some earth mother phase. Hecate for me," Phillipa decided. "Although Heather might want Hecate."

"Heather's the spitting image of Maid Marian, who most certainly was an early Wiccan. Or she could be a Diana."

"The Huntress? Not on your life. What about the Norse goddess Freya? An avenging Viking might suit Heather. Fiona would *have* to be Titania. Can't you just see her wearing a wreath of flowers, a bit askew, ruling the wispy fairies of the forest?" Phillipa's deep-voiced chuckle was as contagious as ever.

"How about Deidre?" I asked when we'd quit laughing over plump Fiona in filmy garments playing *Midsummer Night's Dream*.

We were silent for a few moments, each of us running through our mental Rolodex of mythological characters.

"Well, as she's preggers, how about Ishtah, Babylonian mother-goddess?"

"Sort of heavy for one so petite. I was thinking more along the lines of Iris, wind-footed messenger and goddess of the rainbow. But if we decided to take craft names, everyone would have her own idea, probably nothing we'd ever imagine."

"I might have tagged you with Ceres. Would you have thought of Hecate for me?"

"Sure."

"Well, there you have it. But it's a great question, and we ought to ask it just for fun."

"That's how we started—all for fun. Who ever thought we'd end up burying a poppet in mud?" I shook myself out of this reflective mood. "Robes might be nice, only none of that wretched polyester stuff. Let's bring that up again after we've finished with Gere."

"Or he's finished with us. But you're right about 'real'—just think of Fiona's glamour." Phillipa sighed. "Now *that's* true magic!"

"Most covens—circles like ours—have a name. Maybe we should be 'Glamour.' " I turned on the radio and punched in the button for WCRB, Boston's classical music station, broadcasting from Tanglewood. Strains of Brahms came wafting from the Koussevitzky Music Tent into the snug confines of my Wagoneer. A few generations ago, that would have seemed like the most amazing magical show. Maybe our spells—when they worked—were as simple and explainable, if only we knew the physics involved.

"Why, are we some kind of rock group? Okay, what about calling our circle 'Justice,' or 'Queen of Swords.' " Phillipa took her inspiration from the Major Arcana of the Tarot deck.

"You're assuming that bringing evildoers to justice will be our circle's continuing mission?"

"Yep, partner. We're going to hex all those durned outlaws clear out of Dodge, " Phillipa said.

In Hazel's book, Fiona had found something called *Recipe for Bringing Home*, which she read to us in ringing tones, touched by that glamour that made her taller and us envious. Hazel recommended lighting yellow candles—her yellow dye was brewed from onion skins—one for each of the four directions. The name of the person to be brought home should then be called aloud "to the four winds, over earth and sea, to the moon and the stars." Cords of sweetgrass had been woven around a minature likeness; careful Hazel never wrote the word "poppet" in her book, but her tiny drawing in the book's margin looked exactly like one of Deidre's dollies. When the name was called out, this likeness should be secured by sweetgrass to the kitchen rafters where herbs were hung. The name should then be written on a square of paper. With a blossom of heartsease laid in, the paper was to be folded and anointed with oil. Cinnamon oil, I thought, for its attractive power. Finally, the spell was burned in a place where the smoke would rise and disperse into the air. "Never fails," wrote Hazel, "if you perform it aright."

"Worth a try," said Deidre.

"Cool!" said Freddie.

"Look at this," Phillipa said in awed tones, carefully picking up two sprigs of dried heartease enclosed in the pages.

"Genus *Viola Tricolor.*" I said. "I've brought a few dried sprigs I had on hand but none has a blossom like these. How well the color has been preserved!"

"It's as if Hazel is reaching across time to help us. I think we should use her cutting, don't you?" Heather said. "I bet there's real power in it."

"Who do you suppose she was calling home?" I wondered.

"A kid gone astray," Deidre said. "Or a husband. Our purpose is a bit darker, but it might just work. And we must have this matter settled for good and all."

"So mote it be," Fiona murmured, tenderly caressing the pages of the grimy old book with a many-ringed hand. "Let us not forget to thank Hazel for this gift at Samhain."

"Oh, wicked spooky," whispered Freddie, backing away a little. "Do the ghosts show up and everything?"

"Who knows what may happen?" I said in my deepest "witch" voice, winking at Phillipa. We hadn't actually materialized any otherworldly beings yet, although I did feel the spirit of my grandma surrounding me from time to time.

Deidre consecrated our circle, inscribing a pentagram in the air with her athame, so that we might work "between the worlds." After invoking the guardians of the four directions, we performed the spell just as Hazel had described it. Since we were outdoors in the mild summer night, our yellow candles were scented with citronella, which was all to the good. When we got to the final burning of Gere's name, Heather asked Freddie to commit the slip of paper to flame and to concentrate on its purpose with us. Freddie's amber eyes turned wild as a tiger's when she lifted her hand into the smoke. We watched it rise straight into the air, then turned unerringly north. *Yes!*

"Go get him, Hazel," Heather muttered darkly.

After less than a week's stay, Tip's father was released from Jordan Hospital with assorted prescriptions and a warning to lay off the alcoholic beverages. Tip hurried home to take care of the ill-tempered invalid.

"How's he doing?" I asked when Tip got a chance to visit for a few minutes on the way home from his Animal Lovers job.

Tip's saddened look said it all. "Paw don't always do what the doctors say."

"I'm real sorry to hear that. I know how hard it must be on you." And all I could do was to give Tip lots of hugs and fresh fruit that was never part of his shopping list. *Comfort me with apples . . .*

Tip's father would drink himself to death eventually, but

maybe not before making a worried old man of his son. I wondered if Tip would be able to go out for track, to play in a band again when school started in the fall. It wasn't easy to think good, healing thoughts for S. E. Thomas.

With Tip gone home to cook and clean for his invalid and Freddie dividing her time between the Triple L and being a helpful companion for Heather, Joe and I had the house to ourselves. There's a great deal to be said for being able to retire for a nap in the afternoon with a bottle of wine and a lusty Greek guy, a ship's engineer who never seemed to run out of steam.

It was less than a week before the solstice. Under the circumstances, ours was to be a more somber than joyous celebration of summer's fertile power. We simply weren't up for the usual madcap merriment. We still knew nothing of Gere's whereabouts. "Patience and faith," counseled Fiona. Patience had never been my long suit.

Our back-and-forth cellphone conferencing kept escalating until one too many urgent calls caused Phillipa to curdle a custard sauce, so she called a moratorium to our living in each other's tote bags.

And then, just before the high holiday, Bobby, the youngest member of the Ryan clan, got lost. Deidre didn't know exactly how Bobby had wandered out of their fenced yard, but on one point she was very clear—it was all Will's fault. Will had been working nights, therefore available to watch Bobby during the day while Deidre was at the mall.

It hadn't been a quiet night at the firehouse; three calls, two of them false alarms, the other a blazing summer cottage. Nobody living there yet, but the fire had been tricky to subdue while keeping the neighboring cottages wet down and safe. Not too surprisingly, the weary fireman had nodded off after lunch. When Jenny and Will Jr. got home from school at 3:15, Will didn't really know where Bobby was or how long he'd been gone.

No one envied him having to call Deidre with this calamitous news. To his credit, he called her the moment it became obvious that Bobby had indeed vanished from the house and yard. A few minutes later, the Ryan place was frantic with activity—police, off-duty firemen, a crazed mom, plus neighbors and friends eager to join the search party. Fiona couldn't leave Laura Belle, who was sniffling, but she would "find" at home with her pendulum. Phillipa was in Boston on book business. But the rest of us rushed in to help find the lost toddler: Heather, with Trilby, her bloodhound, Freddie, Joe, Tip, and I.

How far could Bobby have gone in an hour or so? Still, it had not been that long ago when a murderer of young boys had been preying in this area. And now we'd called back a vengeful Gere into our midst. I was in an agony of worry—how much worse must it be for Deidre and Will?

The police chief directed us to fan out and begin searching. Trilby was given Bobby's pj's to sniff and taken out to the wild area in back of the house. I could hear the bloodhound baying on the other side of the fence. Heather called it singing; Trilby did have a curious high-pitched tone.

Tip tugged at my arm, pointing to a few loose pickets in the stockade fence near the jungle gym. "They should have brought Trilby this way. They got her headed all wrong. These push out like a pet door." He showed me how easy it was to do. "I think he went under here, and I think I can track him. I done a lot of tracking up north, you know."

"Did," I replied automatically, then, "okay, *go.* I'll follow you."

Looking back, I saw only Deidre on the back patio, firmly bracketed by two women in uniform, who were no doubt preventing her from racing about erratically or beating her fists on Will. Each cop had a cellphone clasped to her ear. Jenny, Will Jr., and the two poodles were being kept inside the house, the dogs loudly protesting their missing the excitement. No doubt the two children were equally frustrated. Everyone else was already in motion.

Tip and I hurried around to the other side of the loose pickets where the neglected field buzzed with insect life and harbored who-knew-how-many dangerous holes and beyond, a wooded area with a FOR SALE sign. Trilby must be running there—I could hear her strange bark growing fainter. I'd catch a cop or someone on the way to tell about Tip's tracking notion.

But with Tip in the lead, we were moving much slower than anyone else. He studied the tangle of grasses and weeds and even smelled them. "We should have brought one of Bobby's dogs," he said. "They'd know Bobby's smell. Some sugary cereal, milk spit-up, and pee here."

The boy kept moving along the fence on his hands and knees, turning the corner away from the overgrown field to the smoothly-cut lawn between the Ryans' house and their nearest neighbor. A well-trimmed hedge marked the boundary between the two large lots, but the area between the properties was too manicured to offer any hiding places or booby traps where a kid might fall in.

"Bobby sat down here," Tip said. "Not too steady on his feet, I guess, because here he began to crawl." The grass where he was pointing looked like plain grass to me. Again Tip leaned down and snuffled like a dog. "Boy, that kid stinks," he said. "Good thing." Then he lay right on the ground, sighting tracks with his cheek pressed to the grass, his ponytail over one shoulder.

Inch by inch, we crept toward the main road with my heart sinking farther down with every baby step. Surely Bobby didn't get as far as the main road! A dog began barking at the neighboring house. His owners were out in the field with the others, but it looked as if their dog was tethered, unable to follow.

Tip turned toward their house. "The kid came this way," he muttered, rising to his feet and moving faster. Soon we were near enough to see that the barking dog was a boxer hooked to a line allowing shelter under the deck. As we came closer to the house, the animal began to snarl in an ominous way.

"She got pups under there," Tip said. "Look at her tits."

"Tip, you stay away from her. She'll jump you," I ordered. The ugly female was all low-throated growl and bared teeth. Between growls, I was beginning to hear the soft yelping of pups. It seemed to be coming from the far dark corner where the deck met the crawl space under the house.

Then we heard another sound that froze us both in our cautious tracks. A giggle! Great Goddess—Bobby was under there with the pups!

"Don't go . . . don't go . . ." I cautioned Tip urgently. "Bobby?" I took a deep breath, mentally surrounding all of us with the pure white light of love and protection. Then I made my voice calm and soft, almost without tremor. "Are you in there, honey? It's Aunt Cass." The dog's low growl persisted like the steady throb of a motorboat, and she was drooling. But this was no time to doubt my own power.

Another giggle! The boxer hadn't harmed him, or he wouldn't sound so gleeful. With Bobby's milk-and-pee smell, had the pups' mother taken him to be like one of her own—a baby, not a threat? The suspicious animal certainly was warning us off with her ferocious stance. Motherhood was a serious business in her canine world.

"Bobby, can you come out of there, please? Your mommy wants you to come home now."

"Puppies!" Bobby crooned, chuckling.

"No, honey, don't bring a puppy."

"I want one!" His voice trembled, as if he were working himself up to a scene.

"Listen to Aunt Cass, Bobby. It's *very* important. The puppies' mommy wants them to stay right there where she can watch them, because they're still so little. Come on, now."

At last I could see his blond curls, so like his mother's. He was beginning to crawl toward us. Without consultation, Tip and I both turned slightly to one side, so as not to seem to be confronting the mother. We remained frozen in those postures while

Bobby giggled and wiggled his way forward. My thoughts, as active as my body was immobile, were busy planning how I could best throw myself at that boxer if she turned her bared teeth toward the toddler. Meanwhile, I kept visualizing that white light around Bobby, around Tip and me.

I saw that Tip was gripping an overturned plastic lawn chair as if he, too, was making a defensive plan. Bobby was just now raising himself to his feet. He took a few unsteady steps, blinking a bit at the sunlight, after who-knew-how-long in the darkness with the pups.

"That's a good boy," I said. "Come on over here to Aunt Cass, and we'll go home and have cookies."

"Cookies for puppies!" Bobby was lurching forward from beneath the deck, but still too close to the mother dog's range for me to grab him. The animal was crouching down now, ready to spring, her amber eyes fixed on us, her mouth slavering.

Bobby began to run at a reckless tilt until, finally, I caught him in my arms for a hug of pure relief!

Just then a young policeman came around the side of the house and took in the whole scene at one glance—the threatening dog, the child in my arms, Tip with the chair. Hardly hesitating to think, he drew his gun and aimed it at the dog.

"Stop! Don't you dare fire that gun" I cried, thrusting the child at Tip. "Hang on to Bobby, Tip!"

I stepped in front of the hostile dog, hoping I wasn't actually in her reach and that my protective spell didn't have any major gaps in it.

"Step aside, ma'am," said the cop. "That's a mad dog if ever I've seen one. I got to protect you and the kid."

I pointed both my banishing fingers at him (the two little fingers with the silver rings on them) drawing myself up in what I hoped was a full glamour. "You . . . holster your gun at once. That female boxer is protecting her puppies, she's on leash, and as soon as we've gone, she'll be perfectly docile."

Taking in my imperious stance, the cop paled a little. "No need to get all het up. You one of those witch friends of Will Ryan's wife?"

"You'll find out if you keep waving that gun." I pointed my fingers slightly downward to his belt line. It might be an empty threat, but it worked.

He snapped his gun back into its holster. "Say, don't get nervous, ma'am. No need to do anything rash. I don't believe in that hex stuff anyway. Hey now, what do we have here?" The cop turned his attention from the aggressive dog to Bobby, allowing me to move cautiously away from the deck. He reached down with one easy motion and pulled the little boy out of Tip's arms. "*I think we found the kid*!"

With that, he began jogging back to the Ryans' house at full speed, Bobby's head bouncing like a rag doll over his shoulder. "Hey! Hey!" he called to the small cluster of people on the patio.

Deidre pulled away from her guard and ran screaming and crying toward the officer and his welcome burden. "Bobby . . . Bobby . . . oh, thank you, thank you for finding my baby."

The cop was quick and strong, and he easily outdistanced us, since Tip kept pace with me. As I hurried as fast as I could across the lawns, I could see everyone clapping the cop on the back and cheering. Will came racing from the woods, red-faced and, I thought, weeping, to throw his arms around Deidre and Bobby. Jenny and Will Jr. ran out of the house, hollering; the poodles barked. It was a beautiful scene, with only one thing wrong. That young man seemed to be taking all the credit.

"It's okay," Tip said. "Don't get upset, Miz Shipton."

"You bet, I'm upset! I want Deidre and Will to know it was *you* who found Bobby, not that dumb cop." I huffed and puffed to arrive at the Ryans' before the story got too far out of control.

"Please, Miz Shipton. Everyone looks real happy over there. I wouldn't want to spoil it. And besides, I don't like being fussed over. I didn't do nothing special. Just what I learned."

"*Anything* special. All right, I won't embarrass you and spoil the celebration. But later . . ."

"Thanks, Miz Shipton. Say, that was great, what you did with just your two little fingers when that cop had a real gun. Scared him, didn't it?"

"All in his imagination, but who cares? At least he didn't shoot Mama Boxer and make orphans out of all those little baby boxers."

Jimmy Banks, the young cop, not only took all the credit, but wanted the Ryans to know just how dire the danger to Bobby had been. "A damned vicious dog," he insisted, "that ought to be put down before she maims or kills someone." He would speak to the dog officer about that.

I kept my promise to Tip not to say anything right then. But one good thing about our close cellphone connection—it enabled me to set the record straight an hour or so later and rescue Boadicea, as the boxer had been aptly named. I related the real story to Deidre—how Tip had tracked her little boy while everyone else was racing through fields and woods, and how we'd lured Bobby away from the puppies. "Then Jimmy Banks came along and snatched Bobby up for a dashing rescue. Some nerve!"

"We owe Tip a big vote of thanks." Deidre was crying again. Pregnancy was going right to her tear ducts. "And he ought to have a nice gift, too—you know Tip better than anyone. What would he like?"

I thought of the clarinet, which was far too expensive, so I didn't say it.

I didn't have to. Deidre, the witch, ferreted it out of my mind—well, maybe I'd mentioned it once a long time ago—and scrounged around among Will's wide circle of buddies until she found an instrument gathering dust in someone's attic; it only needed a new reed.

Will was still in the doghouse, however. Even his mother gave him grief, but that might have been part-guilt over her bus-tripping to the casino and leaving Bobby in her sleep-deprived son's tender care. As it turned out, Will and his mother were both soon to be off the hook. Deidre, who'd planned to work at Nature's Bounty until her water broke and labor pains forced her into an ambulance, decided after all to retire early—two weeks after Bobby's escapade.

Boadicea got off with a stern warning to her human companions to lodge Mama and her pups in a more secure place—such as the garage—where little visitors were not allowed until the boxer got over her just-birthed defensiveness. A few weeks later she'd be begging anyone who came along to keep those noisy pups busy for a while.

When Tip got his hands on the clarinet Deidre gave him—with effusive, if tardy, praise of his tracking expertise—he was thrilled beyond speech, but his smile blazed brighter than the June sun.

"Tip says he can track even over bare rock," Joe told me. He walked his fingers over my bare breast by way of illustration. This afternoon siesta business was getting to be a lovely habit.

"How in the world does he do that? Rock is rock—tracking is hard enough on leaves and grass."

"Tip says that anywhere dust has settled for a few hours, there will be an imprint, faint but readable to an experienced tracker. And there are pressure points that tell him where to look for the next footstep." Joe continued the trail along my bare skin. Very soon the subject of tracking got dropped for a more fascinating diversion.

But the next time Tip came by, Joe and he got into a long discussion of the finer points of following an animal or a person in the woods. Tip could only explain some of his tracking skill. The boy struggled to put in words a deeper concept, an awareness of the natural environment he understood but couldn't express.

Tracking was an art, and art comes from the spirit. In fact, Tip did say that "the old guys" called this connection *the-spirit-that-lives-in-all-things*.

What Tip had been taught was not much different from the studies of our own Wiccan circle. All of which were soon coming to a test that none of us had foreseen.

Beware of what you spell for should be written on the first page of every Book of Shadows *because you may make it come true*. And we five witches had indeed called Gere home. Only we didn't know that yet.

"Yo, Cass!" Freddie's voice called from the kitchen door on the morning of the Summer Sabbat. "Happy Solstice, and all that. I suppose you're going to leave me out of the woodland romp again."

"Hmmm?" I was concentrating on choosing which herbs I would need. "Come on in, Freddie. I'll be finished here in a minute, and we'll have some iced tea."

"Heather's packing up candles and pretending that nothing special is going to happen tonight. She, like, dropped a few reminders on what to do for the canine crew in case she's late getting back to the manse. Hey, as if I don't know what doggie sleeps where by now. Big fellas in the kennel, little guys in the conservatory. I suppose Heather's never had to worry about a kennel license." Freddie flopped down at the kitchen table and dropped her shoulder bag on the floor; it looked as if it had been made from two red bandanas. Her hair was spiked like porcupine quills, her earrings the usual row of five in one ear, pentagram dangling from the other, and a delicate circlet in one nostril. She was wearing a denim miniskirt and a black tank top that didn't meet it. I noted with a shudder that her navel was pierced with a brand new gold ring. Black sandals on two-inch platforms. "But Heather's a regular person, even if she is stinkin' rich, you know what I mean?"

Scruffy and Patsy trotted downstairs from the guest rooms where they'd been having their mid-morning nap. *The girl is here! The girl is here! Maybe we'll all go run on the beach.*

"Not now, Scruffy. We're busy." I poured two tall glasses of iced mint tea and laid the table with plates, a board of cheddar cheese and bread, and a pot of chutney.

"No time for us *mundanes* on the Sabbat, guys." Freddie gave both dogs a good scratch behind the ears. "No time for Joe, either, I bet."

"Joe's gone to Boston today and tomorrow—some Greenpeace fund-raiser." He wasn't absolutely required to put in an appearance, but he'd decided to go since it was only an hour away and I was going to be busy welcoming in summer. "So, how are you doing with your meditations?" I'd been teaching my protégée a few simple methods of controlling psychic energy.

"I bet they're going to entertain a bunch of *cats* out there tonight, and you guys are *not* invited." Freddie continued to talk to Patsy and Scruffy as she cut thick slices of cheese and piled them on bread. Scruffy's nose swiveled from the cheese to me. He gave me the canine equivalent of a dirty look.

"He understands what you're saying, you know," I warned Freddie.

"*Cats!* And they're all going to have *chicken livers on toast with a sprig of catnip!*" She added a few spoonfuls of chutney and took a big bite.

Scruffy began to bark. *Blasted fur-balls! I'll chase them so far up the trees, they'll never be able to come again..*

"Scruffy, there will *not* be any cats at our Summer Solstice. And no teenagers, either."

"So, where's the party going to be, anyway, Cass?"

"We'll be meeting here tonight—we're having a fire on my beach. Will Ryan got us a permit."

Freddie sighed dramatically. "Sounds groovy. The beach is, like, the perfect place for witches to meet. Moonlight magic by the sea and all that sh . . . stuff. So, when can *I* get in on the big voodoo?"

"You haven't told me yet how you're getting on with your meditations."

"They're, like, putting my feet to sleep, you know what I mean?"

"Did you visualize a favorite place of tranquility where you felt safe and happy?"

"Yup."

"Was it a garden, or a woodland walk?"

"Nope. Disco bar."

"Didn't you find that rather noisy for an exercise in serenity?"

"Nope, I muted it down a bit. You can do that, y'know."

"Yes, I know. Like turning down a radio. So, did you do as I suggested and visualize a spiritual messenger who came to offer you a gift?"

"Yup."

"A wise woman?"

"Nope, a guy in a black turtleneck with sleeves sort of ripped off just popped into my visualization, you know what I mean? Biceps out to *here. Move over, Arnie!* Goddess tattoo, wiggled her butt. Boy, was he hot! So he goes, *Yo, Freddie.* And I go, *Yo, Messenger of the God and Goddess. What you got for me in your pocket?* You want to know what he gave me?"

"*No,*" I said hastily. "You're supposed to keep that to yourself. But somehow, I think you're missing the real spirit of this meditation."

"You expected maybe I'd think about the chapel where the nuns used to have me praying for my sinful soul and along comes an angel with a new rosary?"

"Heaven forbid."

I did feel a pang of guilt at not including Freddie in our celebration. It wasn't one of the four most important Sabbats, like

Samhain, so we really could have invited her to join us. But it was one of the eight great Sabbats of the year, and Freddie just wasn't ready for that sort of intense ritual yet. She was still struggling ambivalently with the dark side of her considerable psychic talent.

When I began my online *earthloreherbs.com* business with Freddie's assistance, the girl's crackling energy had periodically caused alarming computer malfunctions, freak error messages, and downright threats from the ghost in the machine, some of which the manual didn't even list in its Troubleshooting chapter. Often these eccentric warnings had been an excuse to call Adam, Freddie's favorite hot line. Hey, I couldn't blame her—my son had turned out to be quite a hunk once he got out of his computer-nerd phase.

Now, of course, besides working at the Triple L, Freddie was helping out with Heather's canine crew and reveling in her luxurious bedroom at the Morgan mansion. But I noticed the odd poltergeist event still occurred in her vicinity sometimes—a painting banging against the wall, a piece of toast flying across the room, a computer mouse hopping off the desk. Innocent or amusing incidents outside the range of what we call "normal." Recently, when she and I had been walking through the Massasoit Mall parking lot, a number of theft alarms had turned on all the way down the aisle as we hurried toward the Jeep.

"What's going on, Freddie?" I'd asked as we made good our escape before we could be charged with trying to rip off a vehicle.

"Hey, nothing at all. What do you mean?"

"I believe that was *you*, kiddo, turning on all those alarms. Remember that I'm aware of this stuff, so don't try to fool me."

"Yeah, I guess. Maybe it was because that creepy grain and feed guy tried to hit on me while he was delivering an order of dog feed to Heather's place. Chased me around the kennel. Kept trying to pull up my top. When I stomped on his foot, he yanked on my earring. Hurt something awful."

"Nothing bad happened to him as a result, I hope."

"Nope. But he had to quit pawing at me when the van's horn started beeping. I mean, he had no idea whether there was someone in the house who was going to run out any minute. Didn't know I was alone, except for the dogs, of course. So while he was trying to get the horn to quit, I let Rommel out of his kennel. Rommel's not keen on strangers. So the asshole decided to take off out of there pronto, you know what I mean?" Freddie giggled. "I could hear that horn blaring all the way down the road. But I guess maybe I got stuck, too. I mean, doing horns."

If Freddie were going to learn control, she would have to bring her psychic activity up to a more conscious level. I mused on ways to help her do that while I soaked in an herb-scented bath before the Sabbat meeting. She didn't seem to be getting a handle on the messenger meditation. Whatever the messenger brought should be a gift straight from the depths of one's subconscious.

Joe called while I was still lolling in the deliciously warm water. I'd set my cellphone right beside the tub, in case. "I miss you already," he said in his low, thrilling voice. "I wish I could see you right now. What are you wearing?"

"Right this minute, just a few bubbles and a little herbal scent. But *later* I'm wearing a longish blue-green dress for the festivities."

"Then I wish I were there right now."

"Mmmm. Me, too. Keep the good thought until tomorrow, love. So, what are *you* wearing?"

"A lavish Four Seasons terrycloth robe while raiding the minifridge. Looking for liquid courage to face the herd of Boston philanthropists downstairs in the hotel ballroom. I knew I shouldn't have come—now that I'm in Greenpeace's clutches, I'm being given missions. I might have to stay another day or so to massage some heavy contributors."

"They'll be putty in your hands. Good luck, love."

"You, too, sweetheart. Don't dance away into the fairie moonlight."

I promised I wouldn't, but I almost did. We hadn't been practicing Wiccans very long. This was only our third Summer Solstice, and it turned out to be the best Sabbat ever. The stress and fear of the past few months simply lifted away from us as we celebrated another turn of nature's wheel. Part of it was the natural magic of a moonlit beach in June, and part of it was our own evocation of the space between two worlds, our charmed circle. Magic was afoot, and what a dance we had that night!

Stone called me the next day. "There's something I need to discuss with you, but I don't want to do it over the phone. Phil says, why don't you and Joe come for dinner tonight?"

"I suppose there's no point asking what this is all about? Surely you're not afraid that your phone is bugged! Joe's still in Boston squeezing money out of the Back Bay. But I'll be there. What time? Can I bring something?"

"Are you kidding? Phil would be insulted. Sixish. We'll have drinks on the patio. And in answer to your questions, it's too important a matter to take any chances, and how safe do you think *your* phone is from a mechanical wizard like Gere?"

What Stone wanted to talk to me about was Candy Donahue. Over glasses of an inspired Barolo from Piedmont, he said, "Candy and her grandparents were in protective custody temporarily, while we still had hopes of apprehending Gere quickly and bringing him to trial. But the little girl was not faring well. The shock of witnessing her parents' murder, of almost being killed herself, of all she went through to escape and hide—well, you can imagine. Candy has become increasingly depressed— nightmares, bed-wetting, an eating disorder—the works! Bea Hawkins, Candy's grandmother, insisted on getting the kid into a more homelike environment—and she wants the little girl to have the companionship of her dog."

"Yes, of course. Patsy might make a world of difference. A friend from happier days, even a guard who can be depended upon to protect her. And Patsy knows Gere is the enemy, as she has amply demonstrated." I took another sip of the aromatic wine and imagined Scruffy's sad nose pressed to the living room window. "But Scruffy is going to miss Patsy something fierce. Maybe when this is all over, there can be visits."

"You mean, like *play dates*." Phillipa passed a tray of assorted tiny bruscetta. "Really, Cass . . . sometimes I don't believe you."

"That's because you don't have a canine cohort yourself." I put down my wineglass, the better to scarf up a mushroom bruscetta, then an anchovy one, then . . . "Where did Bea Hawkins want to go? Home, I bet. Scituate, was it? That would have been utterly crazy. Please tell me you didn't let her do that, Stone."

"I couldn't force them to stay hidden until I arrest Gere. But I did come up with an interim place that's a lot homier than the motel where they were staying."

As I stared into the red wine in my glass, now reflecting the afternoon sun glinting across the patio, a sign flashed across my inner eye, the one that's supposed to be invisibly located in the middle of my forehead. A sign swinging in the ocean breezes. WELCOME TO . . . The silhouette of a witch against an orange background.

"Say, Stone—did they by any chance rent a cottage in Salem? It's very picturesque. If you give me the address, I'll drive up there with Patsy and no one will be the wiser."

"Nix, Cass." Phillipa refilled the bruscetta tray I had just savaged. "The karma in Salem could be hazardous to our health."

"Oh, don't be such a worrywart. Remember it's my hometown. I'll just drop off the dog and be gone before any of those ghosts-of-evil-judges-past know I've been there. Say, is that delectable fragrance some kind of lamb?"

"Leg of lamb with oregano and garlic. In honor of your absent Greek. *What* did you say he was doing in Boston?"

"Massaging dowagers. Oh, I don't know. Some money mission. Why don't I bring Patsy back to Candy tomorrow."

"Don't go alone. Wait until Joe gets back," Phillipa warned. "I don't like this."

"No, I'm not ready to expose Joe to Salem yet. He'll naturally want to look around the town, and there's so much pseudo-witchcraft at its most commercial. Why don't *you* go with me?"

"Yet it seems to have become a Mecca for real Wiccans today, *so to speak.* 'Witch City,' they call it. Laurie Cabot, et al. I would love to take the day off, just to keep you out of trouble, but alas, I have galleys that have to be back in seven days. Tomorrow is day five, and I'm only halfway."

"That may be because you're still testing and retesting recipes that are already perfect," Stone said.

"I'm edgy about a few of them, I admit. After all, a recipe is a set of directions that someone is going to have to follow, so each one has to be really workable. Maybe Fiona would like a little outing. What could be better than being protected by one of her nondescript glamours?" Not only could Fiona draw attention to herself with an attractive glamour, she could also make herself practically invisible with its reverse. We were all admiration.

"I wouldn't want you to be followed," Stone said, "so I'll arrange for an escort as far as the Weymouth line to make certain that no one is watching your departure."

"Would you have a patrol car do a few drive-bys as well? The house will be empty and tempting. I don't have natural gas, but I understand that doesn't rule out a gas explosion, which I wouldn't put it past Gere to orchestrate."

Fiona was quite willing to ride shotgun. She would leave Laura Belle with her neighbor—a generous and loving friend who always slipped a tract on Christian baptism into the pink tote bag of Laura Belle's belongings whenever she returned the child to Fiona.

I debated on whether to bring Scruffy on this excursion. Perhaps it would be better for him to know what had become of Patsy, that she was with her family, rather than for me to return without her and have to face a betrayed canine.

I put it to him plainly and firmly. "Scruffy, we have to bring

Patsy home tomorrow. She misses her little girl, Candy, and Candy misses her. You know how you'd feel if you and I had to be separated for a long, long time. It's the right thing to do." Whoever thinks you can't explain things to a dog has missed a lot of clues. Most dogs understand a hundred words or so, and some of them even talk back.

Oh, sure, Toots. Just when she was getting friendly, like maybe she was going to be even friendlier in a few weeks. Scruffy was sunk deep in gloom all evening while I bathed and fussed over Patsy's appearance. Patsy had not been fixed, and Scruffy's long-range hopes were going to be dashed.

The next morning was a perfectly gorgeous end-of-June, rose-scented day. Even Scruffy found it difficult to look depressed while wearing the jaunty red bandana I'd tied around his neck to complement Patsy's green shamrock bandana. Leaving a cryptic note for Joe—"Gone to Salem with Fiona. Back late tonight, if I don't get hung up"—I drove off at 8:30 with a patrol car lurking in back. We picked up Fiona at her little fishnet-draped cottage. With the two dogs enjoying the ear-ruffling breeze from the back windows of the Wagoneer, we sped along north, deciding on the most expedient route for avoiding Boston.

Fiona had brought her capacious green satchel, which instead of being filled with childcare necessities, was stuffed as it had been in the old days with charms, potions, cobwebs in a plastic baggie (very useful to stanch blood, Fiona has told me), essential protective oils of sage and rosemary, butterscotch candies, buffered aspirin, and miscellaneous arcane volumes to which she might need to refer. "I've never been to the House of Seven Gables," she said wistfully.

"If there's time after the Patsy-Candy reunion, we'll do the Gables," I promised.

"Ought we to stop for a six-pack of water? We may need to re-hydrate from time to time."

"We're not crossing the desert, Fiona. Oh well, I've brought a gallon of water for the pups. I guess I should allow as much for us." This was a grave mistake, but how was I to know? I stopped on Route 3 at a self-service gas station that was also a convenience store so I could top off the fuel tank while Fiona got her six-pack. Later I learned that I'd been quite oblivious of the Chevy parked around back and the man just coming out of the rest room. But the Chevy's driver had seen and recognized my Jeep Wagoneer. Before ducking back out of sight, he'd noted with keen interest that I was transporting an Irish setter and that a patrol car had followed me into the station and waited for me to leave. When we pulled out to continue on our mercy mission and holiday, we were followed so expertly that neither the bored officer nor I ever caught on. Some clairvoyant I am! To her credit, Fiona had a few uneasy moments.

"Close the back windows for a minute, will you, dear? I'm going to sprinkle some powder out of my window, and I don't want it blowing back into the doggies' noses."

"Okay. Do you want to tell me what you're working at?"

"I'm not exactly sure. Just a little protective sprinkle I concocted on my own. A little pure sea salt, powdered blue chalk, and some other stuff."

"Eye of newt?"

"I never leave home without it."

The patrol car left us at the Weymouth line; the officer beeped and waved us off. We were in Salem by eleven and had no trouble finding the little community of summer places where the Hawkins family had rented a gray-shingled cottage with aqua shutters named Sea Haven, which soon proved to be a misnomer. The front yard was awash with hydrangea bushes of the particular blue that can only be found near the ocean and is therefore a badge of honor at seaside dwellings.

I'd never met Bea and Harry Hawkins, or Candy Donahue, for that matter, but being Patsy's chauffeur was introduction enough. As soon as Patsy hopped out of the Jeep, yelping excitedly, the little girl threw her arms around the Irish setter and cried out with pleasure. She had big, soulful brown eyes, a sad expression, and a mop of sandy ringlets that instantly brought to mind Little Orphan Annie. There was a white scar on her cheek that looked as if it might fade eventually. Perhaps a souvenir of her escape from Gere. When Candy shook my hand and looked up at me gravely, I could feel her tragic memories lumping up in my own throat. Fiona had pulled a lavender handkerchief from her satchel and was dabbing at her eyes with it.

Bea Hawkins, a compact little woman with unlikely blond sausage-curls and very pink cheeks, was herself a little red-eyed watching Candy and her dog catch up on hugs. Her husband, a short and sturdy man with a jaunty air, wearing a Tower of London T-shirt, passed around Blue Willow mugs of steaming coffee, a welcome pick-me-up after the long drive. If the aura of bereavement weren't surrounding them still, they would have been a naturally jovial couple. Their late lamented antiques shop must have been a fun place to browse. But now, with their daughter murdered, their business blown up, and their granddaughter drifting into depression—they were coping with too much to contemplate.

After a few minutes of being kissed and nuzzled by Patsy, Candy cheered up visibly and began an animated game of *fetch-the-stick* with both dogs. They played in back of the house where there was a sandy driveway, an oblong of burnt lawn, and a split-rail fence resplendent in blooming *Rosa rugosa*, those beach roses protected by killer thorns that later would yield a bounteous harvest of rose hips.

"Oh, just look at that child." said Bea. "I knew this would help. Thank God! Now you two will stay for lunch, and I'm not taking no for an answer." Actually, we weren't planning to decline her invitation. We'd spotted the fragrant blueberry pie on the kitchen counter, and Bea had taken a platter of wrapped lobster rolls out of the refrigerator.

After an agreeable hour on the back porch, drinking iced tea and enjoying the North Shore's summer bounty, Fiona and I, with a reluctant Scruffy in tow, left to tour the House of Seven Gables. Scruffy kept looking out the back window with a heartrending expression until the little cottage with the aqua shutters was lost in the distance. Then he sighed and lay down with his nose between his paws for some time afterward, and was far from his usual cheeky self.

We found a deeply shaded parking place where we could leave Scruffy in the Jeep with all four windows open partway to the ocean breezes. He didn't even complain when we left him alone in the car.

Hordes of tourists like ourselves were trooping through the House of Seven Gables, completely diluting any atmosphere of the literary past that the handsome residence of Hawthorne's cousin might have had before it became so popular an attraction. Fiona was quite disappointed, as I knew she would be. When I'd visited the historic landmark as a girl, off-season usually, it had still retained the aura of times past. That was before I knew I was a clairvoyant, so I thought everyone sensed lingering spirits as I did.

After allowing Scruffy to stretch his legs and mark a few trees in a dispirited fashion at Willows Park near the wharves, I took Fiona to the Salem Witch Museum, advertised as a "powerful multi-sensory historical drama, accentuated by thirteen life-sized stage settings—experience it! You be the judge. We'll fire your imagination." The presentation took about a half-hour.

"So, how did you like it?" I asked my ashen-faced friend as we came out into the glorious summer afternoon.

"It certainly was lively, in a deadly way." Fiona held her arms straight out and shook her hands briskly to shake away the frightening scenes we'd just witnessed. Then she dug around in her bag for her essential oil of sage. After rubbing a drop between her wrists, she handed the tiny bottle to me. "Here, anoint your wrists, dispel the vibes," she ordered me.

"So, what's next? The Witch Dungeon or a walk on Gallows Hill?"

Even as Fiona's head was strongly indicating the negative, my attention was caught and held by a picturesque lantern in the square, the sun's rays dazzling on its metal rim. Brilliant effects often throw me into the half-hypnotic state that precedes a vision. (Maybe I, too, needed to learn more control.) In an instant I was transported back to the Hawkinses' rental. I saw a Chevy drive by slowly. I saw Gere at the wheel, studying the cottage. And I saw his brutal expression, his ruthless determination. I screamed.

Tourists milling out of the Salem Witch Museum glanced at me curiously but seemed to take it all in stride, perhaps thinking a distraught woman was part of the act. I clutched at Fiona. "It's Gere. He's here, in a blue Chevy. He's found Candy."

Fiona didn't hesitate for a heartbeat. Taking a cellphone out of her satchel, she punched in 911. "I'm reporting a possible break-in in progress. Look for a man in a blue Chevy. Thomas Gere. There's a warrant out for his arrest," she declared, slowly and distinctly, giving the Hawkinses' address and her cellphone number. Then she turned to me reassuringly. "That will get the patrol cars at the scene. But I don't think they'll get their hands on Gere. He'll take off as if he were shot from a cannon. After all, he's a wanted felon."

Shorter than I, she had to reach up to give me a hug. I was still shaking with fear for Candy, whose sweet brown eyes had witnessed the horror of her parents' murder, and obsessed with guilt at my own wrongheaded part in this fiasco. "We have to get Candy out of there before Gere comes back," I insisted. "Will you call Stone, or shall I?"

"I will. I think if you do, there might be some recriminations."

"He's going to *kill* me," I wailed. "Gere must have followed us. Not only didn't I see him, I didn't even sense his presence."

"Well, we wanted him back and we got him," Fiona declared. "So, now what?"

"As soon as I've talked to Stone, we'll take your dog and walk down to the waterfront. We'll say a really urgent spell for Gere's capture. The ocean empowers magic—that's why people crave being near it, absorbing its strength and peaceful energy."

"You're really calm. You're even giving me a little lecture."

"One of us has to keep her head."

"There's one thing we didn't consider." Self-doubt threw cold water on my rising hysteria. "It was only a vision. How do we know it was true sight? What if we get an army of police down there at the Hawkinses' for nothing at all—a figment of my imagination?"

"What do you mean, *only a vision?* You're a clairvoyant. Have faith! I'll wager there wasn't a single clairvoyant who sailed on the maiden voyage of the *Titanic.* Or stayed in Salem long enough to get hung from the Gallows Tree, for that matter. We can't take a chance on this. We have to protect Candy and those lovely, hospitable people. What's a little embarrassment—if it comes to that—beside saving their lives?"

She made sense, as always, but before I could thank her for stiffening my spine, she was already on the cellphone, tracking down Stone. When she finally got his ear, she spoke firmly. "Cass says we were followed by Gere. Well, either your officer never saw him, or Gere picked up our trail later. The point is, he knows where Candy's living now, and he's making some evil plan to get rid of the child. Yes, yes, we are sure, and you must trust us on this. We've already called the local police and reported a break-in."

There was a pause that might have been longer, but Fiona obviously interrupted. "It was the best way to get help in a hurry—just a little white lie, Stone. Yes, the Hawkinses will be scared out of their shoes. And a good thing, too—fear is a survival mechanism." Another pause. At this point, I was itching to grab the phone and made a motion toward it. Fiona slapped my hand away. "Cass says he's driving a blue Chevy. Light or dark, dear? Yes, she's right here beside me. She says it was dark blue. No, she didn't see the license plate. No, not with her own eyes. It was a vision." There was a slight pause before Fiona continued in a dignified tone. "I knew you'd understand. Thank you for your confidence, Stone. Now you just get busy and rescue that little family. We'll be in touch." Whatever else Stone might have had to say was clipped off when Fiona hit the "end" button with righteous vigor. "There. He'll do the right thing. I know it."

"Fiona, you're a wonder. You even convince me."

"Good. You're much too diffident about your abilities. Now let's get Scruffy out of the car and go for a walk on the wharf. We have some magic to work." Fiona led us firmly and energetically forward. It was not my imagination—she *was* becoming taller and glowing in some powerful way.

Even as I watched in awe, she was wrapping the cloak of a glamour around herself. Surely our words of power would lead to Gere's arrest. Who wouldn't believe in Fiona!

We found a bench near the wharf, where we rested and sipped at our bottles of water, Scruffy at our feet, his body appearing to be completely at rest but his head swiveling about, ears and nose alert for every unfamiliar sound and smell in a new place. You had to admire the way dogs adapt to whatever situation presents itself.

After a mindless pause while I sat there just recovering from the day's events, Fiona launched into what proved to be an advanced lesson in spell-making. "If we want to be truly effective in a spell involving other people, we have to step outside ourselves, dear, and I mean that rather literally. We're all part of each other, you know, like cells of one body, but Nature with a capital N has programmed each of us to believe we are separate and individual. That's a self-preservation thing, you see, so we'll live long enough to reproduce. Keeps us from being indifferent to our own well-being, or too easily altruistic and heroic."

"Step into another reality, you mean?"

"Or out of delusion." Fiona tried to pin back an unruly strand of her braids. Silver bangles chimed together on her pale, plump arms. The pleasant, cleansing odor of sage wafted from her wrists. "Just think about the true connection between all living things, and slip through to that dimension, dear. You'll find it's quite restful not to be yourself alone for a bit. So let's sit here quietly for a moment and let that happen."

I focused on my breathing, as if meditating, and tried to let go of myself. Not easy. But after a moment, I thought maybe I had, a little, because I felt a certain lightness of spirit. "What do you call this, Fiona?"

"Oneness. Oneness. Oneness. Say it over and over to yourself. Any word with the letter N or M in it promotes a trance-like state. It's the humming sound."

I couldn't say how long we sat there murmuring "oneness." It could have been five minutes or a half-hour or even longer—time seemed to have no relevance.

"Now, we will visualize that blue Chevy being stopped, Thomas Gere being questioned and detained. The warrant is activated, he is cautioned and arrested." Fiona's voice was low and hypnotic.

I gave it my best shot.

After a while, Fiona stood up and stretched; the silver bangles rang together again, like temple bells. We gathered up our bags, bottles, sweaters, and Scruffy, and we headed back to Plymouth. There seemed to be no need for conversation on the way home, so I played some old tapes I had in the Jeep—Elizabethan tunes, medieval music, and Gregorian chant. Just the right segue from high spell-making to the mundane world of home.

I wondered what would happen next. Even psychics do that.

In response to Fiona's call, Stone had the state marshals at the Hawkinses' place in less than a half-hour. Thanks to our visit, the distressed family would have to find a new haven. Stone wouldn't tell me where he planned to settle them this time, but he was pleased with himself, so I knew a really agreeable alternative housing had presented itself. I didn't really need to know all the details, but curiosity is one of my besetting sins. Not to worry—

Stone couldn't keep a secret from us very long. If I didn't see the Hawkinses' new home in a vision, Phillipa would get the information out of Stone through her own nefarious methods.

But as it turned out, it was Fiona who ferreted out the place with her dowsing pendulum. She wouldn't even tell me over the phone, but whispered it into my ear when I stopped by with a gift of her favorite rose hand cream. "They're in Little Compton, Rhode Island, dear. Now, who would have thought of that? Charmingly rural and nonthreatening. Looks to me as if they're close to the ocean, too—so nice for the little girl and her doggie."

By the time Fiona came up with this gem of information, Joe had returned from Boston. There's something to be said for separations, even short ones—they do lead to some delightfully passionate reunions!

Esbat of the Thunder Moon

Incredibly, three days later, as July began with a bout of dazzling dry heat, Gere *was* pulled over by a cruiser on highway patrol. No longer driving the Chevy, this time Gere was behind the wheel of a Toyota when he failed to come to a complete stop at a stop sign at an intersection near Silver Lake High School.

The cop, Officer Dan Rosen, who was alone in the patrol car, strolled over to the Toyota and requested that Gere fork over his license and registration. His intention was simply to write Gere a ticket. After numerous complaints about speeding through that particular stop sign, Rosen was there to teach traffic violators an expensive lesson. Summer school was in session, and failure to stop was just as dangerous as zipping past the school at twice the speed limit.

Leaning casually on his patrol car, Rosen eyed the Toyota for any equipment irregularities and called in the numbers of the documents in his hand. A short time later, he was informed that the Toyota was a stolen vehicle and Gere was wanted for murder. What a collar for Officer Rosen!

But Gere had planned ahead for just such an emergency and was ready for the cop. Before the flustered officer could reach for his weapon and cuffs, Gere jumped out of the Toyota, flipped a switch on a small item in his hand, and threw it under the patrol car.

A few minutes later, when a second car came screeching in as backup, all that remained of the patrol car's encounter with Gere was a heap of smoking carbon. Very little was recovered of Officer Rosen.

The Toyota was found abandoned in the high school parking lot. Members of the Plymouth police force quickly searched on foot as well as by car throughout the neighborhood, but somehow Gere got away. They thought it likely that he'd stolen another car, and immediately requested the small group of teachers and summer students to come outside to the parking lot and check their vehicles, but none was missing.

"What went wrong?" I wailed to Fiona, leaning weakly on my kitchen phone after Phillipa's call.

"I blame myself." Fiona sounded more thoughtful than distressed. "The spell was much too specific. There's this trickster nature to the universe that *will* give you exactly what you ask for but in a way that negates the whole purpose. I should have foreseen that. We'll do better next time, dear. Something more openended."

"Too late for Officer Rosen." I couldn't be so easily mollified. "Husband and father of two, both under school age."

"A terrible, terrible tragedy. When's our next Esbat?"

"Esbat of the Thunder Moon. Next week, Wednesday. Freddie's invited."

"Good. Fresh blood. We'll work something potent then, I promise you that. Meanwhile, work on your oneness, dear."

"Fiona's phenomenal, you know," I said to Heather while we prepared the authentic stone circle she'd designed in a clearing between trees. It was the afternoon before our July Esbat, and we wanted no stray pebble, stick, or dog droppings to mar our barefoot ceremony. We used two stout straw brooms to whisk away all debris, and any unseen negativity as well. There was no doubt that having a lot of money could make life beautiful, I reflected as I gazed at the rolling green lawns and groves that surrounded Heather's Federalist home. Heather hadn't had to prune the lower branches of pine trees or tote those picturesque little boulders by herself. "You should have seen her on that Salem wharf. An incarnation of the Goddess herself, so sure and powerful."

"Yes, but Gere escaped and a cop got blown to smithereens."

"I was quite upset myself by the wrong turn that spell took. But I still say she's powerful, and we need to learn more from her," I declared. The serenity of the deep summer day was broken by the sound of periodic hammering in the vicinity of Heather's kitchen entry, and further by the dogs in their spacious fenced enclosure, barking at the intruding carpenters. "How's the reconstruction coming along?"

"The kitchen area will be back to normal by the end of the week. My life, on the other hand, is missing someone who was very special to me, and that will take longer to heal." Heather paused while brushing away litter and looked out over the long lawn. Her patrician profile was stern but there were tears brimming up in her hazel eyes. The sun burnished her long chestnut braid to a lustrous brightness. One could imagine her in the role of the goddess Diana—although realistically, Heather was an avid protester of hunters and hunting in general. Perhaps in an earlier time, she would have run through the moonlit woods in search of deer, but today she was more liable to be carrying anti-gun placards or breaking into labs to rescue beagles. "I must say that Dick has been a tower of strength to me," she said with a sudden glowing smile. "And Freddie's a godsend."

"About Dick . . ." I began.

". . . I don't know what to do." Heather completed my sentence, not as I would have wished. "You may have guessed that he's proposed. In fact, I know damn well you're all talking about this behind my back. But honestly, Cass, after having married three money-hungry, thieving, lying, cheating bastards, I don't know if I have the courage to try again."

"But Dick Devlin, the loyal, trustworthy, upstanding, and altruistic Boy Scout, is a completely different sort of guy, judging from what you've told me about those other three snake charmers," I objected. "And besides, think of how reassuring it would be to have your own personal veterinarian on the premises, not to mention friend and lover."

Heather's broad brow was still creased with worry. "There's that, I admit. He's been wonderful about donating his time at Animal Lovers. And I am incredibly fond of him. He's got such wonderful hands."

I wondered how she meant that, but I didn't ask. Sooner or later all will be revealed among friends. "Maybe you should send out a request for guidance at the Esbat." Heather scooped up the last of the debris with work-gloved hands, and tied the green plastic lawn bag with a decisive twist. I sensed it was time for a change of subject. "I'm glad to hear that Freddie's been useful. She's crazy about staying here, you know. In love with the bathtub in her suite, I understand."

"Let's go back to the house for a nice, cold drink." She hoisted the lawn bag into a wheelbarrow. "Well, you know Freddie. She's great with the animals, but there is the occasional poltergeist event. It really embarrasses her when that happens, so I don't make too much of it. The radio moaning like a banshee on all stations—well, that only lasted for a day or so—or the blender turning itself on—or the fireplace broom sailing across the living room, happily sparing the vases and lamps."

"A broom? How very traditional."

"Listen, Cass, we might as well admit it. That girl is a witch, and it wouldn't surprise me at all if she's not a hereditary one. It would be interesting to learn something about her family. Now, how about a tall gin and tonic?"

"How about a tall iced tea, instead? I want a nice, clear head for tonight. Fiona has another spell planned, more open-ended, she said. This worry about Gere is driving me batty. I think about him day and night. I know I'm obsessing but I can't seem to quit. Except when I'm with Joe, of course. I mean, *really* with Joe."

We dumped the trash and skirted around the work area to the half of the kitchen that was still operable. Heather took an iced blue bottle of Bombay gin out of the refrigerator. "Hmmm. I wonder who'll get blown up this time. Come on, Cass . . . join me in killing a few brain cells? You obviously have too many, and they're working overtime."

This was Freddie's second Esbat, and she was literally dancing on her toes with excitement. Whenever I stood near her, I could feel the energy crackling in her aura. Matching her newly-charged spirits were the jelled spikes of four-alarm red hair on the crown of her head; the rest was still midnight black, a two-tone effect. "Gotta get in sync with the Thunder-and-Lightning Moon," she explained, grinning at me shyly as I studied her new "do." Her amber eyes were fringed with the usual sooty black. All her rings and pendants—for ears, nose, and neck—were silver for this occasion (I'd recently told her that silver was the metal of choice for Wiccan jewelry), her micro skirt and tank top were shocking pink. As a fashion statement, her outfit was purely electric. "I'm ready to zap the living daylights out of Gere," she declared.

"Excellent," murmured Fiona. "You look amazing, dear. Very powerful, indeed. I used to have bright red hair myself in the Sixties."

Even though it was after seven when we met at Heather's outdoor circle, it was not yet dark but a soft lavender twilight with pink strata streaked the horizon, the hot, red orb of the sun having just descended below the trees. The rising moon appeared pale, nearly transparent. The surrounding grove was richly fragrant with deep-summer leaves. Heather consecrated our circle with her silver-handled athame, invoking the spirits of the four directions and their corresponding elements to aid in our work. As the priestess of this Esbat, she drew down the moon's force into our circle.

Fiona lit the small fire at the altar in the center, and sprinkled in it powders of her own devising, probably something she got from Hazel's book. The new spell she cast was indeed more open-ended than our previous attempt on Salem's wharf. It specified only the outcome—an end to Gere's murderous attacks—not the means. I was beside Freddie when we passed the energy around our circle; her hand was so warm I thought she might be feverish. The power moved faster and faster from hand to hand. When the time was right, when we could no longer contain that energy, Heather cried, "Send it out now!" All of us cast up our arms and let the spell fly straight to Gere—"So mote it be!"

Then Deidre, glowing with the authority of her new pregnancy, led us in a protection ritual, for which I added dried branches of sage and rosemary to our fire. Their aroma was pungent and somehow cleansing.

Afterward we chose limbs from Heather's birch and hazel trees to make wands—measured as thick as a little finger, as long as the forearm and hand, to be smoothed and blessed to the work. We'd never depended on traditional paraphernalia to implement our magic—this was a first. We were a new circle, more a gathering of solitaries than a coven, and hadn't got around to all the accoutrements yet. But Deidre, our craftswoman, had been pushing for wands. They'd be fun, she'd assured us, and who knew what else?

"No one needs to know we have them. You don't have to wave them around at the supermarket or the bank." Deidre's face, just a little puffy now, shone with enthusiasm.

"Oh, I don't know. Do you suppose a wave of my wand might make those annoying long lines disappear?" Phillipa winked at me with a look that said, 'I think this is all nonsense, don't you?'

"Birch, hazel . . . what's the difference?" whispered Freddie.

"Birch for you," I said. "New beginnings, feminine power—it's a young wand. Hazel is for the more mature wisdom."

"What will these sticks do?"

"Magic, of course. You can use your wand to conduct energy from natural sources." I didn't know myself what use they would be, but when students press for answers, teachers have to say *something.*

I should have known. As soon as Freddie had whittled away the twigs, cleaned her wand of bark, and sanded the bare wood a bit, she waved it dramatically at the little fire. A tongue of flame shot into the air that had us all dancing around to stamp down the sparks.

"Cut that out!" Phillipa ordered Freddie in an imperious tone. "Cass, you ought to have given her apple, not birch, for goodness sake."

Freddie jumped back from Phillipa's glittering black eyes, swinging her wand wildly. A frisson of light ran down the wire that brought electric power to Heather's house.

"That's only a little power surge, Heather," Fiona said soothingly. "I doubt it will blow the circuits. I hope you don't have too many appliances plugged in, though." She turned and stretched out her hand to Freddie. "Here, dear, you let me have your wand a minute. It needs blessing and consecrating. New wood, you never know what will happen."

"Apple *would* be better," Deidre agreed with Phillipa. Suiting quick action to her words, she grabbed Freddie's hand and sped her off into the moonlit night to where three crooked old apple trees stood behind the dog yard. A few minutes later, they were back with an apple limb of the appropriate size.

"But I *liked* the birch," Freddie complained. "What good is apple, anyway?"

"Apple's for love and giving," Deidre told her.

"Oh. Okay." Her smile flashed impishly. "Like, for love spells? Awesome. Hey, Cass . . . maybe I can practice on Adam."

"*Not,*" I said firmly. I hadn't seen Adam since he set up my marvelous computer system—code name: Ceres. It was possible he wouldn't be traveling up here from Atlanta again until Christmas. Perfectly safe from Freddie, I concluded.

There's no doubt that the spirit of the universe has a sense of irony. Through the inevitable quirks of fate, I was to see all of my children rather soon.

It was late when I got home, but Joe and Scruffy were still awake. And they weren't alone. Tip was with them in the living room watching some Red Sox game run late into extra innings. Scruffy sat attentively near the little bundle of Tip's belongings that lay beside the couch.

The boy is here. He smells sad. Scruffy nosed Tip's hand for a pat, a dog's way of taking a friend's mind off troubles.

"Tip's father had a relapse," Joe explained. "He's back in the hospital for a few days, so I persuaded Tip to bunk here with us. But I couldn't get him to turn in until you came home and gave his visit your blessing."

"*Of course,* you'll stay here, Tip. Anytime. You know that. How's your dad doing?" I had to struggle not to reach out and smooth the straight, dark hair that fell forward on the boy's brow. I also had to struggle not to wish that Tip's bad-news father would disappear from his life forever this time. A dangerous impulse.

Out, out, out, I said to myself. Banish the thought!

"They won't tell me nothing about Dad." Tip's gray eyes were solemn and resigned in a way that made him look much older than his thirteen years. "But he don't look good, Miz Shipton. Real yellow skin, worse than before. And his pee was brown."

"The doctors will know what to do," I promised, the usual lie we give to worried relatives. I would have to do a strong healing meditation for S. E. Thomas, to make up for my self-serving negative thoughts.

After we'd settled Tip in the blue bedroom under the eaves, with Scruffy hospitably camping out at the end of his bed, Joe and I retired to my room. As I slipped into one of the slinky satin nightgowns I keep for Joe's visits—a much-washed, oversized sleep T-shirt being my usual night attire—he said, "I hope that deliciously warm mood you were in when you came home tonight won't be completely dissipated. Because there's more. Some other phone calls this evening, in fact."

"Okay. What's up?" My hand fell away from the light switch of the bedroom lamp that I had been about to turn off, and I waited, not without admiring Joe's bare muscled chest, the gold cross gleaming.

"Adam called. He said that his sister Cathy had flown into Atlanta last night and would be staying with him. They're planning to drive up to Boston this weekend to see Becky, and then, if you wish, the three of them will come here on Sunday. And I believe there's some plan to have dinner with their father also—he's working at the Pilgrim Nuclear Plant?"

"Yes, but Gary lives in Bridgewater, far enough away so we don't run into each other at the supermarket. Wow, this is quite a surprise. I haven't seen Cathy as often as I could wish since the divorce—she's in San Francisco, you know. I can't remember the last time I had all three of my children together—maybe some Christmas past, years ago, actually. What a good chance for you to meet them all!"

Joe looked away from my eyes, like a small boy who knows he's about to be in deep trouble. "And there was another call. From Greenpeace."

"Deserter!" I cried. "Just when I'm about to be inundated with family, you are off on another quixotic mission. Are you sure *you* didn't call *them*?"

"No, sweetheart, I did *not* call them. I tried my best to duck this one. I'm really uneasy about leaving you with Gere still skulking around. But they're short an engineer for the *MV Greenpeace*, and I'm elected."

"What's this—another Patagonian toothfish emergency?"

"And the albatross, too. Don't forget that we were out there saving the albatross as well." Joe smiled his sexy Greek smile. I never seemed able to be truly angry with him when he smiled.

"Coleridge would have been proud of you. So . . . where to this time?"

"I have to meet the ship in Vigo, Spain. My flight leaves Logan tomorrow night." He reached over to take me in his arms, but I wasn't melting. Then he began massaging my back and neck. A thaw was on the way.

"I'm getting tired of these worthwhile missions," I whined.

"But, sweetheart, let's remember that I work for these people—they pay my salary."

"Yeah, yeah. A crisis in every port. What's the big deal this time?" I moved in closer, resting my chin on his shoulder. This would be our last night together for a while.

"We're out to document illegal, unreported, unregistered fishing off the coast of West Africa—mostly Sierra Leone and Guinea. Pirate trawlers—Spanish probably, but flying some flag of convenience—are plundering those waters, throwing away everything except the prawns they're going to sell in Europe, leaving a stripped ocean floor to the Africans. I really did try to get out of this trip, though."

But there it was, just the tiniest undercurrent of anticipation in his voice. Maybe what I loved about him was his adventurous nature. Maybe I didn't want to settle down to a regular live-in lover anyway. Maybe I was going to quit arguing and make him really regret leaving me.

"This is a hell of a job," Joe admitted. "It's always suited me so well until now. But every time we say good-bye, I seem to be leaving you in some dangerous situation. You don't suppose you could stay out of the crime-fighting business for a while?" A deeply worried expression was etched in his face as he pulled me into his arms for an aching kiss.

"You have your missions, and I have mine," I said when we finally broke apart. "Gere is just as evil as any marauding fishing trawler—more so, in fact. Just come back soon—and safe. See if you can stay out of jail this time."

"You, too, sweetheart. Safe, I mean."

Tip, who was waiting in a newly rented car for Joe to drop him off at Jordan Hospital, looked away until we were finished kissing. Scruffy, however, stood on my foot protectively. He'd reached a kind of détente with Joe, but wasn't at all sorry to see him leave. *Want to go for a walk, Toots?* Scruffy cavorted merrily about as soon as the car drove out of sight.

"No walks now, Scruff. It's time to clean house!" Dragging his paws, Scruffy followed me inside, then trudged upstairs to the refuge of the blue bedroom the moment I hauled out his sworn enemy, the vacuum cleaner. Pavarotti's love arias played at top volume while I dusted and vacuumed and worried about which drawers or cabinets would most likely be opened by the children when they descended upon me. The medicine cabinets, of course, and the pantry.

I didn't know why I wanted everything to be absolutely perfect. *An herbalist is by nature a bit of a clutterer, so I might as well relax*, I told myself as I lined up the pantry's canned goods in military formation.

At Becky's Newton home, I'd noticed that she arranged her pantry in alphabetical order, but I decided to settle for logical groupings rather than to puzzle out whether pie fillings should be P or F. Cathy, on the other hand, was the daughter who used to stash dirty laundry under her bed and then complain to the neighbors that she had no clean clothes to wear to school. And Adam had lived in a never-never world of ham radio until he discovered the computer. Plates of food remnants stacked at his elbow, a dangerous maze of electronic hookups at his feet—but perhaps he had changed. I'd never seen his Atlanta apartment. *It would be a kindness not to come off as supremely-neater-than-thou to those two*, I thought. Nevertheless, I polished up the living room, dining room, and my bedroom. Then I searched through the refrigerator, wiping down shelves with a vinegar-dampened sponge. Not a wizened citrus, wilted lettuce leaf, nor molding cheese rind would escape this purge. When the inside of the refrigerator looked like a magazine ad, I turned to the rest of the kitchen. Ugh! The detritus of herbal experiments would have to go. I scoured the counters, put away the fixatives and odd jars of dried herbs, correctly labeled the new tea mixtures: Wise Woman, Celestial Calm, Harmony High, and ESP (Energy, Serenity, Power). Last, I washed the kitchen floor. Scruffy immediately ran downstairs for a long, dribbling drink of water. I booted him out onto the porch to let the floor dry, and while he was out there, brushed his fur, cleaned his ears, and inspected his teeth.

Ouch! Watch out! Easy! He wiggled with every assault on his person.

Would the children be staying overnight? Both guest rooms had twin beds, but Tip had laid claim to one half of the blue bedroom, and I wasn't about to disenfranchise him. Adam could bunk with Tip; the girls could have the rose bedroom. I hauled the vacuum cleaner to the stairs, much to Scruffy's disgust. Grumping loudly, he stalked away to my bedroom while I thumped up the steps. No doubt he'd make himself comfortable on my white chenille bedspread.

But once my cooking frenzy began, Scruffy appeared with a winning canine smile, sniffing appreciatively as he flopped onto his favorite braided rug in front of the rocking chair. *What's cooking, Toots?*

"This is not for you, Buster." I busied myself preparing New England summer standbys—poached chicken, new potato salad, deviled eggs, coleslaw.

I was just putting the finishing touches on a chicken salad with almonds and olives when Phillipa's BMW appeared in my driveway. Wearing black linen slacks, a black halter top, and a large-brimmed black hat—the very model of a modern witch—she carried a hamper whose top lids were bulging up. As she rounded the house, we began talking through the open windows before she ever got to the kitchen door.

"Deidre told me all three of your children are coming to visit," she called in through the first kitchen window. "I bet you're cooking up a storm."

"What's in the basket of goodies?" I wanted to know.

"Desserts, my dear! You know my freezer, otherwise known as Willy Wonka's Chocolate Factory," her voice carried through the second kitchen window. She ran up the steps lightly for someone who never spared the butter or cream, then pushed her way into the back door, hamper first. Scruffy jumped up excitedly, catching an enticing scent of the chocolate that he loved but wasn't allowed to have because it's poison for dogs. "You can never have too many desserts." She heaved the hamper onto the kitchen table, swept off her hat, and hung it on the rocking chair. "But you can have too many children, so I've heard. Are you okay with this? Is Joe looking forward to meeting your family?"

"Joe's gone to Spain. Some strip-fishing emergency off the coast of Africa. It's just that I don't know how long my three will be staying or what their agenda is. Adam had already left when I called back, and Becky hasn't answered my phone message yet. They're planning to visit Gary, too, but I won't have anything to do with that. And I'm wondering if Cathy has mellowed toward me."

"Must have, if she's coming to see you. Maturity. Life experience. Mom's not the enemy, after all." Phillipa's straight black hair fell forward in wings as she unpacked frozen, foil-wrapped bricks and disks with evocative names like *Devil's Enchantment.* "Now, don't you want to hear the latest about Gere?"

"*Of course* I do."

"The death of Officer Rosen has really galvanized the police force—you know how they are when one of their own gets killed. The Hawkins family and Candy have moved again, and Patsy with them—but you know that." Was it my imagination, or did Scruffy's ears prick up at the mention of Patsy? "And Stone has received a tip that someone answering Gere's description was in little Mattapoisett hardware store buying various supplies suitable for constructing a homemade bomb."

"Great Goddess! Who for, do you suppose?"

"Well . . . either he's found out where Candy is . . . or he's after *us*. He's a vengeful bastard, that we know. A history of murdering anyone who, in his mind, wrongs him. Started with that village in Vietnam. Then his faithless fiancée mysteriously dies in a gas explosion. Then the Donahues, maybe his first real hands-on killing. Freddie's letter bomb followed. Poor Ashbery. Officer Rosen and his patrol car. Gere's a madman, Cass. So, who do you think will be next on his shit list? Don't be surprised when Stone sends over a couple of guys in an unmarked vehicle to keep watch on your house. Our house, too . . . and the rest of the circle. Rather stretching Plymouth law enforcement to its limit, but he's had a lot of volunteers, retired guys and the like. We'll all be well guarded, in hopes of catching a cop-killer. Just look out the window, up there by the pines. See that old Pontiac that just drove in and parked?"

I peered out the window. Yes, there was an old blue-green sedan up there, nestled under the pine branches. "Well, that *is* a comfort. Tell Stone how grateful I am. But what will I tell Adam, Becky, and Cathy?"

"Oh, I don't know . . . private detectives? Lovelorn suitors? Bill collectors? You'll think of something." Phillipa's smile was fearless. "And don't neglect to do a protective ritual around the whole perimeter of your property. Sage, rosemary, sea salt . . . you know the drill. The moon is waning, so conditions are ideal for a banishing. I've already called Fiona, Heather, and Deidre."

"A visit from the prodigal daughter and her siblings. An exhusband in the wings. A raving lunatic lurking around in the bushes. Joe off somewhere saving the African fish. I don't know if I can stand the stress, Phil."

"Oh, of course you can." Phillipa brooked no cowardice. "Do your being-of-light meditation. Take a jasmine bath. Think good thoughts. And see that your grandmother's rifle is cleaned and loaded."

Lammas—First Harvest of Fruits and Grains

I really wasn't comfortable with rifles, so in the end I took only a part of Phillipa's advice. I could have asked Tip, who knew everything about cleaning, loading, and shooting, to get us into defensive order, but something inside me drew back from putting a rifle in a teenager's hands, even as seasoned a hunter as Tip. The jasmine bath, however, was as refreshing and energizing as always, even as I lay there in the fragrant bubbles wondering where Gere would strike next. And to think we had deliberately called him back! Yet I knew in my heart that it had been necessary. Now it was up to us to bring an end to Gere's terrifying campaign of revenge.

The hardware store clerk who'd waited on Gere told the police that he'd stepped outside for a cigarette just as Gere drove off in a black Buick. But Gere changed cars more often than some men changed their shirts. A stolen vehicle, I didn't doubt, soon to be swapped for another. But Gere would have to hole up someplace to set up his bomb-making shop, and that might give the police a chance to locate him before he could murder anyone else. Remembering Ashbery, I didn't much like the possible targets that Phillipa had presented to me. At least we knew he was planning on planting a bomb, not skewering anyone with a steel-tipped arrow. There would be time to forestall him.

The next morning, Becky's Land Rover, plastered with *Vote Ron Lowell for Representative* stickers, arrived precisely at ten, as she had promised. The house was shining, the kitchen fragrant with a Dutch apple coffee cake I'd just taken out of the oven. Scruffy was freshly bathed and brushed, not without consider-able back talk, especially concerning the stylish red bandana I'd knotted around his neck. And I, too, was smartened up in a motherly, suburban way, wearing an ecru linen sleeveless jumper, Italian leather low-heeled pumps, and a rope of chunky African beads Joe had given me.

The first surprise was that four young people, instead of the expected three, got out of the Land Rover. For a moment I thought it must be Ron who had decided to join them, but the fourth person was a soignée young woman with straight, short dark hair and a straight, short dark skirt.

The second surprise was that Cathy, my beautiful youngest child, immediately ran to my arms. Her silky, fair hair flying lightly around her, her smile luminous, she looked like a young Guinevere of the Summer Country. She felt as insubstantial as a bird; I wondered if she was still troubled by her old eating disor-der. I was unprepared for the rush of love and concern that flooded me. How long it had been since we were this close! Tears stung my eyelids.

Becky sailed in next, so mature and proper in her demeanor, so inoffensively stylish, she seemed already to have turned her-self into the quintessential candidate's wife. Only the least flicker deep in her dark blue eyes betrayed a spark of rebellion, which I took to be a healthy sign. And my handsome Adam, with the lean, muscular build of a baseball player, sandy-haired, his eyes as green as my own. Everyone hugged everyone, with Scruffy somehow managing to be between us every time.

"Who is *this* furry interloper?" Cathy crouched down to Scruffy's level. "It's surprising to see you with a dog, Mom. You never let us have one at home. I thought you didn't like them."

Scruffy sniffed Cathy's hair appreciatively. *She's okay. Does she play?*

It was Gary who didn't let us have a dog, but I didn't say that. "Oh yes, Scruffy's been my boon companion ever since I moved to Plymouth. Don't you remember my telling you about him?"

"Yes, of course." Cathy stood up, and the stranger stepped forward to take her hand, tugging a bit like a child who felt left out. "This is my partner, Irene, Mom." Cathy looked suddenly shy. "Irene, this is my psychic mom. You two will have so much in common."

I didn't think Cathy meant *business partner* or *half of my song-and-dance team* or *study buddy*. That left one startling possibility. I deliberately pushed away thinking about it right now, while I was in the midst of gloriously welcoming my family back into my life—and all at the same time! *That* was the miracle!

"I've heard so many fabulous things about you, Sandra." Irene's voice was deep and dramatic, unmistakably theatrical.

They must have met in some show Cathy was in, I thought. Adam had kept me informed of Cathy's few small triumphs between long stretches of waitressing.

"All true, I fear. Welcome, Irene. And it's *Cassandra* now—perhaps Cathy didn't realize that I'd changed my name. It's wonderful to meet you! Cathy's been on the West Coast so long, I've got ten quite out of touch with her friends." I tried to keep my tone cheery, not complaining, hoping I wasn't being disgustingly perky.

I served hot, strong coffee and apple bread on the small porch. There were only two wicker rockers, but Cathy and Irene settled themselves on the glider, and Adam sat cross-legged on the floor, his back to the railing and the Atlantic. The ocean was nearly smooth, thinly dappled with daubs of gray and blue in the still summer morning. Scruffy lay along the length of the small wicker coffee table, his nose close to Adam's hand, the one with a piece of apple bread in it. I sent him my best warning glare; he gave me the back of his head.

It was thrilling to have my three children gathered around me. My eyes kept threatening to overflow with embarrassing tears. I almost wished no one would speak. Let no old conflict or new worry break this harmonious mood.

Cathy was explaining that her own and Irene's substantial roles in a revival of *Carousel* had enabled them to put together some vacation money, which they'd decided to use to visit their respective families. Adam, Becky, and I would pass inspection okay, warmly hospitable to Irene and mannerly in general. I didn't know about Irene's folks, but it was inconceivable that they wouldn't love my ethereal, magical Cathy. "Now that you two are here, I hope you'll be staying for a while," I said.

"Just a week or so, Mom. There's a Webber opening rehearsals next month, and we need to be home for the tryouts in two weeks. Irene's never been to Boston, so we're going to cram in the whole tourist scene. Colonial Theater, of course—new production of *Long Day's*. Then all the out-of-towner's stuff— Faneuil Hall, the Freedom Trail, Museum of Fine Arts." Cathy laughed deprecatingly, then added that the four of them were planning to spend the day with me, then have dinner with "Daddy," and they certainly hoped I would join them. "It would be so nice, just like the old days," Cathy said. "I'd like Irene to know us that way."

"Sorry, honey. I'd love to have dinner with you any other evening. But Irene will have to know us the way we really are, which is divorced. I'm sure Becky has told you that I don't see your father."

"Yes, Mom's not into civilized divorce," Becky said, a crack showing in her serene armor. "Not even for my engagement. We had to take Ron's parents out twice to meet Mom and Dad separately. I'm sure they thought it was very strange, very unforgiving. It's not as if Dad was going to drink or anything. He's all over that."

"Oh, cool it, Becky," Adam said. "You had Mom and Dad together at your wedding, didn't you? And very gracious she was, too. So, let Mom have it her way without discussion for once. And let's change the subject. How's the computer working, Mom? Does that funky friend of yours still manage that end of the business?—the gal who calls me her 'hot line.' "

"She'll be sorry to have missed you." Or so I thought. But after a long walk on the beach to show Irene our "stern and rockbound coast," so different from the Pacific, Freddie turned up at my door while Adam was showing my herb gardens to Cathy and Irene, and Becky was in my bedroom, talking to Ron on her cellphone. I was setting out the lunch things, wondering what I'd do with that whole salmon I had languishing on ice for tonight's dinner.

"Yo, Cass! Heather told me you had company and might need some help in the kitchen." Freddie leaned over to pat Scruffy, who'd pranced in with her, and also to avoid my skeptical look. I was in some doubt that Heather had added that last part about "needing help." When Freddie stood up again and smiled innocently, I saw that she'd undergone another one of her amazing transformations, her hair all one color again, a vivid brown, and slicked back behind her ears—no jelled spikes on top—and she was wearing an actual dress. True, it was a tiny dress, clinging and low-cut, but in a very quiet shade of sienna that brought out the amber of her eyes. No exaggerated platform heels, just attractive sandals and a delicate ankle bracelet. No nose ring either. Two modest gold circlets, one in each ear. But she was holding a stick in her hand—the apple wand!

Scruffy, who'd also spotted the stick with interest, began tugging it playfully. *The girl is going to play fetch. Let's go. Let's go.*

Freddie wrested her wand away from Scruffy in one quick, baffling motion and laid it on the windowsill. "I don't have to eat, if there isn't enough," she offered, taking the plates out of my hand to set the table.

"Oh, don't be ridiculous. Set another place for yourself, and behave. I'm delighted to see you. How did you get here?"

"Heather loaned me Ashbery's old Dodge. I parked it up there on the hill beside the fuzz. Don't those guys ever take a break?"

"They change teams three times a day. I don't think Stone will be able to keep up this protection much longer. It's just too hard to justify."

I brought forth the cold dishes I'd prepared and unwrapped them, then began to slice the beautiful tomatoes that had been ripening on my kitchen windowsill. I noted that Freddie had carved a few runes into her wand; she must have been doing some studying. *Ger*, the rune of partnership and love, the marriage of heaven and earth. *Beorc*, rune of feminine energy and beginnings, breasts of the earth mother. This girl was definitely up to something.

Adam came in just then, his rugged frame somehow filling the room with a glow of warmth. "Hey, Ma, what are all those packages out in your garage? Hello, Freddie. Good to see you again." He seemed not to notice his instant effect on Freddie, who stood transfixed, a marble statue clutching a handful of silverware— *Pygmalion* in reverse.

"Oh, just some supplies I haven't had time to open yet," I said.

"Want me to open them for you? Got a box cutter?"

"*No!*" Hearing my own urgent tone, I tried for a gentler refusal. "No, thanks, honey. Can't have you working when we're sharing this lovely holiday."

Freddie came to life. "Might be a boom-boom in one of them, you know what I mean?" she said helpfully. "About that jerkface Gere and all?"

"Let's not go there, Freddie," I murmured.

Becky came into the kitchen just in time to hear Adam say,

"Jesus, Ma . . . are you two on some kind of witch-hunt again?" He looked back and forth between me and Freddie.

"Oh, Mother," Becky said. "You know you promised Ron and me that you'd keep a low profile while he's campaigning. I mean, if one whiff of some sort of Wiccan neighborhood crime watch gets out to the press, Ron will be swamped with embarrassing questions about my family when he should be talking about his vision for Massachusetts in the twenty-first century."

Cathy and Irene were now standing in the doorway, listening in silent fascination. I took advantage of that pause in the conversation to introduce Freddie all around as my associate in the Internet herbal business, with thanks to Adam for his magnificent gift and his electronic guidance. Then I busied myself filling a pitcher with iced herb tea and nudging my guests toward chairs. There was room to spare around my generous kitchen table, a long slab of weathered oak that doubled as a worktable. Scruffy could loll out full length underneath it, his personal den. He went to lie down there now, alert for anything tasty that might fall his way.

Ignoring my attempt to steer the conversation in a new direction, Freddie jumped in with, "I'm also Cass's protégée in Wicca. Cass is teaching me how to control my . . . well . . . my natural abilties."

"How perfectly fabulous!" Irene was all attention now. "What natural abilities are those? Astral travel? Precognition?"

"Oh, never mind that . . . do tell us about the San Francisco theater scene." I started bowls and platters passing around the table, wanting to pass the subject as well.

Explaining that she and Irene were vegans now, Cathy examined the potato salad closely before putting a dab of it on her plate. Fortunately, the hard-cooked eggs were on another platter, deviled. Quickly I scanned the table for vegan edibles. Tomatoes, coleslaw, and the breads, of course. No wonder Cathy was so fragile. My daughter was wasting away for lack of protein. Not to mention Vitamin B$_{12}$, found only in animal foods. My thoughts leaped to irreversible nerve damage.

"What's in this bread?" she demanded.

"Flour, water, yeast, and salt," I said. "The only legal French bread formula. Have some. I hope you two take multivitamins."

"You don't have to worry about us, Cass. I see to that. Go on about your natural abilities, Freddie." Irene took a slice of French bread and passed the basket to Cathy.

"Cass calls it psychokinesis," Freddie said. "That's the ability to move objects, especially metals, with thought power. Whoa! Am I getting vibes that Cass'd rather I didn't spill all that right now! So, okay . . . Cass wants to talk theater. I've never been to San Francisco, or the theater. I mean, other than the senior class play, directed by C. B. Demented, Miss Manson. Were you on a real stage, singing and dancing like the Rockettes in New York?"

Freddie was scooping chicken salad, sliced ham, and cheese onto her plate, never missing a beat of her monologue until Adam snickered over the Rockettes. She flushed then, and looked down at her lap. The fork beside her plate slid a fraction of an inch toward Adam, but I didn't think anyone else noticed.

"Say, Ma—I meant to ask you—do you know there's a couple of guys parked up under the pines?" Adam asked. "They've been there ever since we arrived."

"Just some retired cops keeping us safe. Please don't make a big deal out of it."

"Oh, no! Do you mean to say you're under police protection? *Ma* . . ." Everyone looked at me in varying degrees of dismay.

I got up to refill the iced tea pitcher, taking a moment at the sink to rest the cold pitcher against my forehead. The wand, I saw, was no longer on the windowsill. I glanced back at Freddie; she was holding it in her lap. A ray of sunlight, bouncing from window to the refrigerator handle, hit me right in the eyes. I felt dazed by it, overcome with weariness. I'd better sit down quick before I faint. Of all the times for this to happen!

As my consciousness leaped out of the present scene, my circle of guests faded away. I was in a van speeding along the highway. There was a Route 3 sign on the road ahead. Gere was at the wheel, and I was a wisp of myself, hovering invisibly above him. I could see his tonsure bald spot, his round face sweating and unshaven. A smile played across his pale mouth. There were two bulky bags on the seat beside him. He made a left turn. The sign said CLARK ROAD. I knew where that was but I couldn't say the words. I shivered and fell softly, quietly downward, like a maple seed drifting on the wind.

"She's not having a fit or anything," Freddie was explaining as I came back to myself. "It's this vision thing Cass does, then she sees things that are happening or will happen—awesome, isn't it? Bet you guys didn't get away with much when you were living at home. She'll be okay in a minute. Here, let me rub her wrists."

I felt Adam's strong arms around me, lifting me from the floor in front of the kitchen sink and gently setting me back onto my chair. I opened my eyes to a circle of concerned faces. "Damn and blast—why did this have to happen now?" I wailed.

Somehow I managed to pull the rest of the lunch together by not admitting to my headache and nausea and by adroitly turning the conversation back to everyone else's interests. That and a sharp kick to Freddie's ankle seemed to guide the party into safer waters.

"What did you see, Cass? Did you see Gere?" Freddie whispered while we were clearing the table.

"Later," I hissed. "What do you think you're going to do with that wand?"

"What? Oh, this? Shit, Cass—it's just a stick."

"Not in *your* hand, it isn't."

Freddie gave me a wicked grin and waved the wand toward my guests, who had changed into bathing suits and were carrying sand chairs to the beach steps. Could have been a coincidence, but I saw Adam turn his head to gaze intently at the window where we were standing.

"Cut that out, Freddie. He's much too old for you." I dialed Phil's number and got the answering machine. I dialed Stone's extension and got his voice mail.

"But what a hunk!" Freddie was frankly staring at Adam, who was poised on the top step near our totem pole, a parting gift presented to Joe by the Nuxalk nation. "Great buns."

"Listen, Freddie, pay attention. I want you to do something for me. Drive over to Phil's and wait for her. She's probably just gone to the store or something. Tell her that I've seen Gere. He was headed for an inland area, a cluster of small ponds: Long Pond, Little Long Pond, Gallows Pond, Bloody Pond, and some other I can't remember. Tell her to pass that on to Stone to check out, that my children are all upset with my involvement, so I can't leave now to chase down Gere. Say that I'll call as soon as they leave. They're having dinner with Gary, so I'll be free then. Can you do that?"

"Hey, is this for real, Cass? You're not just trying to get rid of me?" Obviously, Freddie had been looking forward to following Adam as soon as we finished in the kitchen. I wondered what kind of minuscule bathing suit she might have on under her dress.

"It's for real. A real vision."

"I'm on my way," said Freddie, gamely choosing adventure over romance. "I don't suppose you'll give Adam my love?"

"You can say good-bye yourself, if you connect with Phil early enough. But you drive carefully, you hear?"

Just before everyone left at six to meet Gary at Bert's Restaurant, Freddie careened into the driveway, and Tip arrived on the Animal Lovers company bike. I introduced the boy as Heather Morgan's right-hand man at the shelter, and explained that he was staying with me while his father was in the hospital. Nodding politely to everyone, his clear, gray gaze quickly sought out Freddie and stayed there, with that soft, wet, adoring look common to boys in the throes of their first love and puppies in search of a home.

Waving at the departing BMW, I wondered, despite promises to the contrary, if I'd really see Cathy again during the busy week they had planned. Cathy had wanted Irene and me to meet, had needed me to understand the nature of their relationship, and that requirement was now satisfied. Adam, of course, had to hurry back to his demanding job in Atlanta. Becky's involvement in Ron's campaign duties occupied much of her time and energy. I'd done what parents are supposed to do, raise the young to take off on their own, I thought dismally as I watched Becky's car disappear around the turn into the pines.

I shook my hands briskly to fling away negative thoughts. The bond of love would never be broken, even when we weren't a part of each other's daily lives. Pinching off a few slender stalks of blossoming lavender, I inhaled its bracing scent and stuck the tiny bouquet into my jumper's decorative high breast pocket where the fragrance would continue to refresh me. My children weren't the only ones who had taken wing; I was moving into a new life, too. Freddie and Tip both needed me, and they had become as dear as family. Joe would be coming home sometime soon, coloring my life with exotic passions and subtle shades of friendship. My Wiccan circle was strong and supportive. And I had a mission: stopping Gere before he killed anyone else.

"You talked to Phil. She talked to Stone," I verified the lines of communication with Freddie. "Right?"

"*Wrong.* I cooled my heels on the Sterns' patio for *hours*, then I figured it was really Stone you were after, so I drove over to the Middleboro HQ. The great man himself had just got back from some break-in over in Carver. So he's real surprised to see me, and he goes, 'Freddie, what are you doing here? Is everything okay?' And I go, 'Cass had this, like, dynamite vision of Gere at the ponds, Long Pond and the rest, and she wants you to check it out.' And he goes, 'Another vision, eh?' Looking up over his glasses, just like my high school principal, only cuter. And I go, 'Yeah, and you better believe it.' Not to worry, Cass. Message delivered, and Detective Stern is on the case. And by the way, don't bother to call your friend Phil. She's in Boston wining and dining with some high-flying foodies. Won't be back till the day after tomorrow. If any of you gals asked, she told Stone to say, 'In plenty of time for Lammas,' whatever that is. I'm guessing—summer sex magic?"

"Lammas, August 1, High Sabbat. First harvest of fruits and grains, last harvest of magical herbs, and that's what I should be doing right now, not chasing after apparitions. Although, who's to say what's the business of a witch? You'd know all about Lammas if you'd been studying those books I gave you. Beltane was sex magic, Lammas is a festival of bread and thanksgiving. Did Stone say he'd go after Gere right away?"

"Oh, yeah—Lammas. I remember. Stone promised he'd check it out. Send a patrol car and what-not. Asked me what Gere was driving. So I go, 'Sorry, Detective. Cass couldn't make the vehicle, except that it was some kind of van. But she did see a couple of packages lying on the front seat.' "

Sitting at the kitchen table with a glass of milk and a plate of lunch leftovers, Tip was following this exchange with avid interest, but without interrupting. The boy's talent for silent attention was quite unnerving.

I called Stone again, got the same voice mail. The desk sergeant said Stone was onto something and had left the building. "You can reach him, can't you?" I asked.

"Depends," said the sergeant, "who wants him, and why."

"Tell him it's Cass. Ask him to call me. It's the Thomas Gere case, and it's urgent." I gave him my cellphone number. I could have sworn he wasn't even writing it down.

Totally frustrated now, I decided the only thing left to do was to follow up the vision myself. What harm would there be in just riding through the pond roads with all my psychic senses open? Maybe some clue buried in that vision, some flicker of recognition would help me to identify Gere's car. But Gere knew I drove a Wagoneer. "Freddie," I said, "I'm going to borrow the Dodge for a little while, okay? Do you want to stay here with Tip, or shall I drop you at Heather's?"

"Hey, Cass, this is me, Freddie, not some kid." Casting a scornful look at Tip. "I know the score here. So you'd better let me drive. Otherwise you're going to be looking so hard for Gere you'll wrap yourself around a tree."

She had a point. "Tip, I'll leave you to take care of Scruffy. He hasn't had his dinner yet, and he'll need a good walk afterward."

How about some of that chicken and ham, Toots? At the mention of his name and the word "dinner" in the same breath, Scruffy was prancing around the kitchen on happy paws.

"He can have a few bites of the chicken in his chow, and a half can of dog food. No ham. No sweets. Two biscuits for dessert."

"Okay, Miz Shipton. But I don't think this is such a good idea. How about if you and Freddie just wait for the police to clear things up, arrest Gere and all. That dude is dangerous."

"Oh, cut out crying about danger, infant," Freddie said. "Cass and me will throw a hex into Gere, don't you worry."

Tip flushed, but that didn't stop him from continuing to give advice. "Please, Miz Shipton, if you latch on to Gere's trail, give Detective Stern a shout. Or if you can't reach the detective, call here, and I'll keep trying until I get him. This is, like, a hunting expedition, and we need to keep in contact, right?"

"Oh, sure," Freddie said. "First party to be charged by a rutting moose sounds the alarm, is that it? Should we maybe synchronize our watches?"

"He's making sense, Freddie." I warned her off teasing Tip and ostentatiously picked up my cellphone from the tiny kitchen desk, stashing it in my leather handbag. "I just hope this thing's still charged."

"Hey, Miz Shipton, if you call and don't get me, it'll be because I'm out with Scruffy for a few minutes." Tip's face was creased up like a worried old man. "So you'll keep trying, right?"

"Right. We only have a couple or three hours before dark, then we'll be back. No sense chasing around those ponds after sunset, when we don't even know what car we're looking for. So, you hold the fort for a while, okay?"

"You can count on me, Miz Shipton. See you later, Freddie."

"Later," Freddie echoed, not even glancing back at the eager boy.

"Tip's only a kid," I said to Freddie when we were under way in the Dodge. "You could be a little kinder and more understanding, you know." The air conditioning wasn't working, so we opened the windows to catch a breeze. Sultry summer poured in.

"I don't know what he keeps mooning around us for. Honestly, don't you get sick and tired of him and his long face and his daddy?" Traveling north on Route 3 to connect with Clark Road, Freddie was not letting the grass grow under our wheels. I realized that I'd never asked her whether she had a driver's license. Perhaps now was not the ideal time.

"No, I'm very fond of Tip—he's a fine boy. His father I can do without, though."

"So . . . if the old man drops off the twig, you're going to, like, send the boy back to his mom in Maine?"

"Not a great idea. The last time Tip was there, it got so bad with his stepfather, he ran away."

"Well, he's still got that uncle down in Wiscasset, right?"

"The uncle might not want to put a major crimp in his bachelor lifestyle." Freddie was taking me over ground I'd recently traveled in my own thoughts.

"Shit," said Freddie, swerving to avoid a cat streaking across the road.

I tried to distance myself from her angry aura, rather like the vibes that sometimes arise between step-siblings, so I could open myself psychically. It was a rare thing for me to enter that dimension on purpose—it's never failed to conjure up trouble and sorrow of the kind that eavesdroppers encounter—but I did so now.

Leaning my head back against the car seat, I tried to relax completely. I gazed intently at the slanting rays of sunlight where it gilded the landscape.

I thought: Let the light guide me and keep me safe.

"Okay, Clark Road comes to a dead end here. Hey, Cass—this is no time for a snooze. Left or right on Long Pond Road?" Freddie slowed the Dodge a bit to make a turn and tapped impatiently on the steering wheel with a shocking pink fingernail. All her fingernails were painted the same shade, and in a color not reminiscent of the dead. If only Adam would appear more often!

In my mind's eye, I saw water shimmering in that same shade of pink, then turning as dark as the Red Sea. Monuments of stone rose into view. "Go right," I murmured with great effort, caught in the lassitude of my vision. "Bloody Pond. Somewhere around there." I pulled out the crumpled bouquet of lavender and sniffed its revitalizing fragrance—better than smelling salts. I stashed it back in my pocket like a boutonniere. "If you see a cemetery, stop there."

"Shades of Edgar Allan Poe," Freddie said. "Is this for real, or have you been down this way before? Because, look—there *is* a little cemetery on the left side of the road. Awesome!"

"Take the dirt road just past the cemetery. Turns up by the cranberry bogs, I think."

Freddie made the turn as directed. In the midst of deep summer, the road was so overgrown as to be almost impassible. The Dodge bumped and bucked over the dry ruts. Thickly-leaved low branches whipped against the car; we rolled up our windows.

"Uh-oh," I said. "Better stop right here. I think there's a car blocking the way ahead of us. And a bog worker's hut on the right side of the road. We'd better retreat and call Stone."

"Jesus, Cass . . . there's no room to turn around here. I'll have to back up all the way."

"Then do it, Freddie." I heard and felt the rising anxiety in my voice. "Back up any way you can. And do it fast."

Freddie swiveled her head around easily—supple as a ballet

dancer—so she was looking straight into the road behind us. The tires dug in and last year's leaves sputtered and squished beneath our wheels. My insouciant driver navigated the Dodge to the rear on the rutted road between dense patches of woods. Even so, our progress was slow on the twisted route, often bringing us into danger of being wedged between slender birches and bushy pines.

While Freddie exercised her driving prowess, I tried in vain to rouse Stone at police headquarters. I have to admit that I'm not exactly proficient on the cellphone, and often have been known to cut off my own calls, so I wasn't exactly surprised to find I was having trouble making a connection. After a few feverish tries— as we bumped backward—I pressed the digit 1, which was set to dial my own house, and got through immediately to Tip. Relief poured through me like cool water.

"Hi, Tip. Now don't you be worrying. I want you to catch Detective Stern as soon as he's available. Tell him to check out a cranberry worker's hut on Bog Hill Road near Bloody Pond *right away*. I think Gere's holed up in there."

"You bet, Miz Shipton. And I'll call to let you know as soon as I have an answer. I got your cellphone number right here. But . . . you're not anywhere near Bog Hill, are you? Stern is going to say for you to get out, you know. They're probably going to want the place clear for a SWAT team."

"We're backing up out of Bog Hill Road right now. Freddie's driving. Listen, get off the phone and make your call. Talk to me later. *Oh, oh.*" I punched the "end" button just as Freddie came to a crashing halt. We still had about a quarter of a mile to go.

I swiveled around to see why she'd braked so fast. Great Goddess! There was Thomas Gere in the flesh, standing in the middle of the road holding a crossbow with what looked like a steel-tipped arrow. The only way out of there would be to drive straight through him. *Good idea!* was the thought that flashed through both our minds without the need for conversation. Freddie started the motor revving again, her mouth set in a grim line, her chin staunch with determination. "Try to go around him, Freddie. We can't just run him over . . ."

"We sure as shit can . . ." Freddie pressed her foot all the way down on the gas, causing the Dodge to hurtle in reverse, barely missing Gere as he jumped smartly to one side. We got about thirty yards beyond him when both of the back tires blew. Later, when I had time—too much time—to think about it, I realized that he'd spiked the road behind him. But right then, I couldn't make my brain think of anything. Gere dropped the bow and yanked the driver's side door open. In one quick, powerful motion, he pulled Freddie off the wheel into his arms, holding a gleaming hunter's knife to her throat. I could see it pressing into her flesh.

"So it's you two fucking witches again! You were together at the funeral, too." He hissed the words out between clenched teeth. "Shipton, is it? Called the police, have you?"

"They're on their way now, Gere. You'd better drop the girl and run as fast as you can." Freddie was making no sound at all, her eyes wide with horror. I could not only imagine what she felt, I could feel it myself, the nemesis of a clairvoyant—blood turned to icy slush, chills galloping from neck to spine to fingertips. I prayed Gere wouldn't harm her before taking off to save himself. Just when you need it most, spiritual protection is hardest to summon.

He smiled, his pale, round face glistening with sweat, his glasses glinting in the lowering sun, opaque as mirrors. "Get out of the car, and give me your cellphone, Witch Shipton," he said. I did as he asked with shaking hands. Just underneath the phone, I could feel the travel-size can of hair spray in my bag. If I sprayed it in his eyes, would he still be able to harm Freddie? Too close to risk.

"Please don't hurt the girl," I pleaded. Meekly handing over the cellphone, I let my mind flip madly through every conceivable wild scheme to defend ourselves. With his right arm still holding Freddie tightly against him, the knife at her throat, he took the phone with his left hand and stuffed it in his pocket. Looping my leather handbag over my shoulder, I got out of the car gingerly, like someone who'd been injured, but actually it was Freddie's feelings that were hurting me. Her denim bag was still in the car. Good—that would let Stone know we hadn't left willingly.

The car parked ahead, which must be Gere's, wouldn't be able to drive past the Dodge, disabled and squat in the middle of the road. The road didn't go much farther, just turned around the bogs and came back this way. Where could he take us? Would he hold us as hostages in that hut, soon to be surrounded by Stern's SWAT team? The blast of hatred coming off Gere seared the air between us. I knew by the images flashing up before me that this man wanted us dead, and worse than dead. There was no hope that a negotiator would talk him into letting us go. It took only a microsecond to reach the only logical conclusion. This was a single combat—him or us.

"Walk ahead of me to the cabin, witch." His voice was ugly and rasping, thick with threat. He tightened his hold on Freddie. I saw a trickle of blood at the place where his knife blade pressed against her throat. I had no choice but to stumble ahead. "Look straight ahead and move it!" he ordered.

Keeping my bag close, I did as I was told. It wasn't far, but it seemed as if that short walk to the cabin took hours. I could hear Freddie whimper from time to time—Gere's rough hold and the pressure of the knife must be painful. Sweating from fear and dreading the black hole of the cabin door, I stopped frozen on the threshold. His foot kicked me through. I sprawled on my knees. My bag went flying off into a dark corner. Spinning around as fast as I could, I sat on my backside on the rough floor. I had to see Freddie. And I had to see what Gere was going to do.

He pushed Freddie down beside me, holding the knifepoint between him and us. His smile was a repulsive sight. As he reached down beside the door, I saw there was a knapsack and another bulky thing sitting there. In an almost leisurely fashion, he stuck the knife in his belt, reached into the knapsack, and took out a neat, small gun, which he pointed directly at my head. A flood of emotions darkened my sight.

We can't end here, like this!

As if he read my thought, he laughed with malevolent pleasure. Without taking his gaze away from us for a moment, he removed a coil of nylon rope from the second bag, something like an airplane carry-on, this one bulging with lumpy packages. He flipped the knife out of his belt, awkwardly cutting two lengths of rope with his left hand. He tossed one at Freddie.

"Turn around, witch. And you, Freddie, my little spy, you tie her hands together really tight, because if I see even a fraction of an inch of slackness, I'll shoot her in the head and have done with it. Fast! Make it fast! We don't have much time."

I turned around immediately. "Do exactly as he says," I said to Freddie with as much reassurance in my tone as I could muster. Freddie worked quickly; a minute or two later she was done, and my wrists told me she had followed directions too well.

Pushing me into a corner with his foot, Gere ordered Freddie to face the wall. He used the second length of rope to tie her wrists behind her back, always keeping the gun near his hand. I kept hoping she'd seize some moment when his head was turned, checking on me, to jump out the door, but she did not. She knew I would die if she ran.

Then it was done. We were both trussed up, but still alive. It's true that life is hope, and I had not given up. Deep inside me that little flame was still flickering. Gere threw the knapsack over his shoulder and picked up the carry-on with his left hand, the right holding the revolver steadily pointing toward us. "Get cracking," he growled. "We're getting out of here."

We stumbled out the door. It had been dark in the cabin, some old rags shielding the few windows. Now the sunshine made us blink and squint. With the gun as a pointer, Gere waved us behind the cabin, then pointed toward an impenetrable stand of bushes, a wall of leaves and entwined twigs. "Go through right by that maple tree. You can do it, if you turn sideways. Either that, or I'll finish this right here and now."

"Someone will hear the shots," I said lamely. Did I hear the wail of a siren in the distance?

"Can't be helped. But you're right. I do prefer the bow for just that reason." Gere's voice was almost pleasant now, which was even more terrifying. "Now go or die here!"

We went. I'd motioned Freddie to go first, and I followed her. Carefully edging around the maple. Without our hands as shields, the prickly bushes scratched our arms and faces. Beyond the maple we saw that a trickling brook, hidden away in these dense woods, eased its way in the general direction of the bogs.

"Walk in the water, upstream," Gere commanded. With my back to him, I ducked my head down, and with my teeth, pulled out a sprig of lavender from my pocket. When I heard Gere lurch and curse, I opened my mouth and let the sprig drop on the bank of the brook just as we entered the water, praying he wouldn't notice the slight thing fall to the ground. But when I glanced back, I saw that Gere had tramped right over it as he entered the brook.

Gere was wearing heavy leather work boots, but we were not so stoutly shod, especially Freddie, who was wearing those sandals with insubstantial straps. My low-heeled pumps were not much better, the leather soles treacherous when wet. The chilly water was ankle-deep, the brook's bed slippery with worn-smooth stones and uneven places that continually tripped us. We inched along without arms to balance and hands to steady ourselves. Sliding and stumbling were inevitable. Freddie managed to keep upright, but once I sat down rather heavily. A sharp stone rapped my coccyx. Gere picked me up roughly and shoved me ahead of him. "Clumsy bitch," he muttered. "You slow us up, and you're herring food."

That hidden brook went a surprisingly long way through the woods. When we arrived at a mini-waterfall where it poured over some galactic round boulders, Gere allowed us to step out onto a stand of pine. Ordering us to stop, he checked the bonds at our wrists. While he was peering at Freddie, I dragged out another sprig of lavender with my teeth and let it drop. In my mind's eye, I could see a vision of Tip crouched down at the cranberry bog cottage, examining the ground for clues.

Satisfied that we were still helpless, Gere shoved us forward through the trees. It was easier going now, less underbrush. The pine-needle carpet was thick and soft, cushioning the sound as Gere prodded us, literally, with the gun. I judged us to be traveling northeast, which proved accurate enough when we emerged at tiny Dugway Pond. Around one side of the pond, there was a cluster of small summer cottages looking desolate and uninhabited—no children, no dogs visible—although there was an old Pontiac in one driveway and a black Chevy van in another. It was getting late. The sky through the tree branches reflected a rosy pink from the setting sun, but the woods were now quite dark. I saw a light click on in one of the cottages, the one with the Pontiac. Would someone hear me if I screamed? Maybe, but we'd be dead a minute later.

I hadn't dared to ask any questions. I'd been fully occupied with keeping myself from falling and trying with all my spiritual force to cast a protective aura around Freddie and me, a difficult thing to do when one is already frightened out of one's wits. But now, after what seemed like an hour of tramping in silence, I got up the nerve to ask, "Where are we going?"—not knowing if I really wanted to hear the answer.

The answer was laughter, a low, giggling burble that teetered on the edge of madness. Gere dropped his carry-on, fished out car keys, and opened the back door of the black van with his left hand. The little gun, always pointed at one of us, never slackened for an instant.

When Gere turned toward me, I saw Freddie glaring at the back of his neck, mouthing some words silently. A curse, certainly. Gere actually stumbled forward, but caught himself and whirled around. But Freddie was faster, looking at the ground

with a meek expression. I used that split-second when his attention was fully on Freddie to pull out and drop another sprig of
lavender.

Gere must have stashed a backup getaway vehicle at this deserted cottage while he'd been holed up in the cranberry bog
hut. Quick and clever, he'd been trading stolen car for stolen car
ever since this manhunt began.

"Get in there, bitch," he said, shoving me into the van. "Your
Girl Friday will ride in front with me. Can't have you two working on knots, now, can we?" Freddie and I simply looked at each
other, saying with our eyes that we were still alive, still intent on
saving ourselves, and our chance would come. Freddie's face was
ashen but calm. The thin line of blood on her throat looked like
a scarlet ribbon choker. I crawled into the van as she turned to
step up into the passenger seat.

"I have to pee," Freddie said, her first words since Gere had
taken us.

"Tough titty, little spy." Gere laughed again, a shade more
sanely this time.

"Be a shame to let go right here in your van." I couldn't see
Freddie's face, but her tone was bold and firm.

"You better hold it tight, if you know what's good for you.
You'll get your chance in a few minutes," Gere said. I tried to figure out what that meant—in my mind's eye, I saw a shadowy
building.

It wasn't a long trip—I judged just a few miles before the van
stopped again. Before the back door opened, I dropped another
sprig—my trail of bread crumbs. Then I was hauled out of the car
in that purple hour of twilight that is nearest to full darkness.
"Get out and get inside," Gere snarled to me. Freddie was already standing beside the car, the gun held against her back.
Gere was still carrying his knapsack on one shoulder, the carry-on
in his left hand. I dragged my gaze away from the gun to see
where we were—it was the deserted parking lot of a school—a
school I knew. I'd been here before with Deidre, to pick up

Jenny, who was enrolled in a summer course of remedial reading to combat her dyslexia.

"What do you want here?" I asked, but I already knew the answer. Everything in my stomach wanted to rise up out of my throat, but I fought down the nausea. I thought about Denise Donahue, smothered in a plastic bag. I would not go quietly. He would have to fire that gun if he wanted to kill me or Freddie. Maybe someone, hearing a gunshot in this residential area, would call the cops.

"Straight ahead, both of you. Not a sound or you're dead." Gere gestured to the basement door. At the few metal stairs that led downward to the basement, Gere dropped the carry-on just long enough to reach ahead of Freddie and open the door with a key. I wasn't even surprised that he had one—he seemed capable of anything. But I used that blink of time to spit the rest of the lavender onto the stairs.

We entered a large playroom, smelling faintly of cookies and sneakers. Gere pushed us toward the little stage at one end. "There's a john on the right." He opened the door halfway to reveal a single lav and looked at his watch. "If it takes you more than one minute to piss, I'm shooting your friend here."

Freddie dashed in sideways, leaving the door ajar, not fully open. I heard her relieve herself and wondered, since I couldn't see her, how she'd managed it with no hands. She was back in a few seconds.

"My turn," I said. Listening to Freddie had made the matter truly urgent.

Gere looked at his watch again. "Half a minute," he growled.

Inside the lav, I looked around for anything I could use to cut my bonds. The place was disappointingly clean and empty. Using the side of my arm, I worked my dress up over my hips and peed through my panties. It was drippy, but it was better, by a very small margin, than having it run down my leg. A few moments later, I was back beside Freddie. I felt disgusting.

"Get your asses over there," Gere ordered, gesturing to a door at the opposite end of the room from the stage and lav. Again, he put down the carry-on so that he could throw open the door while keeping the gun pressed against Freddie's back. We were in the true basement now, a room of massive gray pipes.

Gere marched us to the other side of an enormous furnace where there was a cubicle furnished with an old oak desk, a matching swivel chair, an army cot, and a small TV on a triangular shelf—the janitor's quarters. He lined us up facing him, our backs to the cot.

"I want you to know this, bitch-witches. You made a fatal mistake when you chased after me." Gere almost spat at us, his breath fetid, his eyes empty of any human emotion. "I always pay my debts. Now it's your turn, and the blond witch, too, with the cute little girl. I'm going to take care of the others as well before this night is through. Turn around and face the wall. Goodbye, witches."

The gray expanse of the wall was punctuated only by a slick, new *Sports Illustrated* swimsuit calendar. That was my worst moment yet. As our knees pressed against the cot's edge, I felt certain that my last sight on earth was going to be that red-haired model smiling over her shoulder with the thong of a blue bathing suit running up the crack of her behind. Gere was going to shoot us in the back. "I'm so sorry you're here, Freddie," I said. "I love you a lot."

"Me, too. Never say die, Cass," Freddie answered, a break in her voice.

Then for a fleeting moment, I was certain that I was dead. There was a searing pain, and all sensation of life departed in a flash.

When I woke up, my head pounding like the mother of all hangovers, I was lying on the cot on my side, still facing the wall. Not only my hands but my feet, too, were bound in excruciatingly tight ropes, and my mouth was closed with tape. I could taste stomach acid. With agonizing slowness, I turned my body around. It was dark, but not completely; a light seemed to be shining in another part of the basement. My heart as well as my head was pounding—what would I see? What had become of Freddie?

In the dim light of the janitor's cubicle, I saw that Freddie was tied into the swivel chair, bound hand and foot as I was, with a similar strip of duct tape over her mouth. As my eyes grew accustomed to the gloom, I saw a wincing expression in her half-closed eyes, now ringed with running mascara. It looked as if she, too, had been hit over the head with the revolver and only recently had come to her senses again. She gestured with a feeble tilt of her head toward the desk. I looked. In the middle of the blotter sat an ugly, squat box. Wires ran from the box along various pipes in the ceiling. A digital read-out in red numerals shone cheerily in the murky gloom of the basement. As I watched, the second hand moved, then moved again.

What time did the janitor come to work? His cleaning routine must begin when the summer school program closed for the day. On Sunday, he wouldn't have been here at all—a clear field for Gere. With my hands tied behind me, I couldn't see my watch. The teachers would unlock the doors at seven-fifteen in the morning, and the children would begin arriving as early as seven-thirty. I knew that Deidre would be dropping off Jenny at quarter to eight. Soon a hundred or more children will have gathered for reading workshops and math reviews. Looking at Freddie, I could see these thoughts mirrored in her eyes. She tilted her head toward the wall behind the furnace, a place she could see but I couldn't. There must be a clock on that wall.

Freddie shut her eyes twice, waited a moment, then blinked two times again. She was telling me the time. I nodded. We had perhaps six hours before that lethal little robot, the bomb Gere had left, was going to blow up, taking us and everyone else in this building to Summerland.

If eyes could speak, mine, looking fixedly at Freddie's, said, *What can we do?* and hers replied, *I will try.* She nodded at me once, then swiveled her chair around so that she was facing the bomb. I knew, as if she had spoken aloud, that she would attempt to stop or at least slow the clock mechanism. However impossible that seemed, there was at least a chance. I wondered if I could send her some of my energy, providing I had any left. Why not? Isn't that what we did at every Sabbat and Esbat? Conjure up energy and send it off to accomplish our wishes?

Closing my eyes, I began by invoking the spirits of the four directions, summoning the energy that each could impart—and then I reached out to the infinite force of the universe, male and female—the Creator of all. Make of me a channel, I prayed. Send your power through me to help Freddie, who can move things with her mind. Send your power through me to warn the others—Dee, Heather, Phil, Fiona. *Stop Gere! Stop Gere!*

If the natural psychokinesis Freddie could unleash against the bomb miscalculated even a little bit, if she didn't control it as carefully as a laser beam and it came up in its poltergeist mischievous guise, it was possible that the device would detonate early. Perhaps before the school opened. Goddess knows I didn't want to die, but if I had to die, the end would be quick, and a premature explosion would save lives.

As I continued to send all the energy I could gather to Freddie, I felt as if I were one huge, beating heart sending my essence out in waves. At that point, from terror, fatigue, and a kind of weakness that was probably hunger I couldn't feel, I entered some kind of timeless state, a fugue. I was conscious of where I was but unconscious of the passing of moments, minutes, hours, suspended in another dimension, the place between the real world and the world of spirit.

I had no idea of how late—or early—it was when I heard the sound of heavy feet running. Then a bright light was in my eyes, blinding me. It was as if I were being blasted out of a dream, only I hadn't been sleeping, exactly.

"Okay. It's okay. You're okay, Cass," a voice said to me, then in a louder tone, "Get the bomb squad in here." What a welcome sound! It was Stone's voice, and beside him a guy looking like Darth Vader was swinging an automatic weapon around to sweep the room.

I tried to speak. I couldn't. I felt a sharp, stinging sensation across my face. The tape had been ripped off. I took a deep breath. "Freddie," I gasped. Across the room I could see her, still focused on the black box and the red digital readout. Two more black-armored men picked her up, chair and all, and ran with her through the basement into the playroom. A thrill of joy swept through me. Stone was cutting my bonds with a knife. My hands, bloodless and numb, were free to move. Then my feet. He took my hand, clasped one long, strong arm around me, and bundled me toward the door. Two more guys, in helmets and padding, pushed past us going in the opposite direction. "They better stay out of there," I mumbled. "What time is it?"

"They're going to defuse the thing. It's six-thirty, Cass, and all's well. If the school doesn't blow up, that is. We've got Gere in Jordan Hospital under police guard. Fiona spotted him moving around her house in the middle of the night, and she shot him. Got him in the foot, then called Phil."

That's as much of an update as I got before I found myself in an ambulance with Freddie. We threw our arms around each other, crying out so many things we'd wanted to say for hours that neither one of us could understand the other. Then we were rushed into separate cubicles in the Emergency Room at Jordan. Beyond wrist and ankle abrasions, sore mouths, stiff muscles, aching groins, dehydration, empty stomachs, and filthy clothes, we were fine. We were better than fine—safe, secure heroes surrounded and embraced by a loving circle of friends. Phillipa, paler than I'd ever seen her, was pouring Freddie and me cups of a hot liquid out of a thermos—very sweet, very strong tea. Deidre, her face tear-streaked, her mouth softened with overflowing emotions, unable to speak. Fiona looking triumphant, in full glamour. Heather and Dick Devlin, close to each other, both

smiling broadly, gingerly hugging Freddie while she sipped the
reviving liquid.

"Is Tip all right? Scruffy? Tell me everything that happened,"
I demanded. "And let's go home. I don't even want to be in the
same hospital with Gere."

"Tip's already at the house with Scruffy. But boy and dog have
been out with Stone tracking you two most of the night."

"I've got to crash," Freddie said in a weak little voice. "I think
I fried my brain. Maybe I better give up on this psychokinesis
thing."

"No way," said Phil. "Wait until you hear what you did."

"Nobody talks until these girls get a shower," Phillipa ordered, as Heather, Dick Devlin, Deidre, and Fiona crowded into
the house with us. Tip and Scruffy leaped up to greet us, each in
his own way, Tip with blazing smiles and Scruffy with licks and
scoldings. *Hey, Toots, where were you? You shouldn't have gone away
without me. The boy and I got hungry and tired looking for you in the
woods.*

Phillipa hustled Freddie into the first-floor bathroom and then
helped me to the second floor. At that point, I needed her strong
arm. I was near collapse. Scruffy wedged himself on the other
side as we went up. He refused to leave the bathroom while I
bathed, although the wintergreen in my body-soother bath mix
makes him sneeze.

When we gathered in the kitchen again, Phillipa was fussing
over a soup pot on the stove. Freddie was wrapped in a terrycloth
robe. I was warm and comfortable in my soft old sweats, a towel
turban around my hair, ensconced in my padded kitchen rocker.
At last we heard, in various installments, from several sources,
the rest of the story of Sunday night and Monday morning—the
saga of how we were saved.

After Tip's call, Stone and the SWAT team had swarmed into
the woods at Bog Hill Road. They found Ashbery's Dodge with

two flat tires and Freddie's denim shoulder bag on the front seat, then a second car, an old Chevy, abandoned farther along the road. Scouring the woods, the officers came across the discarded crossbow. When they broke into the shack, my leather handbag was still in a dark far corner. A workbench revealed snippets of wire, a dusting of powder, and a forgotten pair of pliers. It was clear to the men that Gere had been there, possibly constructed an explosive device, but somehow had escaped without his vehicle, taking Freddie and me as hostages.

Gere couldn't be very far ahead of the SWAT team, Stone decided. He called Tip at my house, just to rule out our return by some other means. But Tip hadn't heard from us again. Stone told the boy that Gere must have gone through the woods with the two of us on foot.

"Listen, Mr. Stern—I been trained to track through the woods down Maine," Tip declared. "You better get me over there before the signs are lost with all those SWAT guys trampling the trail." Stone mulled that over. It was unconventional, and might get him into trouble later, but he dispatched a patrol car to transport Tip and Scruffy to the scene. He also called Phillipa, who roused the circle to action.

"Look here," the officer driving the patrol car complained to Tip. "No one said nothing about a dog."

"Scruffy's an unofficial search-and-rescue dog," Tip said. "Detective Stern has used him before, in that case of the missing boys last year."

When they arrived at the scene, Stone equipped the boy with a cellphone that clipped to his belt and a powerful flashlight. The oncoming darkness hadn't prevented Scruffy from picking up my scent at the cabin and following it out back to the maple tree where we'd penetrated the woods. But after trailing us to the brook, the dog had stopped in confusion, snuffling up and down the banks and yipping in distress. It was Tip who'd found the sprig of lavender crushed in the mud by Gere's boot.

"Look, Miz Shipton was here all right, and I bet she left us a sign on purpose. They must've gone upstream. Downstream would have taken them smack into the SWAT team," the boy told Stone. "I'm going to follow the brook until I find where they got out—it has to be there along the bank somewhere. Be a lot easier in daylight, but I done night tracking, too. And nothing will stop Scruffy if we pick up another scent."

"Go," Stone said. "And keep that dog on leash. I don't want to be hunting him, too. The instant you find anything, hit the number 1 button on the phone—it's set to ring me. And listen—this is important—don't try to do anything or accost anyone on your own! We'll all be out searching the woods, but you're right, we are going to trample the ground, so I'm giving you a few minutes head start while I round up this crew and divide the territory."

Meanwhile, Phil talked to everyone in the circle. News of our probable abduction got everyone moving. Phillipa joined forces with Heather at her house so they could keep an eye on the well-being of the dogs while Gere was on this vengeful path. Fiona and Deidre, both housebound with children, decided to team up at Deidre's. That way, Fiona would stay with Laura Belle and Bobby when it was time for Deidre to take Jenny to summer school. No one knew yet that Gere had rigged the building.

At this point in the story, Deidre cursed roundly, belying her girlish prom-queen persona. "I had *no idea* what that madman had conceived," she wailed. "I'll always wonder if some warning would have clicked in before . . . before—" She stopped abruptly with her hand on her stomach.

By the early hours of Monday morning, they were all picking up urgent danger vibes, and they responded with every protective spell in their grimoires. While they waited for Stone to report his progress in finding Gere and his hostages, Fiona borrowed a silver pentagram from Deidre and began dowsing over a map of Plymouth.

*   *   *

Tip moved slowly along the brook, keeping Scruffy not only on leash but on heel as much as possible, to prevent the dog from trampling the sign. He could hear Stone's team crashing and thrashing through the underbrush somewhere behind him. Although the moonless night made the woods seem nearly impenetrable, Tip moved with an ease born of natural talent and experience, slowly scanning every inch of the brook's banks with his flashlight as he went. At home in the woods, he was unfazed by tracking alone at night.

Telling this part of the tale, Tip grinned in triumph. "Took a while before I seen that sign you left near the little waterfall. You know, where you got out of the stream and headed toward Dugway. No problem for Scruffy to pick up your scent once you got out of the water. And I could see your tracks, no prob—'specially with wet shoes, you going first, then Freddie's sandals and the man's big boots. But Scruffy was way ahead of me. He pulled so hard at the leash, I had to run to keep up with him."

The nose is quicker than the eye. Scruffy looked from Tip to me with the canine equivalent of a supercilious smile.

"When we got to the end of the track, Scruffy ran around and around, nosing that scrap of motor oil on the driveway and your footprints, where they ended, and that last sign you left, the herb twig like the others. So I called Stone. He was there, like, in two minutes, and the officers rapped on every door, even woke up a guy in the last cottage."

"Lavender. It was the lavender that I had in my pocket. Pontiac in the driveway?" I asked, sipping at the mug of strong chicken broth that Phillipa had thrust into my hand.

"Yep. Turns out the guy in the cottage seen something Sunday evening. A black van, might have been a Ford, and some little gray man that had been living in that cottage off and on. Only this time he was with a woman and a girl. Something looked funny about the way the three of them acted, but not funny enough for this guy to call 911. He watched them out his bedroom window, though—and he remembered that the license plate began with LS."

"Hey, Tip. Got to hand it to you. You were awesome," Freddie said. "Maybe sometime you could show me how you do this tracking business. I like to learn hot new things."

Tip couldn't have looked more pleased if he'd won a gold medal at the Olympics.

In the early hours of Monday morning, Stone called Phillipa to let her know they'd reached an impasse. Gere had eluded them in the woods and got through to his backup vehicle stashed at Dugway Pond. He'd been seen to drive off with Cass and Freddie. There was an APB out for the black van, possibly a Ford, license plate beginning with LS—"Approach with caution, suspect is a white male, armed, and has two hostages." Every patrol car was out looking for Gere, but the trail had gone cold.

"Listen, Stone," Phillipa said, "Fiona called. She's been dowsing. She says the van is no longer on the road. It's parked somewhere near Indian Hill. She thinks she might actually be able to pinpoint the exact street if she had her own pendulum, that crystal thing she favors, but she's at Deidre's. She's driving home now to get the crystal. I know I said I'd leave your line free, but I'm going to call you if anything develops. Fiona is an incredible finder."

Fiona found an amazing thing, indeed, while she was in her own house at three that morning, looking for the crystal, which Omar had buried. Just as she reached under the tasseled velvet cushion that the cat preferred and closed her hand around the familiar coolness of the crystal pendant, she heard a strange noise outdoors.

"It was a kind of scratching against the house, as if someone were fastening something on the electric meter," Fiona explained. "I didn't like it. Sure, it could have been a raccoon, but why were the hairs standing up on my neck, and on Omar's neck, too, for that matter? So I crept quietly into the kitchen, which was still dark. I'd only turned on one lamp in the living room, you see, because I had a very good idea that my darling might have hidden my crystal in the special place where he likes to keep his treasures. He's such a little devil!"

"Yo, Fiona," Freddie prompted. "Get back to the noise under the window."

"Oh, yes, that. As I say, the vibes were speaking to me loud and clear, so I armed myself with that pistol my late husband gave me. He always used to worry so when he was off fishing that someone would break in and harm me. What a grand, thoughtful man he was!"

"Earth to Fiona," Freddie insisted. "And *then what?*"

"Well, I took a moment to put on a shadowy glamour—have I told you girls about that one?—and I opened the window ever so softly. I could see his head bending over a package—I recognized the tonsure, you know—and I said, 'Good evening, Mr. Gere. What are you doing there?'" Fiona laughed, that deep infectious chuckle that came from deep within her. "You never saw such a shocked expression as was on Mr. Gere's face when he looked up and saw, what? A shadowy kind of thing speaking to him, I guess. He started back, holding the package. I thought he was going to throw it at me, I honestly did. And the next thing I knew, he was lying on the ground, screaming and holding his foot. When I looked at the pistol in my hand, I realized it had gone off all on its own, more or less. Maybe the ghost of my departed sweetheart . . ."

"Oh, knock it off, Fiona. You shot him, and that's that," Phillipa said with some satisfaction. "It's not magic, but it's damned effective."

Fiona called Phillipa, her voice trembling as she tried to explain what had happened.

"Are you hurt? Is Gere there now?" Phillipa demanded.

"You'd better hurry, dear. I think he's trying to crawl away. It's his foot, you know. I don't want to have to shoot him again. Maybe I could just hit him over the head. Now, where did I put my cast iron frying pan?"

"I have to hang up now, Fiona. For Goddess' sake, don't do anything else!" Phillipa yelled into the phone. A moment later she was alerting Stone. Several patrol cars rushed to Fiona's, and Gere, who'd left a trail of blood as he crept into the shadows, was taken into custody. They found the black van parked on a side street two blocks away. Even before the rescue wagon arrived, Stone tried to get Gere to talk, threatening to let him bleed to death if he didn't tell where he'd imprisoned his hostages. Gere just gritted his teeth and laughed as Stone pulled him back to where the lights from patrol cars shone into Fiona's front yard. At one point, Gere tried to reach the package he'd dropped, but Stone stepped on his hand. The bomb squad arrived to take charge of the package, bearing it away in the "bomb pot" to the vacant field where they could dispose of it properly.

All the way to the hospital, Stone badgered Gere, and Gere turned his head away. The only words that passed through his lips were, "Those bitches deserve what they're going to get." After that, he was silent. The trauma unit at Jordan Hospital sedated him and got to work.

Before he left to accompany Gere to the hospital, Stone had warned Fiona that shooting a man, even an intruder, with an unregistered pistol was going to take some explaining, but that would come later. She seemed too shaky and distracted to take it all in, so Stone had directed the driver of a patrol car to drive her back to Deidre's. Tip and Scruffy were sent along home at the same time. Although drooping with fatigue, they complained mightily about being benched just when the action was heating up. "You've done enough—and what you did was great—but tracking won't help us now." Stone ruffled Tip's hair and patted Scruffy, but remained firm.

At Deidre's, after a restorative cup of tea with a liberal shot of Irish whiskey in it, Fiona continued to dowse over the Plymouth map, this time using her powerful crystal pendant. Before Gere woke up in a hospital room and Stone got to question him again,

Fiona called Stone with fresh information. "It's the school. They're at the school. The one in the Indian Hill area. That must have been where I saw Gere parked, before he left to come after me. Deidre's screaming in my ear to tell you, it must be Pilgrim where her Jenny takes a summer reading workshop. We think he may have rigged a bomb to go off when school starts."

"And that's how we found you," Deidre said through a fresh batch of tears. "Thank the Goddess, we were in time."

"Did they see the last of the lavender on the school stairs?" I thought about how dangerous it had been and what split-second timing was involved in marking our trail.

"No way," said Tip. "Those SWAT guys just run over everything, flash and smash. The whole story could be right there under their feet for anyone to read."

"Not anyone. Just a clever tracker like you," I said. It was time for another round of hugs.

"But wait, there's more—as they say in the TV commercials," Phillipa said. "Stone tells me that the bomb Gere left at Pilgrim was completely addled. No one can tell what time it would have gone off—early, late, or ever—because the clock mechanism— Gere's specialty—was garbage. The bomb expert said it was like being set for the Twelfth of Never. Now how could that have happened, do you suppose?" She beamed at Freddie.

Freddie smiled modestly. "See, you need me. I mean, in the circle. If you're going to keep getting into trouble like this."

"I do think we might invite this girl to join our Lammas, don't you?" Fiona suggested, referring to our next High Sabbat. Up to now, Freddie had only been invited to Esbats, monthly celebrations of the full moon.

I agreed. Freddie had earned her participation, as a full-fledged apprentice.

Heather, who was sharing a chair with Dick Devlin, rolled her eyes upward, but she smiled. "Freddie is worth her weight in silver pentagrams. A very talented young lady."

"What does she mean, 'keep getting into trouble'?" Dick asked. The vet was a comfortable-looking man with bushy hair, shining brown eyes, and an innocent expression, rather like a teddy bear. What a nice change, I thought, from Heather's predatory ex-husbands.

"I'm serving notice right here and now," I said. "No more chasing murderers for me. I don't like the part where they turn around and come after us."

Everyone laughed at me. I guess that's what friends are for—letting you know when you're fooling yourself.

After Freddie limped up to the rose bedroom, looking more exhausted than I have ever seen her, I crashed with the light of dawn into one of those deep slumbers of unremembered dreams that feels more like falling into a coma. By the time I woke up, the sun was past its noon high and I could hear quite a commotion in my kitchen. Hadn't everyone been as tired as I? I thought they had gone home.

Scruffy raised up wearily from his sheepskin bed. *What's up now, Toots?* He trotted dutifully into the kitchen to check out the premises. I threw on a robe and prepared to shuffle into the bathroom. Was that the smell of bacon wafting my way? Scruffy began barking excitedly.

Becky, Ron, Cathy, and Irene were in the kitchen with Tip, apparently making brunch. Cathy rushed over and threw her arms around me. I could feel tears on her cheek where she pressed it to mine. I cried, too, with the sheer joy of this unexpected family gathering.

Soon Becky was hugging both of us. "Detective Stern contacted Ron last night," she explained. "He wanted us to be informed that you were missing, probably in a hostage situation, but he thought Ron should be the one to break the news. We were nearly *frantic* with worry all night—until we got the call that you were home safe. This young man heard us drive up. He let us in but wouldn't let us wake you—which was quite right, of course." She gave Tip an approving look.

"I reached Adam on his cellphone just as he had deplaned in Atlanta," Irene chimed in, beaming. Ron cracked eggs into a blue-striped bowl and checked on a pan of bacon in the oven. "He's catching a return flight to Boston right off. He'll pick up a rental and drive himself here. You slept like the dead. And I bet you're really hungry now."

"Famished. Overwhelmed."

"Adam's coming back?" said a weak voice from the stairs. Freddie appeared, wearing my big pink shirt and little else. "Shoot—I don't have any clothes. All my good stuff is at Heather's. Okay if I borrow your Jeep, Cass?"

I made a mental note to investigate the matter of her driver's license—later. "After you eat a proper breakfast. Adam won't be here for hours."

Becky looked at me with a raised eyebrow. "Adam's her computer mentor," I explained. "Freddie has a kind of love-hate relationship with things electronic. And she probably saved our lives last night, zapping that bomb."

"Bomb!" "What bomb?" "Detective Stern never mentioned a *bomb.*" Everyone seemed to be exclaiming at once.

Over breakfast, I related the whole story, my bare-bones version, glossing over the horror and minimizing the witchcraft angle. But while I ate ravenously, Freddie filled them in with some of the colorful details I'd omitted.

"Good Lord, you're a pair of heroines," Ron said. "Solving the Donahue murders, saving the school . . . I bet the press will be swarming in here any moment now." He didn't look displeased.

"It's Fiona they'll be after, not us," Freddie said. "She's the one who shot the son of a bitch. Too bad she didn't aim a little higher."

After we'd feasted and talked through the night's adventures and found our way out of those terrors into the easy laughter of families, Cathy and Irene drifted upstairs to settle themselves in for an overnight stay, while Ron and Becky cleaned up the kitchen and Freddie raced back to Heather's for fresh clothes. I poured myself one more half-cup of Irene's excellent coffee and wandered out to the herb garden with Scruffy trotting beside me. Perhaps I'd harvest a handful of fresh dill for that humongous whole salmon still languishing in my freezer. There would be a festive dinner party when Adam arrived. Looking at the shimmering July sky, the rich, dark shades of green in deep summer foliage, the ocean beyond with a light blue haze hovering above the water, I felt an inexpressible wonder at the beauty and rightness of every cloud, leaf, and wave. I had escaped, I was alive, I was needed and loved. Dizzy with happiness, I had to sit down in one of the Adirondack chairs to savor this miracle of being.

Scruffy put his head on my knee. "What a good dog you are," I said. "A hero in every way." He sighed. Dogs know when a moment is too perfect for words.

Freddie underestimated Fiona, who soon tired of microphones and cameras being thrust into her face and sicced them onto us. Then Una Grimm called and demanded that we do a follow-up segment, giving *AFF* credit for Gere's apprehension.

"Mrs. Shipton will get back to you." Freddie had taken on the job of answering the phone, her voice crisp and businesslike. "Right now, she's dickering between Larry King and Oprah. Heavy schedule, you know what I mean?"

But when Freddie answered the next call, the eleventh that morning, she said, "Here, you'd better take this one." She slapped the receiver into my hand and sprinted outside where Tip was weeding the herb gardens and tossing the occasional orange sponge ball to Scruffy. From my kitchen window, I saw her sit cross-legged on the grass to talk to Tip while he worked.

"Hello," I said in a cautious tone.

"Hello, sweetheart." It was Joe!

"Where are you?" As always, my first question. "Did you hear what happened to us?"

"I just landed at JFK airport. Yes, I heard. I'll hop on a shuttle and be in Boston in an hour or so. Not in time to rescue you, but not too late to scold you."

"That's wonderful, darling! But *how* did you hear?"

"One of those gals who interviewed you and Fiona was a CNN reporter, honey. They gave you at least thirty seconds. A couple of my coworkers caught the story, thought you might be the Plymouth woman I've been dashing off to see between assignments—news like that gets around fast in the Greenpeace organization. They got in touch with me through the ship's computer. I got another engineer to fly in from Amsterdam so I could book the next flight home. You're all right, you and Freddie?"

"A few scratches and bruises, that's all. They're nearly healed now. Hey, you should see the other guy! Did you also hear that Fiona shot Gere? He was in Jordan Hospital, but he's been transferred to Bridgewater for a court-ordered psychiatric evaluation. It's the state hospital lockup for loonies."

"Okay for now, but I want to see Gere put away forever. In fact, I'd like to do it myself. But never mind him—that bastard has taken enough of you. I want you to promise me that you'll never get mixed up with a criminal investigation again."

"Let's not talk about that now. Soon you'll be up in the clouds, descending on Boston like Zeus in a shower of gold. Mmmm, what a pleasant prospect."

"Listen, Cass. I love you. I want you to be safe. I want to marry you. I want to take you home to meet my mother."

"You mean, like, to Athens?" I pictured a little old lady with a black shawl over her head, her eyes glittering malevolently, holding out a silver cross as she cursed me in Greek. Possibly I'd seen too many foreign films.

"My mother will love you. I know you two are going to have a lot in common," Joe said.

"And my children will adore *you*." I hope, I hope. Alcohol, I thought, has twice the usual effect at high altitudes. "Joe?"

"Yes, love."

"Did you have an in-flight beverage or two?"

"Just breakfast, honey. But yes, I am drunk. Drunk with love."

"Me, too? Fortunately, the furor of my fame is dying down. The children have gone back to their lives. We'll talk and plan—and whatever.

"Good timing."

"Good timing is my specialty—as you know."

I felt caught up in a warm whirlwind of desires that I'd been keeping locked away ever since Joe left. "I forget," I said. "You'll have to show me again."

Joe arrived in another Rent-A-Wreck late that afternoon. Freddie, who was fast becoming a model of discretion, drove Tip home and herself back to Heather's canine mansion. She was becoming all too fond of Ashbery's Dodge, now sporting four good tires, but Heather seemed grateful to have such a willing volunteer for errands. S. E. Thomas was out of the hospital again, so Tip had resumed his caretaker role, although he kept working odd jobs because they needed the money. At least now everyone's mail would be arriving on time, including Thomas's workman's comp checks. And I would always keep an eye on the boy's welfare.

So we were alone and free—how wonderful! That night Joe and I did indeed renew our "good timing," spinning off into that oceanic oneness that is the gift of loving sex. As we lay clasped in each other's arms, not yet separated into two striving individuals, I felt as if I were moving weightlessly in that place between the worlds where magic happens.

A long time after, when we came back to ourselves, he said, "So what do you say? Will you come with me for a week in Athens, meet my mother and the rest of the family? Would you rather be married there or here?"

"Yes, yes, yes," I breathed in his ear. "But I think we should be married here, maybe at the Garden of Gethsemane, to please my children. Then we Wiccans have a ceremony we call a hand-fasting. In the Celtic tradition, a man and a woman jump over the broom together."

Joe's grip tightened and he sighed. "Okay, but not too high. I'm not a young man, you know."

"I don't believe that for a moment." And as that beautiful night went on, it did seem as if we were growing younger. When we finally drifted off to sleep, my head on his shoulder, I whispered, "But if we get married, will you quit roving from disaster to disaster?"

"Will you?" he murmured, pulling me closer.

Phillipa's kitchen was full of the delectable aromas of bread baking—a bread made of several rich whole grains with honey for sweetening and an egg-wash to make the crusts shine. Our Lammas priestess hadn't been able to resist baking the man-shaped loaves that are traditional for this High Sabbat. We would eat the flesh of the grain god. A Wiccan version of gingerbread men, the question always being, what to eat first?

Deidre brought a basketful of handcrafted corn dollies and a smile of joyous expectancy that suggested she had, after all, accepted the largess of her fertile body. Fiona carried a cache of old-fashioned straw brooms "to brush away the negativity of Gere."

Phillipa raised her eyebrow at the brooms but accepted one and even tried a few dancing sweeps around her immaculate kitchen. "Banish Gere to a far, far place forever!" Heather unpacked a hamper of bottles, some kind of delicious honey-mead brewed only in Norwood, and sang the improvised chant along with Phillipa, adding a line, "Banish him to silence, unlock him never."

And as I had promised, I brought Freddie—this was to be her first High Sabbat. Freddie had reverted to what I now thought of as her "Adam" outfit. Slicked-back brown hair and fawn eyes, summer-tanned skin and short, leafy sundress—a cross between Winona Ryder and a child of the faeries. Until she opened her mouth: "Yo, witches!" she exclaimed. "How high can you fly on those brooms?"

"They're not for flying, Freddie," Fiona said. "They're for sweeping."

"No sh . . . No kidding. What about all those Halloween silhouettes—moon, witch on broom, bats?"

"Whoever started that tale had partaken of too many herbs and mushrooms, dearie. You know what *I* mean." Fiona's authority in historical matters could not be questioned.

The rites took place on Phillipa's patio, a perfect, starry August night. We welcomed Freddie as our official apprentice, in a simple initiation of our own devising, with garlands and blessings and hugs all around.

"You've *earned* this, honey," I said when I saw the tears rolling down her cheeks. "You're so talented, and you've learned so much."

"It's like having a real family," she sobbed.

"And so you have," I agreed. We'd decided to take responsibility for the training of this spirited girl, to teach her how to use her psychic gifts without letting herself become a prey. But she was strong and canny. The dark hearts that were greedy for such powers would never get the better of Freddie.

The long, narrow patio lent itself to our barefoot dance in the figure eight, the sign of infinity. As we moved through the steps, chanting the old round song, "*We are one with the Earth, Mother Earth, we are one,*" the rhythm soared faster and faster. But that night, instead of sending out our wants and wishes in a burst of energy, we sent our gratitude to the Creator, male and female, of us all—for our endurance and our triumph, and for the harvest of good, bright love we continued to gather. *Blessed be!*